Ford shook his head, even pouted, as he delivered the statement in his most pathetic poor-me tone.

"Are you looking for pity?" Shay slipped her hand into his hair, as she always did.

"I'm willing to do almost anything to lure you into bed," he said in a heated voice.

"Interesting." And more than a little tempting. After all, he was an expert with that tongue, and not just for talking.

He pulled her in closer, wrapping her in his arms and pressing his chest against hers. "Next time we'll have to schedule in some phone-sex time while I'm gone. Pretty damn hot."

Before she could laugh, he lowered his head and treated her to a welcome home kiss that had her wanting to tie him in a chair to keep from leaving again. Hot and firm, he took control and dragged her under.

PLAYING DIRTY

BAD BOYS UNDERCOVER

HELENKAY DIMON

A V O N

An Imprint of HarperCollins*Publishers*

This is a work of fiction. Names, characters, places, and incidents are products of the author's imagination or are used fictitiously and are not to be construed as real. Any resemblance to actual events, locales, organizations, or persons, living or dead, is entirely coincidental.

AVON BOOKS
An Imprint of HarperCollins*Publishers*
195 Broadway
New York, New York 10007

Copyright ℗ 2015 by HelenKay Dimon
ISBN 978-0-06-233005-5
www.avonromance.com

First Avon Books mass market printing: February 2015

Avon Trademark Reg. U.S. Pat. Off. and in Other Countries, Marca Registrada, Hecho en U.S.A.
HarperCollins® is a registered trademark of HarperCollins Publishers.

Printed in the U.S.A.

10 9 8 7 6 5 4 3 2 1

To my agent, Laura Bradford,
for coming up with the perfect pitch and
then negotiating the deal while on vacation.
I am lucky to have you on my team.

PLAYING DIRTY

1

Ford Decker balanced on his elbows with his stomach dragging in the wet grass and wondered how he'd managed to pull this shit assignment. Adjusting his night goggles, he stared across the open field to the brick building sitting below him at the bottom of the slope.

"Target approximately hundred meters at your center across the heath." Harlan Ross's Oxford-educated British accent cut across the still night.

As one of the supervisors of Alliance, Harlan waited and watched from 3,600 miles away in the Warehouse, the team's high-tech operations center outside Washington, D.C., but his voice echoed in the silver disk in Ford's ear. One word grabbed Ford's attention. "Heath?"

Weston Brown—West to anyone who knew him for more than two seconds and wanted to breathe for a third—didn't make a noise as he held still in the pile of leaves to Ford's right. "Sounds made up."

"Fucking Brits." Ford mumbled the comment.

Harlan had landed at Alliance, the newly formed joint intelligence task force handpicked from members of the CIA and MI6, and independent of both agencies, from the Special Reconnaissance Regiment, a division of the British Army with roots in operations in Northern Ireland. He might sound smooth, but under all that properness lurked a nasty temper and crack shot.

Ford wasn't in the mood to test either. He turned to West, his number two on Bravo Team. "What exactly is a heath again?"

"That will teach you to ignore the nonessential parts of a briefing."

"Gentlemen." Harlan managed to load the word with sarcasm. "It's the grassy open area of land in front of you."

Ford continued mumbling. "Then just say that."

"We have heat signatures on all three floors." A low rumble of conversation and rhythmic clicking from what sounded like a keyboard played behind Harlan's voice as the muted sounds of the Warehouse magnified tenfold in that cavernous room. "Limited movement."

"Because it's two in the morning." Prime surveillance hour, which made it the worst time to move, in Ford's mind. Too obvious.

West snorted. "You think terrorists work nine-to-five?"

"I think we have bad intel."

"According to the chatter we're picking up, the man renting that house is in the process of setting up an auction to place a deadly toxin on the open market." Harlan could have been reading from the briefing notes. Since he possessed what he insisted be called an eidetic rather than photographic memory, the recall likely matched verbatim.

Not that Ford needed a review of the intel. He stayed loose and kept the sarcasm turned to maximum, but he didn't fool around when it came to strategy and completing an operation. He studied, memorized, did whatever he had to do to put the plan in his head.

"A terrorist's wet dream," he mumbled as he shot West the side eye.

Harlan droned on. "So, we have talk about a meeting in Yemen, and a deadly toxin missing from a U.S. government lab."

West let out a low whistle. "That's a lot of ways to get fucked."

Ford understood the pieces but they didn't connect in his head. "You're talking Yemen and I'm looking at a scene out of a Dickens' novel."

"As if you've read Dickens," West joked as he scanned the horizon.

Fucking up what should have been an easy snatch-and-run was Ford's real concern. Tree-lined cobblestone streets and expensive houses. Not to mention the freaky sense of quiet. No way would this high-end neighborhood tolerate strangers hanging around. This place with the ponds and walking paths had neighborhood-watch-protected written all over it. Or whatever the British version of that might be.

The man coming up from their right, watching the same house while stomping through the high grass, did challenge that theory. The careful footing raised a flag, but it was the gun the guy carried that ruled out an innocent evening walk around the neighborhood.

So much for Dickens.

Ford motioned for West to drop. On command and

without a word, the big man flattened, slithering on his stomach as the wind covered the small amount of noise his pants made sliding across the ground. He shifted out of sight within seconds.

On his own, Ford hunkered down. Staying still until even his breathing slowed and the sounds of the neighborhood echoed in his ear, each one magnified and highlighted so he could separate the man from the surroundings.

The grass crunched and the thud of footsteps grew closer. Ford heard a click, as if the guy tapped his finger against the side of his gun. If he kept it off the trigger, Ford would have an extra second or two. Not that he'd need it. He had surprise on his side . . . and West. They could take on ten men and come out on top. One guy wandering around as if he'd lost his dog hardly amounted to a real problem.

Ford waited until the last second, until the guy's shoe came into his line of vision, then jumped to his feet in a crouch. Another step and Ford stood, lifting his elbow and nailing the guy under the chin in one swift move. The gun dropped and the man's head snapped back on a sharp intake of breath. Before he could recover, Ford slammed a heel into his stomach and sent him flying. He landed on his ass and sat there, doubled over and coughing.

Ford knew that was too easy. He leaned in and the guy came alive. Rage showed in every line of his body and in the flat line of his mouth. His guttural roar had Ford shaking his head as the guy launched himself. The man's full weight barreled into Ford's midsection.

The breeze kicked up around them and a dog barked

in the distance. Ford heard shouting in his ear over the com and ignored it all to concentrate on staying on his feet as the guy backed him up and attempted a spine-cracking throw-down.

Ford would shoot without blinking. Truth was, gun beat wrestling every single time, but he didn't want to draw attention. Not that the guy seemed to realize that. He grunted and tried to shove Ford off balance, knocking him from one side to the other but not standing up and planting his feet like he should have.

Fucking amateur.

Ford tired of messing with him. When the guy got lucky and landed a shot to Ford's chest, Ford declared playtime over. He kneed the guy in the jaw and heard a crack. The vise grip around Ford's waist eased a second later. He took advantage of the break with a quick stranglehold around the guy's neck. A few defensive kicks and grabs at Ford's arm then the man passed out.

Dropping the dead weight, Ford stepped back and surveyed his supposed attacker. The guy could have used more bodyguard training. The whole scene lasted a few seconds. It only went on that long because Ford didn't immediately end it. Next time he would cut it short and get back to surveillance faster.

Bent over with his hands on his knees, Ford stared at the lifeless form at his feet. Then he checked pockets for ID, not expecting to find any and not disappointed when he didn't.

A movement off to his side had him glancing up. West stood there wearing a stupid grin. That was annoying as shit. "You'd think a supposed terrorist could afford better talent," Ford said.

"Hey, he did get one shot in against you."

Ford gave his teammate the finger.

West laughed. "Just reporting what I saw."

The chaos on the com finally pulled Ford into responding. "Stop yelling,"

"We're fine." West touched a hand to his earpiece and answered as he scanned the area before his gaze landed on Ford again. "What were you saying about Dickens?"

Not a topic Ford wanted to discuss right now. "You run out and get a sandwich or did you get confused about the concept of backup?"

West shrugged. "You were doing fine."

Not convinced the unconscious guy didn't have a friend hovering nearby, Ford motioned for West to duck down. After a quick visual sweep of the area, Ford glanced at one of the upstairs windows, on the tick of movement he sensed rather than saw.

Screwing with West gave Ford a second to think about the best way to scale the wall. "For the record, your sister likes when I read Dickens to her before sex."

"Does this imaginary sister think you're a dick?"

Ford had to laugh at that. "That's just you."

"No, it's not," Harlan said, breaking through the byplay he despised and repeatedly insisted should have no role in an undercover operation, boring shit that he was. "Are we clear to move?"

Ford spared the downed man one more glance. "I was ready twenty minutes ago."

"Right." Harlan exhaled. "We need eyes and ears in that building. It's the only way to know if Ford's instincts are misfiring."

Ford shot West a let's-kick-ass grin. "While I'm playing with tech toys, you stand guard and shoot anyone who gets near me." Which Ford viewed as the more interesting part of the operation.

Sneaking in, planting devices, all while ducking gunfire and nosy neighbors, required someone with the patience to sit and not move for hours, if needed. Not Ford's usual thing, but even less so for West. His specialty was killing, so Ford got stuck with the boring role this time around.

"Negative on the shooting." Harlan's accent sounded sharper now. A little less refined university and more like the MI6 asshole willing to do anything to finish the job and sacrifice anyone in the process.

Looked to Ford like Harlan continued to forget the usual MI6 and CIA rules didn't bind Alliance. They operated off the grid and without any of the usual restrictions of the intelligence agencies.

"Boss man has no sense of humor." West made the comment, which made it even funnier since the guy ran low on the amusement gene.

"Fucking Brits." Ford calculated he'd made that comment at least ten times a day since throwing in with Alliance. Almost hourly when dealing with Harlan.

"We need an in and out. No footprints," Harlan said, ignoring the open talk about him.

"This whole op is going sideways on us." Ford thought he should point that out, if only to be able to say "I told you so" later, when the time came, and it would. He'd bet the nineteen hundred dollars in his cover ID's bank account on that.

"No firepower," Harlan said at the same time.

Fuck that. "Screw you, Ross. If someone shoots at me, I'm shooting back."

Several voices filled the line but Harlan talked over all of them. "Nullify targets as final solution only."

Ford nodded. "Dad has spoken. Move in."

Crouched and jogging as they fanned out, Ford increased his distance from West as they moved in on the target. The noises of the night fell around them. The whisper of the wind through the long grass and the scurry of animals provided background noise, but Ford focused on the house at the bottom of the small hill. A Georgian-style brick residence you'd find wherever rich people live. Windows in the back and only a few lights on upstairs.

It was totally wrong as a potential terrorist's hideaway. Too out in the open. Not secure or easily guarded.

The shadow he'd been concentrating on moved, and Ford raised his fist. West, a perfectly trained Marine killing machine, stopped in mid-step, and Ford didn't hesitate to confirm. "We've got a body at the back door."

"Copy." Harlan's voice stayed steady. Cool and unruffled, as if this amounted to nothing more than a practice exercise. "Hold."

"Easy for him to say." West stepped closer as he and Ford eased down, balancing on the balls of their feet.

"That's a negative on heat signatures," Harlan said.

Ford saw West mouth *What the fuck* and silently agreed. "Then your equipment is malfunctioning because I'm looking right at the guy. What are you seeing on your end?"

Shuffling and orders to the tech team came first,

then, "We've lost contact with your cam. Switching to CCTV as backup."

Britain's notorious closed-circuit television surveillance. Reports set the number of cameras across the country at more than four million. Relying on the system rather than Alliance's internal intel kicked the ticking at the back of Ford's neck up to a constant banging.

"What the fuck?" West didn't bother to mouth it that time.

"I've got a bad feeling." An understatement, but since they were basically pinned down in the middle of a field without cover and no eyes up above, Ford decided downplaying was the answer. He'd launch into yelling and hitting later. "We're a go on this end," he said. Sitting there made him antsy. "We've got one hostile at the door and a shadow on the second floor, far right window."

Harlan exhaled then started again. "We're not seeing any of it."

"Then your satellite is aimed at the wrong town." This is why Ford didn't believe in relying on all the tech shit. Equipment went bad and malfunctioned. Sometimes the humans working it failed or fell down. The only truly reliable intel came from what he could see and what he heard from people he trusted, and there were very few of those.

"Hold," Harlan shot back.

Enough of this shit. "We're circling to the side for a better look."

Ford didn't wait for the go signal or approval. He took off and motioned for West to follow.

At sixty meters they dropped lower and cut off communication. Voices would carry in the open space. One breeze blowing in the right direction and the guy outside could pick up the wrong sound and the dark sky would light up with gunfire.

Not the plan.

Just as they swung out wide to the right side of the house, the guy guarding the back door shifted. After a telltale touch to his ear, he left his position. Two steps and he abandoned the steps and stood under the window. And he kept going.

Ford knew from the schematics and photos that a parking lot and three-stall garage sat in that direction. It meant cars and a possible getaway, and he was not in the mood for a chase across the countryside. "Hostile heading left from our current position."

"Stand down." Harlan didn't leave a lot of room for improvisation with that response.

Right or wrong, the waiting ticked Ford off. "Damn it."

West's response was more measured, as he kept his assault rifle aimed on the guy. "Follow?"

"Negative." Anger edged into Harlan's voice. "Position? We're still not seeing what you're seeing."

"Closed in to twenty and—"

Ford's breath jammed in his throat as the night turned deathly still. A wall of heat slammed into his chest a second later and his ears popped. A series of concussive booms thundered around him as an invisible wave pushed his body up and back, kicking him off his feet.

Noises, unidentifiable at first, roared to life around him. His gun dropped from his hand before he could tighten his grip, and his body shot up then careened toward the grass, ass first. His bones rattled as gravity won out and he came to a sudden stop with his head slamming against the wet ground. For a second, light blinked out. Thoughts, fragments, spun through his mind but he couldn't grab onto anything.

He couldn't tell if the strange blankness lasted ten seconds or ten minutes before his brain rebooted. When he opened his eyes again it took several attempts before he could focus. The automatic off switch on the goggles prevented flash blindness, but the burning smell choked him as much as the dark smoke rolling through the once clean air.

Flames danced, filling the sky. He heard the telltale whoosh. The cracking and slamming that echoed as walls fell and fire engulfed buildings. Ignoring the ache in his shoulder and twisting in his lower back, Ford rolled to his side, scanning the area for signs of life. For West.

The shouting in his ear registered as he spied West struggling to balance his upper body on his elbows. Ford tried to call out but his voice didn't register above the din.

"Report." Harlan's yelling and the rumble of noise in the background on the com wiped out the sounds of the raging fire. "Ford!"

"We're here." Sirens wailed in the distance and lights flickered on all around the area. People stood in huddled, hugging groups. A few brave souls tried to rush into the crumbling hull of what only seconds ago had been a grand house, only to get beaten back by flames licking through the structure. The fire spread fast and wild, overcoming the houses on either side, which now burned with abandon.

West shook his head. "What the hell?"

"Not just a fire. It was an explosion." Ford expected a fuck-up but this exceeded any anticipated problem. There would be bodies. Innocents caught in the cross fire. Questions it would take meticulous piecing together to answer.

And then someone would need to explain why their intel was so piss poor and who warned the bad guys they were coming.

"Target and other buildings on fire," West filled in as he turned over and shuffled on his elbows in the grass, to drop next to Ford.

The com went silent. No background noise. Not even a hint of Harlan's usual Brit bullshit. Ford was on the verge of demanding new orders when Harlan broke in again. "Transport at RAF Mildenhall. Rendezvous back here at the Warehouse in forty-eight hours. Cutting communication."

Then nothing. Even the subtle hum of the mic in Ford's ear cut off.

West sat up but kept his body low as they blended into the smoke-filled night. "We could just go to the London field office."

Alliance stayed mobile but did have set offices, one of which was nearby on the Thames. An imposing white and blue building, referred to as Legoland, housed the British secret intelligence, and deep inside sat a nerve center used by Alliance. From there, they had the ability to spring into action when international security threats popped up around the world.

But this order adhered to protocol. No matter where they were, operatives reported back to the Warehouse rather than remain in the field when an assignment blew up. The brief time delay from disaster to meet-up allowed for separation between the people in charge and the people who risked everything—them.

Ford knew the drill. Drop IDs, hide weapons and evidence, pick up alternative travel documents. If someone meant to terminate him, it would happen now and headquarters could maintain deniability. "This is a full field op fuck-up."

West swore under his breath. "And we'll be blamed."

History suggested yes. "We need to get back before Harlan hangs this around our necks."

West took off his knit hat and shoved it in one of the utility pockets of his pants. "Fucking Brits."

About time someone agreed. "That's what I've been saying."

2

SHAY ALEXANDER heard the dueling sounds of off-key humming and a blaring radio as she entered her first floor condo. Closing the door shut out the traffic noise and mumble of conversation from people walking by on the sidewalk, but the bad singing remained.

Town houses and stately old homes converted to apartments and condos lined this street in the Dupont Circle area of DC. The Metro sat a few blocks away, and the prime real estate location kept the prices high, which was good since she managed the building and two others for her uncle. She lived alone in the Beaux Arts–style place that had served as a home to one family in the forties and had since been divided into a twenty unit complex.

Her small one-bedroom came with the job. The perfect size for a single person, but she'd been fitting two of them in quite nicely on and off for the last three weeks. Which brought her mind back to the not-really-singing thing happening at the back of her condo.

The deep male voice lured her through the family room to the kitchen that ran along the side of the old building. From the doorway she noticed half of the contents of the navy toolbox lay scattered over her tile floor. A can of soda and open bag of chips sat on the edge of the sink. She didn't know where the snacks came from because buying chips inevitably resulted in her hoovering the bag in one sitting, so she never stepped one foot into that aisle in the grocery store. That was as far as her chip self-control extended.

The radio, set to deafening, sat on the small table pressed up against the opposite wall. She spied the sneakers next and tiptoed, careful not to tramp down too hard with her boots. There was no need to give away her position. Not when she could steal a moment of looking at him.

Legs, long and lean, stuck out from under her sink. A sliver of bare trim waist peeked out from the space where his faded jeans and the bottom of what looked like a T-shirt should meet. The unexpected sight of a guy on the floor might scare another woman, but not her. Not those legs and surely not the impressive male body attached to them.

She winced over a particularly rough note and reached over to turn the radio down. The chips were right there, so she grabbed one. Then two.

"You're back," she said, munching over the salt and fat frenzy in her mouth.

Tools clanked and something thudded. An impressive string of profanity came next. "Shay?"

"Who else?" She still hadn't seen that hot face, with the dark scruff around his chin and those intense green eyes. The guy was of the pure Tall, Dark, and Oh-So-Hot variety. She hated to admit she could stare at him for long periods of time. Look, and totally miss whatever he said.

After rubbing the salt from her fingertips on her jeans, she crouched down, balancing on the balls of her feet, and tried to get a peek at his T-shirt of the day. The graphics ranged from ridiculous to innuendo-filled. None could be classified as appropriate for outside the home. She had no idea where he got them, but she sure enjoyed the ongoing show.

"Hey." He lifted his head and clunked it off the side of a pipe. "Shit."

"Smooth."

He rubbed his temple. "I'm seeing two of you right now."

The scruff was thicker than usual, and wasn't that the sexiest thing ever. "You deserved that."

"Hey, I'm fixing your leak." He slid out. The move rolled his shirt up his torso and showed off skin . . . and muscles . . . Yeah, forget the T-shirt.

Minor handyman tasks fit in with her job description, but ever since he moved into the two-bedroom across the hall, he'd volunteered to help out. He worked as an IT specialist, handling computer systems for large companies and always on call. But, man, he looked good with a wrench in his hand. She liked him best bare-chested and fixing something.

His smile reeled her in, but she pretended to be immune, or at least a little in control. "You're a plumber now?"

"Want to see my tools?"

The eyebrow wiggle almost did her in. "Wow, that was terrible."

"Yeah, sorry about that." With one hand wrapped around the lip of the sink, he pulled his body up and stood, stopping only for a quick kiss on her mouth. He extended a hand and brought her up beside him before her mind could take in every amazing inch of his six-foot frame. "It was the only line I could think of after a few hours of restless plane sleep and armrest wrangling with the guy in 15B. Give me a few minutes and my moves will catch up to the time zone jumps."

He traveled all the time. In and out, always grabbing a duffel bag and heading off to fix some emergency. Sometimes texting her at one in the morning to announce he'd gotten back, then knocking on her door to come in for a visit. He'd moved in three weeks ago. The sex started about two days after that.

The relationship—or whatever it was—ran on fast forward from the first day. She'd seen his T-shirt with the piglet playing poker on it, and for some reason her control nosedived. Never mind that it was then October and cold and any sane person would wear a jacket or at least a sweater. He claimed DC was the South and warm. She guessed that meant he grew up in the Midwest or Vermont or, hell, even Canada. Somewhere cold. Not that he'd shared any part of his past with her . . . yet. His body, yes. The basic information, no.

She pushed the nagging thought out of her head and ran a finger over the prickly scruff on his chin. "How was the conference?"

"Long and tedious."

"I imagined you hanging out in a bar talking computer code over beers."

He snorted. "More like security measures. Firewalls and rotating IPs."

With that, her already limited interest in the subject of computer tech fizzled out. Him putting his hands on her waist didn't help her focus one bit. She ran her hand over his shirt and smoothed it down over his torso. Today's version featured a cigar-smoking rat.

Of course it did.

"That is something else." The graphic, the abs . . . the comment worked for both.

He backed her up until her backside balanced against the counter. "Yeah, I've been subjected to some pretty boring lectures and bad conference chicken."

She kicked the wrench rocking under her heel to the side and lifted her arms to circle his neck. "You poor thing."

"And my bed was very cold." He shook his head, even pouted, as he delivered the statement in his most pathetic poor-me tone.

"Are you looking for pity?" She slipped her hand into his hair, as she always did. Something about the length, as if he were growing out a military cut, appealed to her as she wove the softness through her fingers.

His eyebrow lifted. "If that would work."

"You're getting there."

She'd been so sure he was former Army—or something—and asked him about it the first week. Nothing in his renter's agreement talked about military service, but she got the vibe. Service members moved in and out of DC all the time. She got the routine, and recognized the straight stance and assured conversation. And he had the confident walk and toned body down.

He'd listened to her assessment and laughed it off,

insisting his smartass ways would have gotten him kicked out on the first day. She pretty much agreed with that.

"I'm willing to do almost anything to lure you into bed," he said in a heated voice.

"Interesting." And more than a little tempting. After all, he was an expert with that tongue, and not just for talking.

He pulled her in closer, wrapping her in his arms and pressing his chest against hers. "Next time we'll have to schedule in some phone-sex time while I'm gone. Imagine me ordering you to touch yourself. Pretty damn hot."

Her heart did a little jig at the thought. Saying "next time" meant whatever they had wasn't going away. For now, knowing that but little else was enough. Soon she'd need more. "You gotta tone down this sweet-talking or it will go to my head."

Before she could laugh, he lowered his head and treated her to a welcome home kiss that had her wanting to tie him in a chair to keep from leaving again. Hot and firm, he took control and dragged her under. His hands rubbed up and down her back as his mouth crossed over hers. When that sweet tongue slipped inside and met with hers, she dug her fingernails into his shirt. Almost bit through the cotton to hit skin.

He pulled back just far enough to stare down at her. The room spun and she held onto his shoulders to keep from falling down as babble filled her brain. "What?"

"I can spit-shine my lines until they're clever but we both know you're the gatekeeper."

She wasn't exactly sure what he was talking about but she liked the sound of it. "Damn right."

"And I am your sex slave." His voice dipped low until it skidded across her senses.

She clenched her fingers even tighter against his shoulders. Had to clear her throat a few times before finally spitting out a word. "Nice."

Those strong hands slipped down her back to land on her ass. "The green light is totally in your control."

His touch had her stretching up on the tips of her toes to brush her lower body against his. Not her most subtle move but then nothing about them being together was. They'd shifted from simmering to raging heat from the beginning. Skipped right over the get-to-know-you phase on the way to the bedroom.

She knew about his job and tried to keep a handle on his erratic schedule. His renter's application included his social security number, which led to his impressive credit score and the glowing report from his last landlord in Virginia. The rest remained a mystery . . . except for the information she found in a few hundred Internet searches trying to make sure he wasn't a wanted serial killer. Or married.

A woman had to be smart about these things. She refused to feel guilty about the dating recon after hearing one horror story too many from her friends. A guy with a hidden wife and an anger complex here. A guy who liked to wear women's bikini underwear over there. Then there were the looking-for-money types. Yeah, no thank you.

Playing coy wasn't her thing, and the attraction between them that sparked on the initial walk through the condo had burst into full flame by the time she handed over the keys. He'd asked her out a few weeks after. She refused. Two days later he brought pizza over and they'd been seeing each other ever since.

Seeing as in sex. Lots of sex. The guy might work with computers but he knew his way around a woman's body. Hands, tongue, mouth . . . lord.

After a rocky last relationship, the physical play with him and limited dating contact due to his work schedule appealed to her. It didn't matter that the need to know more about him kept picking at her. She'd vowed to turn off her preference for being prepared for anything and just let things unfold without trying to steer them.

In that spirit: "I thought you were blowing out my pipes."

He chucked in the middle of nibbling on her ear. The sound was so rich and deep, so sexy it hit with the force of a superpower. "I would love to do that, yes."

She felt his arms around her waist with hands caressing her ass and the back of her thighs through her jeans. The dual blast of touching and closeness had her breath stuttering in her chest. She inhaled and caught his scent, the same hint of black pepper she associated with his soap.

Unable to resist his face and that firm chin, she smoothed her fingertip around his mouth, letting the stubble of hair tickle her skin. "You should be resting from your boring conference and long flight."

"That is not what I had in mind when I came over here."

"My pipes, right?" She'd given him a key and the

alarm code before he left on his latest trip. He'd been in and out working on the steps to the front door of the building. The argument about needing to get to the supply closet without tracking her down proved compelling. And the idea of him spending his first few hours back in DC fixing the plumbing problem she mentioned on his way out was just about the sexiest damn thing ever.

"Do your pipes need blowing?" He kept a straight face.

She had no idea how. "You make everything sound dirty."

"Give me ten minutes and I'll show you how dirty I can be."

There it was, the flirty talk that drove her doubts away and had her handing over keys even though a little voice inside her head told her to be more careful. But there was no need to fight it. She didn't plan to make him wait or work for it. Those days were behind them, and they had passed fast.

That left only one thing. "I have two words for you."

One of his eyebrows lifted. "Which are?"

She leaned in until her mouth hovered over his. "Green light."

He pulled back as his gaze searched hers. "You sure?"

Since she'd been giving him the go sign pretty much from the beginning and he'd been speeding ahead with her, his hesitation now struck her as odd. But those knowing hands skimming along her sides let her know he was ready when she was.

The answer was now.

"Are you playing hard to get for, like, the first time

ever since I've known you?" She pulled him in tighter, rubbing her body against his until his mouth dropped open and a sharp exhale escaped.

His hands clenched against her sides for the briefest of seconds then relaxed again. "Never."

"You know . . ." She kissed her way down his throat to that delicious spot just above his collarbone. "I think there's something in the bedroom that needs your attention."

His fingers went to the button at the top of her jeans, then the screech of her zipper filled the room. Her mouth covered his just as his fingers slipped inside her underwear. Down and over her. Into her.

She held the back of his neck as her mouth slipped over his again and again. The counter dug into her lower back as his body rocked against hers. None of that mattered. Just his heat and those fingers and his warm breath brushing against her.

When he lifted his head again, he was on the verge of a full-fledged pant. Balancing his forehead against hers, he went to work on the white buttons of her oxford shirt. "What do you need in your bedroom?"

"Just you, Ford Decker."

3

As DIRECTED, exactly forty-eight hours later, after landing back in the U.S., Ford and West stepped through the doors of the National Counterterrorism Center in Mclean, Virginia. They passed through security check-ins and gates and an array of retinal scanners and other means of identifying the cleared humans from potential threats inside the massive facility known as Liberty Crossing.

They walked across the operations floor, consisting of analysts sitting at desks scattered around a high-tech space. Steps led to a balcony packed with more desks, where the watch officers and higher-ups sat. A central twenty-foot monitor hung off the main wall with slightly smaller ones to each side. Everywhere Ford looked he saw a computer screen and watchful eyes staring back at him.

He didn't fault the questioning looks. Not wearing a suit was only one way in which he stuck out around here. These people were trained intelligence officers with a wealth of experience. They didn't joke around and wouldn't hesitate to hit the panic button or reach for a weapon if he got too close.

Paranoia qualified as a necessary personality trait in undercover work. The locked-down facility included both the counterterrorism center and the headquarters for the Director of National Intelligence. That meant, in theory, all intelligence operations across numerous U.S. government agencies contributed to what happened inside these walls, and it all passed directly from here to the President. One wrong step in this building guaranteed being taken down by armed guards dressed in black who shot first and only checked badges on the fallen bodies after.

So Ford and West did what they always did. They kept walking, ignoring the stares and not saying a word, until they reached the private area at the far side of the room. Several more rounds of security, including a fingerprint reader and body scanner, and they entered the steel-walled elevator that took them underground and into the official Alliance headquarters. The room where the tech folks and administrative types sat. Not Ford and his team.

When in town, Bravo and Delta teams ran out of the Warehouse, a building on the Liberty Crossing grounds that housed the important things like a shooting range and gym. These offices and the conference rooms and all that by-the-rules crap struck Ford as unnecessary to Alliance's very simple directive—get the job done, no matter the cost and body count.

He'd left the CIA to escape all the intelligence-gathering, overseas-only restrictions and all they'd cost him on his last assignment. If a bad guy landed in Kansas, Ford refused to turn the job over to local law enforcement or the FBI, which is why Alliance and it's "do anything to get the job done" charter appealed to him.

In this job, the people at the top watched but didn't interfere. They let Harlan and Ward Bennett, the CIA's chosen command counterpart to Harlan's MI6 supervisor position in Alliance, run the show. In return, the U.S. and UK got an expert kill squad not bound by the restrictions in either country or by international law, and complete deniability about its work outside of the Warehouse's walls. Even the two thousand employees working in Liberty Crossing above and loaded down with security clearances didn't know exactly what happened out in the Warehouse or what Alliance did with the intel the analysts uncovered.

It all sounded good, but right now, in practice, Ford thought it amounted to a load of shit. He signed on to stop terrorist attacks before they launched or expanded operations. That required top tier information. So far on this assignment they'd had anything but.

Nearly being incinerated would have been bad enough, but he'd messed up. Jumped the gun and tied up his work life and his personal life against orders. Just thinking about Shay sent his mind spinning. Lying to her, having the type of mind-blowing sex that had him squirming in his seat on the plane ride back home from thinking about it. She represented everything normal and safe and honest . . . and he was fucking her in every way possible.

He thought his time as a CIA field operative had sucked. He'd reached a new level of suck shoveling over the last few days.

Harlan greeted them as they entered, all tall and thin

and British. He wore a permanent frown and at forty-
three his hair started to show more gray than black.
Likely it had something to do with dedicating his
entire adult life to black ops. He'd infiltrated the IRA
and spent years on an assignment with French intelligence in Rwanda before moving into administration
and agreeing to set up Alliance. Those bright blue eyes
were always watching.

Right or not, Ford traced the Hampstead failure
right back to Harlan.

Ford stopped right in front of his makeshift boss
and asked the only thing that mattered. "How many
are dead?"

"Seven. Two guards and five from the neighborhood. The guy you took down ran and got lost in the
neighborhood."

"So, an excellent operation the whole way around."
Loss of life and they got nothing. That pissed Ford off
more than anything else.

Harlan's gaze didn't shift. He never broke eye contact. "We've talked about your choice of clothing
before. A bit much, isn't it?"

Ford knew the long-sleeve tee with the beer adver-
tisement pushed the informal code, but he didn't care.
His nerves ran right on the edge and he wanted answers, not lectures. "I don't wear a uniform."

"I'm done arguing about this." Harlan turned and
walked deeper into the room. He stopped at the conference table, on the opposite end from Ward, with files
stacked in haphazard piles between them.

Monitors lined the walls. The only other people
in the room were the tech specialists, who rarely saw

field action. They sat and typed and collated and did a whole bunch of crap Ford knew was important but had no hand in.

Additional screens on the desks on either side of the long table displayed a constant flash of images. One set showed the building's internal and external security images, covering thousands of square feet. The other set ran news programs from around the world.

Ford had no idea what the two monitors with lines of computer code referenced. He might play an IT specialist on the current job but he sure as hell wasn't one.

As he pulled out the closest chair and watched West circle the table to sit across from him, Ford focused on all the gadgets that had failed them so far. Monitors filled with information. Folders stacked in front of them. None of that had warned of an explosion.

Harlan used a remote control to change the images on the main monitor. Live footage of a forensics crew sorting through the fire rubble in Hampstead held the prominent position. In daylight the situation looked far worse than the nighttime version. Scorched land and blown out husks of buildings. Ford could almost smell the smoke.

"Our clean-up crews moved in first," Ward said.

Ford didn't want to know how that happened but he imagined searchlights and fake police personnel played roles. "Any chance we found the guy who is supposed to be fronting this toxin auction?"

Ward exhaled. "Not yet."

"He wasn't there." West fiddled with the edge of the file in front of him, opening the cover then shutting it again without reading.

"Let's stay focused." Ward put a hand on the folder and dragged it closer to him. "We don't know that yet."

"Do we know anything for sure other than some pissant piece of garbage walked out of a secure US government facility with a vial of deadly shit and disappeared?" The news hadn't leaked, and as the days ticked by the chances increased. Ford knew from experience these things had a way of getting out even with the tightest net thrown around them. People panicked. They talked. Then his job went from impossible to whatever crap storm came after that.

"Admittedly, we had an intelligence failure."

Ford didn't wait for Harlan to come up with a second sentence. "No shit."

"That's enough of that." Ward used his remote to bring up all the data they had on Trent Creighton, the young scientist who went missing along with the toxin. Photos of him and his apartment filled the screen. His passport and security clearance documents. "We're tracking every piece of paper Trent ever signed or even read and trying to tie him to this supposed auction that's scheduled for less than two weeks from now."

"That's fine," Ford said, "but West and I were five steps away from having our memories reduced to stars on the wall at Langley." He lounged back in the leather chair even though he felt anything but relaxed.

Ward kept clicking through photos. "You don't technically work for the CIA anymore, so your heirs shouldn't count on a star ceremony."

Talk about not getting the hint. "Is that the point?"

Ward slammed the remote on the table hard enough to crack the plastic. "I'm trying to get you to calm the fuck down."

If Ward wanted a fight, Ford would give him one. They'd worked together for years. Stormed into situations where the chance of survival hovered around five percent, yet they walked out again. Ward understood the dangers in the field, how a situation could turn in a second and bodies would stop dropping. He sat behind a desk now, but Ford knew deep down that wouldn't make a difference.

"This isn't working," he said.

"What is the 'this' in your sentence?" But the do-not-cross-this-line scowl on Ward's face suggested he knew.

"Alliance. Joint resources. You billed this whole team-up as a way to ensure that bullshit like two days ago never happened." It was why Ford had transferred over from the CIA rather than just leaving the service as planned. That and because the CIA didn't want him anymore. He considered it a mutual breakup but he wasn't sure his old bosses did.

Truth was, the bad guys were winning the ground game. They combined forces and communicated through back channels. They traveled on faked documents and didn't play by any rules. The number of killings mattered most to them—the more the better, and the bigger the destruction the greater the reward. Collateral damage didn't bother them because they refused to see anyone as innocent.

The fight had become so stacked against those trying to prevent disaster that Ford now measured successes in terms of the bodies left standing. Blood stained his hands and deaths weighed on his shoulders. He'd watched good men fall and stood there while others disappeared.

His final CIA operation left him hollow and raw and

he'd wanted to step away. Needed the fresh air and days free from confronting piles of bodies on a daily basis. But Ward had made promises. Talked about cooperation and resources that could finally pinpoint the madness and crush it before it grew. Ford threw in.

Alliance trained together for three months. Since then, Bravo and Delta teams conducted raids and recovered kidnapping victims and weapons. Stopped attacks and eliminated targets. The usual ops for a group getting its footing and finding a rhythm.

But in this thing with Trent Creighton, the danger magnified as the minutes passed. This guy, little more than a kid, developed GB-19, an odorless gas, a more lethal version of its cousin, sarin. No treatment, and too easy to weaponize and disperse with a guarantee of large-scale annihilation.

"Hey, man." Josiah King, leader of Delta team, walked in and nodded in Ward's direction. Dumping his keys on the table, Josiah shook Ford's hand before dropping into the seat next to him.

"The one Brit I trust," Ford said.

Josiah possessed a clean-cut look in his khakis and buttoned-down shirt and had a connected father. Ford liked his counterpart anyway. They worked together without battling for control. On the very first op, Josiah stepped up, ready to sacrifice his life for the team, and proved he'd earned his leadership position with his tactical abilities and expert shot, not from a nasty case of nepotism.

Ford earned his position as Bravo team leader the hard way—by working his ass off. He'd known Ward since their time at the Farm, the CIA training facility where they learned everything from paramilitary tactics to flying a helicopter. Ward was two years older and just crossed over the magic over-thirty-five line. He'd settled into a desk job. Ford would rather be dead.

"Can we get back to work?" Harlan asked.

"Maybe we could call in a contact in Mossad." Ford had more than one of those. This job was about forming relationships with the right people. Knowing who to trust and when to pull back. He wasn't the smartest guy in the room, but he had those skills down.

Harlan frowned "Why?"

"Since Brit intel sucks so bad, I thought we could try another country."

Everyone waited, except Ward, who shoved a stack of files to the side and leaned forward to eye up Ford. "You're not funny."

"I'm not kidding." Ford tapped a stray pen against the glass overlay on the table. A steady click, click, click that beat in time with the ticking of the nerve at the back of his neck. "I'm willing to try the French."

"We could go with GIA," West suggested.

Ward swore under his breath, something he did often enough to consider it his trademark move. "Don't help him."

"What country is that?" Ford asked at the same time.

"General Intelligence Agency." West closed one eye and stared at the ceiling as if he were trying to remember even though he clearly knew. "Mongolia."

"How do you even remember that?" Josiah shook his head as he laughed. "Have you been studying again?"

"Give him credit." Ford spun his pen across the table, and West stopped it with the slap of his hand, which only impressed Ford more. "Nice drop, man."

"Are you all done?" An unexpected smack had them looking to one end of the table. Harlan held part of his remote control in his hand. Two other pieces lay on the table where he'd banged the device. He fidgeted, trying to get the back cover on again but finally dropped it all and folded his arms in front of him. "If so, let's get back to operational details, shall we?"

Ford stopped whatever the other man was going to say by launching into a heavy dose of truth. "This was a rope-a-dope, a sting . . . hell, a suicide mission. Call it whatever you want. Point is, we got played. Shitty intel brought us in, the tech went bad and the sky lit up."

"Poetic," Josiah said.

"Yeah, well. You weren't almost toast." Ford still couldn't come down. The adrenaline coursed through him.

He'd meant to land, debrief, and stay away from people until he cooled off. Instead his brain turned off and took his common sense with it. Despite every silent promise he'd made during the long flight, he headed for Shay's condo and worked off some excess energy having sex. But not enough.

"Which is why we need everyone on this." Ward glanced over at the tech table. "I want Bravo and Delta to muster within forty minutes."

Ford swore under his breath. "More bodies aren't going to save this op."

"We need intel on this supposed auction and to locate Trent Creighton now, before he sells or loses or unleashes, or whatever the hell he plans to do with his new toy." More photos flashed on the screen as Ward scrolled through Trent's last known contacts and the contents of his apartment and work space.

"Have we figured out how he got the GB-19 out of the government facility in the first place?" They were missing something. Something obvious. The pieces clicked together in Ford's head, and he said them as he thought them. "Employees are searched when leaving, yet this kid smuggles a deadly toxin into the open and fucking disappears with it? No way."

"No one knows." Harlan flipped the pages in front of him. "Creighton is supposed to be a novice."

Ford didn't buy that either. "Doesn't seem like it."

Young and socially awkward, but Trent had made all the rights moves so far. He stayed under and cut contact, making the fear that he was a true believer in whatever cause he planned to use GB-19 to support a real possibility.

That was the danger. Greed, bribery—those were easy to combat. Martyrs to the cause couldn't be reasoned with or turned. The only answer was a bullet, and Ford didn't relish the idea of killing Trent Creighton . . . for many reasons.

"Ford is right." Josiah folded his hands together then stopped and did it again. The cycle kept repeating.

"I'll be the one to say it," Ford said. "Trent's getting help."

"We've got eyes on the father and cousin." Ward clicked a button and two more photos flashed up on the screen.

The faces blurred. Ford rubbed his eyes to focus on the problem at hand instead of the woman on the screen whose face he knew all too well. He'd handle that personal disaster later. "That's not the kind of assistance I meant. A few drops of this toxin could wipe out thousands. Tens of thousands, depending on the conditions."

"Then stop him," Ward said.

Harlan nodded. "Best and brightest and all that, right?"

"I think you're mixing up your American war story references." Josiah tapped his fingers against the table. "But, you know, if there's an issue, Delta team can take lead."

"Bite me." Ford treated the threat for what it was—a joke. He and Josiah had an unspoken agreement not to poach. More than likely Josiah's dig was meant to issue a challenge and get him on track. And it worked. No way was he handing this job over. "You Brits have fucked this up enough already."

"How do you figure that?"

"Call it a case of pants-on-fire." Ford winked. "Lucky for you, Bravo team is here to clean up your mess."

4

Two HOURS later Ford sat on a locker room bench in the Warehouse gym and looked around at his team. No monitors or fancy equipment. No bullshit briefings or plodding through a list of possible actions. Just an informal meeting with the three most lethal men he knew. Men he would die to protect and could trust at his back.

He'd handpicked every one of them, even Lucas Garner. The order for Ford to put a Brit on Bravo sent him digging. Lucas came from something called the science division of British intelligence. It made him sound like a nerd but it really meant he could get in anywhere, blow up anything. The guy liked fire and found a job that let him set them without getting arrested. Ford admired anyone who could walk that line.

In addition to Lucas and West, a guy with a mysterious past and sharpshooter skills, Ford chose Reid Armstrong. One look at his file convinced Ford that Reid belonged outside the rigid structure of most intelligence agencies. He'd infiltrated terrorist cells as easily as sneaking into a movie. Add in the fluency in more languages than Ford knew existed and the guy proved the perfect addition.

"Let's cut through the bureaucratic bullshit. We know what's going on." The "we" meant Bravo. There was Alliance and then there was *his* team. Ford relied only on the latter.

"Right." West leaned against the row of gray lockers. "Purposely bad intel."

"On one hand we have an auction. On the other a kid who walked out of a government facility holding deadly crap in a tube and no one tried to stop him. That can only mean inside job and we all know it." No other explanation made sense so Ford refused to dwell on them. Let the admin types run through options and follow protocol. He was hired to get shit done.

"And the need for better screening in those jobs." Reid mumbled the comment.

"You think Ward or Harlan is a problem?" Lucas stood at the end of the aisle keeping watch. As the youngest member of the team, that often turned out to be his role—making sure none of the rest of them got shot or stabbed. Getting garroted was also out. "Is that why we're meeting in here instead of the conference room?"

"No." Ford really only trusted Ward. They had a past, and the man had proven to be rock solid more than once. "Though, admittedly, I'm not so sure about Harlan."

Lucas stopped pacing and watching. "Because he's British?"

Straddling the bench, Reid sat down facing Ford. "Because he's a condescending ass."

"Well, there's that." West delivered the comment in a dry tone, which was starting to be his normal tone.

The talking it through partially worked for Ford. He

knew the guys needed to blow off steam and sometimes that meant verbal battles or going back and forth. If they had more time, he'd encourage it, but they needed to get prepped and ready to fly. That meant he had to explain to Shay one more time why he'd drop out of her life for at least a day.

Lying and deceit came with the job. He'd been trained in subterfuge and subjected to random screenings and lie detector tests while in the CIA. He now counted beating the machines and skirting the truth among his skills. When he tracked terrorists or killers or hung out with assassins and mercenaries, that was fine. But Shay deserved better.

He walked in out of the darkness with the slime of his work still clinging to him and she hit him like a burst of light. With long wavy brown hair and big blue eyes, Shay would qualify as pretty by any standard. She had this wide smile and smokin' hot body. All of it worked for him.

But there was something else. Something that reeled him in and had guilt kicking in his gut. He wasn't one to be lured by a sweet face, and he'd had perfect bodies and skilled mouths in his bed before. His job had him facing off on a regular basis against trained female operatives who exchanged sex for information or used it to survive. He understood and accepted how the game was played, but nothing had prepared him for Shay.

The simple things about her comforted him. Him, the same guy who never sought out comfort or security in his life. She brushed her hair while sneaking peeks at him over her shoulder and his insides went wild. She would make him dinner and shake her hips, so slight, as she stirred something in a pot, and he all but ripped the kitchen towel out of her hand.

Hell, he caught her changing a lightbulb and got hard. It was as if she represented everything solid and good, all the things he fought for but eluded him in his personal life.

And he'd spent every single minute since he knew her lying to her.

He pushed away thoughts of her and how open she was in bed and how giving she was even as he limited his time with her, and focused on how to get through the next few days without walking into a toxic cloud. "We need to treat all intel with skepticism from now on. Believe none of it. Plan for the opposite. We get a lead or intercept chatter, we doubt it. Go in thinking we're going to be fucked from behind and prepare two or three extraction options."

Reid swore under his breath. "It's like I'm back in the CIA."

"Except there are people we can trust." Ford gestured to all of them. "Us. Bravo."

West nodded. "Damn right."

Lucas kept up his steady scan of the room. "Do we tell Ward?"

"Not yet." Ford trusted Ward with his life but sometimes you needed to slip around the rules. Like now. "We're not putting him in the position of having to keep our secrets from everyone else in Alliance."

"I have a feeling we're about to do something stupid that could get us thrown in jail." Reid held up his hands as if in surrender. "Hey, I'm in. I'm just saying I see it coming."

Jail would be a positive outcome compared to some of the other options, but Ford let that drop.

"At some point we're going after this kid Trent Creighton, right?" Reid looked around the group. "He's on the run and a novice. I'd like to think even with being fed bad intel we could track down that little piece of shit and take him out."

"I could feed one of those toxic vials to him." West shrugged in the way only West could when talking about killing someone. "Hard to sell it when you're dead."

"I like where your heads are." Keeping them on task would be the trick. Ford knew he could unleash them and the combined firepower in the room would put an end to most problems, but they had to sweep up all the pieces, and right now he wasn't sure what those where.

The day likely would come when he had to put a bullet in Trent, and soon, but not today. Not before they collected more information and knew all the players. And if the kid coughed up the intel, he might get to live. He owed Shay that much. More, actually, but the least he could do after screwing her was not cut down her relatives in front of her.

Trent was a stupid kid, but the person running the auction ranked as the most dangerous under Alliance's watch because if he couldn't get the toxin from Trent, he'd look elsewhere, and that meant the danger would lurk and grow until he got caught or killed.

"Under all of this we have the prick who provided the bad intel and got innocent collaterals killed in Hampstead." The person Ford tagged in his head as the inside man and vowed to wipe off the planet. A potential mole who would die ugly and slow at Bravo's hands.

West raised a hand. "I get to put a bullet in that guy."

"Only one?" Lucas asked.

"Sure." West mumbled under his breath. "After I cut him into pieces."

Ford wanted a front row seat to that. "That will teach him to try to set a match to your ass."

"So, the plan is?" Reid asked.

Looking around, Ford knew he had their attention. They were engaged and ready. They'd follow his lead and throw their bodies in front of the toxin, if necessary. And it could come down to that, but right now he needed to sneak them out of the country. "We have a lot of blind spots in this thing, but we can collect our own intel. Do it right and get out clean."

"Let me guess," Lucas said. "You know a guy."

"An old asset in France. He won't be happy to see me but we can convince him to talk." Ford shrugged. "That's what guns and hitting are for."

West nodded. "Sounds like we need our passports."

Since they all possessed multiple sets of those, Ford knew that wouldn't be a problem. "We plan the op on the plane and fill Ward in when we get there. Well, after we have the asset and he's giving up intel."

"Dad is not going to be happy with this plan." But Reid smiled as he said it.

Adrenaline bounced around the room, pinging off every surface. The tension, the possibility of shutting this down before it became a nightmare, sent a shot of energy moving through all of them. All but Lucas, who frowned. "I'm in but I wonder if we should take a run at the people closest to Creighton first and apply a little pressure until someone gives him up."

"I have a few minutes to spare." West pushed off from the bank of lockers and twisted the lock on the one closest to him. "I like the idea of finding Trent and killing the little fucker."

"We need to attack this from both ends," Ford said. The middle, the side . . . he was willing to do whatever worked. And he had the resources to get them all where they needed to be. "I have a plane ready to go tomorrow morning."

Reid's eyes narrowed. "You know the most interesting people."

Ford noticed none of them said no. They didn't balk at undermining Alliance command. He talked about shitting all over their office and bosses and taking off to chase a possibility, and they signed up on his word. That was the kind of loyalty and trust he never got in the CIA. Something that made Bravo team and Alliance worth fighting for, even with the bullshit and stuff with Harlan.

"A pilot who owes me a favor." Ford had known that unsanctioned run into Libya to hunt down that missing seaman would pay off one day.

"Is this friend of yours bringing bail money?" Reid asked.

"As if we'd qualify for bail." Ford tried to make it sound like a joke but truth was, no. One screw-up, one word to the wrong person, and they'd be dead.

It was almost four o'clock in the afternoon when Ford walked into Shay's apartment. One firm knock, then the keys jingled in the lock before she could get up from the kitchen table. Seeing him walk in—was that a beer ad on his shirt?—had her brain misfiring.

His biceps bunched under the edge of his tee. Between the scruff around his chin, big smile, and dark brooding good looks, she felt something gurgle in her throat. It was as if she were treading water and getting tugged under. She'd talked about having someone steal her breath before. With Ford she lived the sensation.

While she loved seeing him, she had no idea why she was right now. He worked long hours and four o'clock qualified more as lunch than his quitting time. With one leg crossed over the other and her foot bouncing against the floor, she stared him down. She held her pen in a death grip to keep from fidgeting and flinging it around.

The more still he stood there, leaning in the doorway, the more nervous she became. Energy rolled through her, all jumbled and making her twitchy. Maybe if he'd stop staring back. "Ford?"

"That's hot."

She followed his gaze to her hands. The edge of her checkbook dug into her palm from where she clenched it. With her elbows balanced on the table, she tried to ease the tension in her shoulders and relax, though that rarely worked with him around. "What?"

This time he gestured with his chin. "You. Right there."

She lifted her hand and pointed the bottom of the pen in his general direction. "I'm writing a check."

"Exactly."

"You should see me vacuum." She wanted to laugh but no sound came out. His effect on her scared her sometimes.

"Are you trying to break my concentration?"

"I don't even know what you're doing here at this time of the day." Standing, leaning, generally making her insides jump and jiggle.

"Staring."

She noticed that, too. "Okay . . . why?"

"All that traveling, all those times I leave . . ." His voice trailed off as he pushed away from the door and came toward her. "I want to remember your face."

That sounded like a goodbye or a break. Like something she did not want and would fight to fend off. "Are you telling me you're leaving again?"

He kept walking until he stood next to her chair. "Just for twenty-four hours."

Just. "Honestly, Ford. Who needs this type of non-stop computer service?"

He made a face. "Uh, everyone?"

She was starting to curse her e-mail. Everything about computers ticked her off right now. She associated technology with him and that led to thinking about him leaving . . . again.

Her friends joked about her making him up. Never one to pick a guy she dated over lifetime friends, she'd inadvertently done just that. He came in and out with little notice and no set schedule. She'd moved plans around and canceled a dinner here and there. Every invitation included Ford, but he never tagged along.

She bit back her disappointment and growing anger. They didn't have a dating understanding and she'd gone into this not wanting more of a fling. Those days were long gone. She was the one changing the rules, but damn it, they needed to be changed. Not tonight, but soon.

She blew out a long breath, one packed with a you-are-right-on-edge drop of frustration. "Where are you going this time?"

"Omaha."

Not exactly a boondoggle. For a second she thought about tagging along, but Omaha? Nah. "That doesn't sound very fun."

He leaned against the table and ignored the creak of the wood under his weight. "So, we should go out tonight."

Her leg slid and her foot hit the floor with a thud. "Out?"

"On a date."

He could have used any word right there. Date, refrigerator, apple, and she would have had the same response. Dry-throat shock. "Really?"

He eyed her up as he pushed off from the table and moved in closer. Kind of like she'd lost her mind. "You've heard of the concept, I'm sure."

Yeah, but not from him. They mostly stayed in. Not that she complained about the sex or the cuddling on the couch while they watched the disaster movies he always seemed to find with the remote. Well, not much. Getting coffee or grabbing a burger—hell, even going for a short walk around the block with him—sounded good, but he'd never shown any interest.

She'd understood. He traveled all the time. Wanting to be home and stay there made sense. Still, she yearned for something bigger. Only a few weeks had passed but she craved a deeper connection.

"As in leave the building." He hesitated between each word. "We go outside and see people and—*Oompf.*" He rubbed his stomach. "What's with the hitting?"

He was probably trying to be funny with that tone. She was too busy trying to catch up to appreciate any amusement. "You usually want to stay in."

"Oh, we'll come back and then stay in until morning. Count on that." That sly smile telegraphed exactly what he had planned for later, all of it likely while naked. "But you deserve a normal date."

The shock hadn't faded. She didn't want to question, but still . . . "What brought this on?"

"A reality check."

She understood all those words but not in this context. Leaning in, she put her hand on his thigh. "I don't know what that means."

Capturing her hand in both of his, he lifted and placed a kiss on the dead center of her palm. "Sign your name so the electric company doesn't get pissy, then we'll get dressed and go out for an early dinner."

She wanted to repeat the word "out" one more time just to be sure, but refrained. The clouds started to clear from her head . . . sort of. "You're paying."

With her fingers slipped through his, he glanced at the register in front of her. "I can see your checkbook balance and I'm thinking you should."

She definitely heard the joking in his voice that time. Even without it, she'd never believe her twelve hundred dollar balance beat his, so she played along. "How badly did you want to get to those after-dinner activities?"

He flashed her a sexy smile. "Like I said, dinner is my treat."

"Smart man."

5

DRESSED IN street clothes but armed for attack, Ford and his team spread out as they walked down the narrow street in Paris's Marais district. Art galleries and shops filled the hip historic area. The famous Pompidou Centre, a modern building with brightly colored tubes and metal railings that scaled seven stories and stuck out among the older architecture, sat a short distance away. People milled and café seats were filled.

Basically, it was the worst place to conduct an interrogation, but Ford didn't have a choice.

As agreed, they were going in blind and without backup. No tech and no support from Ward or the Warehouse. If anyone but Bravo team tried this op it would be doomed to failure. Ford knew his guys could handle it, get in and out without anyone in the neighborhood knowing they were there.

Without a word they broke off. Lucas slipped into an alley and circled around the back of the building over the tea store. Reid stayed out front. West and Ford went in.

The outer door to the apartments above was unlocked. They stepped into a small alcove lined with mailboxes and a locked door right in front of them. Ford pressed the buttons beside every apartment number except the one without a name. A few people said hello, then the door buzzed. The click came next.

West reached for the handle. "I could have broken the lock."

"This was faster." There was something about human nature where people let strangers in during the day but not at night. As if criminals stuck to a darkness-only schedule. Ford shook his head as they passed through the inner door and headed up the stairs to the fourth floor. "The people in this building could save some money by not paying for security that doesn't actually secure anything."

"People are fucked up."

Amen to that. "That could be the Bravo team motto."

They reached the floor and headed down the hall-way to 4G. With each in position on either side of the doorway, Ford nodded.

West yawned.

Ford couldn't help but stare. "Am I boring you?"

"Not yet."

He took out the burner phone and dialed. He'd always had a memory for numbers, and this was one he kept in his mental Rolodex. The phone rang in his ear and on the other side of the door.

Cutting through the chitchat, Ford dove in as soon as someone answered. "Rupert, how are you? I'm in town and we need to talk."

The line disconnected and Ford could hear a series of thuds from inside the apartment. Shuffling and swearing, then the door flew open. Rupert ran out at top speed. West knocked him to the ground simply by putting his arm out.

Ford pressed his boot against Rupert's chest and held him down. "Going somewhere?"

Usually well-dressed and composed as part of his cover as a gallery owner, Rupert looked anything but. His hair fell over his eyes and he sputtered and squirmed as he tried to shove Ford's foot away.

Rupert groaned and blinked as if the hard fall jarred something important loose. "I . . . what are you . . ."

West nudged Rupert's shoulder with the tip of his shoe then glanced at Ford. "I don't think he's happy to see you."

That was the plan. Terrify, then get him to spill. But they were going to need privacy. "Let's go inside and talk."

After a nod from Ford, West reached down and lifted Rupert. The guy's knees gave out as soon as his feet hit the floor, but West held him upright with one hand. With a good shove, Rupert flew backward and tripped his way into the middle of the sunny studio apartment.

As soon as he found his balance, he turned on Ford. Rupert's cheeks reddened and his voice came out in a furious whisper. "You can't be here."

The dramatics didn't impress Ford. "Yet, I am."

"You have to—"

Ford stopped whatever Rupert planned to say by slamming him against the wall and trapping him there with an elbow pinned across his throat. "Stop talking."

"Technically, we need him to talk." West walked around shutting the curtains and flicking on lights. He stopped at the kitchen table to the right side of the room and studied the food spread out there. "I think we interrupted his lunch."

Ford pretended to care. "Did we, Rupert? Ah, man. Sorry about that."

"The cafe a few doors down looked good," West said.

"Is he right, Rupert?" The man shook under Ford's arm, so Ford squeezed tighter. Jumpy people did stupid things, and Ford didn't have the time to clean up the blood that came with that kind of mess.

West used the tip of his knife to move the cheese around on Rupert's plate. "We should talk fast or the bread will go stale."

"You're right." Ford made a tsk-tsking sound as he turned back to Rupert. "He's right."

Weaker, but smart enough to guess he was in trouble, the man clawed at Ford's arm but couldn't move it one inch. "I don't know anything," Rupert croaked out.

Now that was interesting. "I haven't asked you anything yet."

"I heard a denial," West said.

Ford almost smiled when West ripped off a piece of bread and popped it in his mouth. "You're eating his lunch?"

West cut off a piece of cheese. "If he keeps denying, he won't need it."

"Good point."

Rupert's heels thudded against the wall as his face turned a weird shade of purple. One that matched his argyle sweater. Only Rupert could pull off a fussy sweater and striped pants. "Very stylish outfit, by the way."

"Shame he might die in it."

Ford pretended to wave off West's concern. "Don't listen to my friend. You're only in trouble if you don't tell me what I need to know."

Rupert shifted and turned his head to the side. "I can't."

"You still don't know the question." Ford made a show of opening his knife with a snap. Waved it right in front of Rupert's face.

The man's eyes crossed. "This is about the auction, right?"

"See, now we're on the same page." Ford ran the tip of the knife along Rupert's throat.

He panted as his eyes widened. Was probably ten seconds away from wetting himself. "We're friends."

The man had an odd sense of friendship. Apparently it included attempted homicide. "You tried to kill me the last time you saw me." Ford still had an attitude about that, which likely explained why he leaned so hard on the guy's windpipe.

West made a noise somewhere between a hum and a sharp intake of breath. "To be fair, I've been tempted, and we're friends."

Rupert tried to shake his head but could barely move. His fingernails dug into Ford's arm. "That was a misunderstanding."

"You stabbed me," Ford pointed out.

Back then Rupert thought his cover had been blown and tried to run. Ford still had the scar across his stomach from where Rupert sliced him. One he'd explained away as a camping injury to Shay. Just another lie to her on top of so many others.

"A knife, Rupert?" West sighed. "Bad move."

"The auction." Just thinking about those days brought Ford's anger rushing back. He didn't make many mistakes, and letting this weasel get the jump on him pissed him off. "Talk now."

"I don't know—"

"Anything. Right." Ford dragged the knife across Rupert's chin, shallow but enough to draw drops of blood and make the guy whimper. "Let me tell you what's going to happen. This big guy here, after he eats the rest of your lunch, is going to beat the shit out of you. I won't go into details, but there will be blood and broken bones."

The whimpering grew louder and the muscles in Rupert's legs gave way. Ford had to ram a knee into Rupert's thigh to keep him upright.

"After he's done, I'm going to take a turn." Ford doubted he'd get through that without killing the guy. Seemed he had some leftover stabbing rage to work off. "Then I have some friends outside and they will each want to land a few punches."

West shook his head. "Rupert will be unconscious by then."

"Right." Ford looked from West to Rupert. "There's some good news. You won't be awake for most of the beatings."

Rupert swallowed as he tried to pull Ford's arm down. "You don't understand."

"Let me try." West's fist shot out. Right to Rupert's nose.

His head slammed against the wall. "Fuck."

"And I was holding back."

Rupert wiped his nose then stared at the blood on his hand. "Jesus."

West snorted. "He's not coming to help."

Ford had hours of control left but he wanted to get out of there. He lifted Rupert's head and pressed him back against the wall. Blood smeared his face and dropped onto his once pristine sweater.

Rupert weighed all of 150 pounds. A few more hits and he'd slam to the ground.

Ford grabbed a shirt off the nearest chair and held it to Rupert's face. "Talk before you pass out from blood loss."

"You broke my nose."

West nodded. "That was the point."

"Fine." Rupert's hands dropped and the stained shirt dangled from his fingertips as he balanced his head against the wall. "Benton."

Now there was some damn bad news. "He's the one behind the auction?" Ford asked.

Everyone in the law enforcement and intelligence communities knew Benton. No one had seen him for almost two years but every bombing and every attack carried his fingerprints. He didn't have a political agenda except to upend any legitimate government. The guy thrived on chaos. He stole weapons, bought them, traded in them. His network reached across every continent and the devastation rippled through country after country.

Looked like now he was branching out into chemical weapons. Wasn't that fucking fantastic.

"That's the word," Rupert said. "He wants something that will eat through protective vests and gear."

There was a nightmare scenario. Letting a madman with that sort of power get his hands on a toxin no one was prepared to counteract was the very reason Alliance was created. To stop end-of-the-world disasters like this. And they would.

Ford needed to know more first. "Give me the details."

"I don't have them." Rupert shook his head, and when West took a threatening step forward, he threw up his hands. "No, stop! There's talk but I can't confirm anything."

The wild-eyed panic suggested he'd coughed up all he could on that issue. Fine, but Ford had pieces he needed to fit together. "There was a fireball in Hampstead a few days ago."

"Right." Rupert nodded. "Someone fed intel to Jake Pearce. It was meant to throw you off or be a warning. I've heard both."

Pearce. Ford knew him by reputation. Had met him a few times. Talked to him a few months ago. He was a veteran of the CIA's Clandestine Service, retired but brought in as a free agent to assist in setting up Alliance. Ward trusted Pearce and had worked with him. That relationship explained how Alliance got the intel on the Hampstead house to begin with. Shame it was so damned wrong.

Something in Rupert's explanation caught Ford's attention. "A warning about what?"

"To let anyone who heard the chatter know who's in charge."

"We still don't," West said.

Rupert spared West a quick glance before looking at

Ford again. "The auction is being set up in Yemen in less than two weeks."

They had a ticking clock and a lot of players to identify, locate, and take out before then. No problem.

"What exactly is for sale?" Ford knew but wanted it confirmed.

"Some nasty chemical shit. No cure and no way to stop it. Word is, Benton's claiming he can weaponize it."

"No ego there." Ford hadn't planned to break the top international arms dealer this week, but that task just moved up to number one on his list. "Where's the kid?"

Rupert frowned as he dabbed at the trickle of blood that continued to seep from his nose. "Who?"

"The scientist who made the nasty shit," Ford said.

"No idea. I was told—" Rupert winced.

As if Ford would let that fly. "Don't stop there."

West motioned toward the table. "Unless you want me to use your cheese knife on you."

"I don't know about any scientist. This auction is way above that level. This is doomsday stuff."

Rupert's tendency to overstate and overact worked in this instance. Ford thought the phrase actually fit for once. "And you didn't call to warn me."

"You threatened to kill me the last time we talked."

The guy had a point. "Is Benton in London now?"

"No way. He hasn't shown up anywhere since the hotel bombing, and the drone strikes on his compound after." Rupert didn't explain, but the attacks in Morocco happened right before the attack on Benton's rumored home in Algeria, so drawing the line from one incident to the other wasn't a stretch for anyone in the know. "Some of us thought you got him."

Ford wasn't taking responsibility for that fuck-up. "*We* would have." And now it was time to go. "What else do I need to know, Rupert?"

"Nothing." He tipped his head back, then checked his shirt one last time. "I swear."

Ford studied Rupert for a few more seconds before nodding to West. "Go ahead."

Ford and West switched positions until West stood right in front of Rupert and clamped a hand around his throat.

The squirming started right on cue. Rupert flailed and tried to break contact. Between coughs he managed to get out of few words. "Wait, I told you what I knew."

"Now we're even, but we still need to turn your place upside down and you'd rather be asleep for that." Ford snapped his fingers. "But you need to agree not to talk. I'd hate to bring my friend back and watch him kill you."

"No, I wouldn't—"

Whatever else Rupert intended to say got cut off. West applied the right amount of pressure, cut off a few seconds of breathing, and Rupert crumpled to the floor unconscious.

"We're coming down," Ford said into the com, knowing Lucas and Reid had heard everything, then turned back to West. "So, we're dealing with the guy at the top of every watch and wanted list who somehow found Trent Creighton."

"Can we kill that kid now?"

So very tempting. "We need him alive."

And they did. If Trent had a link to Benton, Ford

intended to exploit it. Whatever they had to do to make that happen, they would.

West swore under his breath. "That's a shame."

"Also looks like it's time to check in with Ward."

West walked over to Rupert's bookcase. "The boss man is going to yell."

"Ward doesn't scare me." Little did other than failure, and Ford vowed not to lose.

He'd been too late once. Not this time.

6

FORD HAD been home for two out of three days. Even with working long hours, Shay thought that might be a record.

But for the first time in weeks he was not the only man on her mind. Her cousin held the title of Most Difficult to Pin Down at the moment. He had not checked in for about a month. Texts and calls went unanswered. No one opened the door at his apartment when she stopped by.

She used her emergency key to get in, which she knew he'd hate because he got all sorts of prickly about privacy, but she'd bet he would have hated the smell of rotten trash in his studio even more. She handled that and the expired milk in the fridge and acted like his big sister, or worse, mother, more than like a twenty-six-year-old cousin who grew up with him.

Hoping to get some direction, she'd left her cousin's house and went directly to her uncle's place. Now, she sat on the stool at the impressive carrera marble breakfast bar in his kitchen. The pristine white and gray room sparkled as if no one ever cooked in there, which was pretty accurate.

Uncle Anthony had built a commercial and residential real estate empire in the DC metro area. Worked his butt off for years accumulating and managing his holdings. When he lost his wife eight years ago, he abruptly cut back and started spending some of his hard-earned wealth. A cook was the first addition to the household staff in his red brick minimansion on Massachusetts Avenue, right across from the Japanese Embassy.

Shay smoothed her fingers over the handle of the coffee mug and fought the urge to grab her phone and try Trent one more time. She glanced up at her uncle instead. "He left me four messages and then nothing."

Anthony waved her off before diving into the pink box filled with doughnuts and all sorts of sugary goodness. "I talked to him that week. He'd been running for days straight on adrenaline and caffeine when he called to borrow your car. He came off manic and we talked about it."

"And?"

"That's it, really. He said he had a big project coming up." Anthony shook his head. "You know your cousin. He gets lost in work."

"It was more than that." She couldn't quite name it, but something had been festering for a few months now. Trent had retreated to his old ways of dealing with stress—by ignoring the people around him and becoming shorter and grumpier with each conversation.

Maybe he didn't mean it and it stemmed from his big brain and all that, but he could cut off the people he cared about without thought. Be mean. He had an anger management issue that had calmed as he got older but only after Anthony threw therapist after therapist at the problem. At this point Shay would almost welcome his sharp barbs to his recent silence.

"Shay, he's twenty-one and obsessed with his work. He gets wound up and you worry. None of that is news." Anthony dropped a glazed doughnut on a napkin and slid it across to her. "You've been doing this dance since you were both kids. He's . . . difficult and you're a fixer. It can be a rough combination."

Growing up with Anthony, living in his house from the time she turned fourteen, she knew that dough-nuts qualified as cooking to him. Not that she could fault him since she'd become the take-out queen. If she couldn't buy it already prepared or in a box, forget it.

"Still, bad mood or not, busy or not, he usually checks in." She picked at the edge of the doughnut then ripped off a piece and popped it in her mouth.

"Maybe he finally found a girl." Anthony settled on a long john slick with a thick layer of chocolate icing. "About time, if you ask me. Science geek or not, a guy his age should date."

"He will, you know. Eventually. Find a woman . . . or possibly a guy." Shay couldn't tell which Trent would go for. Men and women hit on him all the time, but he never seemed to notice. Between his cute face, the sly smile, and hair that straddled the line between blond and brown, he looked more star baseball player than stereotypical nerd. He happened to be both.

She peeked over the mug's rim to see Anthony's re-action to her comment.

This time he shrugged. "I checked with him a few years ago and he said it would be a girl, but who knows. He doesn't share, and if you ask the wrong question . . .

well, you know how he can go off. But I'm still thinking female is the answer."

"Because Trent would tell you." Though they were
close, so Trent might.

"I'm his dad."

Anthony didn't need to say more. Trent lost his
mother young. By that time his natural brilliance had
already spiked. He'd outgrown his classes and teach-
ers and moved on to special tutors to supplement the
education his impressive private high school provided.
Anthony made all of that happen over Aunt Marianne's
pleas to keep Trent's life normal. Anthony had known
even back then that Trent needed something more.

"I know I push him hard but I don't want him to
waste his gift."

"By working for the government?" She'd heard this
justification many times over the years. About how Trent
had skills other people didn't and needed to capitalize
on them. Inherent in the comments was Anthony's frustration over Trent's decision to go the public sector route
instead of throwing in with a private company.

Anthony's relaxed lounge against the counter ended.
He stood up straight as his lips flattened into a straight
line. "Stop putting words in my mouth."

"Right." This time she gave in and picked up her
phone. The anxiety spinning in her stomach whirled at
super speed at the continued lack of a response.

In the past, Trent would go long stretches without
touching base. She was used to that, but he always re-
sponded within a few days when she texted and asked
for a status check. It was their code, but it failed this
time.

She tried to think of a way to approach this, skipping the sour notes about Trent's employment choices. Fact was, Anthony looked calm, but she'd guess he was worried and calling in favors and ten seconds away from going to Trent's boss for help. He was an overprotective dad. She knew because he'd played that role for her for years. It could be suffocating. She'd found her way through it. Trent had a harder time with the coddling.

Still, her worry kept multiplying. Much more and she'd camp out in the hallway of Trent's Capitol Hill condo. "It's just that he hasn't been to his place and—"

"Let me worry about this." Anthony grabbed the coffeepot, the one appliance with which he was very familiar, and refilled her mug. "You have a new boyfriend to keep happy."

That sounded . . . well, awful. Wiped most of the worries about Trent right out of her head and filled it with a please-be-kidding sensation. "Ugh."

Anthony's smile came back full force. "What, too old fashioned?"

"Only by about fifty years."

"I just think the younger generation of women would benefit from being more attentive to their men."

She held up both hands to beat back the words. "Oh my God, stop."

"Fine." Anthony pointed at her while he shot her with his most serious expression. "But I want to meet him soon."

Yeah, that was a dinner she didn't relish. Anthony could be intense. Ford could be vague. The idea of those worlds colliding while she tried to choke down linguini didn't appeal to her. "Maybe."

"I know his work is important, but so are you." Anthony dove into the pink box for pastry number two.

Clearly he had switched the target of his lecturing from Trent to her. Yet another reason Trent needed to show up soon. It was time for him to take one for the team. "You really think I'm going to let Ford take me for granted?"

"I didn't say that."

She picked at the uneaten half of her doughnut, suddenly not hungry for much of anything. "What are you saying?"

"Let me check around. Ask a few questions about the guy." When she opened her mouth, Anthony talked over her. "More than the standard reference check for the rental."

"You mean you want to investigate him? Like call-in-the-FBI type check him out?"

"It's prudent."

Shay noticed that Anthony didn't laugh off her attempt at sarcasm. That's part of what scared her. "It's insulting."

She forced her body to relax when she realized the tension running across her shoulders had turned into a neck cramp. Truth was, her objections zoomed right past feeling uncomfortable about Anthony poking around into Ford's life to something deeper.

"I'm more worried about your safety than hurting your boyfriend's feelings."

"He's private." Their relationship was new and in a tenuous phase. She didn't want to drag Ford in front of her uncle. Her *very* wealthy uncle.

And there it was. The real fear. Her last boyfriend

proved more attracted to Anthony's bank accounts than her. She didn't want to live through that again.

"Which is exactly why I'll be careful," Anthony said.

She needed him to back down. Maybe spend as much energy on finding Trent as he was on her love life. "No."

Anthony lowered his doughnut back down to the box nice and slow. "I'm not asking for permission, Shay."

"Good, because I'm not giving it." Nothing in his expression suggested she'd won the argument. "I'm not kidding. Absolutely not."

Anthony nodded but didn't bother looking up. "I hear you."

That's not what worried her.

Alliance team members moved in and out of the main room of the Warehouse. Most of Delta Team wore exercise clothes and headed to the showers after the mandatory gym session called by Josiah. Bravo team had hit the weight room early and now gathered around the conference room table going through the paper trail computer analyst Ellery Kimball compiled on Trent Creighton.

Ellery could track anything. She liked guns but only on the practice range. She showed no interest in field-work. Cute and petite with fiery auburn hair, she stood up to the men in the office and could seemingly track any money transaction anywhere with only the thinnest of leads.

Ward had to laugh at the men's reaction to her. Ford called her skills spooky, but none of them ever mistook her pretty face for a sign of weakness. Despite how protective they all were of her, they listened. Sometimes Ward thought she had better command of the room than he did.

Wade sat in his small glass-walled office and watched it all. None of them were good at waiting but they needed a solid lead on the scientist, so they poured over every frame of video and every line of document.

They'd connected with sources. They would find him. Ford and West would leave a pile of bodies behind them, if that's what it took. They clearly had no trouble sneaking off to France on a twenty-hour turnaround without authority to rough up a former asset. Ward knew he should be angry and threatening disciplinary actions, but he would have done the same thing in Ford's position.

The men weren't the only ones who sucked at waiting. Ward opened and closed his right hand. He kept thinking if he strengthened it enough, loosened his muscles the right way, he'd get the feeling back. Not fucking happening. After all the rehabilitation and hours of work, the doctors said he should be happy he could make a fist after having a knife rammed through his palm. He thought they should kiss his ass.

But the main reason behind the act that caused his injury was on the way to visit him, and seeing her reminded him that he'd take a stake through the heart if it meant keeping her safe. Natasha Gregory, former MI6 agent, current Alliance director, and the woman who flipped his life upside down until he couldn't imagine a day without her.

They met in Fiji when they were both on an assignment for their respective agencies—he posing as a tourist and she as a bartender—and neither knew the other's true identity. Their operations overlapped. She threatened to kill him more than once. He couldn't help but fall for her.

In the end he got the woman and Alliance was born. He considered it the best operation of his life, even though it did sideline him permanently from the field.

His cool blonde didn't disappoint back then when tracking down a brutal dictator, and she didn't disappoint now. She walked across the main floor in khaki utility pants and a long-sleeve black tee, with her long straight hair up in a ponytail. The confident walk highlighted her lithe frame. Tall and sexy and very much in charge.

She pushed open the door and entered without knocking. "The energy is thrumming on the floor, isn't it?"

He loved everything about her, but that British accent was so damn hot. He'd tell her, but they had a deal he would not breach. At work they were all business. She demanded to be treated as the boss and she'd fucking earned it, so he didn't test that limit.

"The team doesn't exactly excel at sitting." Shooting, yes, but Ward didn't let them touch weapons in the office except at the indoor practice range.

"Then it's good I brought this." She dumped a file on the edge of his desk.

He didn't touch it. "What is it?"

"We have a waterfront construction worker in southwest DC who reported some odd activity in a run-down building." She flipped the cover open and pointed at a photo. "Sounded like nothing. The police checked it out. It only got flagged for our review because some smart analyst noticed the expensive and seemingly new alarm system on the gate."

"Someone earned his pay." That old kick of adrenaline pounded him. Tension started building inside him and he itched to put on a vest and grab his guns.

"You can thank Ellery." Tasha shrugged. "She has some program that sorts these things out."

"I figured as much."

"A quick look at the deeds led to a rabbit hole of corporations inside of corporations, and after some stone overturning, finally back to Anthony Creighton."

Ward was starting to hate that family. "More than interesting."

She turned away with her back to him and faced the floor. A few seconds passed before she spoke again. "Ward?"

"Yeah?"

"Are you staring at my ass?"

He pulled his gaze away from that very impressive part of her when he heard the amusement in her voice, but not without some effort. "Yes, I am."

"We're at work."

"Which is why I haven't bent you over the desk and dragged those pants off." He had to push the mental image out of his head before he started squirming in his chair.

She shot him a smile over her shoulder. "Later."

"You can fucking count on that."

"In the meantime, it looks like your boys have something to break into." She put her hand on the door handle then stopped. "Where's Ford's head in this?"

"Meaning?" But Ward knew. He'd served with Ford.

The guy was rock solid but he lacked the gene for tolerating bullshit. Tact was not in his wheelhouse either.

"I know about the Paris trip." She spun back around and crossed her arms over her stomach. "Then there's the issue between Ford and Harlan."

"I wonder who told you about that." Ward admired his cosupervisor, but the guy was all about the chain of command. That put Harlan on a collision course with Ford.

"Not Harlan, if that's what you're suggesting."

Ward balanced his palms against the edge of the desk and pushed back, straightening his arms. "Ford handles disappointment with sarcasm."

She treated him to one of her you've-lost-it eye rolls. "You sound like his father instead of his boss."

Ward decided to ignore that. "Ford and Bravo should take the lead on his."

"If you think he's ready."

The "he" in question stopped talking with his group on the main floor and stood up, staring straight into Ward's glassed-walled office Ward took in the determined scowl and the fury bubbling beneath the surface. Ford would do anything to stop Trent and whomever the kid was working with, and Ward agreed there was someone.

More than once Ward had put his life in Ford's hands, and he'd do it again. "I do."

"Fantastic." She reached for the doorknob again.

"One question."

She froze, looking more wary than curious. "Yeah?"

"Why are you investigating warehouse deeds and minor trails on your own instead of letting the folks down here handle it?" When she didn't immediately jump in, he tried again. "Seems a bit beneath your job description."

She threaded her fingers together in front of her, held that pose for a second before dropping her arms to her sides again. Not one to fidget and shuffle her feet, she looked to be fighting off a major case of both right now. "We're not engaging in a pissing contest, Ward. That's part of our deal."

The defensiveness reminded him of how they first met, arguing over who got to bring down a dictator hiding in Fiji. "Just making sure we're still on track here."

She came away from the glass door and stood at the edge of his desk. "Some little shit with a drop of catastrophic toxin is not taking out a city on my watch."

Now that he understood. "Agreed."

"I thought you would." She blew out a long breath before going back to the door and opening it to call out. "Ford?"

He didn't hesitate. He practically jogged the distance to the office and nodded his welcomes as he walked in. "Hello, Director."

"Tasha is fine."

Ward grabbed the file and held it out to Ford. "We have a lead."

"What is it?" he asked as he flipped through the first few pages.

Tasha slapped her hand against the top sheet. "First, I need to know that you're going to be a team player on this and not hijack a plane and head out for Iceland."

Ford dropped his arms and switched his frown from

Tasha to Ward and back again. "If there's a lead in Iceland I will."

She smiled but looked as if she wanted to fight it. "From anyone else I'd be forced to give a chain of command lecture."

Ford peeked at her over the top of the file. "Please promise you're going to spare me."

Not one to back down, Tasha didn't now either. "Find me that damn kid scientist and I will."

Ward had seen this before. These two had their battle down. He doubted they needed him but he stepped in anyway. "It's all about finding the right incentive."

"Sure is." Ford nodded. "Challenge accepted."

7

"COME ON, baby. Open up for me." Ford shifted his hand to the right as he kept up the steady string of sweet talk. "That's it. Let go."

"I feel dirty listening to this." Reid didn't even twitch as he stood in full battle gear with his assault rifle at his side. "Not that I'm going to stop, of course."

Ford ignored him and the other members of the Alliance team hovering around him. They stood just outside the ten-foot security door to the front gate of the run-down Atlantis Food Company building. The sun had disappeared hours ago and only security lights from the surrounding warehouses brightened the deadly quiet area of the southwest DC waterfront.

Water lapped against the dock, and the sharp scent of rotting fish wrapped around them. Ford blocked it all and focused on the task in front of him.

Josiah separated from Delta team and looked over Reid's shoulder. "With that kind of sex talk, I feel sorry for Ford's last girlfriend. Remind me, what did she do for a living?"

No way was Ford touching that, since the last woman in his life that Josiah knew about turned out to be a spy for North Korea. Not that one minute of those ten days were a secret. The men standing around him right now knew because it happened two months into his employment at Alliance and the beginning of the team. The second damn overseas field operation, in fact.

He'd figured it out right after they had sex. She did a good job of searching his stuff in the hotel room. Avoided most of his traps and kept everything exactly as she found it. She was good. He'd been better. Still, he'd had no choice but to neutralize and report.

The guys had given him shit for weeks for not sniffing her out before they hit the sheets. Which was a welcome relief compared to the threats of dismissal from Harlan. Between that and what Ward liked to refer to as his shitty attitude, Ford was still on informal probation. At this rate he'd always be.

In reality, with his CIA career in shambles and his choices slim, Alliance had been his last stop. He liked to say he chose to switch jobs when Ward came with the offer, but the truth was, he had few options because he wasn't qualified for anything else.

Ford had been there for seven months and had no intention of blowing the gig, even if he did find the operation parameters the CIA and MI6 tried to hand down for Alliance fucking ridiculous. Pages of regulations made up by men who spent their days sitting behind a desk. No real life experience. No discussion with anyone in the field. As if the bad guys followed protocol.

Good thing Tasha and Ward ignored all of that garbage. They insisted on moving fast and hard once they cleared the intel. They expected the teams to be on call and ready to go. That's why Ford hated having time off. Too much opportunity to think.

And then there was the problem where his mind went soft after a few days of his dick getting hard. Shay had him spinning in circles. The mix of sexy and smart, grounded without taking herself too seriously, reeled him in. The husky voice, the walk that made his brain sputter.

But the attraction tunneled deeper than the surface. He liked the way she led her life and supported him . . . or the guy she thought he was. She didn't run around in circles or panic. She took things in stride. She was rock solid, and he'd known so few rock solid types in his life. People who wanted something or broke rules and made excuses, yes. Someone who was exactly who she claimed to be, no pretense or games, no.

She was supposed to be a job. He was supposed to be watching from a distance. He blew right through both of those terms of his assignment and now had a disaster brewing.

She was related to Trent, which meant she could be dirty. At the very least Ford expected and dreaded a spectacular explosion when she figured out he'd lied to her. And if Trent died in the fallout it, Shay would come gunning for him. Ford predicted it, saw the train coming at him but could not seem to back away from her.

Damn women.

Not that staying was an option. To keep his edge, he needed to keep moving. Needed to be at work. He'd learned that the hard way more than a year ago and could still see the red stain of a woman's blood on his palms when he turned his hands over.

He used those same hands now. The electric pick knocked the internal pins clear. Twenty seconds of grinding and the tumblers in the old-fashioned lock gave way. With that out of the way, Ford slid the box's front panel to the side to reveal the computerized second lock underneath.

Adrenaline poured through him. He lived for this. The chase, the find, the hunt. And he had a handy way to solve this part. With his handheld computer clicked into place, numbers flashed across the small alarm screen, flipping one after another until they revealed each number of the code.

The final one snapped in place. "We're in."

After a click, Ward's voice came over the com. "We've got a green light, gentlemen."

No one moved because they all knew the alarm amounted to the first step of many. They'd studied the building's layout and watched the tapes. They had to get through the small courtyard and to the back side of the building before the missing scientist bolted.

First they had to know how many hostiles they had inside.

"How we looking?" Ford asked the question, knowing Harlan followed the action through their helmet cameras and the surveillance back in the Warehouse. Despite being a general pain in the ass, Harlan knew his stuff. He kept in top physical condition and could pick up a weapon if the moment called for it.

"Two heat signatures to your northwest," he said.

Two against eight. Ford loved those odds. With both

Alliance teams on the job and some serious planning, they could take on the full military power of some small countries. "Still in the corner room?"

"Affirmative."

They'd walked through the plans several times back at the Warehouse and agreed Ford would take his men inside. Josiah's team would secure the perimeter. Or that was the theory. One explosion or wrong turn and the whole op could flip upside down on them. That's why Ford wanted to know where all the players stood. "Movement?"

"One hostile is walking around in the doorway," Harlan said. "Likely a guard."

Ford motioned for his team to take their positions. "Eyes open."

He waited until Josiah's team cleared out before clicking off the com. Just for a second, but the message needed to be said: "Be prepared for a fuck-up. This intel came through official channels."

West nodded. "I don't like it."

"Let's say I'm skeptical." Ford didn't trust anything he couldn't track on his own.

Tasha had handed this over, and that carried some weight, but she got the tip from another department in Liberty Crossing. From someone not affiliated with Alliance, which made Ford's inner alarm blare a warning.

"Getting this far undetected was too easy." Reid's attention never slipped from his visual scan of the area.

"For you, since you just stood there while I did the work." Ford went for sarcastic but inside he agreed with Reid. With a nod, Ford turned the com back on and snapped into attack mode. "Going in."

He and Reid slipped into the opening first, taking positions just inside. Weapons up and gaze roaming, they moved a few feet so the other two men on the four-person team, West and Lucas, could step behind them and watch the flank.

Ford sent Josiah and his team spreading along the outside of the building. They all stayed silent, depending on hand gestures and Harlan's directions to guide them to the man with the deadly toxin. Turned out the boss's precise nature helped in cases like this.

Inside, Ford blinked several times, forcing his eyes to adjust to the stark darkness. They'd skipped night gear for fear of being unexpectedly blinded by hostiles because the Hampstead setup showed they were dealing with professionals.

Stray rays from the lights outside snuck in through cracks in the boarded-up windows. The scent of rancid fish and stale air mixed to create a gagging stench. But there was little else in there. They'd stepped into a large empty room. Remnants of machinery had been pushed up against the walls and wires hung from the exposed ceiling. Stray pieces of metal and crushed cement crunched under the soles of their black shoes.

Looking around, he couldn't figure out if someone was in the process of breaking the place down or building it up again. Except for the eye-watering smell, none of what they found amounted to a surprise.

Having the electronic model in the office match up with the real layout this time would be nice. No unexpected rooms to weave through, which also meant nowhere to hide.

According to the briefing, at the far end, about a half

a football field away, a doorway led to a series of hall-ways and small offices. What they needed—who they needed—was behind there. Ford opened his hand and pointed in the direction of the door.

Without another word, they broke into a light jog. In formation, from one end to the other, they moved. Never stopping and taking in every inch of the surroundings.

When they reached the opposite end, Ford stood to the side and put his hand on the door, feeling for heat or any sensation. Nothing. With the doorknob in his palm, he turned, half expecting another lock. Instead, the door opened. A creak echoed through the near-empty building as he pushed it a few inches.

Reid winced and Harlan swore over the line, but Ford kept moving, heading through and into the next open area. A left turn, a right turn, then a straight shot. That was the plan, and they'd execute it. Grab the weasel science wunderkind and save the world. What he hoped would become a typical day for Alliance, but they had to get out of there alive first.

The fall wind whistled through the small spaces be-tween the warehouse's broken boards and rattled the walls. The building creaked and their clothing rustled from their swift movements and bulletproof vests.

They made the first turn and Ford closed his fist to stop them before the second. A wave of heat smacked him in the face. The temperature didn't make sense with the cool outside breeze. Someone could have the heat on, but the place didn't look like the wiring would hold and this was too hot for normal.

A nerve at the base of his neck twitched. He glanced over at Reid and read his flat mouth and saw West's stiff shoulders and the small shake of Lucas's head. They all knew something was off. Maybe just a fraction, but that's all it took.

They were in tune with their surroundings and each other. They were also on alert, and it looked as if they were walking into a second trap thanks to bad intel fed to them through supposedly friendly channels.

Yeah, the mole, if there was one, was going to go down screaming.

Ford scanned the open ceiling tiles. Harlan and the tech team had blocked cell phone signals into the place and scanned the area for devices. Even now they monitored the power usage on the building, just as they had been doing for the last twenty-four hours since word came down this could be either a hideout or a place to find the toxin.

All evidence pointed to this being a solid lead. Trent's rich daddy owned the building. Not the usual expensive condo or high-priced commercial property in Anthony Creighton's portfolio. The tip from the waterfront worker informant triggered an investigation that led to round-the-clock surveillance and photos from every angle. Trucks had pulled in and out at all times of the night and the men took precautions not to have their faces show up on film.

Still, Ford was having trouble imagining some guy in a lab coat testing GB-19 in a place without a high level of security. Never mind that it reeked of dead fish.

Once they learned about it, governments would want Trent's research. Powerful people would fight to own him or kill him. Knowing that, the lax setup didn't make sense.

The ticking at the top of Ford's shoulders kicked up to a nonstop hammering.

After a final visual check for cameras and company, he used the small mirror in his right pocket to check out the hallway. Nothing. The door at the end stayed closed. If someone was pacing, they did it inside and out of sight.

Yeah, it was fucking official. Ford hated this op and wanted to beat the hell out of Trent.

Taking the lead, Ford turned the corner and hugged the wall. The rest of Bravo team filed in behind him.

"Bravo's a go." Harlan sat miles away and still whispered over the com.

"We need the kid alive," Ward added.

They had to know how and why Trent Creighton slipped out of his lab. The kid, all of twenty-one, was considered a Superman of toxic research. Him going missing—or worse, going rogue—pointed to all sorts of nasty possibilities. Terrorism, espionage, bribery. None of which headed down a positive road and seemed to collide in a potential auction in Yemen.

This substance was a death sentence. A terrorist's dream weapon. Mix a short incubation period and a very limited time in which to apply the antidote—something that wasn't even fully tested and vetted yet—and you had a near guarantee of death and destruction on a massive scale. Trent had created a catastrophic virus and no solution.

An auction would touch off an End of Days countdown. It would mean Trent, or a partner, or someone holding Trent, planned to fuck up everything in the vicinity of exposure and make a shit ton of money doing it. Which was why Ford would stop him, even if doing so meant a bullet to the kid's head.

Once again Shay's face flashed in Ford's mind. He blinked it out before the guilt clenched at his gut. It was an unusual sensation for him but one that kept kicking up when he thought of her.

They got to the door to the offices. With Ford on one side and Reid on the other, they waited. Heat rolled over Ford until sweat broke out over his eyes and across his back. This wasn't a furnace gone wild. Someone was playing with the temperature.

Keeping his voice as low as possible, barely above a rumble, he tried to send a warning. "Heat."

"Negative on fire," Josiah answered from his position outside.

"The temperature is rising in the target room. The heat signatures are blurring," Ward said over the shouts of voices behind him. "Could be subterfuge to hide their presence or could be an incendiary device. Pull back and assess."

Ford's gaze shot to West and Reid. They both shook their heads. No shock there. Not from a Marine and a guy so deep into black ops that whispering his old program's name would get you killed.

Lucas was the odd man out, but Ford trusted him and his skills. They all were trained to fight until the end, to give everything, even if it meant handing over their lives. Ford just hoped today was not that day.

Losing this kid, Trent, this lead, meant chasing the toxin out in the open. In liquid form, GB-19 could enter the water system, and then forget any talk of antidote. Death was instantaneous when ingested. As a gas, the

Metro, museums, government buildings, even residential neighborhoods, could become testing grounds.

No, doubling back wasn't the answer. The domino would not fall on his watch, even if that meant hurting Shay, which was just about the last thing he wanted to do.

"Stand down, Bravo."

Harlan was running this show. Ford really wished Ward would shove the Brit aside and unleash the men to end this.

"Negative." Ford whispered the response, then signaled to move.

Harlan said something else but Ford stayed focused on the path ahead. Through the door, take out the guard and grab the kid. Simple . . . unless they had a repeat of Hampstead and all burned to death first.

Reid slammed into the door, going low as West and Ford went in high and Lucas covered the back. The hot air wrapped around them like a blanket, thick and suffocating. Ford struggled to breathe over the ripping inside his throat.

With only the light from an open refrigerator as a guide, he conducted a quick visual sweep of the room in less than a second. Empty tables and bare shelves. Papers scattered around the floor and shadows shifting in front of him.

A red dot raced across West's chest. Before he could reason it through, Ford knocked his teammate to the hard ground. Not easy since West was almost six-three with a massive chest and not an ounce of fat on him.

As they fell, gunfire rang out around and over them. Sparks shot in every direction as the back wall exploded, glass rained down, papers kicked up and plaster sprayed.

Through it all, Ford kept moving. Remaining stationary meant being a target. He rolled, drawing the guards' fire away from West. They were both on their feet and in constant motion.

Unable to tell a scientist from a guard in the confusion and smoke, but figuring the science guy wouldn't be holding a Glock, Ford shot at will. He could make out figures ducking from the rubble crashing in on them. Still, no one surrendered.

The series of concussive thuds stopped but the ceiling broke away and crashed to the floor. Before Ford could scramble to his feet, Delta team rushed through the new hole they'd created. Bullets continued to fly as one guard went down, leaving Josiah standing right behind him.

A second later West swore. He clutched his arm and his knees buckled. Lucas caught him on the way down.

The remaining guard spun around as Delta swarmed. When Ford raised his weapon in West and Lucas's direction, a shot hit the guard's leg and another one clipped his throat.

The man's eyes rolled back as his hand went to the gush of blood at his neck. Air gurgled as he fell down. Ford dove for him, thinking to stem the blood and get him talking, but a chunk of ceiling crashed to the floor between them, making Ford jerk back as smoke and debris spun through the room again.

The smell of burning electric cut through the wall of heat. Pieces of the ceiling continued to fall and booms rang out. When Ford uncovered his head, he spied the guard in a motionless sprawl on the floor five feet away. Blood puddled on the floor and seeped under his head.

"Fuck me. He's down. They all are." Ford didn't even try to get to his feet. He crawled over the piles of debris, ignoring sharp cuts into his palms and knees. With a hand pressed to the guard's throat to stop the flow of blood, he screamed into his face, "Where's Creighton?"

Alliance members moved through the room, turning over the larger pieces of drywall and checking every inch of the space. Ford willed this guy to live but his chest wasn't moving and the blood ran like a river, soaking his right side and into Ford's black pants.

. "Ford." Reid dropped on the other side of the downed man while Ford kept yelling into his closed eyes. Reid grabbed for Ford's arm and started issuing orders. "Hey, man. Ease up."

Josiah's hand touched Ford's shoulder. "Yeah, that one is gone."

Finally Ward's deep voice registered in Ford's brain. He'd been hearing this constant stream of noise and chalked it up to the chaos spiraling around him, but now he knew Ward was barely holding onto his temper as he demanded a status. "Someone talk to me."

Ford sat back on his haunches with his hands on his thighs. "We've got two down and no scientist."

Harlan mumbled something that sounded like swearing, even though he rarely did that. He threw in a "bloody" now and then but that was about it. "Body check."

"West got hit," Lucas said with a proper British

accent that mirrored Harlan's but didn't annoy Ford nearly as much.

Until Josiah made the comment, Ford had forgotten about the injury. His head shot up. Big, tough, say-as-little-as-possible West stood against the wall cradling his arm and leaning against Lucas while waving Josiah off.

"I'm fine." With his jaw tight and his voice rough, West sounded anything but.

"The cleaning crew is on the way. Get to medical." Harlan's exhale caused a crackle on the com. "Either guard alive?"

Ford swallowed back a coughing fit itching to grab hold and forced the word out. "Negative."

Reid got to his feet. "Creighton's in the wind. No equipment that I can tell either."

"*What?*" Harlan shouted the question.

Ford grabbed onto Reid's hand for an assist. As soon as he was on his feet, Ford conducted a mental body check. Except for some aches and the drip of blood down his leg from what he guessed was a cut around his knee, the special gear and vest held.

"Just a lab where some nasty shit used to be," he said.

"The forensic squad is headed there." Ward's voice trailed away, as if he was talking to other people in the room and had given up on the lab recon.

Ford wiped the last drips of sweat from his forehead. Despite the cool air blowing in from the new hole in the wall, the heat still lingered. Damn, but he'd been right. Just as Ford predicted, it had been a setup, a way to lure them in then block their ability to tell one figure from another.

The score read something like: Bad Guys two, Alliance zero.

At least Bravo team had one win. Ford was determined to add to their side of the score. Thanks to the impromptu trip to Paris, Alliance knew that Benton was in on the search for a toxin. The manhunt for the weapons supplier had kicked into hyperdrive. But not grabbing Trent now started a new plan in motion. They'd hunted the kid down through other means. Now it was time for pressure.

Josiah clapped, gaining everyone's attention. "Looks like it's time for Plan B."

"Shay Alexander." Reid whistled. "That woman is smokin'."

Now there was an understatement. Long brown hair, big blue eyes, and an ass that made him speechless. This was the last avenue Ford wanted to drive down, but now he didn't have a choice. His team didn't know he'd jumped the gun, moved in and started sleeping with Shay. He'd laid the groundwork for this part of the job for weeks. He just hated thinking of her as a job.

Now he really liked her, which meant he fucking hated this assignment.

"Yeah, Ford. Looks like it's time to make contact with the pretty cousin," Lucas said.

Too late. "Right."

"Lucky you." Josiah shook his head. "You get to search and squeeze and do anything else that needs to be done."

It all sounded so cold-blooded, but Ford couldn't blame them. He'd made similar comments about other operations in the past. The ones where he didn't lie to the target.

"Guess that means I'm up." Ford dreaded the ongoing subterfuge and how high he'd have to turn up the lying to get answers.

Reid snorted. "What a hardship."

"We don't know that she's involved in any of this." Ford hoped to hell she wasn't. He couldn't see it. Didn't want to see it.

"That's your job to figure out." Josiah clapped him on the back. "Be gentle."

Good advice, and since he would rather tangle with terrorists than an angry woman any damn day, Ford decided to take it.

8

Shay threw her head back and let the winding sensation inside her grab even tighter. Her bare thighs pressed against the outside of Ford's as she rode up and down on his erection. When his hands clenched on her hips, she slapped a palm against his headboard and dug her fingernails into the leather for leverage.

She wanted him deeper. Harder.

One of his palms found the back of her neck and he pulled her head down. Lips met lips in a mind-blowing kiss that had her head spinning even as her orgasm exploded inside her. With her breath catching in her throat, she moaned against his mouth. When he lifted his lower body one last time, a fresh tremble raced through her sensitive inner muscles.

Every part of her shook as her hips continued to flex and buck without any signal from her brain. It was pure sensation. The amazing friction of skin against skin that sent heat spiraling through her.

"So fucking good." He ground out his words as his lips traveled to her neck.

The kisses, firm and hot, wet and intensely wild, skimmed down to the base of her throat. One hand slid up her back and the other snuck down to cup her ass.

She lifted up on her knees then sank down again, gasping as her body closed around his. "Yes."

His hands moved all over her now as his mouth traced her collarbone. He touched her like he always did, with a frantic desperation that said he couldn't get close enough, fast enough.

He understood her body. Had learned just where to lick and how to caress. From that first night when he'd knocked on her door holding a pizza, it had been combustible between them. She didn't crawl into bed with men she barely knew, but something about this one, with the broad shoulders and sleek athlete's build, had her drowning in stupid from the second he smiled at her.

And she wasn't about to slow down now.

Her fingers slipped into his hair and pulled his mouth tighter against her heated flesh. A shiver shook through her as his shoulders strained. When she shifted her hips, he groaned. So she did it a second time, grinding against him and letting the rub of their bodies send him tumbling over the edge.

They'd been all over each other. Touched and tasted every inch. Still, she never tired of watching him as he came. The orgasm slammed into him now and he didn't fight it or hold back. When his hips finally stopped moving, his shoulders pressed back into the pillows. Those eyes drifted shut as the tension ran out of him, leaving nothing but a sprawl of glorious male.

Before she could lift up and off of him, he tugged her closer. His eyes open now, he brushed those fingertips down her body to the juncture between her thighs. When the pad of his finger slipped over her, she jerked, unable to hold her body still.

His eyebrow lifted. "Sensitive or sore?"

She noticed his voice still shook from the force of his heavy breathing. "Satiated."

The room spun as he pressed a hand against her lower back and rolled her to the side. Her back hit the mattress and 180 pounds of sexy male loomed over her a second later. She loved this position, being surrounded by him. Smelling him and seeing a close-up spark in those intelligent eyes.

With their bodies still joined, he balanced his upper body on his elbows and ran the tip of his finger around her left nipple. "I like your use of S words."

She touched him then because she couldn't *not* touch him. Her palm danced over his chin then across his cheekbones. "Just how bad was that service call?"

His face went blank as he stared down at her. "What?"

This she didn't love. She asked one question too many and all the emotion drained from his face. His practiced look of disinterest sparked doubt in her. The kind of doubt that had her wanting to take her uncle up on his suggestion of a big investigation into Ford Decker's past. Not that she was proud of the snooping temptation, but being a building manager, going in and out of strangers' apartments, she was more cautious than most.

Then there were the frequent calls that took him out of the house. She didn't understand everything an IT specialist did, but clearly the job description included some sort of be-on-call-all-the-time provision for Ford.

"You got the text yesterday, took off, and when you got back an hour ago . . . well, I'm not complaining about the getting back part." She stopped because it was too early in their relationship, if that's what it even was, to make a list of demands. But she did want some respectful ground rules. "A woman loves being swept off her feet, but you carried me across the hall and almost forgot to shut my front door before you stripped my bra off."

He glanced over his shoulder in the general direction of his family room and the front door beyond. "Did I actually get it closed?"

"Yes, but you were very focused on getting naked."

The corner of his mouth kicked up in a smile. "Do you blame me? Those jeans you had on, all tight and perfect in the way they frame your ass, had me crazed."

"Sweet talker." The things he said, the way he looked—it all worked for her.

His thumb went to her bottom lip. "I missed you."

And wasn't that the sexiest thing ever. "Me, too, especially since I didn't know when you'd be back."

Or *if* . . . that was the unspoken word she dropped from the sentence. Her last relationship was with a gigantic asshole with an even bigger secret. His betrayal taught her to ask questions and not trust blindly. She kept telling herself that laying the groundwork with Ford didn't matter because this was just sex, but her head and every other interested part of her were at war on this one. Three weeks in and she'd started spinning tales of things they could do together in the future.

Ford wasn't Devin. This was about pleasure, not about using her. But the doubts weaseled their way into her brain. Ford didn't offer any information about his life. He didn't have family photos or talk about past loves. He worked, took her to bed, and spent a lot of time on his phone. That was about it.

All the evidence suggested he was single and available. If it turned out he was married or Devin the Second, she might just throw him in the middle of traffic.

"Sorry." Ford whispered the word right before he kissed her.

An apology? She was still waiting for one of those from Devin. The dumbass.

In her mental wanderings, she lost track of the conversation. She needed to rewind. "For what?"

"I get to work and it's nonstop action. It's kind of the nature of the gig. Somebody always wants something."

Part of her knew that. She'd seen Ford come in off a days-long shift with the tension pulling around his mouth and eyes. More than once he'd explained away a limp by too many hours sitting in one position as he tried to figure out some complex but confidential computer issue affecting a multinational corporation.

Still, she wished he'd slow down and find a speed other than off or racing. "Your life is all emergencies and no down time."

"But that's no excuse." This time the kiss lingered and he only lifted his head when she wrapped her legs tighter around his trim hips. "Next time I'll at least text."

Her heart skipped. Actually did this rat-a-tat-tat thing that made her freeze for a second. "You don't have to—"

"Shay." He placed a finger across her lips. "I said I'll text. You deserve that much."

The mood morphed into something deep and a little scary. Still smarting from her last relationship gone wrong, jumping into a new one that seemed stuck in super speed terrified her. From that first impulsive night together, she'd promised herself the time with Ford would be light and fun. But the days passed and something shifted and now everything he said made her insides dance and spin.

Yeah, she was definitely drowning when it came to him.

She tried to joke even as her stomach tightened and the lightness whooshed out of her. "Well, as your landlord, I would have to report you missing if I didn't see you for a few days."

He put a palm on each cheek. "As the woman who's sharing my bed—the only woman sharing my bed, in case that's not clear—you get to know where I am."

Those words meant too much. She tried to slam on the brakes. "I . . . okay. Sure, um, we can—"

"And I want the same from you."

She waited for him to push too hard. For the idea of something bigger to overwhelm her and be too much. But the usual anxiety didn't come. It always came, even with Devin and that time she should have listened to the quiet voice inside her head. She wondered why the hell it was on vacation now.

"I'm almost always here at the complex. This or the one two blocks down."

"I'm actually trying to make a point here, Shay." That deep voice sounded so serious.

She swallowed. It was either that or climb right up on top of him and . . . "Which is?"

"I'd like us to have some obligations toward each other. Monogamy, communication. The usual."

"That sounds serious."

"Grown-up even." He pretended to shudder. "What's happening to me?"

With that the building tension seeped out of the room. "All kinds of sexy times could happen for you if you don't go all jerky on me right now."

"I'm going to take you up on that, but first I need a shower." He slipped out of her as he lifted up and shifted to the side. "Damn, you feel good."

"A shower? Now?"

"I should have taken care of that before I came over and snagged you as part of my caveman routine, but I was pretty desperate to rip those jeans off you."

She glanced around his king-sized bed and the sparse blue bedroom, looking for any sign of her clothes. She didn't spy so much as a sock. "You're very talented."

"Want me to show you my shower skills?" He wiggled his eyebrows as he leaned down again.

She stopped him with a laugh and a hand against his chest. "I'm familiar with those, but I think we need to find some food first or we'll both pass out."

He sighed as if the weight of the entire male race rested on his impressive shoulders. "Damn."

The world had shifted back into alignment. This she could handle. The banter and flirting. This part didn't bring memories zinging back or open her up to pain. "You shower. I'll find food and I'll meet you in the family room."

His gaze did a little roaming and the heat sparked again. "Naked."

She scooped up the sheet and held it against her chest as she searched for something of his to wear. A few more minutes without clothes and they'd never eat. "I am not cooking naked."

He frowned. "You ruin all my fun."

"I know. Women are the worst."

"Exactly." He stood up, not doing anything to cover up or hide the stirring down below. "But you should feel free to ogle me while I walk away."

Oh, she definitely planned on doing just that. "So romantic."

With a final wink, he slipped into the bathroom and out of sight. She waited for a return performance. He'd pulled that move before. Leave then storm back in for a kiss that turned her knees to pudding and her brain to mush. But this time she heard the shower spray.

Dropping the sheet, she reached for the gray T-shirt folded on top of his chest of drawers. For a second her hand hovered near the biggest drawer. It was so tempting to look inside, to find some clue about what made up the complex and sexy man she wanted in her bed each night.

She settled for bacon instead. Just thinking about it made her smell the nonexistent stuff.

With her stomach growling, she walked through the family room, ignoring the tightly drawn curtains. Thank goodness for the alcove dining area. Ford used it as an office and the shade was up for once, letting the bright fall sun pour in.

On the way to the kitchen her foot snagged her discarded panties. Then she spied the jeans thrown on the floor. She grabbed the clothes she could find and stopped when the heaviness in her hands reminded her of the missed call, and she went digging in her pockets for her phone.

She unlocked it and scanned the incoming call list. Her uncle and a few tenants but nothing from Trent. He'd ventured so far out of touch this time she worried about his safety every minute. Looked as if she needed to ask Anthony a third time to call the police. If he still balked, she'd do it. Let Trent get pissed off. He had earlier this year when she asked for a wellness check. She doubted this time would be different.

Her uncle would hate her going behind his back, but his thing with Trent getting lost in his work and disappearing for weeks at a time didn't work for her at all. She didn't care about the phone call Anthony got from Trent's boss yesterday reassuring him that Trent had camped out at work in a frenzy to finish some project.

All she needed was ten seconds of conversation with Trent. A hello. She didn't think that was too much to ask.

She sighed and glanced toward the bedroom. The water shut off at that moment and she had to smile. Nothing like going from thinking about one mystery man to another. Her cousin, Ford . . . both shook her sense of security, but in very different ways.

She set the cell on the granite breakfast bar with a click and headed for the fridge. Her fingers had just hit the handle when the doorbell buzzed. The sudden sound broke through the silent room and had her jumping. She may have even yelped.

Tugging on the bottom of the soft T-shirt, she rounded the corner and peeked through the peephole.

Even through the blur of the tiny window Shay made out a figure, blond and female. Definitely female.

Forget all the fancy thoughts and his talk of monogamy. Ford was a dead man.

Without thinking, Shay threw the bolt and pulled the door open. She tried not to stare but the woman on the other side did the up-and-down thing, which was just about the rudest thing ever. From the shirt barely skimming Shay's upper thighs, it wouldn't take a genius to know what Ford had been doing last night. If that made Shay the "other woman" without knowing it, she really would find that busy intersection and heave Ford in it.

Without the glass distortion, Shay got a good look at the woman. Tall and lean with high cheekbones. Really pretty in a put-together, both-men-and-women-would-stare kind of way. Her hair lay straight and perfect, falling over her shoulders and partway down her back.

Shay felt like an unmade bed. She pulled her fingers through her hair in a feeble attempt not to look like she wore a small dog on her head.

She studied the woman in front of her. She was one of those women who worked out at the gym but barely broke a sweat. She had smooth skin and big brown eyes. If there was an inch of fat on her, she hid it well, and the hint of makeup enhanced rather than detracted, making it tough to pin her age to anything other than somewhere between her late twenties to her early forties.

"Hi." That's it. That's all Tasha could get out. The other woman smiled. "You must be Shay Alexander."

Shay had no idea what the whole personal greeting thing meant. "Do we know each other?"

The mystery woman's smile didn't quite reach her eyes. "No, but we will."

9

EVEN WITHOUT the British accent, Ford recognized that cool voice coming from his family room. He dropped the damp towel on the floor on his way to the dresser for a tee. He nearly did some serious damage when he zipped on his jeans.

Breaking speed records, he stepped into the family room a second later. Just in time to see Shay's ass from where her borrowed shirt rode up in the back. The contrast with his boss, who stood at the front door as if conducting a silent countdown to shoving her way inside, proved pretty interesting. Since that same boss never traveled anywhere without a weapon, Ford walked faster.

Stopping next to Shay, he reached out and tugged the cotton down until his shirt covered as much of her as possible, but his focus stayed on his unwanted and lethal guest. "Tasha?"

Shay's eyes narrowed into tiny slits as she looked between Tasha and Ford. "You know each other?"

Tasha kept smiling. Didn't blink or move. "We shared a birth canal."

And with that Ford's mind went blank. He couldn't

have come up with a coherent response if someone pointed a grenade launcher at his head.

"Excuse me?" Shay pulled the edge of the shirt down in front as she backed up against him. She didn't stop until her butt rested against his thigh.

"Not really. I'm messing with you." The laughter came next. Tasha burst out with an uncharacteristic giggle. "I'm his sister."

"I, ah . . ." It took Shay a second to get the sputtering under control. "I didn't know he had one."

Neither did Ford. He'd analyze that after he got over the sight of Tasha performing the perfect carefree giggle. The woman could drop a grown man with the heel of her hand. Hell, she once drugged Ward and tied him up. Ward, a career black ops expert.

But Ford had a bigger problem. He'd been careful not to provide personal information to Shay other than the work and education basics. He searched his memory for any drop about siblings to figure out if he had to fix Tasha's quick thinking.

He settled for an answer that gave him room for wordplay if needed. "Half, actually. Our parents married when she was little, and I came along right after."

"But my timing is usually better." Tasha slipped the rest of the way inside and shut the door behind her. "I'm sorry for not calling first and messing up your morning."

Ford hoped Shay would skim over the part where Tasha got around the main door alarm and into the building without a key or a code. "No problem."

"Okay, yeah." Shay's bare feet finally unfroze from the floor. She looked around, her gaze zipping to the pile of clothes on his breakfast bar then all over the room. "I'll just go . . . find underwear."

Tasha's smile appeared genuine this time. "I can see where you would want to."

With a nod and a quick jog, Shay grabbed her clothes and dashed into his bedroom.

Ford waited until the door slammed to move in on Tasha. "Why are you here?"

"Since we're asking questions, let's start with one of mine." Tasha slipped around him and headed for Shay's abandoned purse on the edge of the couch. "How did you go from watching Ms. Alexander at a safe and impersonal distance to having her in your bed twelve hours later?"

"I'm good at my job."

The corners of Tasha's mouth fell. "Oh, please. Not that good."

She picked an envelope out of the side pocket of the purse with two fingers. Scanning the room and peeking at the door, she stopped her watch only long enough to glance inside the bag.

Ford wasn't in the mood for Tasha's covert stakeout of his family room. He grabbed the envelope and stuffed it back in the spot Shay assigned to it. It was bad enough he checked all of her mail and personal papers. She didn't need two people working overtime to violate her privacy.

"You're like the idiot younger brother I never wanted." Tasha's British accent slipped out.

Ford guessed that was on purpose because this woman didn't do anything by chance. "Your brother is a professor at Oxford."

"Yeah, I already have a smart brother. I was considering you for the role of the dumb one." She glanced over Ford's shoulder. "You're back."

Shay walked in wearing her jeans with his T-shirt. She hopped on one foot as she slipped on a sneaker without untying it first. "Do you want some coffee?"

Tasha bit her bottom lip. Actually looked genuine in her sorry-for-intruding act. "I'm good, but I actually need to talk with Ford about some estate stuff."

The last of the wariness faded from Shay's face. A concerned calm washed over her as she took his hand. "Who died?"

Ford waited. Tasha had veered off cover script. It was up to her to drag them back to the information he memorized in the file.

Tasha's glance was so quick—a bounce down to their joined hands then back to Shay's face—that someone not looking for it would have missed it. Ford picked it up and knew a list of questions clicked together in Tasha's impressive brain. He planned to ignore most of them.

"An uncle, more than a year ago," Tasha said, without even a blip on the lying scale.

Ford wondered if Ward knew about her ability to deliver line after line of false information without registering even the smallest sign of deception. The skill was both impressive and a little freaky. Clearly her home country got its money worth out of her intelligence training.

"I'm sorry."

Tasha waved off Shay's words. "No, I'm sorry for messing up your morning."

There was a beat of silence before Shay clapped her hands. She grabbed for her purse and looped the strap over her shoulder. Next she treated him to a quick kiss on the cheek as she hovered on the verge of bolting. "I need to run some errands anyway."

That was news to him. "You sure?"

"I want to check on my cousin." Shay's grip on her purse handles tightened until her knuckles turned white.

Forget whatever Tasha needed to say. This mattered. Shay hadn't dropped one hint about Trent but now she went there. This could be the chance to poke around, to get on the inside without having to push in a way that felt manufactured and risked his cover.

Ford rubbed a hand up and down her arm, hating Tasha's presence in the room with every pass of his palm. "Everything okay? Do you want me to come with you?"

Shay shrugged. "You're busy and—"

"It's no problem." He jumped before she talked herself out of unloading whatever was on her mind. "I'll be over to your place in twenty and we'll go."

"You should visit with your sister." But Shay didn't sound all that convincing.

Hooked. She wanted him to go with her. Wanted to share. It was the in he'd been looking for. He just wished they didn't have an audience for the moment. "We'll go see your cousin and then we'll be done with family obligations for the day."

"I did only plan to come in for a few minutes then go," Tasha said. "I doubt I even need ten minutes."

Shay smiled at both of them. "Tempting."

"Then make it fifteen minutes." Ford took it slow. Reeled her in.

Hated every fucking minute of it. This, the whole setup, made Shay a mark. Part of him knew she could be involved in Trent's schemes up to her big brown eyes, but his instincts screamed no. And if she happened to be an innocent bystander in all of this, his actions made her collateral damage. His, not Trent's.

On most jobs he shrugged that off and chalked the waves of danger up to an untenable but necessary job hazard. Something about Shay turned him around and had him hating the game. He didn't want to analyze his wavering or even think about it, but this operation was different. Not just because the stakes were higher if he failed. No, this one hit on a personal level when he didn't even know he had a personal life left.

"Fine." Shay shook Tasha's hand then gave a little wave on her way out. "Nice to meet you."

By the time his front door closed behind Shay, Ford's temper sparked over Tasha's unexpected intrusion. Rage spewed inside him. "Really, Tasha. What the fuck are you doing here?"

"You might want to remember you work for me." She paced around the condo as if she were casing it instead of handing down some bit of work news.

"I don't—"

"And you broke protocol." Tasha brushed by him then turned around again. At five-ten with those high heels on her boots, she met him head on. "How long have you been sleeping with her?"

He knew he'd been busted. Tasha wasn't dumb, and Shay barely wore anything when she opened his door. Still, Ford was not in the mood for a conversation about his sex life, protocol or not. "That's not your business."

"We both know it is."

"I made contact earlier than planned." The answer said something and nothing at the same time.

"Try again."

Since he'd learned that skill from Tasha, it was no wonder he couldn't slide it by her. He leaned against the arm of the couch and crossed his arms in front of him.. "I seem to remember a certain operation in Fiji where you started sleeping with Ward."

She stopped flipping through his unopened mail and glared. "Be careful what you say next."

No doubt he deserved a punch, and he knew from experience she could. land one that would have him gasping, but Ford kept pushing. It was his nature and he couldn't always control it. This time he didn't want to. "I was there for the start of your romance."

Her eyebrow lifted. "Is that what you're having with Shay?"

Damn. "No." Shit, he didn't know.

He shifted, crossing and uncrossing one foot over the other. He finally went with standing up.

"Then you should also remember Ward and I kept cover. We weren't casing each other. We didn't know the other was working a covert job."

"I'll refrain from making a joke."

Tasha dropped the mail and it whapped against the counter. "Smart man."

Ignoring her useless poking around, since it was not as if the paycheck stubs were even real, Ford went right to the heart of the issue. "Look, it turns out we may need Shay to find Trent. Consider my premature actions lucky."

"This time." Tasha opened his refrigerator.

He had no idea what she thought she'd find in there. He half wondered if she was so accustomed to searching that she couldn't turn it off. "Everything is under control."

"We'll see."

"Ready to tell me why you're really here and making us come up with a revised cover as we talk?" With a palm against the stainless steel, he closed the refrigerator and cornered her in the galley-style kitchen. "Last I checked, I have a phone. Harlan doesn't hesitate to use it at all times of the day to call me in. I'm guessing you wouldn't either." But since he never got assignments straight from her, Ford didn't know. He reported to Harlan and Ward. They reported to her.

Tasha looked him up and down. Just stood there, not talking, drawing out the moment. The woman was a pro at making people squirm. Under her intense scrutiny, he fought the urge to shift his weight. They'd both been trained but no question her stamina for this type of bullshit outlasted his.

She finally sighed. "I suspected you'd gone rogue on this job."

"No way." He'd talked to Shay too early but did not ignore the end goal. After a fuck-up of epic proportions that left two people dead at the end of his time with the CIA, he'd reined his actions in. Or at least he tried, but the Paris trip might suggest the tendencies still lingered.

"Since I'm here, we can discuss your evening plans." Tasha leaned the side of her arm against the refrigerator. "The waterfront employee."

The partial sentences didn't confuse Ford. He kept up fine. "What about him?"

"We're thinking he was paid to plant the warehouse information. It's possible his 'help' wasn't as innocent as it seems."

Just proved that convenient clues were often anything but. "When do we move?"

"He likes to drink after work. Bravo team can grab him at his favorite bar tonight and engage him in a little chat since that worked so well with poor Rupert."

"Who else knows about this?" Because too many ears seemed to be a problem lately.

Her smirk looked like it should accompany an eye roll. "I'm not dumb. I know you're worried about a mole, so this is limited to me, Ward, and now you."

Ford picked up his phone and typed in the go code to his team, along with the time he needed them to muster at the Warehouse for prep. "I'm assuming the assignment is to get the information however we need to."

"Do it fast."

Adrenaline pumped through him. Every cell burst to life as his body and brain revved up to go in. "Sure, sis."

"And leave your new girlfriend at home."

Now that was just insulting. "This isn't my first day on the job."

"Since you stopped following the rules, I thought I'd make sure you remembered that one."

An hour later, Shay typed in her cousin's alarm code and opened the door to his basement studio with Ford at her side. A car horn honked and two guys argued over a tight parking space outside of the row-house apartment just off Capitol Hill, but she focused on the lock that always stuck.

Trent worked for the government and didn't make anywhere near the kind of money he could from a private firm, but he could afford a better place. One bigger than five hundred square feet. The neighborhood housed Hill staffers and law students, as well as young couples who liked the buzz of the city. It was safe and not owned by Uncle Anthony, which Shay assumed played a big part in Trent's reason for living there.

Trent had developed am I'm-not-my-father complex lately. It kicked in right about the time his anger came flaring back.

Even though he was really young when he graduated with his doctorate, he'd insisted he needed to stop living off of his dad's dime. Shay suspected Trent's choice to go with the public sector job also had something to do with Anthony pushing in the opposite direction. Her uncle was old school and believed you went to the highest bidder and made piles of cash while you could. He'd yelled for weeks when his son turned down lucrative positions for the top-secret one.

She admired Trent's spirit but still wished he lived in her building, where she could keep a closer watch on him. That likely was also a reason Trent took this place. The last time they talked, he sounded off about needing control and being an adult, so a lack of interference could be a compelling draw.

The lock finally clicked and she ushered Ford inside. Questions had been swirling in her brain since meeting his sister. A kind of nagging sensation that something wasn't right there. "Are you and Tasha close?"

"She treats me like an annoying little brother."

Well, that answered that. Shay couldn't really see Ford in the role of little boy, since he was all man now. She'd guess the battle of wills between the siblings bordered on epic.

"Were you?" She dropped her keys on the small table by the door and walked inside with Ford right behind her. The smell had cleared out but the place, with the curtains drawn, resembled a tomb.

"She would say I still am a bad boy."

Shay glanced over her shoulder, saw the devilish gleam in his eyes and put the brakes on before they traveled too far down that road. "I'm not touching that."

"Why?"

"It seems wrong to talk dirty when we were just talking about your sister."

"Good point." Ford went to the bookcase and cocked his head to the side as he skimmed a finger over the spines and read the titles. "Tell me about this cousin."

"Trent. We grew up together, so he's more like, well, an annoying baby brother." She followed almost the same path Ford had to the bookcases but her steps caused the parquet floor to creak. She had no idea how Ford, who weighed a lot more than she did—at least she hoped that was true—managed to avoid the sticky areas.

He glanced over at her. "You haven't really mentioned Trent before."

That was a bit of a sore spot, and she didn't know why. What they had was new and still finding its footing, but having a sister pop up out of nowhere threw her off stride. "Then we're even because I didn't know about Tasha."

A sexy smile broke across his lips. "Touché."

She walked into the bedroom area and then through the closet to the bathroom. The spaces flowed into one another and hadn't changed at all since her last visit. No clothes out of place and his suitcases still stacked on the top shelf. She counted the sneakers, still not understanding why Trent needed thirteen pairs, and none had disappeared.

When she turned the corner and walked back into the living area, Ford had moved. He now stood by the front door. Staring at the doorjamb, he ran a finger along the crack, leaning in close to examine the imaginary line he drew.

"What are you doing?" She looked around, trying to calm the bubble of anxiety expanding inside her.

He stopped and glanced at her with a shy sort of you-caught-me expression on his face. "Maybe I've seen too many movies, but I was checking to see if there were any signs of a break-in."

The boy-investigator thing struck her as cute, but the words sent a shot of anxiety spinning down her spine. "Are there?"

"Not that I can tell." He dropped his arms to the side and scanned the apartment from one end to the other. "What are we even looking for?"

"I don't know, really." That was part of the problem. She had no idea what Trent's job entailed other than he couldn't talk about it at all. Even the little she did know she couldn't share with Ford.

Trent didn't have much of a social life, due to his long work hours. He dated now and then but usually only short-term, so there was no one for her to call on that score either.

"His keys aren't here and the apartment is in good shape," Ford said, "so I would say he's off somewhere."

"How do you know about the keys?" She had checked for those and Trent's wallet first, but something about Ford mentioning the obvious had her focus splitting.

He gestured at the room. "I don't see them anywhere, do you?"

Okay, she was officially paranoid. She kept dissecting and analyzing. Poor Ford said one stray thing and she ran off on a tangent. She chalked it up to stress. "No, you're right."

"When was the last time you talked with him?"

"I saw him about a month ago and he stopped answering texts and calls right around that time." She knew the exact date because she slept with Ford for the first time exactly one week later, but she kept that piece of information to herself.

Ford's face went blank. "What did he say?"

She couldn't tell if he thought four weeks without contact was too many or if it painted her as overly cautious. His expression gave so little away. That ability to look neutral no matter the circumstance shook her. "Nothing really. That's the point. Trent didn't offer an explanation for his lack of communication or warn me about this absence. He just said work was out of control. His mood was different. He was different."

She walked over to the love seat and dropped onto the cushion. "He's been out of touch longer than usual. I can feel something is wrong."

"Yeah, I can see where that would be the case." Ford picked sitting on the coffee table over the other chair in the room.

She assumed he was thinking about how people normally carried on their work and private lives. But Trent never worked along those lines. He battled with his father and tended to think professors and bosses singled him out for harsh treatment. He carried a bit of paranoia that became problematic when it combined with his anger issue.

He could be so charming, winning over even the toughest critic, but at other times he dwelled in an odd state of victimhood. Shay didn't always understand Trent but she did love him. Which was why she wanted to see him now. Just see with her own eyes that he was fine.

She tried to explain Trent's difficult and sometimes confusing personality to Ford. "Trent checks out. He has this important job that keeps him in the office overnight, for days on end."

"Doing what?"

"Something in a lab. I really don't know because it's confidential."

Ford nodded. "I can understand that."

She had to laugh because the men in her life had only a passing acquaintance with the telephone and the concept of keeping in touch. But as much as Ford's schedule kept her head spinning, his trips usually lasted only a few days. "You're slightly better at checking in than Trent is, but then you are supposed to be older and wiser. He's twenty-one. You're . . . what?"

"Thirty-four, and I promised to work on my checking-in skills. Or if I didn't, I am now." Ford shuffled the papers and magazines on the coffee table next to him. "As a fellow workaholic, I feel some kinship with Trent. Are you sure he's not in the office now?"

"His boss talked to my uncle and said everything was fine. Trent's working on a big project and got pinned down in the lab."

Ford's eyes narrowed but then the concern left his face as quickly as it came. "Well then, you likely have your answer."

"It doesn't feel right, you know?" She had to move. To burn off the extra energy pinging around inside her. She got up and walked back to the kitchen. "You ever just feel like something is off and you can't quite grasp what?"

"Once or twice." Ford got up and joined her. Wrapped his arms around her and pulled her against his chest. "Maybe if you talked to your uncle."

Her head fell into that reassuring space beneath his chin, and the heat of his skin penetrated her clothes, making her feel protected. "I tried that, too."

"Do you want me to give it a shot?"

"He's already itching to meet you." She looked up in time to see Ford's mouth drop open. "All the color just drained from your face, by the way."

"I wasn't expecting that." He flashed a look at his shirt with the dancing alligators. "Warn me so I can wear something that doesn't scare him."

"Uncle Anthony is overprotective." And gruff and pushy and far too driven, but he loved her and she never forgot that. "He took me in after my parents died in a car crash."

"Damn, Shay." Ford brushed a finger over her bottom lip. "I'm sorry. I didn't know."

"I was fourteen and sulky and determined to hate everyone, and he didn't give up on me." She leaned her head on Ford's shoulder again because cuddling against him felt better than anything else. "I owe him."

"Is that why you're looking for Trent?"

That was an easy question for her to answer. "No, I'm looking because he's family. You don't mess with that bond."

10

LATER THAT night Ford crouched in the back of a large van with West and Reid next to him and Lucas up front in the driver's seat. From the outside it looked like a nondescript moving truck with a generic company name. Inside, however, it was a minicommand center filled with electronic equipment that monitored every angle of Whicken's Bar from a block away as they waited for their mark to stumble out.

Reid cleared his throat. "Let me understand this—"

"Here we go." Lucas exhaled as he balanced an arm on the steering wheel and watched the street through the windshield.

Ford thought about ignoring Reid and moving to the front seat with Lucas.

"While the woman was in the next room playing in the closet, or whatever," Reid went on, "you made a press copy of her key to her cousin's apartment and planted cameras in the bookshelves just in case Trent or someone looking for Trent came by?"

"Her name is Shay." Ford had no idea why he felt the need to point that out. The team referred to Shay as "the woman" or some neutral form on purpose. It kept her status to that of a collateral in the assignment, or if things went wrong, a statistic. Giving her a name made her human, and that was not their job. It wasn't his either, but fuck that.

"So, that's a yes?"

Even in the dark interior Ford could see West's eyebrow lift as he asked the question. Since a few words were about all West could manage at a time, Ford dropped the sarcasm before he answered. "Yes. Ellery is back in the Warehouse watching the camera feed now for any signs of activity."

"No way the science genius is dumb enough to stop back home on his way to unleash a deadly toxin." Reid pulled at the collar of his buttoned-down shirt. "We are never that lucky."

He ran a hand over his sleeves then went back to concentrating on the scene flashing on the monitors. They all wore street clothes, figuring it would be easier to blend in and grab a guy off the street without wearing combat gear. That meant protective vests went under the shirts, and Reid, usually a smooth operator in the "right" clothes for every occasion, wore a plaid shirt held together with snaps.

Ford fought the urge to take a photo for future harassment potential. "I was thinking the cameras might clue us into who else is following Trent or watching his place."

"This kid is a pain in the ass. Makes me happy I sucked at science." West's words ticked in time with the clomping of his heavy boots against the metal of the van floor. Despite a recent injury, West kept his movements steady, as if to prove he could get hit by a building and keep going.

Reid snorted. "I'm not sure I see this as an excuse for you failing high school chemistry, but okay."

Not that he didn't like the sitting and bullshitting that went with surveillance, but while they were all captive in the twenty-four-foot van, Ford thought it seemed like a decent time to fill in the pieces of his afternoon. "Unlike you guys who just sat around knitting all day—"

"That's offensive," Reid said in his most serious voice. "There's nothing wrong with dudes knitting."

"—I waited until Shay said she was working on bills before circling back to Trent's place to check his mailbox, go through the entire apartment, and stomp on the floorboards in the hope of finding secret compartments. No luck on that, but I got back to Shay before she noticed I was off searching."

West's head shot up. "How many bills does she have?"

"What?"

West's serious expression didn't waver. "Seems like you'd have a short window to get all of that done."

Before Ford could ask what the hell that had to do with anything, Lucas piped in from the front seat. "I thought our guys checked the apartment already and we had people watching it round the clock."

"Not someone I control. Harlan's guys, maybe." And Ford was not taking a chance on losing Trent to the sloppiness of some government drone in a suit.

Reid rolled his eyes. "You're a paranoid freak."

"And annoyingly anti-Brit," Lucas added.

"To be fair, I don't hate *all* Brits." Ford kept his focus on the monitor showing the bar's front door. Two minutes later it paid off. "There's our guy."

Reid looked over Ford's shoulder at the screen. "I was hoping he'd be wasted and stumbling."

"The assignment file called him a functioning drunk." Not that Ford knew exactly what that meant. Impaired was impaired, and he was hoping this guy was. "Starting the countdown. Everyone in position."

"We've got potential collaterals all over the street," Reid said as he maintained his position guarding the truck's hidden side door.

That meant potential rescuers, or worse, potential casualties. Groups of guys roamed around and shouted. A few slipped from the target bar and headed toward the opposite end of the street to a second dive. That gave Bravo a very abbreviated window. Grab the target before he went from one crowded spot to another.

West and Ford jumped out of the truck using the side door facing the road and away from the sidewalk, hiding their advance from the target. West broke off and crossed to the other side of the street then Ford lost sight of him. For a big man, he could disappear like a ghost.

Their target walked alone and made every mistake. People came out close to him but he didn't stay bunched with them. They peeled off and he stayed on his own and kept going. Didn't stay on guard or act as if he lived in a city. He kept his head down, staring at his phone. Talk about the perfect target.

Ford touched the disc in his ear, opening the line of communication with the Warehouse from his end. Harlan and Ward and possibly others listened in but stayed silent, leaving control of the operation to him. "Ellery? Who is he calling?"

"No one." She had tapped into their target's phone

and performed whatever tricks she needed to track his movements and calls. "He's offline. I think he might be playing a game."

"That should make this easy." Ford gauged the distance to the target.

The man came toward them, less than half a block away now and walking with slow measured steps. His path took him in and out of the shadows from the streetlights. He never looked up, and if he heard the footsteps from where West circled around behind him, he didn't show it.

When the target was twenty feet away, Ford slipped past the end of the truck, heading toward him. They'd practiced this sort of takedown a thousand times before, in every scenario and using cameras to help them improve. It was all about incapacitating and timing. Having a distracted mark helped.

"In four . . ." Reid began the countdown, and it played in all of their ears over the com.

A couple lingered down the block, walking faster than the target and gaining distance. Ford prepared to go in a beat early, if needed. He swept around the vehicle to the sidewalk as Reid's numbers echoed in his head. Matching the target's pace, Ford pulled up beside him and a half step behind. The guy shot him a quick glance then returned his attention back to the phone.

"Two . . . and go."

On Reid's signal, Ford slipped the small needle cradled in his palm right into the target's neck. The guy stopped and his hand flew to the wound. Just as his mouth dropped open, Ford caught his arm. A step later

West swooped in and lifted the target from behind as Reid opened the truck door.

A crack sounded as his phone hit the concrete. By the time they got him up the dropped steps, he'd morphed into dead weight. West bent to grab the cell then jumped into the truck. In less than six seconds they'd drugged and dragged him off the street, with people walking nearby.

Ford slapped the back of Lucas's seat. "Get us out of here."

Now it was the Brit's turn to show off his driving. Blend in but move. They drove from their spot at the bar near the convention center to a fenced-in construction yard in southeast DC. An area without witnesses. Not that they needed to hide. The target was out cold, and would be for a few more minutes. That gave them time to get into the prearranged location and get set up.

Five minutes later Reid passed the smelling salts under the target's nose. His head flipped from side to side and his body jerked. But he didn't get far now that he was hog-tied to a chair in the middle of the truck bed.

Reid crouched in front of him. "Have a good night of drinking?"

"What's going on?" The guy struggled against the ropes and tried to pull his hands apart, but the zip tie stopped him.

"We wanted to say hello." Reid actually smiled as he said it. "Oh, and feel free to scream. There's padding on the walls. Of course, no one is alive outside to hear you anyway."

"You have the wrong person." The target shook his

head and looked frantically from one man on the Bravo team to another.

That was Ford's cue. Time to clue the target into how much trouble he was facing. "No we don't, William Roosevelt Franklin. Very patriotic name, by the way."

"What?"

So much for the guy having any sense of history. "You live at 411 G Street Southwest."

"What . . . how do you . . ." Billy shook his head as if trying to clear it. "I was just getting a drink."

Ford leaned down with his knees bent and his hands balanced on his thighs. He stood just out of reach. Menacing but not close enough to become a casualty. "But before tonight you were very busy telling lies. Weren't you, Billy?"

"I don't know what you're talking about." He kept shaking his head but his eyes cleared a bit.

"You filed a complaint." Ford held out a hand and Lucas dropped a file in it. The folder held blank pages, but Billy couldn't see that.

"No."

Ford hauled off and punched him in the jaw. It sent his head flying to the side. "Try again."

A few seconds ticked by as the guy swallowed and shook his head. Usually it took ten seconds from trying to chew through the bindings to curling up on the floor.

Ford took another step forward. "Billy?"

"This is about the warehouse on the waterfront?"

Looked like their man was getting smarter. "Good guess."

Billy froze. His gaze traveled around the enclosure one more time before his chest started to rise and fall in rapid succession. "Look, man, I didn't see anything."

Ford stood there paging through the sheets in the file, pretending to read. "That's not what you said here, Billy."

"I saw movement in and out of that beat-up place." Billy's gaze flew to Lucas and stayed there. "That's it. I reported it or it would have been my job. My boss is a douche. You know the type?"

Looked as if the target wanted to connect with Lucas. Ford stepped in front of his teammate to break whatever bond Billy hoped to build. "You can't blame this on someone else. You did this."

Billy shifted in his chair but didn't get far, thanks to the bonds cutting across his chest and upper thighs. He tried to look around Ford, maybe find a friendly face, and finally gave up as his chest hitched on a long exhale. "You've got this all wrong."

Ford kept pushing. "Who gave you the report, Billy? Who told you to call this in?"

"What?" Billy sounded confused, but he didn't look it. Not now. The haze from the drugs and confusion seemed to have cleared. His voice hesitated, wary now instead of panicked.

"Someone told you to plant that report. I want to know who and why." Ford walked around his target, treating him like prey and going in for the kill.

Billy fidgeted and tried to spin to face Ford as he moved. "I don't . . . you've got—"

"I'm done waiting for your memory to reboot." West stepped in front of Billy. One button at a time, West stripped off his shirt to reveal his protective vest underneath.

Billy's shoes scuffed the floor. He banged and pushed as if he wanted to move the chair away from West's broad chest. "What's happening?"

"Now you've done it." Reid made a tsk-tsking sound as he shook his head. "You've made him angry."

"Dumbass move." Ford shoved his thighs against the back of the target's chair to hold him steady, give the sensation of the walls closing in.

"What's with your shirt? I don't get what's happening here." Billy squirmed even more. "Come on, guys."

West shrugged as he moved in closer. "I didn't want to get blood on my clothes, but don't worry. I'll put it back on after."

"After what?"

West snorted. "Oh, Billy."

"Hold it." Billy's voice rose with each word. He yelled and the words rushed out of him. "Wait, this is a misunderstanding!"

"How so?" Ford asked.

"I didn't do anything."

Wrong answer. Ford motioned for Lucas to take his spot, then moved around to stand next to West. Billy wore the expression Ford wanted—one of paralyzing fear. For the second time in a few days Ford stood over a grown man who looked ready to piss himself. That was fine. Billy could do whatever he wanted so long as he got chatty because Ford needed answers and Billy had them.

"Billy." Lucas shook his head as he balanced against the table with the back of one thigh on the top. "You need to think this through."

"Because we are about to unleash the fiercest fighting force on earth on your sorry ass," Ford said, adding to the pile-on. "A pissed-off Marine."

"Fucking-a right. Hold this?" West removed his holster. Next came the gun by his ankle and another that appeared out of nowhere. Two knives followed.

Ford half expected him to whip out a rocket launcher for effect.

"See, Billy." West rubbed his hands together as he walked around Billy's chair then stopped in front of him again. "I don't have to use weapons to get you to talk."

Fear pounded off the guy now. Tension filled the truck to suffocating, and Billy kept swallowing as if he needed to clear the taste from his mouth. "You can't do this to me."

"Oh, I can." West crossed his arms in front of him, making his biceps and the vine tattoo of barbed wire peek out from under the edge of his T-shirt. "You wouldn't be my first, and you won't believe how much I'll enjoy it."

Even Ford thought that sounded creepier than hell. He made a mental note not to piss West off.

"I don't need the guns or those fancy knives." West bent over, moving in close and giving Billy nowhere to turn. "Want to know why?"

Billy visibly swallowed. "No."

"Because I can use my hands to rip every bone in your body out of its socket."

"Oh, God."

"Yeah, Billy. Praying is smart." West nodded, stepping away. "Won't help you, though."

Darkness fell all around them. The lights from

the site snuck in the front window, but the night had plunged the back in shadows. Only two lights set up on the floor showed the chair. The equipment had been moved into the corner to keep all the focus on the man who looked ready to puke up blood.

To prevent that, and because Ford could see West's face just fine and couldn't believe Billy could withstand the combination of West's size and scowl, Ford stepped in. "Last chance, Billy."

"I didn't . . ." West took a menacing step forward, and Billy slammed his eyes shut as he winced. "Okay, okay. I got paid."

There, that was exactly what they needed. Accurate intel and confirmation. If they could get it by scaring the guy and not touching him, all the better. Ford just hoped he actually knew something. "We're going to need more details."

"I got an e-mail . . ." The details rolled out of Billy now. He spoke fast as his words ran into each other and the machines in the truck recorded them "They deposited money into my account and promised more if I did this one thing."

"Who is 'they'?" Ford asked.

"I don't know." Billy stared at Ford, but his scared gaze kept shooting to West, as if tracking his movements. "Whoever it was knew my bank information. The money actually did show up as the e-mail promised. Like, a minute after I got the e-mail, so I knew it wasn't one of those Internet scams to get my account number then screw me. But I don't know how they got it. I'm careful. Change passwords every month and all."

Ford almost rolled his eyes. "Finish the story."

"The next e-mail said there would be more money for me if I did the thing . . . I mean, filed the report."

West took the guy's dropped cell out of his pocket and shook it in the air. "Do you have access to your e-mail on your phone?"

"What?" Billy's eyes narrowed as he looked at West's hand, then the lightbulb seemed to go on. "Oh, yeah. You can get it on there."

"So, you did this 'thing' and got paid again," Reid said. "Then what?"

"Nothing. Got the last of the money and spent some tonight." With each question, Billy's gaze shot to the person who spoke to him last. "Look, it was no big deal. Just a statement about activity at an old warehouse. I figured someone was screwing an insurance company or getting back at a former boss or something."

The patsy didn't even know he was a patsy. That was just fucking sad to Ford. "You might want to know that warehouse blew up."

"With us in it." West had made it to Billy's side before dropping that comment.

The rest of the color leached out of Billy's face. "That's not my fault. You have to believe—"

One touch of West's hand at the right place on Billy's neck and he passed out. Stopped mid-sentence and slouched down as far as the bonds tying him to the chair would allow.

West glanced over at Ford. "Think that's the truth?"

"Unfortunately, but we should take him in for further questioning. Let Delta team take a shot at him. Maybe something can be done with the e-mails, a trace of some sort, but I doubt whoever left them was dumb enough to leave a trail."

"I'll handle the transfer to interrogation." Lucas frowned at the sleeping man. "The car is outside. He'll fit in the trunk."

The plan was to leave the truck and take the equipment and Billy with them. They had a car and a smaller van, and protocol said they split up to head back in. Ford didn't veer from it this time. "Take West with you. He can carry the dead weight."

Lucas looked his makeshift partner up and down. "He has to get dressed first."

West scooped his shirt off the floor. "You said intimidate him."

"Not perform a striptease," Reid mumbled before blowing out a long breath. "Okay, now what?"

Ford needed to call the Warehouse. Ward had listened in to the takedown and questioning but stayed silent. That meant he was thinking. So was Ford. "We now know someone is trying to wipe out anyone who might be following Trent. In this case, us."

"And we know an operation works if there are a limited number of people who know it's about to happen," Reid pointed out.

That part ticked Ford off. It meant the mole theory was no longer just a theory. Someone on the inside could be working for Benton, and that set off a fiery explosion in Ford's brain.

This all had a calculated feel. Like, someone with knowledge of operations and tactics was pulling the strings. Someone who understood Trent would become as much a target as a prize and moved in to buy him time. "We need to look deeper into Anthony Creighton's background and contacts and see if he has the skills to pull this off."

Lucas nodded. "He definitely has the money to pay the right people, and him being the owner of the waterfront property is too much of a coincidence."

"Then maybe it's time for you to meet Uncle Anthony." Reid sounded far too pleased with the idea.

West laughed while he finished buttoning his shirt. "Think how much fun that family dinner will be."

Ford didn't find any part of this amusing. "Lucky me."

11

SHAY CUDDLED closer to Ford and inhaled the clean fresh scent of his soap. Her back leaned against his chest. One hand covered his on her stomach while her other palm brushed up and down his blue-jean-covered thigh.

Sitting in between his raised legs, feeling the warmth of his arms as they wrapped around her, it all felt right. She loved the quiet moments with him. They didn't get that many.

Last night he'd been called in to fix a server problem. Tonight they lounged on her couch watching an action movie where alien ships rose out of the water and took out most of the East Coast. Between the sound of his husky chuckle by her ear whenever something unbelievable happened on the screen, and the soft kisses he placed in her hair from time to time, she could stay there forever.

When the aliens outmaneuvered the military for the hundredth time on screen, Ford slid his free hand over hers, trapping it against his leg and entwining her fingers. "You feeling any better about Trent?" he asked.

Now there was a subject that could chase the calm

right out of a peaceful moment. "Not really. Each day that goes by without contact makes me more nervous for him."

She and her cousin had set a new record for non-communication. Trent hadn't come up for air, and she refused to believe any project could keep him that enthralled for that many days in a row.

"What is your uncle thinking about all of this?"

She wished she knew. Anthony had never been all that transparent. He made his fortune conducting quiet commercial real estate deals in back rooms. By negotiating and refusing to back down. He'd raised Trent the same way, skipping the emotional support and even the negotiating and going right to demands and high expectations. "Anthony says it's fine, but I can see he's starting to worry, and he never worries."

"How?"

She turned a little to get a better look at Ford's expression. "What?"

"How can you tell?" He lifted their joined hands and kissed the back of hers. "My dad is the strong, silent type. He says about three words at a time and I never know what he's thinking. If he were worried, I have no idea how I would tell."

"Your mom must love that."

"They've been together for thirty-six years, so I'm guessing she's used to it by now. But it drives me crazy. I have to fight the urge to go through his papers and check his medication bottles just so I have some idea what's happening."

Ford traced his thumb over the back of her hand. The soothing gesture had her falling boneless against him. She had to struggle to concentrate on the conversation and not turn around and straddle those impressive thighs.

They got so few moments of sitting and relaxing that she wanted to savor them. "You ever do that?"

"The medicine thing? More than once." Ford pressed his lips against her temple. "I know it's sucky behavior but sometimes you have to dig a little to find the truth. To make sure everyone and everything is okay."

She tried to imagine the open land Ford grew up on. He'd described his Montana hometown as having three stop signs and four churches. Properties stretched for miles and the days started early. Hardworking people who thought a traffic light would ruin the farming community.

She'd grown up outside of DC in Virginia horse country. Her mom rode and her father wore a suit all the time. For some reason that was her most vivid memory of them. She never thought of them together or of the family trips mom insisted dad take them on. When Shay closed her eyes and tried to conjure up the smell of her mother's perfume or the sound of her dad's voice, she found the details had faded.

Her memories were limited to moments and pieces of conversation. She pictured them now as she'd seen them back then, through a young girl's eyes. Dad coming home late and mom standing in the kitchen in her riding boots. That and the night her uncle came to pick her up early from a sleepover at her friend's house with a policeman at his side.

Photos helped her with the timeline of life back then, but Anthony never talked about losing his sister.

It was as if he cried at the funeral and then packed his emotions away forever. All of them.

She lived with the agony of loss that lessened over time but never fully disappeared. With the guilt of not being there when they died because she insisted seeing her friends was more important than some stupid play. Life spun on and the sadness crept up on her every time something happened where she would naturally call her mom, but she survived.

"Anthony is always so in control and solid. He doesn't stray from his schedule much at all. Like, I could tell you where he is during the day just by the time."

"Hmm." Ford's brief hum rumbled through him and into her. "Sounds rigid."

"He is, but he's always been good to me." She nibbled on her top lip as she tried to decide how much to say.

"I would hope so."

It struck her as oddly disloyal to talk about Anthony, and so hard to describe him without making him sound tough and cold. That's not how she viewed him and not how he ever treated her. "You see . . . oh, I don't know."

Ford turned her slightly until his eyes met hers. "What is it?"

Maybe it was the warmth of Ford's body or his calming touch, possibly his low voice that vibrated through her when he spoke. Something made her want to talk, to spill her worries and share.

The sensation was so foreign to her. Her last boyfriend taught her to hold it all in. Devin acted smooth and talked about loving her, but every conversation was calculated to get something out of her. To get him closer to Anthony. Closer to the money.

With Ford, she never felt that tug of insecurity. If he cared about her uncle's money, he'd played it so cool she had no clue. He was too busy working to even notice. And that *was* a problem.

She shifted and had to smile when Ford snagged her legs and dragged them across his lap. "That was smooth."

"I thought you'd be more comfortable talking this way."

More like she was one move away from trying that straddling move she'd been thinking about since they sat down. But first, the worries. "Well, for the last week Anthony has been making calls and leaving work. He's disappeared for hours at a time. There's nothing on his calendar and he comes back distracted and frustrated."

"I think I'm lost again." Ford smiled. "How would you know what's happening at your uncle's office?"

"I talk with his assistant, Andrea, all the time. She keeps me updated." That came out a bit more stalkery than Shay liked, but with Ford she didn't feel the need to weigh her words. Including him lessened her anxiety.

Sharing was not easy for her, thanks to Devin and the limited ties she kept in her personal life. But from the beginning, letting Ford in resulted in him seeing more of her, knowing more about her. The reality didn't cause panic to bounce around inside of her, which was a nice change.

Ford gave her thigh a gentle squeeze. "As I said, sometimes you have to sneak around to get the information you need."

"Thanks for getting what I'm saying and not think-

ing I'm creepy." The easy acceptance confirmed what
she already knew—Ford was worth the risk of trying
again.

"Never." His palm slipped up her back, under her
shirt. "Any chance whatever is bugging your uncle is
not a work thing or a private thing?"

"Like what?"

Ford closed one eye as he winced. "Not to hit on
a potentially touchy subject, but could he be dating
someone? You know, maybe sneaking around because
he's worried you or Trent might not approve?"

"No." Not a touchy subject but not possible either. In
reality she thought both Anthony and Trent could stand
to let their good looks work for them and enjoy more
interesting personal lives. Concentrating on something
other than work might ease some stress. She knew from
her time with Ford that the concept worked for her.

"That's an emphatic response."

She didn't bother to explain how Anthony focused
all his attention on the office now that her aunt was
gone. Since Ford appeared to be made from the same
mold, and close to her uncle on the workaholic scale,
she let the topic drop. There was no need to start down
a road that could lead to arguing. Not tonight.

Right now she had a bigger problem. "I'm going to
contact the police if we don't hear anything concrete
from Trent by tonight."

"Hmm."

There it was again. Humming twice in two minutes
was never a good sign. It was the sound men made
when they thought women were making wrong turns.
She wasn't a fan. "Just spill it."

Ford laughed. "Your mind-reading skills aren't working?"

"They've been spinning overtime on Trent and failing miserably."

"Right, sorry." Ford placed a quick kiss on her lips but pulled back before it deepened. "Maybe wait on calling in the police on Trent."

"I have."

Ford brushed a hand over her hair as his eyes softened. "I know, but Trent is an adult."

That sounded like some sort of guy thing. A groan rumbled in her throat but she cut it off before it could wind up.

She tipped her head back, balancing on his arm and staring at the ceiling. "Now you sound like my uncle."

"From your tone, I'm not sure that's a compliment." Ford touched her chin and brought her head up to face him again. "I'm just saying Trent might not appreciate the babysitting when he comes home."

Clearly, Ford sided with Anthony in thinking they had to tiptoe through the minefield of Trent's fragile male ego. Her fears burrowed deeper. Right to his safety and their failure to step in and ensure it. "Don't you get it? I'm worried something happened and he won't be able to come home."

"I know, babe." With his hands on her hips, Ford turned her until she hit that straddling position and stared him down eye-to-eye.

The term of endearment threw her off and had her brain cells scrambling. The delivery, so low and caring, with the softness of a caress, pushed past her frustration. She'd seen him sweet and hot and sexy, but this sounded almost loving. The way her heart hammered in response had her bouncing between excitement and terror.

Before she could pick one, Ford continued. "Look, I know some people who have contacts. I can make some calls and see what I can find."

The offer snapped her out of her stupor. She slipped her palms up his arms and settled them on his shoulders. "Are you being purposely vague?"

One of his eyebrows lifted as he pulled her tighter against his body. "Well, I do have some computer skills that can help in situations such as these."

"You'd hack for me?" It was wrong and an invasion of privacy, but the offer came from a good place. A caring place. For some reason that made her almost giddy. She'd heard friends talk about getting hit with this wave of happiness and feeling as if light poured through them. She'd had no understanding of the sensation . . . until now. "Interesting."

"But?"

"No buts. I'm not the kind of woman who says no to solid help. If you can do something, please do it, just be careful not to get in trouble, and try to limit the information to what's necessary to confirm Trent's safe." She'd deal with the angry cousin fallout later.

"Guess that means you don't want to know about his porn collection, assuming of course a guy his age would have one."

"God, no." Trent was an adult, but there were things she didn't need to see.

But she did want to know about Ford's needs and maybe fulfill one or two. She wrapped her arms around his neck and leaned in for one of those burning kisses that would have her touching her lips hours later in memory.

With only an inch between their mouths, he pulled back, pressing his head into the couch cushions. "We do need to talk about one other thing."

He got so many things right. She hoped he wasn't taking a sharp turn into wrong. "Uh-huh."

His hands soothed up and down her back, slipping under the edge of her T-shirt to caress bare skin. "I'll be gone for about twenty-four hours. I'll be in town but I have to help a company move. That means breaking down the system and bringing it back up as fast as possible so they don't lose precious work hours."

The news plowed into her. He walked in and out of her daily life, and she knew to expect that with his job, but that didn't mean she liked it.

She tried to smile but the corners of her mouth refused to lift. "If you say so."

"Hey." He cupped her cheek and forced eye contact again. "This is me trying to let you know what's going on so you don't think I just disappeared without warning."

The words mattered. So did the pleading for understanding in his eyes.

Frustration blinked out and satisfaction took its place. This was better. The traveling would continue but now he clued her in, gave her advance warning.

The unexpected warmth flowed through her again. "Well, look at that."

"I can be taught, you know." His fingers slid under the clasp of her bra as he pressed a line of kisses down her throat.

She felt a tug and the band around her middle loosened. Then his hands shifted until her breasts filled his palms. The way he flicked his thumb over her nipple as that hot mouth kissed the dip at the base of her neck and headed across her collarbone had her head falling to the side.

Her eyes closed as she breathed in his scent and concentrated on the way his tongue and lips inflamed her skin. "It is that hope that keeps women coming back for more."

"If you want more, I can give you more." Using his nose, he moved the V-neck of her shirt down and swept a tongue across her nipple.

"Dirty boy." And thank God for that. Heat exploded and his hands traveled over her skin. It took all her control to ignore the heartbeat pounding in her ears as blood rushed through her.

Her lips went to his cheek, to the rough brush of hair over his chin, then found his mouth. The kiss hit her with a zap of electricity and had the need inside her spiking.

Something snapped then. Her body rubbed against his and her hips rode up and down, building the heat through their clothes. She held him close. Fingers slipped into his hair. Their mouths crossed over each other once then twice. Then she lost count.

Just as her fingers switched to his T-shirt and started tugging, his body jerked. His hands went to her sides and he shifted her off his lap as he sat up straighter.

"Ford, what are you—"

The front door clicked shut. "Hello?"

Hearing her uncle's voice had her flipping around on

Ford's thighs as she struggled to shove her shirt back down and prevent a disturbing peep show. She noticed her uncle, imposing in his usual dark suit. "Anthony?"

"I see you have company." His dark-eyed gaze stayed on her face then drifted away. "It would appear I shouldn't have used my key."

"Probably not," Ford mumbled as his fingers went to work putting the clasp of her bra back together.

She nearly fell over trying to get up off the couch. His thigh trapped her leg and she had to yank to stand up. Between the heavy make-out session and the wrestling to get her clothes back in place, her bra strap had twisted and dug into her skin. At least he walked in before all their clothes hit the hardwood floor.

Forget about being a grown-up and in her own damn house, heat rushed to her cheeks and she stumbled over her words trying to explain. "We were just—"

"I can see what you were doing, Shay."

"Well, this is awkward." Ford whispered the comment into her hair.

She didn't bother to whisper her reply. "You think?"

She heard a long exhale as a puff of breath blew across the top of her ear. Hands went to her hips and moved her body a few inches away from the couch. Before she could blink, Ford had his hand on her lower back and guided them to stand in front of her uncle.

Ford held out a hand. "I'm Ford Decker."

"I figured." The men shook hands. "Anthony Creighton, Shay's uncle."

She was transported back to being fifteen and getting caught making out in the back of Paul Freeman's car. Years had passed, but her uncle's disapproving frown, the one he wore then and now, had the power to have her shifting her weight from foot to foot. "Now that we all know each other."

"I was just telling Shay the other day that we should all have dinner together." Anthony spoke directly to Ford in what came off as a serious man-to-man discussion.

"Absolutely, but did you need to talk with Shay about something now? I can wait in the other room." Ford talked with an easy grace and stood tall and confidant, as if getting caught with his hands on her breasts didn't phase him at all.

And maybe it didn't. This seemed to be her issue, not his. She didn't associate sex with shame and refused to apologize for the choices she'd made about men, but there was something about disappointing Anthony that always made her twitchy. He'd taken her in, let her grieve, gave her focus and handed her a job.

She had tried for years to pay him back all he'd given her by being perfect, and had failed miserably. She didn't possess Trent's smarts or Anthony's business ruthlessness. The most she could do was manage his properties so he never doubted his investment in them or her.

But right now he was intruding, and she'd need to take him aside at some point and remind her about things like privacy and knocking. "Why are you here?"

"Right." Anthony finally glanced at her again. "I've been searching around and finally heard from Trent. He needed a few days away so I sent him to my property in Charlottesville."

Ford's eyes narrowed. "Virginia?"

"You saw him?" she asked at the same time.

"I own a place by the university." Anthony put his hands in his front pants pockets and rocked back on his heels. "A small condo complex."

The pieces didn't make any sense to Shay. The searching spoke to Anthony's work absences but not Trent's behavior or why he didn't answer his phone or at least return a text. "Did he give you an explanation?"

Anthony smiled. "This has all been about a young woman."

With that, Shay's mind went blank. "What?"

She struggled to make sense of what her uncle was saying. Good genes blessed Trent with sunny blond looks and big brains. Neither qualified as an excuse for his recent bout of rudeness.

"Someone in his office. I got the impression they worked long hours, something happened and . . . well, things didn't go as Trent planned. He's embarrassed and upset."

She waited for the wave of relief to hit her but it never came. The story raised more questions than it answered. All of it highlighted her need to hear Trent's voice. Maybe yell at him for a few minutes for all he'd put them through.

"Okay." She had no idea what to say, so she went with that.

Ford's hand continued to rub over her back. "Kind of an extreme reaction to young love, isn't it?"

"He can be intense, and that spills over into his dating." Anthony held up a hand. "Well, look. You two are in the middle of something."

She rushed to direct the conversation before her

uncle turned it to her private life. "Thanks for telling me about Trent. I'm annoyed and kind of want to drive down there and shake him, but at least he's safe."

"No problem." Anthony treated Ford to a guy nod then leaned in and kissed her cheek. "Call me about that dinner."

"Sure." But she said the word to the closed door.

Anthony had disappeared as fast as he came. He'd swooped in and dropped the information then took off again. That summed up his behavior lately—never staying still long enough to answer hard questions.

"You okay?" Ford asked.

When she focused again, he stood in front of her, all handsome and reassuring. "Just trying to process it all."

His arms encircled her hips in a loose wrap. "Want to drive to Charlottesville and check on Trent?"

Ford would pile them into a car and drive a few hours without complaining. She could tell by the way he asked. The guy got hotter by the minute.

"Maybe later." But she didn't mean that. She was exactly where she wanted to be, with him, right there.

"And until then?"

She slid her hands under the edge of his T-shirt and trailed them up his chest. "I need some help with my bra."

Heat filled those sexy eyes. "I hope you mean—"

"Taking it off and keeping it off this time."

His palms slipped over her ass and he pulled her in closer and rubbed his erection against her. "I'm your man."

Yeah, she was beginning to think he was.

12

FORD DRAGGED his sorry ass into the Warehouse the next morning. He'd been undercover for most of his career. He took on other personas, used everyone, played games, stole whatever needed to be stolen. Shot and blew up people and things, all in the name of national security. For reasons he couldn't explain but could name—Shay—the stakes increased exponentially on this job.

The end goal wasn't exactly difficult to figure out. They had to stop a reckless genius from wrecking the world. That meant pulling every string and tracking every lead in the search for Trent Creighton. Ford understood the game. He just fucking hated it this round.

Sitting on the couch with Shay, sleeping with her, dragging his mouth all over her hot body, qualified as part of his assignment. He'd done it before, pretended to be attracted to this person and acted the role of a long lost grandson to that one. His whole work life boiled down to one long hand of "the end justifies the means."

It had never been okay with him before, but he had justified and tolerated it. With Shay, the betrayal kept him in a constant state of agitation, as if his skin didn't fit and every word he said to her had to be ripped out of him because with her it wasn't an act.

He didn't realize he'd stopped in the middle of the Warehouse floor, staring at his feet, until another pair of shoes broke into his line of vision. He glanced up to see Jake Pearce standing there, crooked smile in place and hands folded together in front of him.

"You okay there, Ford?"

With the glasses and brown hair graying at his temples, Pearce could be a professor. That happened to be one of his most effective covers. On a joint CIA/MI6 operation years ago he taught at a university in Germany, gathering intel on emerging radical groups. Those poor kids never knew the guy pacing in front of them in a tweed blazer could whip out a machine gun and take out a town without one ounce of regret.

That was just one of the man's skills. Ford had heard more than once about how impressive Pearce was with the ladies. If the CIA needed to charm information or weapons or drugs out of a woman, the people in charge sent in Pearce. Ford thought the whole "model good looks" thing was way overblown, but he couldn't deny Pearce's ability to drag the most obscure piece of information out of nowhere.

Ford reached out and shook the other man's hand. "When did you come in?"

"After the royal fuck-up."

That described the entire job to date. "Be more specific."

"I was talking Hampstead but I heard about the DC warehouse debacle." Pearce shook his head. "Starting to look like this assignment is spooked."

That's not quite how Ford saw it. "Or being sabotaged."

Ward joined them with a welcome clap of a hand on Pearce's shoulder. "Hey, man."

For a second Ford blocked his memories of Shay, the flash of images on the screens around them, and Ellery's frantic typing and moving from one desk to another compiling information. He boiled his concerns into two simple sentences he knew the men standing with him would understand. "Someone is spinning us around. That can only mean this Trent kid is getting help from someone connected and dangerous."

Ward nodded. "I agree. No way this kid—brilliant or not—could make all this happen without someone running interference."

Pearce hid his thoughts behind a blank expression, as he always did. The guy never gave anything away, which was one of the reasons he was so effective in the field. Rumor was, he'd withstood torture in the Sudan by singing to his captors, and survived being thrown in a hole and nearly buried alive in Afghanistan by reciting a book he'd memorized. The man might look pretty but his veins were ice cold. Had to be to live through what he'd gone through and still be standing.

"We're really thinking this kid got mixed up with Benton somehow?" Pearce asked. "Any ideas on how they got together? I mean, Benton doesn't normally look for science types."

"All options are on the table." Ward leaned over Ellery's shoulder at the nearby desk. A few clicks of the keyboard and a diagram of potential targets filled the screen. He gestured to the mass of lines connecting photos to each other. "You're welcome to help us trim this mess down."

They had to wade through all of it, but Ford sensed they needed to dig deeper in another direction. One that would plant a gulf between him and Shay the size of the Grand Canyon. "We should look at his dad, Anthony."

Ward nodded to Ellery. A second later personal information on Anthony and his companies filled another screen. Photos, bank statements, corporate documents. All private but none of it problematic. Ford knew the real information would be buried somewhere, and he depended on Ellery to work her voodoo computer magic to uncover it.

"Rich, connected." Pearce stood close to the screen with his hands on his hips as he took it all in. "This relative angle makes sense."

"Add to that the fact Anthony lied his ass off to Shay yesterday about Trent and we have a reason to dig." Between the smooth delivery and genuine tone, Ford's internal alarm had started buzzing. Maybe Anthony thought lying would put Shay at ease and justified it that way, but Ford sensed something else was at work. "Shay didn't blink, but I did."

Pearce glanced over his shoulder. "Uh, Shay?"

Yeah, that tone wasn't good. "Anthony's niece and Trent's cousin."

Pearce laughed. "I think you're missing my innuendo."

Not exactly. Ford would have to be the worst field agent in the world not to pick up on the direction of Pearce's thoughts. "Ignoring it, actually."

"What did the uncle say exactly?" Ward asked, cutting through the crap and bringing them back to the job.

Ford appreciated the conversation assist. "He said he talked with Trent and the kid was lovesick and needed some time away to heal a broken heart."

Sounded like pure bullshit to Ford. The kid supposedly worked such long hours that he slept on a cot in his lab, yet had enough time to fall for some girl? No way could anyone sell that line.

"So, daddy supposedly sent the kid to his property in Charlottesville to recuperate from getting his feelings hurt?" Ward swore. "I'm not buying it and nothing in the intel supports it."

An understatement as far as Ford was concerned. "Join the club."

"Wait a second. Go back." Pearce whipped around. "Shay told you all of this?"

"Anthony did. I was standing right there." Which was the other reason Ford questioned the too-convenient story. Her uncle had seemed all too eager to have the conversation overheard. He didn't break off and call her aside to discuss a private family matter. No, Anthony made sure he got the news. Felt like covering his tracks to Ford.

"Shay didn't buy the heartbreak thing, did she?" Ward asked.

Relief smacked into Ford. Sounded like he was not alone in thinking they had a new direction to investigate in the uncle. "She clearly wanted to, but she's not dumb."

"Interesting." Ward made a humming sound. "Makes you wonder if Uncle Anthony is looking for a new way to make money, and piles of it."

"While we're digging into backgrounds, we also need to take a closer look at Trent's boss at the Center for Scientific Research." Ford scanned the screens for the man's name. "Matt Claymore."

"I have experience with that group." Pearce leaned against the desk, right next to Ellery, who kept on typing. "He's been vetted and has a solid history. To hold that job he needs a top secret clearance and has his assets checked often, along with being subjected to random lie detector tests."

Ford added *Claymore being too clean* to the list of things he didn't like about this assignment. "True, but every employee who goes in or out of that building gets searched. So, if everyone is above reproach and following the rules, explain how the toxin got out."

"I'll put Delta team on the Charlottesville angle, just to be safe." Ward wrote something on a notepad and handed it to Ellery. "They can also handle walking back through the people who work and guard CSR."

"Claymore is mine," Ford said as he watched the by-play, knowing Ellery's next move would be to call in the Delta team from combing through the warehouse area and squeezing the last bit of information out of Billy.

"Funny but it sounded like Shay was yours." Pearce picked now to break his blank expression and be a sarcastic smartass.

Ford refused to play along. "She's not involved. She's collateral."

"Have we definitely decided that?" Ward asked.

Ignoring all of them proved a pretty big temptation. "She's worried about Trent and looking all over for him."

Pearce dropped his arms and grabbed the edge of

the desk behind him. "Or she's a great actress and is working with her uncle to throw you off Trent's trail."

"She has no idea what I do. She thinks I'm a computer tech guy." She also viewed him as honest and decent and a whole bunch of positive shit Ford knew he could no longer claim.

"Maybe she's in the dark, but I'm not trusting anything we *think* to be true on this job but don't know for sure. I don't trust the intel or the people digging for it." Pearce looked at Ellery and held up a hand in what looked like mock surrender. "No offense."

She snorted. "Whatever."

The frustration in Ford's gut kept building and rumbling. He let it spill over and work its way into the anger in his voice. "Speaking of which, your half-assed info almost got me blown up in Hampstead."

Pearce didn't even blink. "My contact is missing. I keep waiting to hear his body has been found in a dumpster somewhere in London."

"That's fucking great." Just what they needed. Another dead end—literally.

"So . . ." Ward drew out the word as he shot Ford a calm-the-hell-down look. "We lock this down. Limit access and keep to Alliance members for all info gathering and clean-up. No upstairs help."

Pearce shrugged. "That leaves me out."

"Nice try. You're an Alliance honorary member." Ward didn't usher Pearce out but something in his tone suggested it was time for Pearce to hit the streets.

He must have heard it because he straightened away from the desk. "Okay, let me see if anyone is hearing anything else while I check into this auction."

"There's news on that angle?" Ford had been waiting for movement there.

"I'll fill you in." Ward waved off the conversation and nodded to Pearce before turning back to Ford. "I need to talk to you anyway."

Not good. "That's usually bad."

Ward didn't even try to smile. "Think positively."

Yeah, really not good. "Now I'm positive it's bad."

13

WARD WAS impressed they made it the whole way into his private office before Ford started rapid-firing questions. "The auction?"

"Yes." Ward kept moving until he got to the opposite side of his desk and stared Ford down.

Ford threw out his hands. "Well? Any chance you're going to explain what's happening?"

This part of Ford, Ward knew and accepted. They'd worked together during Ward's last year at the CIA. He cut out first to set up Alliance. Ford stayed behind, insisting the CIA was the right place for him, until his assigned partner and his fiancée bled out in front of Ford.

That kind of death changed a guy. Made him harder. They'd all seen some rough shit. Watched innocents get blown apart and had to pull the trigger more times than any human should.

They all had a number. The lives that weighed on their shoulders. For Ward, thirty-seven. There were many more he couldn't save, but thirty-seven where he'd done the deed. But he'd never had a partner shredded in front of him. Ford couldn't make that claim.

Being emotionally ripped into pieces made it tough to ever be whole again. Ward watched Ford function despite the inner turmoil, then a few weeks ago something changed, which was why they stood in the private office right now.

But first the disaster they couldn't duck or ignore. "Pearce got confirmation. The auction is a go but there's no word on the location of the toxin. Not that it matters to the pricks prepared to buy it. The worst of the worst are sending representatives. Apparently, homicidal maniacs all over the world are excited and emptying their bank accounts."

Ford shook his head. "No surprise there. Benton knows he has a hot property or is about to get his hands on one."

"Harlan is working the Benton angle."

"That is not comforting."

"The guy isn't that bad." Testy and anal as hell, but determined. Ward had to admire the man's past, especially since the setup of Alliance had them sharing power. Neither the U.S. nor the UK held the upper hand. It was smart, but annoying as shit.

"For the sake of office morale," Ford said. "I'll go with no comment."

"As if you give a shit about morale." Time to dive into the real topic Ward wanted to discuss. "Though I do have to wonder if ignoring problems and getting pissed off is your answer for everything these days."

Ford froze in the act of crossing his ankle over his opposite knee. "What is that supposed to mean?"

No one would call Ward the ideal human resources person. He wanted to come in and work and stay as far out of the personal lives of his team as possible. When he'd repeated that mantra to Tasha the evening before, she treated him to a "you're so stupid" eye roll and told him to man up or step down. Not his favorite evening with her.

Taking a deep breath and preparing for the swearing, Ward leaned forward on his elbows and dove in. "Anything you need to tell me about this assignment?"

"This job is rigged to get us all killed, and Harlan is a douche."

"True on both counts." The muscles across Ward's shoulders tightened as tension spun through the small room. "Anything else?"

"Are we playing games here? Just say what you're trying to say."

For fuck's sake. "Shay Alexander."

Ward expected a kick of anger. Instead, all emotion drained from Ford's face. It was as if he'd taken a lesson from Pearce in hiding the thoughts running through his head.

"She's not involved in the auction." The words sounded as if they were ground out of Ford, as if a wave of fury was locked inside him and screaming to get out.

"Let me be more specific. We need to talk about your feelings for Shay Alexander."

After a moment of shrieking silence, Ford spoke again. "We're not doing this."

"I'm your boss."

Ford's jaw tightened to the point of cracking. "You gave me this assignment. You set up the cover."

"And I'm wondering if I should take you off this one

and pass her surveillance on to someone else. Josiah would love for Delta to take lead."

Ford's eyes narrowed as he leaned forward. "You think you can have me go out of town and have Reid or Josiah take my place in her life and her bed?"

"I didn't say—"

"What the fuck, Ward?"

The reaction told Ward everything he needed to know. There was no hiding the rage now. Ford wore it like a robe. It showed in the way he seethed and clenched his teeth together, in the stiffness of his body and hands balled into fists on the armrests.

The air in the room was thick, enough to choke them both. "Because you hate the thought of Shay with another man."

"She's a human being, not a commodity to be passed around between us."

Not that Ward ever meant to suggest that, but the way he saw it, Ford's feelings, jumbled and confused as they might be, were the real problem. Ward knew his friend no longer saw this woman as a job. He saw her as a woman. Possibly his woman. That had the power to fuck up everything.

He cleared his voice, thinking one person in the room should stay in control. "I think she's more than a commodity or weapon to you."

"Don't do this." The legs of the chair banged against the floor as Ford stood up and paced to the far wall.

"You moved in too fast." Ward talked louder with each word, thinking Ford intended to storm out, but he turned and came back to the desk instead. Not that facing Ford head-on helped this uncomfortable conversation. "You failed to tell me you'd made contact and went from watching from a distance to sleeping with her. I only knew because Tasha caught you."

"Caught me? What am I, some kid who violated probation?" The defensive hackles rose with each word.

"Don't make this about my word choice. You know perfectly well what I mean."

Ford took a threatening step forward then stopped again. "Not everything is your business."

"This is." Ward forced his body to remain still. "Look, I see you walking around here, double-guessing your decisions and feeling guilty about playing her."

"Stop analyzing me, Ward. I fucking mean it." Ford's mouth dropped open and it looked as if he planned to say something else before he reconsidered and shook his head instead. "Just don't."

"It's part of my job to test your decision-making."

"I gave you space in Fiji. I didn't get in between you and Tasha. I didn't call it in or report it."

That fast, Ward's anger built up and exploded. This was the one topic sure to have him come out swinging. At the last minute he clamped down on the energy pounding through him and stayed focused, but just barely. "She was not part of my cover. Tasha wasn't a mark."

"I hate that word."

"And the situation is different, don't you think? I live with Tasha. I love her." Those three words didn't begin to describe how he felt about the woman who sat at a desk upstairs. "I'm trying to figure out if you've crossed that same line with Shay."

"She's innocent in all of this. I'd stake my job on that."

Ward watched Ford wage an internal battle and heard him talk in circles. Little did Ford understand it all gave him away. "I trust your instincts on her involvement but we both know I'm talking about something else."

"I know." Ford still snapped out the words, but the heat behind them had died down.

"You may have to put her cousin down in front of her."

Ford broke eye contact. "Right."

This was too important for him to retreat or worry about tact, so Ward aimed right for the jugular. "You will likely need to drag her uncle away while she begs you not to and screams about how much she hates you. Take the two people she loves, including the man who helped raise her, and order their executions in a hail of gunfire."

Ford rubbed a hand over his face before meeting Ward's gaze again. "Your point?"

They both knew where the conversation was heading. Ward didn't want to say the words, but he had to. He owed it to all of them, including Shay. "The way to end this might be to kill her, you get that, right? If Trent is the piece of shit we think he is—and all evidence points in that direction—he could use her to get to you. Make you choose."

Most of the color leached out of Ford's face. "I won't let that happen."

"You know how this works. We can plan and protect, and Trent could still grab her and put her right in front of the toxin." They arrived at the bottom line. A line similar to the one that had convinced Ward to stop punishing his body in rehab and leave fieldwork. "When it comes to the woman you care about, there could come a day when you have to put a bullet in her head on your way to grabbing the bad guys."

"Okay, enough." Ford smashed his fist into the desk, and the thud rattled the wood and had the legs screeching across the floor. "I get it, I'm fucked."

"That depends on how into her you are."

"I'm not breaking cover. Not yet."

The nonanswer told Ward what he needed to know. "That bad, huh?"

Ford balanced both fists on the desk and dropped his head. "Damn it."

"If you can't separate—"

His head shot up. "I can do my job."

Ward expected those answers. In Ford's shoes, he would have said the same things. But Ward couldn't afford to just hope. Delaying decisions was not an option in his new role. "We still have time to move you out of there. It's not your call. It's mine."

"Trust me to hold it together." Ford didn't beg and plead. He wasn't the type, but desperation filled his voice.

"You're solid, but this woman matters to you. If your loyalties are divided—"

Ford straightened up again. Tall and rigid, as if he'd regained control and was determined to show it. "They're not."

They had danced around the real issue for days. Now Ward moved in. "Kelly Mackenzie was not your fault, but if something happens to Shay or, worse, if you have to make an impossible call and kill the woman who is sharing your bed, you will shoulder that blame. But you can get out. Right now while I'm giving you the chance."

"Kelly is dead because of me. Tom is dead because of me. I didn't get to them in time and a madman cut them down while I watched. I'm not making the same mistake with Shay. I will be right there, with her, if anything happens."

Ward had seen the file about the hit on Ford's last CIA partner. Blood splattered the walls and stained everything. It had been an assassination meant to carry a message. Not a single gunshot. A battle with knives that took out Kelly first and paralyzed Tom.

Forgetting the details took Ward months. So many nights he closed his eyes and saw the carnage of glass and bodies. He couldn't imagine the movie playing in Ford's head. Ford had passed the mental health checks and Ward got him into Alliance, but Ford still had to be shaky. That was the constant worry.

Rather than poking into his friend's pain, Ward went with simple concern. "That's a lot of pressure, man."

"It's nothing compared to burying someone else I care about."

This time the circle landed on the spot that most concerned Ward. "I'm going to pretend you didn't say that last part and that you're neutral when it comes to Shay."

"Okay."

Ward knew the expression. He could remove Ford from the assignment and he'd weasel his way back in, get the guys to include him somehow. Hell, having Ford go rogue sounded almost as bad as having a deadly toxin on the loose.

But there had to be rules. Ford hated them and bucked against them, but Ward would try. "I will pull you, without warning, if anything smells wrong to me. You're going to keep me in the loop, and if you get in even one inch deeper with Shay, you are going to warn me."

For the first time since he stepped into the office, Ford smiled and the sharp line of his shoulders eased. "You know that sounded—"

"Pretend that wasn't loaded with sexual innuendo."

Ford nodded. "Done."

One knock sounded before the office door opened and Tasha slipped inside, bare leg first from where her navy skirt pushed over her knee. "We okay in here?"

Ford scoffed. "Fucking great."

"That's believable." She gave him an up-and-down look. "A boring navy T-shirt? Are all your other shirts in the laundry?"

He glanced down at her. "I hate this assignment."

The easy back and forth seemed to make Ford relax. Certainly lowered the shouting volume of his voice. It had been this way from the beginning with these two. They had a rapport. Almost a big sister–little brother thing. The dynamic fascinated Ward. Made him smile, since they were two of the most lethal people he knew and about the same age.

"Imagine thousands of people dying the instant the toxin gets out in the open," she said. "That will motivate you."

Ford frowned. "To what?"

Ward knew the answer to that one. "Scream into your pillow."

The last of the tension drifted away, and Ford's usual smartass grin returned. "Are you talking about the assignment or what happens when you two get home?"

Ward had to admit he'd walked into that one. Still, Tasha stood right there . . . within kicking distance. "Out of line, Ford."

She snorted. "Absolutely."

He had the smarts to wince. "Sorry."

"For the record, Ward is the screamer." Tasha's deadpan response broke through the last of the tension.

"Too much information." The amusement in Ford's voice killed the comment. "Speaking of which, I better get back to paging through boring stacks of information before Trent holds an auction or hands off to Benton to do it."

Tasha made a noise somewhere between a groan and a sigh. "I hate that kid."

"I plan to beat the shit out of him when I finally meet him." Ford gave Ward a nod. "I'll go work on making that happen."

Tasha watched him go and closed the door behind him. It took her another few seconds before she turned around to face Ward again. "So, we're pretending his attraction for Shay isn't kicking his ass?"

Her smarts or that face—it was a constant battle for Ward to figure out which he loved more. "For now."

"I hope we don't regret this."

That very fear kept Ward up most of last night. "This is my call. You have deniability."

"Don't make me beat you down while your team watches through the window." She frowned as she spoke. "As with all things, we're in this together."

"That's pretty hot." Since she looked ready to head out, he indulged in a quick bit of flirting. "And, for the record, you're the screamer."

"And you are the one who makes me scream." She winked at him. "Now get back to work."

14

SHAY SAT on a stool at her breakfast bar and watched Ford move around the kitchen. He'd popped up a half hour ago and after a quick kiss made a beeline for her refrigerator. He stood with the door open and the cool air pouring out as he stared at a hundred dollars worth of groceries and frowned.

As if she wanted food right now. She hadn't worn the silky dress with the buttons down the front and skipped the underwear so they could eat pizza on the couch. It had taken most of the half hour since he texted about being on the way home and coming over to achieve the just-out-of-bed mussed look with her hair.

Not that he noticed. He looked half ready to hoover the butter. The intense focus made her wonder if he'd eaten a meal since the last time she saw him.

Her bare toes curled around the stool's cold metal footrest as she drummed her fingernails against the marble countertop. Maybe it was the way his faded jeans rested on his hips or how his broad shoulders formed a perfect vee to his waist, but something had energy buzzing through her.

The longer they dated, the more she hated being

away from him. This time he called and texted, which qualified as huge progress. He even suggested they engage in phone sex until someone called him away to work and ruined his plans . . . and her evening. Just seeing him there, realizing how right and comfortable it felt to have him around, had her spinning stupid fantasies about the future in her head.

Ford stopped foraging long enough to glance over his shoulder at her. "Have you eaten?"

For a smart guy, he seemed to be missing some pretty big clues. Like the lip gloss and absence of a bra. "No."

He shut the refrigerator and turned around to face her. "Want to go out?"

He had that distracted, not paying attention expression. Looked like she needed to be a tad more obvious.

Maybe she should have skipped the dress completely. She'd like to think he'd notice naked. "Nope."

He leaned down on the counter across from her and took one of her hands in his. Fingertips touched her palm and a thumb brushed over the heel. "Okay, well, I can order in. What are you hungry for?"

She fought to keep the shiver running through her. "Nothing."

"Really?" He shot her one of those sexy smiles that made her insides spin.

"Yeah, Ford. Really."

He lifted her hand and kissed his way up her wrist. "You're not exactly being helpful in the 'we need food' department."

This time her insides did a little dance. The tumbling sensation had her locking her feet around the bar footstep to kept from pitching forward. "I don't want food."

"Then what . . ." He peeked up and his eyes widened, all signs of distraction clearing in record time. "Oh, I think I'm catching up here."

"Finally. Thought I'd need to get out smoke signals soon."

She slipped her hand out of his. Her fingers fumbled on the little white buttons of her dress, but she got the top two undone. Peeling back the edges, she revealed the tops of her breasts. She didn't have to guess if he'd figured out the braless thing. His gaze locked on her skin until she thought she could feel the warmth of his stare rush over her.

He swallowed twice when her hand moved to the next button. "I prefer stamina over quickness."

"I was just thinking the same thing." The third button slid out of its hole, and the cool air of the condo mixed with the heat from his eyes. She leaned forward, giving him an unbroken view of the shadow between her breasts and miles of skin.

"Nice dress."

About time he picked up on that. "I chose it specially for your homecoming."

His gaze bounced up again. Traveled to her hair and over her face. "How did I miss how amazing you look tonight?"

Much better. "You should see what I have on under this." She undid two more buttons and let the dress gape to her waist.

"It looks like nothing, and I sure as hell hope that's the case."

"It is." She slid the material off her shoulders, letting it pool on her arms and dip down to her bikini line . . . if she had been wearing one.

He walked around the counter to stand in front of her. "I like where your head is tonight."

"Want to prove it?" She took his hand and slipped it inside her open dress.

"This thing where you take the lead?" He took over then with both hands roaming over her body, stopping to brush his thumb over her nipple and bring it to a tight bud. "So fucking sexy."

"Having me strip down in front of you doesn't make you feel like a dirty old man?"

His low chuckle filled the quiet room as he took her hands and brought her to her feet. "I'm not that much older than you."

"Seven years."

Leaning in, he pressed his mouth against her neck then trailed a line of kisses down and over her collarbone. To the tops of her breasts. "So beautiful."

"Thirty-three or sixty-three, you're still impressive." She cupped a hand over his erection. Rubbed back and forth over the bulge and felt it grow under her palm.

"I try." Slow and steady, he pushed the dress down from her waist and let it slip to the floor. The material puddled at her feet. Before she could kick it free he bent down and licked her nipple.

Fingers and mouth, the joint pressure made her breath hiccup in her chest. He sucked and kissed until her mouth dropped open and her body pressed in closer. She fought for air and tried to keep her heartbeat even, but the blood thundering through her veins had other ideas.

One hand slid around her stomach to her ass. The move dragged her hard against him as his mouth found that sensitive place behind her ear. He nibbled and licked until her knees turned to jelly.

She grabbed fists full of his shirt and tugged it up his stomach and over his shoulders. While he skimmed his tongue over her the top of her ear, she dropped her head into that sexy space where his neck met his shoulders. Resting there, she inhaled his scent, all warm and minty like the soap he used each morning.

"My head will explode if I don't get inside you soon," he whispered against her cheek.

The words vibrated through her. She pulled back and cradled his face in her hands. "That's not quite how I was going to say it, but yeah."

When she wiggled her eyebrows, he smiled. "But I love when you throw out the dirty talk."

With him, sex ranged from fun to heart-stopping. He laughed, they joked. When he entered her, fast or slow, her heels would press into the mattress. And she needed to get them there right now.

"Do you like this?" Her fingers went to work on his belt. The sound of the zipper screeched through the room as she lowered it. The only thing better was his soft groan when she reached inside the material and wrapped her fingers around his length.

As her hand moved up and down, his forehead dropped until it touched hers. "Damn, Shay."

"Should I stop?"

His hands smoothed over her back and down to her ass. "God, no."

"Are you begging?" He was loaded with confidence

and liked to be in control, but she knew from experience he didn't shy away from asking for what he wanted in the bedroom . . . or the kitchen or the shower.

"I'll get on my knees, if you want me to."

"I'd like that." She kissed him then. Not teasing or light. A searing kiss that had her body plunging into a heat storm.

His hands tightened against her lower back as he rocked her body against his, rubbing and igniting a flame in every cell. Her fingers speared in to his hair. Hands pulled at him, grabbing and touching, wanting to get closer and melt into him.

One minute she was hugging and caressing him and the next she held nothing but air. Before she could protest, he slipped out of her arms. Bent his legs and slowly sank to his knees. She looked at the top of his head. Her muscles shook and she snagged the counter behind her in a death grip as he opened her legs to fit between them.

Fingertips slid up the inside of her thighs and a breath of hot air blew over her. When he trailed his tongue inside her, over her, her hips bucked. The waiting plus the prolonged foreplay had her body on edge and her blood pounding through her.

She reached down, thinking to push him back so she could drop to the floor in front of him, but her hand hit his shoulders and stayed there for balance. Her nails bit into his skin. If the sting bothered him, he didn't let it show. He used his fingers and mouth to wind her up until every muscle in her body clenched as if begging for relief.

"We should get to the bedroom." She blew out a

rough breath as his finger hit the spot that made her heart stop.

She was wet and ready and five seconds from crawling all over him. When her knees buckled, he caught her around her thighs and brought her down until she straddled his thighs. The rough denim rubbed against her bare skin but she barely felt it. Sensations bombarded her as they kissed and his palms caressed her.

One hand dipped between then and a finger pressed up inside her. "You are so fucking wet."

Words jammed in her throat. She couldn't say anything.

"I can't wait." He flipped her and the room spun.

When her back hit the carpet, her thighs dropped open to make room for him. He slid over her. The friction of his clothes against her bare stomach had her squirming for more.

"God, I can't stop wanting you." His finger pressed and her body pulsed in time with the intimate touches.

"Don't." She mumbled the words between kisses.

Not sure if he heard, and not caring, she focused on wrapping her legs around his hips and clinging to his broad back with all her strength. Everything inside her clenched. His heavy pants and her soft moans hung in the air.

She was on the pill but her mind flashed to protection and the condoms they'd agreed to use. She would have offered a reminder but her mind kept blanking as thoughts whooshed into her head, scrambled, then left again.

He did this to her. He flooded her senses and had her forgetting about every man that came before. Took her life and control and shook them until they scattered.

"I have to . . ." He sat up before he finished the sentence.

His hands never stopping, he stripped off his jeans and the boxer briefs underneath. Instead of his usual smoothness, the moves were jerky and wild, as if a fever gripped him. He moved quickly and didn't slow until he was naked and staring down at her again.

With a hand on the inside of each knee, he pushed her thighs open. "So fucking beautiful."

All embarrassment and every doubt gone, she let her legs fall to each side. She craved his touch and the feel of him pulsing inside her. Her hands landed on his, guiding him closer to the spot she needed him to touch.

"Ford, now."

Her sharp order seemed to snap him out of his stupor. He stopped staring at her stomach, loving every inch with his gaze, and scrambled to the side. Half on her, half off, he reached for the leg of his jeans and pulled the pants closer.

She tightened her hold on his hands. "What are you—"

"Condom." He pulled the small packet out of his pocket and held it up.

Before she could blink, he ripped the package open and rolled it on. She had to fight off a laugh at his determination. It was a stark contrast to how he'd acted when he first came in. He sure saw her now.

And here she was getting all pissy because he kept eyeing up everything including the leftover Chinese food containers in the refrigerator. "I thought you only came here for dinner."

"I planned to eat first, but then . . ."

"Make 'then' now and we can work our way back to food later."

"Yes, ma'am."

Balancing some of his weight on his elbows, he pressed against her again. His palm slid over the back of her thigh, lifting her leg higher on his hip. Their mouths fused together as he guided his length inside her. Stretching and pushing, he thrust into her long and deep. He cradled her head in one hand while the other skimmed over her leg and then up to her stomach.

In and out, his body pumped into hers. Each pulse sped up the thudding of her heart. The guttural sounds he made matched the buck of his lower body against hers.

They'd been sleeping together for weeks. Sometimes slow and lingering, sometimes hot and fast. Always smoking and shared. Never selfish. He made demands of her body and gave back equal measure. He didn't hide his need or desire. Never judged. The feminine power he unleashed had her more confident to ask for what she wanted.

Right now she wanted more. "Harder."

The rhythm increased. When he shifted his hips, her head dropped back against the floor. With her back arched and tension coiling inside her, she held on tighter to his forearms. Their harsh breathing echoed around them as her body thumped against the floor with each press of his.

She ached for release. Her body, so primed for him, silently begged to break free.

Without a word, his hand snaked between them and his finger found her clit. He rubbed and circled. His body pressed in and out and sensations swirled around her. She couldn't breathe. Couldn't think.

When he lifted her hips and pressed her thighs back toward her stomach, he took her even deeper, her lungs squeezing and the last bit of air leaving her body. She clenched her fingers in his hair and held onto him as the orgasm hit. Wave after wave pummeled her. The clenching inside her released in a rush and her body clamped down on his.

The moan coming from deep in his chest had her lifting her hips. The need to drive him wild swamped her need to relax. Her body had gone boneless but she held on, waiting for his control to snap.

The press of her hand against his lower back did the trick. Sweat gathered on his skin and heat radiated off of him. His mouth left hers and his head dropped. His jagged breathing drowned out everything else as he drove into her in one long last push.

He didn't shout, but whispered her name as he fell heavier against her. "Damn."

"Yeah." That was all she could manage. Once she figured out how to send a signal to her brain to ease up on her hold around his waist, she'd work on words.

Seconds, maybe minutes, later he lifted his head and stared around the kitchen and family room areas. "We didn't even make it to the couch."

"Was that the original plan?" In her mind she'd only gotten as far as stripping the dress off. She'd figured he'd take it from there, and he had.

He looked down at her. All the tension he carried with him after coming home from the job had disappeared. From his relaxed muscles to the sexy way the corner of his mouth kicked up, he seemed satisfied. Happy even.

That made one of them. She was too busy fighting off how good this felt. Last thing she needed was to fall this hard this fast.

From the beginning, she'd hidden him away and kept him from her friends. He'd only met her uncle because Anthony used his spare key to get into her place. Until now they'd thrived on privacy and stolen moments between his work assignments. Tonight struck her as something else. He came in keyed up and\ his attention scattered. She brought him around but the heat between them had her brain misfiring.

She couldn't be in love. But, damn, this felt like something big.

He brushed the hair off her forehead. "What are you thinking?"

That falling for a guy she barely knew was a stupid move.

Pushing the doubts and attractions away, she focused on the moment. "We should use the bed next round."

His smile grew. "Then let's get there."

Ford told himself he wanted water. Nothing else. Two hours had passed since he'd scooped her up and carried her to the bedroom for that promised second round. He'd been all over her, unable to get enough. Even now he was amazed his legs carried him.

He was so fucking lost where she was concerned. She didn't hold back or even try to protect herself from him. The trust drove him nuts because he didn't deserve it.

Now, as he got out of the still warm bed, she dozed. They'd rolled across the sheets, ending with her on her knees and him behind her. Ten minutes after sex, his instincts had screamed at him to get up and check her condo. To slip on his briefs and conduct some quick recon, sick prick that he was.

Battling back a serious case of self-loathing, he concentrated on the job. On Trent and the destruction he could bring down on the city. On the world.

The emotional back and forth gave Ford a nasty case of whiplash.

Still, he pushed on, walked through the condo, turning on a light to keep from tripping over furniture. Making his way from one end to another, he double-checked the devices he had planted in her place. One look at the camera hidden in a picture frame on the mantel and he froze. The equipment relayed the video back to the Warehouse and Ellery's terminal. He hoped she had the sense to fast forward through the sex.

Until tonight he'd been careful up to confine his time with Shay to the bedroom, where at least a sheet could hide some of the deed. Rolling around naked on the floor hadn't been in his plans until she unbuttoned that dress and he lost his fucking mind with the need to take her right then.

Refusing to think about the show they'd put on, he went to her purse. Flipping through the pockets and scanning the contents of her wallet, he didn't see anything new or interesting.

Next came her computer. She worked on it all day. With budgets and bills and collecting rents, she had a steady amount of accounting to keep track of. Ford was more interested in her e-mail account. He'd been all over the computer and sent a copy of the hard drive back to Ellery to analyze. They'd found nothing. But that didn't mean Shay didn't have something new now. Possibly some way to bypass whatever trace Ellery had on her account.

He lifted the top to the laptop and hit the space bar. Shay hadn't logged off, and her word processing program popped up. A few clicks of the keys and Ford got right into her e-mail in box because her computer automatically filled in her user name and password. Her convenient choices made his life easier, but she needed to be more careful. Not that he could think of a way to broach that subject without giving away his snooping.

After scanning a few e-mails, he hit on one that grabbed his attention. Not the right one. One from Shay to a friend that mentioned him and dating and talked about him not being anything like Devin, her piece-of-shit former boyfriend. The guy with all the debt and no boundaries.

Ford knew the name and the broad strokes from her file. He wanted an address and a few minutes scaring the shit out of the guy to teach him a lesson.

He sat there clenching and unclenching his hands until the need to punch something passed. The keys almost cracked under the force of his typing as he deleted the browser history and covered his tracks.

Now for a quick buzz around the room to make sure he hadn't left anything telling for her to uncover. Seeing their clothes scattered across the floor stopped him. He bent over and scooped up her dress before dumping it on the armrest of the couch.

"What are you doing?" Her voice cut through his mental checklist.

Damn, that never happened. She actually got the jump on him. He didn't hear her until she spoke. Even now she lounged in the doorway to the hall wearing nothing more than a short see-through white robe, and he only knew that much because she announced her presence and gave away the upper hand.

Unable to fight it, his gaze wandered over her, remembering every naked inch. "I thought you were asleep."

She squinted as she glanced at the clock on the stove. "It's only ten."

"So I didn't knock you out with hot sex?" That made one of them. He barely had the strength in his legs to move.

"Only temporarily." She smiled as she pushed off from the wall and stepped over the piles of clothing to stand in front of him. "Why are you walking around mostly naked?"

"Should I be all naked? Because that is my preference around you."

"Actually, yes." She went up on tiptoes and wound her arms around his neck.

He had to kiss her then. Long and deep, the kind of kiss you broke off then started again because it's never quite enough.

When his body revved up again and his erection pressed against her stomach, he pulled back and spat out his planned cover story. "Food."

Her eyes narrowed. "What?"

As far as covers went, this one had significant roots in the truth. "I never had dinner."

Even in the mostly dark room, understanding showed in her eyes. "You poor thing. I can make—"

"No." The heat from her body seeped into his and his priorities shifted. "It can wait."

Without thinking, his fingers found the tie holding her robe together. The silk slipped through his hands as he undid the knot. Opening the edges, he slid his hands around her trim waist to her bare back.

"This," she said between kisses. "This is the sort of thing that caused you to miss dinner in the first place."

The need built inside him again, fast and clean and so focused that his brain shut off to anything else. "You trump food."

"Isn't that sweet."

"There is nothing sweet happening in my mind." X-rated and hot, but not sweet.

Her hand found his hair. "Tell me about it."

"We'll start with me licking you." He kissed his way down her neck. "Then move on to touching you." He dipped his head and trailed his tongue over the top of her breast as his fingers touched the very heat of her and found her wetness all over again. "Here."

"Keep going."

"You'll be grabbing the sheets and begging me to fuck you." The game backfired when the words fueled his need.

Her fingers tightened in his hair. "Do it now."

"Say it."

"Fuck me." She whispered the words against his lips.

Yes. "Until you scream my name."

15

FORD STARED across the small conference room table at Matt Claymore. He had two doctorates and enough ego to fuel a dictator. Despite being brought in the back of a van to the room adjacent to the Warehouse and led through long halls to the bowels of Liberty Crossing, the guy acted like he was doing them a favor by coming in for questioning.

If he was intimidated by the way West, Lucas, and Reid stood around the room, leaning against the walls with weapons on display, Matt didn't show it. His only reaction when he'd been shown into the dark-gray-painted room holding the conference table and two chairs, was to frown.

Arrogance hung over the head of the Center for Scientific Research. He used three words when one would do and seemed to hold the mistaken belief he couldn't be touched, as if he held his position until death like some damn king.

In sum, Matt was a total dick. But that didn't make him Trent's partner or a terrorist friend of the mysterious Benton. Unfortunately, Ford met the type all the time and had the same reaction every time: back away and ignore. He couldn't write the guy off this time. Ford needed answers and had to go through him to get them.

Ford pulled out the chair, letting the metal legs drag against the cement floor in a long scraping sound. "Okay, Matt. Let's have a little discussion about your office oversight."

He sat across from Ford and tugged on the bottom of his suit jacket. Next came a brush of his hand over his lapel, as if he'd stepped into an unsterile environment and faced a germ attack. "I'd prefer if you called me Dr. Claymore."

"I'm sure you would." Ford used the first name on purpose because guys like Claymore viewed it as a sign of disrespect. To be fair, in this case it was. This guy was in charge of top secret Department of Defense labs, and no matter how much dodging and weaving he did, the final responsibility for the toxin getting out rested on him.

"Anything you want to share with the room?" Pearce asked the question from his position directly behind Ford.

Questioning usually occurred one-on-one, but Pearce had a history with Matt. Ward and Harlan thought that could make a difference in how much the guy talked. Ford would bet West's size would have more of an impact.

"Actually, we don't care if you want to share or not." Ford put his hand on the file in front of him. He had no idea what was inside because he'd just grabbed the first stack of papers he saw purely for effect. "Just do it."

Matt's eyes narrowed as he did a visual sweep over Ford and made a face that suggested he wasn't very impressed with whatever he saw. "I don't like your tone."

"No one does," Reid said.

"I also don't appreciate being put in a defensive position. There are ways to handle these situations, through channels and appropriate department reviews." Matt leaned back and crossed one leg over the other, acting as if he were in charge.

West snorted. "Who the hell talks like that?"

"Educated people."

From his smirk, Ford guessed Matt believed he'd landed some sort of verbal punch. Not even close. "You don't actually think you can hurt my feelings, do you?"

"And just so you know, we prefer shooting things," West pointed out.

"Who are you all again? I didn't see badges." Matt's gaze traveled over the room, hesitating on Lucas then coming back to Ford. If possible, his voice dripped with even more disdain than before.

"Matt, listen." Pearce pushed forward and rested his palms against the table as he leaned in. "We don't really have the time for tact and briefings. The toxin is out there."

"I am aware of that."

Every sentence this guy uttered added to Ford's fury. "Are you aware how that happened?"

Adrenaline shot through him as the need to get out there and solve this overran common-sense caution. This was about more than Shay and the guilt that pummeled him whenever they were together. This was about death on a massive scale. About a security failure that shouldn't have happened and no one could explain.

Matt shifted in his chair. The first sign of discomfort. "Trent Creighton."

A convenient answer but not the full answer. "We know about the kid. How did he get through your security?"

"Trent's IQ is—"

"Not something I care about at the moment." Ford had just about enough of hearing about how smart Trent was. Seemed pretty damn dumb to Ford to steal a toxin and wave it around in the open.

"You asked, I answered."

This guy had an annoying response for everything. "I assume the people who set up the security system at your building were pretty smart, too, so try again."

Matt's leg began to swing back and forth. "We're looking into it."

"They're looking into it." Reid glanced at Lucas. "Hear that, we're fine because they're looking into it."

West shrugged. "I feel better."

With a shake of his head and an exaggerated move to rebutton his jacket in what looked like four separate steps, Matt stood up. "Unless you have something else—"

The pounding in Ford's temples ratcheted up and his temper exploded. "Sit the fuck down."

"Excuse me?"

That sounded a lot like *Fuck you* to Ford. Maybe that's how hoity people said it.

Pearce put a hand on Ford's arm. "We should—"

"No, enough of this." Ford decided it was time for threats and innuendos. The head scientist needed to sweat. "You, Matt Claymore, have a huge problem. Your employee smuggled your toxin out of your building."

"I know—"

Ford talked right over the other man. "Instead of helping, you're offering excuses about how this isn't your fault and giving government-speak about vague investigations. It's bullshit and you know it."

"You know what that smells like, Matt?" Reid asked.

Lucas kept his arms folded across his chest and his gaze locked on Matt. "A cover-up." Matt sat back down and scooted his chair up to the table as he struggled to make eye contact with Pearce. "Jake, you know me."

Lucas stood closest to Matt now, hovering right over him. He used that to his advantage when he stretched out his leg and moved Matt's chair with a grinding screech across the floor. "And he works with us."

The explosives expert usually took of a more wait-and-see strategy. Sometimes charmed with that British accent. Seeing him take the shot reinforced Ford's frustration. He wasn't alone in needing to race through this.

Ford balled his hands into fists. "So, let's try this again."

The small movement had Matt's gaze dropping to the table then over to Lucas. "I told you what I know."

"Don't look at the Brit. Even though he sounds like the queen, he's as likely to cut off your arm as we are." More like he would wire a bomb and blow the guy up, but Ford figured the threat got the job done.

Lucas smacked his lips together as he nodded. "Very true."

"I want my attorney."

"Not an option," West said.

Reid joined in, starting as soon as West finished, the

two of them in a practiced back-and-forth rhythm that sounded genuine and shored up the ganging-up-on-Matt vibe they had going. "If you don't stop ducking soon, you're not even leaving this building. And by that I mean ever."

"You can't do that." Sweat broke out at the edge of Matt's receding hairline as he flipped his head from side to side. All jittery and a second away from bouncing in his hard metal chair, he was in a full-fledged panic now.

It didn't take much to get him there. Then again, Ford never thought it would. This guy had a small sphere of impressive power. His employees obeyed and he strutted around as if his security clearance gave him a personality. Breaking that type tended to go fast.

Ford drove the point home. "We are in the process of yanking your security clearance. You will no longer be welcome in the agency you run."

Reid held his hands behind his back and tapped a palm against the wall. "By the end of the day you won't be able to get in there to deliver mail."

"You don't have the authority to impact my position." Matt made a grab for the file in front of Ford.

Pearce pulled it out of reach. "Yeah, they do."

"You mean to tell me some amateur kill squad filled with—"

West came off the wall and took a threatening step forward. "Amateur?"

"I'd be careful with my words there, Matt," Lucas said after a loud exhale.

"They have a say in my job?" Matt looked around and pointed and didn't keep the pleading out of his voice as he stared at Pearce. "How is that possible?"

"Matt, look . . ." Pearce hesitated long enough to produce a silence that only the buzz of the lights overhead filled. "I know this is all rolling back on you and it sucks, but we have a potential disaster here."

Ford's already waning patience snapped. "So talk and do it now or I unleash West. He's the big Marine in the corner, in case you're wondering."

"The security guards have been interviewed. Our security protocols have been reviewed." Matt let out a tsk-tsking sound. "I have cooperated as much as I can under the circumstances."

Ford had no idea what that nonanswer meant. It was as if the guy wanted to be punched in the throat. "How did Trent get out of the building?"

"The same way most employees do, through the garage."

Reid rolled his eyes. "And to get in the garage he had to do what? Go through a scanner or get a pat-down from a guard? Spill it."

Maybe it was the way they all crowded in on him or the combination of the small room and angry men, but Matt's shoulders fell. He rubbed his hands together as he bowed his head and he talked to the floor. "There is a missing guard."

It took a second for the words to register in Ford's brain. When they did, a hot seething rage poured through him. He had to grab onto the edge of the conference table as he battled back the temptation to flip the damn thing.

"You waited until now to tell us this fact?" That meant lost time and blown leads. Trails went cold fast, and Trent's would be icy. The guard could be anywhere.

"How did you manage to cover that up?" West asked.

"He left for another position two days after Trent's last day." Matt didn't hold back now. He rushed through the explanation without taking a breath. "The paperwork was in order and I received confirmation that he'd been transferred to another secure facility."

West hadn't blinked in two minutes. "Confirmation from whom?"

"That's just it. During the investigation and all the questioning, I figured out the paperwork wasn't authentic."

Interesting how the guy didn't bother to share that information with anyone until now. He'd be lucky to avoid being shipped to a quiet cell somewhere without a trial. "I've read the file," Ford said. "You said all of the guards on duty that day and in the lab still worked there, and that you presented them for questioning."

"In other words, you falsified the records." Pearce hesitated over each word.

Ford didn't blame Pearce for his shocked reaction. He'd vouched for Matt. Now it looked like Matt had blocked all attempts to resolve this right away. His actions raised questions. The kind that guaranteed he'd lose his prized access forever.

"More telling, he had to fix the electronic logs to cover up his lies." Reid swore under his breath as he paced over to the door to the hallway. "You've been poking around and checking and I'm wondering how that wasn't detected."

"Covering his ass." West joined Reid, forming a wall of pissed-off team members.

"No, I thought I could track the guard down and get an explanation."

From a guard who was likely a killer. By Ford's way

of thinking, Matt wasn't really as smart as he thought
he was. He'd basically broken the law, ignored protocol, and put a target on his back. A true genius.

"No way do you get that security clearance back."
Ford put a voice to the reality in everyone's minds. Hell,
he'd volunteer to go to an internal hearing to make sure
Matt never worked anywhere again, let alone on complex security issues.

Red washed over Matt's cheeks. "You don't get a say."

"Maybe you don't understand me." This guy was
not getting the picture at all. "You're not leaving this
building."

"That's not—"

Matt moved as if to stand, and West slammed him
back in the chair with a hand on his shoulder. "Sit."

"Okay." Pearce held up both hands and signaled
for everyone to take a step back. "Matt, hold still for
a second."

"Or forever," Lucas said.

"Gentlemen?" Pearce gestured toward the door.
"Let's step outside."

Taking a break might be the answer, but Ford didn't
like it. Energy pinged around inside him. His nerves
rode the edge as adrenaline washed over him. Every
instinct screamed to keep pushing Matt until he broke.
This could be a case of covering his ass because of his
job, but it also could be something more sinister. Ford
wanted to know which one.

Forcing his questions back, he slipped into the hall
and kept going until he reached the room next door.
Ward and Josiah stood there, manning the video monitors. Matt's likeness showed on the screen with tiny
jumping lines underneath.

Little did the guy know they'd monitored him the whole time he spoke. Taped everything for later assessment. Matt had basically just admitted to interfering with a federal investigation and a whole host of other crimes. Ford couldn't muster one ounce of sympathy for him.

Ward stood with his arms crossed on his chest and his attention focused on Matt's as he squirmed in his chair. "That went well."

"Got more out of him in ten minutes than anyone else did in two days of questioning." Ford wondered how much more they'd have by the end of the day. A few hours without food or counsel and this guy might spill something really big.

West shrugged. "And we didn't even get to torture him."

With that, Ward broke eye contact with the screen and scowled at West. "Let's not joke about that, okay?"

"You two were watching?" Pearce asked as his gaze went from Ward to Josiah.

Josiah nodded. "Every second."

"Are you sure we can't shoot this pontificating idiot?" Reid stepped closer to the screen and the desk under it. He picked up the file on top of the stack.

Ward didn't hesitate, probably because he knew the team viewed silence as approval. "You can't kill him."

"The word you're looking for is 'shouldn't.'" West took up his usual position, slightly away from the group and leaning against the wall. "I really *could* do it."

As far as Ford was concerned, there had been enough chitchat. Time ticked by and Trent stayed hidden. None of those factors qualified as a good sign. "Now what?"

"We take his story apart, piece by piece," Ward said.

About time. Ford headed for the door and a second round. "Fine, let's go."

"Josiah will do it."

Silence descended in the room as Ford's steps slammed to a stop. He turned to face Ward, ready for an epic verbal battle that would bring security running. "How do you figure that? The guy already hates me. I can use that."

"Yeah, I picked up on the hate."

That settled the question is Ford's mind. "Then?"

"I need you in the field, going through every inch of that lab and the building."

It was shit work and Ward knew it. From the mumbling in the room, West, Lucas, and Reid knew it, too. "So, Josiah gets to walk all over this guy, beat the hell out of him, and we get stuck with the forensic team in a science lab?"

Josiah laughed. "Works for me."

"All of this recon has to be done." This smelled of busy work to Ford. Alliance didn't do grunt work. That was the point. Forensics teams could go out and collect evidence. The CIA and MI6 needed Alliance to wade into the action.

"I think West is right," Reid said. "We should just shoot this guy."

Ward kept his attention on Ford. "That won't find Trent any faster."

"But we'll feel better." The words added to the brewing tension, but Ford didn't care. This issue was too important to back down.

No one said anything but he got the sense he'd walked into a power struggle of some sort. Could be

Ward thought to punish him for the Shay issue. Ford accepted his fuck-up on that score, but he was in, and no one else was getting near her. Not negotiable.

Ward nodded. "Your feelings aren't part of the job."

That was the first thing anyone had said that felt like an absolute. "No kidding."

"I should get in there before Matt figures out a way to back out of what he's already told us," Josiah said as he opened the door and stepped into the hallway.

"I'll come with you," Pearce said as he filed out behind him.

"Right." Reid clapped his hands together and gestured for Lucas and West to join the others. "We'll go suit up for some forensic work."

No need for a high IQ for this one. Ford saw the room clear and felt the tension pressing against him. He hadn't moved but he'd lost ground. Priorities battled inside him. Shay, his need to overcome his past, loyalty to Alliance. The responsibilities crushed him, and he hadn't even added in the ultimate goal of shutting down a toxic Armageddon.

Ward waited until they were alone in the room to hit Ford with one of his long suffering exhales. "You sure being pissed off is about Claymore and his lies?"

A red haze moved in front of Ford's eyes. "Don't start."

"Maybe you're stalling so you don't have to move in on Uncle Anthony."

That struck too close to the truth. Not that he gave a shit about Anthony or his business or how he raised his kid, but Ford did care if daddy's checkbook financed this deadly nonsense. He cared if Shay's family had somehow dragged her into a catastrophe.

Hell, he just plain cared about her.

Still, even in a place like Alliance there existed a small pocket of privacy he should be able to hold onto. "Boss or no, you're getting close to crossing a line."

"Funny, I was thinking the same thing about you."

"We have a lead." Matt and his idiocy.

"We have many." Ward picked up a file and held it out to Ford. "Your job is this one, unless you're ready to bow out."

Ford looked down and saw Anthony's name on the sticker. Recognized the challenge in Ward's voice and stiff stance.

Ford grabbed the folder but didn't open it. Didn't have to. He had the thing memorized. "I'm ready."

Shay entered the alarm code and turned the key to the front door of Ford's condo. As the building manager she had both, but hadn't tried to use either up until now. Standing at the threshold, she listened for any sound. The shower or a radio—something.

"Ford? Are you in here?" She stepped inside and closed the door behind her.

This didn't count as a condo manager visit. There was nothing official about her showing up here. She could have called but something about wading inside appealed to her. It made her jumpy but she felt compelled to do it anyway.

"Um, hello?" She walked through the living room, her gaze touring every inch to see if there was anything out of place. "I was thinking instead of takeout we'd go out like normal people. It's called a date, in case you were wondering."

As she did every time she came over, she took in the mantel and the coffee table. No personal photos. No bills. No evidence that a human being even lived there. Maybe one of these times he'd surprise her and put up a picture . . . or something.

She'd been in the sterile environment many times. They'd had dinner there, slept there. He talked about her place being cozier, which was true. She had knick-knacks and things she'd collected as she moved through life. She'd always assumed everyone did until she met Ford.

She opened the closet by the front door and stared inside. Coats, a vacuum. Nothing out of the ordinary. A quick look at the answering machine a few steps away showed zero messages.

For some reason the absence of life kept her moving and looking. She walked up to the desk in the family room, brushed her fingertips over the edge then looked at the tips. No dust. Everything was clean and in its place. A real estate agent could come in tomorrow and show it.

"Ford?" She walked back down the hall toward his bedroom.

Half of her hoped she'd open the door and find an unmade bed. Something human. She tapped on it then pushed. A navy comforter pulled tight and two pillows that looked as if a head hadn't touched them. He denied the military service but she continued to see signs everywhere.

The top drawer of his dresser called. She stood in front of it for what felt like hours with her hand on the knob. *Just pull,* the little voice in her head kept saying.

It wasn't as if his underwear was all that sacred. She'd seen him in it dozens of times. But he was there at those moments, and her underwear gawking hadn't been hidden. This was different. The sneaking grated against her.

Still, her fingers stayed fastened on the knob.

"One pull and a quick peek." The room didn't answer.

She made a bargain in her head to open and shut it real fast, then backed out a second later. Certain things she could justify, like looking in his fridge and stealing a bottle of water. This was pure snooping.

She dropped her hand and turned around. Going back out to the main living area, she opened the coat closet a second time, as if something drew her there. Not giving herself time to think about it, she slid a hand into his coat pocket, the black raincoat-style one she'd seen him wear to cut the morning chill. She patted around and . . . nothing. It didn't even have the usual collection of lint.

Not having family photos wasn't the oddest thing. She repeated that in her head several times, trying to convince herself.

Ford was sweet and sexy, hot and charming. She enjoyed spending time with him and craved more. When her mind started flipping through memories, she clamped down. Tried to blink out the temptation to rummage through everything.

Bottom line was Ford Decker liked to live a life with few ties. He didn't get many bills. He didn't show any outward signs of caring about other people. In short, he was the guy she should have run from. It was a shame her heart had very definite other ideas.

In one last visual tour of the rooms, she memorized every inch. For the first time in her dating life she missed seeing a guy's stray sock on the floor. Looking for one thing out of place—a sign that an actual human lived there—she failed.

She felt a twinge of doubt and questions peppered her brain, though not as many as she should have had because Ford wasn't Devin. She repeated that refrain several times.

One last look and nothing jumped out at her. Still, she couldn't kick the nagging sensation that something was very wrong. And this time, her growing concern centered on Ford, not Trent. She just wished she knew why.

16

ALL OF Shay's doubts washed away later that night while she sat across the dinner table from Ford. Well, most of them.

She ran a finger over the shiny silverware and the crisp white tablecloth. A low mumble of conversation and clink of glasses sounded around them in the busy restaurant. Waiters rushed across the hardwood floor and an impressive crystal chandelier hung above her. They occupied a two-person table in the corner of one of the city's impossible-to-get-a-reservation hot spots.

A fancy chef owned the place, and the reviews called it groundbreaking. Shay wasn't clear what could be so new and inventive about a steak restaurant but she showed up for the company. The fact that Ford set all of this up on a few hours' notice qualified as miraculous. So did the suit jacket he wore. No silly tee. He put on dress pants and looked like he'd stepped right out of a high-powered office . . . only much hotter and absent any douchelike behavior.

"A nice dinner in a special restaurant." She twisted the white linen napkin on her lap. "This is a surprise."

He smiled at her over the top of his menu. "I got your message."

That look, sweet with a mix of the devil, got to her every time. Those knowing glances made her hot and jumpy and ready to peel his clothes right off him. And that was part of her late night plans. She'd worn the black wrap dress for him, counting on him to peel it off her later.

Her hand ached from her hold on the napkin, so she smoothed it over her legs. "I think I was pretty clear."

"Let me see." He shut one eye as if trying to call up a memory. "I believe the text said, 'Make a reservation somewhere or else,' with one of those frown emoticons. It was clear you didn't want to go back to the burger joint we went to the one other time we went out."

"No one ever accused me of being subtle." Neither was the woman two tables down who kept staring at Ford.

Shay didn't blame her. The white shirt showed off his dark hair and those scruffy rough-and-tumble looks. She'd almost jumped him in the car on the way over but refrained.

But the best part was how Ford didn't appear to notice the leggy blonde. His gaze didn't wander. He never scanned the place or shot secretive glances at other women. Shay loved that he made her feel as if she were the only woman there, the most beautiful woman in DC. Neither of which were true, but enjoying a few minutes of the being-wanted sensation warmed the night's chill right out of her.

"Subtle or not, you couldn't be quiet and blend in with that dress." His gaze dipped to the vee between her breasts. "It makes me want to get the food wrapped up to go."

Not happening.

She'd finally lured him out for a real date and would not cut it short now no matter how delicious he looked and smelled. She held up a finger but stopped right before wagging it. "No."

"Yes, ma'am." He nodded then went back to reading the menu.

The comfortable quiet gave her the opportunity to study him. They had so little downtime, just relaxing. From a few feet away she noticed his lean fingers and strong hands. Clean nails and a sturdy black watch. He was a no-nonsense guy. Not one to slick back his hair or insist on designer labels.

But in the universe of what she knew about him, that was about it. The facts were limited to what she could see and the bits he shared, usually as a result of her asking questions on some topic. After the sweep of his condo, getting him to open up had become her sole focus.

Operation Get to Know the Real Ford started now. It was either that or continue to sort through his stuff when he wasn't home, and that made her feel crappy and wonder about the kind of woman she was.

She fiddled with the top of her wineglass but stopped when it made a whistling sound. "Have you seen your sister?"

"What?" Ford slowly lowered his menu and laid it on the stack of plates in front of him.

Up until then the conversation had looped around like any other, but for some reason her heartbeat sped up now. Breathless and on edge, she tried to inhale long and deep to calm the rat-a-tat-tat beating through her. "She popped up and then disappeared."

"You just described my life with Tasha." He leaned back in his chair, and apologized when his arm brushed against the older woman behind him. "She goes in and out. It's her style."

Her finger slipped over the side of the glass, following the drip of water down to the base. "Do you ever miss a more normal existence?"

"Is there something abnormal about the way I live?"

His expression stayed blank and it made her want to push. To cause a reaction. "You're never home. You travel all the time and get pulled out of every date, formal or informal, to head to the office."

This time he winced. "Uh-oh, this sounds like a life-style lecture."

One she didn't really have the right to launch into. He hadn't changed. This didn't count as some kind of bait and switch. He was the same guy with the same priorities as when they started dating. She just yearned for more.

Only seemed fair if she was falling in love with him that he try to love her back a little.

Because the one thing she could control was her behavior, and since she had no interest in being the jealous mistrusting type who skulked around and depended on investigators, she spilled her big secret. "I was in your condo today."

He put his elbows on the table and leaned in closer. "Did something happen?"

Not exactly the response she expected. "I don't understand the question."

The waitress picked that moment to swing by. She introduced herself and talked about the specials. Shay was so eager to get back to the conversation that she raced through ordering and practically shooed the woman away.

Before she could drag them back to the topic, Ford downed the rest of his drink and started in. "Why were you in my place? I mean, you've been there before. There's nothing much to see."

She wasn't really sure how to answer the question so went with what she knew would be viewed as a stall. "Does the idea upset you?"

He tipped his head from side to side. "I'm not sure."

She'd practiced this speech. The guilt had gnawed at her for snooping, but the unease at not knowing him was very real. "I feel weird that I did it, so that's why I'm admitting it."

"See, I get the sense there's something else happening here, and I don't—"

"Do you have anything you're trying to hide?" Blurting it out like that . . . well, not her best work. Still, the question hung there and now she wanted an answer.

"Uh, okay." His eyes widened and his head shot back. "So, you think I'm keeping another woman across the hall?"

Cheating managed to be the least of her worries. "Don't minimize this."

"Sorry." His mood turned more somber and he seemed to straighten up in his chair. "Tell me what's going on."

She rested both hands on the table and picked at the spoon, then the knife . . . then returned her palms to her lap. At least that way she'd keep the visible fidgeting to a minimum.

"Shay, just tell me."

"The secrets." And now they had the second blurt of the evening.

"What are you talking about?"

"Trent is locked away and not talking. My uncle is acting odd. You're in and out to the point where I wonder if you're keeping a family in another city." She closed her eyes. When she opened them again Ford sat right there, staring and looking concerned and not being a dick. It was a nice change in the men department.

"Sounds like this concern has been building for a while."

"Do you blame me?"

"No." He reached across the table and held out his palm until she put hers in his. "Look, there's no question I'm not good with settling down and checking in. My job has me jumping, and until recently that was fine with me. I'm not used to being accountable to anyone else, but I'm trying."

That all sounded good. Kind of warmed her from the inside out in a girlie reaction she hadn't felt in . . . forever. "Until recently?"

"Until I met you." He did that thing where he cradled her hand in both of his.

The gesture soothed and inflamed her at the same time. Before him she didn't know that was even possible. "That kind of talk might make me forget about some of your reclusiveness issues."

"I know you want to understand me, but there's no sob story in my past. My parents are stable and decent.

They gave me a good upbringing but it was in the middle of nowhere and my whole life I've been looking to break out." He kept up the steady massage of the back of her hand with his thumb.

They sat in the middle of all those people, but the setting still came off as intimate. A man's blowhard voice and overly loud laughter floated by her. People kept getting up and moving and tables turned over. But she needed him to understand. "Losing my parents the way I did, being a kid, I've spent my entire grown-up life in search of those sort of roots you're trying to cut."

"I guess we have to figure out how to make those two mind-sets work together."

A wave of sadness crashed over her. She'd pushed for this conversation and now part of her regretted it. "Is it possible?"

"I'm willing to try." The waitress stepped between them with the salad dishes and he dropped her hand. "Oh, thank you."

The pretty brunette returned Ford's smile. He didn't flirt but he charmed without trying. It was one of the things Shay loved about him. And the longer she was with him, "love" turned out to be the right word, which is what made the day so surreal. It also scared the crap out of her.

"What were you looking for?" he asked after a few beats of silence.

She stopped moving the lettuce around on her plate and put her fork down. "What?"

"In my condo."

"Honestly?" When he nodded and smiled at her, she smiled back. "You."

Nothing about that amounted to a lie. She didn't go in there with the plan to check his bank account records and listen to his voice mails. She'd had numerous opportunities to check his phone and listen in on his work calls. She avoided all of it because, at heart, she did trust him. Despite the shitty hand Devin had dealt her and all his lies, she still believed there were good guys out there.

Ford finished chewing. "It's probably easier to call me than try to track me all over the city."

"Probably." She watched him, fascinated how his hunger kept spiking while the tense topic sucked it right out of her. "There was nothing to see anyway."

"I travel light."

Since the discussion had gone better than she expected, she decided to poke a little more. "Does that philosophy apply to women as well as furniture?"

His hand bobbled for a second on the way to grabbing his glass. "Not anymore."

"Good answer."

He pushed his half-eaten salad to the side. "Am I in trouble for something?"

They'd come full circle. She'd teased out the clues and tiptoed around the rougher topics. She wasn't convinced she knew more now than she did an hour ago, but he hadn't balked. He stayed calm and answered. Gave her a peek into how he handled a woman when she insisted on being heard.

Once again Ford Decker impressed the hell out of her.

Least she could do was promise not to lose her mind and scour his condo. "No, and I won't go in your place without you again."

He shrugged. "You can."

After all that . . . "Really?"

"I'm not hiding anything from you, Shay."

His eyes softened and her insides turned all gooey. "You're not Devin."

The last part slipped out before she could call it back. Even in a nice moment Devin crept into her mind to ruin things.

Ford nodded. "The infamous ex."

"He's a dumbass." She'd told Ford bits and pieces when they performed a cursory review of their recent dating lives and confirmed each of them was single. That came right before the birth control talk but after the kiss that sealed their attraction.

"Good to know you get that."

She battled with the idea of telling him more. When her stomach didn't squeeze in panic, she took the risk. "He used me to try to get a high-powered position in Anthony's firm. Took me out, made promises. It was all a lie."

"Okay, then I'd say calling him a dumbass isn't strong enough." An edge moved into Ford's voice. "Where is this guy now?"

"Why?"

"I may want to run him over with my car."

She laughed but stopped when she realized she was the only one taking what he said as a joke. "It's long done. He doesn't matter."

"It sounds like something about him does. Maybe you're not over the way he treated you."

But she really had overcome that hurdle. Ford came into her life and pushed out many of the bad Devin memories. She appreciated so much about him, but specifically that. "People suck sometimes."

"Very true." Ford picked up his roll but didn't butter it or make any move to eat it. "How did you figure out what Devin planned?"

Hunger hit her out of nowhere. She dug into the salad, croutons first. "An investigator."

"You hired one?"

"Anthony did." She stabbed the crouton a bit harder than she intended and sent it skipping off her plate.

Ford watched it bounce then picked it up and put it on the side of his plate. "I guess that's one of those family things you were talking about the other day."

"He's protective." Choking that out ended up being tougher than expected.

She loved Anthony but didn't have any illusions about him. She never prettied up his actions or made excuses. He didn't pretend to be anything other than what he was. He proved difficult to deal with and judged those around him with a harsh mental checklist no one could live up to.

Devin hadn't stood a chance. Then again, he didn't deserve one. He used her. The fact that he lived down to Anthony's minimal expectations made her hate Devin even more at the end. Devin had played a dangerous game and ticked Anthony off. She instinctively knew Ford wouldn't be that stupid.

"I'm not interested in Anthony or his money," Ford said, as if he'd read her thoughts.

She believed him. Ford was a self-made man. And all man.

Maybe she wasn't hungry for food after all.

Shifting her leg, she ran the tip of her sling-back pumps up his pant leg. "What are you interested in?"

Desire burned in his eyes. "Figuring out how fast I can get you out of that dress once we get in your door."

"I have faith you can beat your old record." Though she did question how they'd have the patience to wait for the valet. The real debate would be if they should get home or pull the car over on the way. "But if you'd rather sit around and eat then maybe order dessert . . ."

He motioned for their waitress. "I'm suddenly not hungry."

17

THE NEXT morning, Ford headed into the Warehouse early. He threw on the nearest clean T-shirt, which advertised a video game he'd never played. He'd already been in contact with Ellery by the time he hit the main floor. He had her tracking down information.

Fact was, Shay had him spooked. Looking through his condo and talking about secrets. He always prepared for this sort of thing and didn't keep anything in the apartment that could lead to his real work. Other than cameras and some traps to see if anyone looked at specific items, he purposely didn't add security because that would only raise suspicion. But her discomfort added to his.

By the time dinner ended last night they seemed to be back on track. He'd barely made it in the door before he stripped off her sexy dress. Afterward, she slept curled into his side as he replayed every word, every question she asked that night, to make sure her doubts were of the who-am-I-sleeping-with variety and not something related to his cover.

No matter how much he fought back the idea, the possibility of her being involved in Trent's schemes still lingered. Unlikely, but he knew he couldn't let his guard down over a pretty face and great sex, no matter how compelling he found the woman underneath.

Now, Ford hovered over Ellery's shoulder, staring down at her auburn hair and watching in amazement as she typed faster than he could think. "There's one more thing I need you to do for me."

Her fingers stopped but held over the keys. "Hit me."

Yeah, this was the tricky part. The request would raise questions. If the rest of Bravo found out Shay spent the afternoon shuffling through his stuff, they'd lose it. He could almost see the joint disappointment and hear the calls to bring her in.

Ford wasn't ready to blow cover. "I need to see the video from my condo for yesterday afternoon."

"Why?"

"What the hell?" Ford jumped at the sound of Tasha's voice behind him. She was one of the few people who could sneak up on him without making a sound, and she practiced the skill a little too often for his liking. "Where did you come from?"

"My office upstairs."

She acted so cool under pressure. Nothing ruffled her. While Ford admired the qualities in a field agent, they annoyed the piss out of him in a boss. She could be everywhere, checking everything, and he'd never see the walls closing in until it was too late to duck and push.

"Are you ever actually in your big office? Because I see you down here on the floor a lot lately."

The question brought a minute of silence. Noise filled the room twenty-four hours a day. Conversations among the men and the hum of the equipment. But he'd managed to throw out a comment that drowned out everything else.

Even Ellery glanced up at him. "Wow."

"Listen to Ellery and be very careful with the words you choose." Tasha crossed her arms over her stomach and stared him down. "That's your one warning."

She'd started in MI6, then headed up Alliance's first office in London. She traveled back and forth but the best bet for finding her was to look for Ward. He'd made it clear that the two of them being apart for long periods of time wasn't an option. Not that being in love softened either of them.

Ford had given him all sorts of shit for falling so hard and being lead by body parts other than his brain. Now Ford feared he might have to eat those words. He never got the whole anything-for-a-woman spiel. It sounded like some dumb line from a bad movie. That was before Shay.

"I was nice enough to wait until you finished your request to Ellery before moving in." With the British accent, Tasha's comment sounded regal instead of threatening.

Ford knew which it really was. "Uh, thanks."

"You can tell me what you were asking for and why, or she will." Tasha's head fell to the side and her hair swept over her shoulder. "And you can apologize at some point to Ellery for dragging her into whatever personal mess you're cooking up."

"I figured you heard all of that when you snuck up behind me." He chalked up her imposing demeanor and covert abilities to her past. Once an agent, always an agent. "Ward must hate that, by the way."

A smile played at the corner of her mouth. "No, he doesn't."

Ford already had a front row seat to this romance. He didn't want a replay. "I don't want to know."

Tasha's eyebrow lifted. "I could have come to your house and asked all these questions but I worried I'd interrupt you with your girlfriend."

Ford noticed Ellery started typing what looked like gibberish on her screen. It could have been computer-ese. He had no idea but highly suspected she'd perfected her ability to eavesdrop while pretending to work.

He shifted so his back faced her then pitched his voice low to talk with Tasha. "Don't call her that."

"Your mark? Your cover?" Tasha didn't bother dropping to a whisper.

"Calling her Shay is fine."

"Uh-huh." Tasha tapped her hand on the back of Ellery's chair. "Would you excuse us for a second?"

"Sure." Ellery's chair spun as she got up.

Lines of text scrolled across her screen but everyone had cleared out, leaving only Ford and Tasha in the area. He didn't like his odds.

"Who is Devin Pinter?" Tasha moved over to lean against the desk Ellery had just abandoned.

He bit back a string of profanity. "What?"

The question hit Ford like a body slam. He'd expected the communication loop to land the request on Ward's desk eventually. Looked like the chain buzzed faster than expected.

"Don't pretend not to understand me. You asked Ellery to check him out."

"Ten minutes ago. How do you know about it?"

"Big brain." Tasha tapped a finger to her forehead. "And, for the record, I know everything that happens here."

Not that he doubted her, but still. "That's creepy."

Activity kicked up in the room as Harlan and Josiah walked in. Josiah took a seat at the conference room table and talked with his team. Harlan circled around to the desk area he shared with Ward and sat down.

Ford hated the sight of them all sitting around. He'd ordered his team to assemble to put together a plan to move in on Anthony. The clock kept ticking down to the auction, the chatter had ceased, and the usual assets weren't talking.

"Feel free to spend time with Harlan instead of me," Ford said. "He's the one who needs help. And isn't he supposed to be breaking Matt?" Which is where he wanted to be. He knew he could get something out of the guy if he had ten minutes and West by his side.

"Harlan is fine. He also works for me." Tasha gripped the desk on either side of her hips. "You might want to remember I handpicked him."

Except for that one choice, Ford agreed with all of her decisions at Alliance, including her insistence that the team was needed in the first place. "Why is that again?"

"You all have skills."

Ford watched Harlan smooth down his tie then do it a second time. "Being a pompous prick is a skill?"

"You're not that bad."

Ford's gaze shot back to Tasha. "Funny."

"One of *my* many skills." She fingered the top page of the notepad next to Ellery's keyboard. Ellery had scribbled a few things down while he talked earlier but the writing looked more like wavy lines than words. "Now, stop stalling. Devin Pinter. Explain."

Ford knew from experience when Tasha fell back on a monotone delivery of staccato sentences that his time was up. "This Devin guy is someone I thought we should check out."

She sighed at him. "You mean someone who once slept with Shay on a regular basis and in your jealous rage you want to hunt down and beat the shit out of."

And that would teach him to try to hide anything from Tasha. Ford made a mental note to not try again, or to at least get better at his office subterfuge skills if he did.

"He's connected to her uncle." The guy also treated Shay like shit. Not the same way Ford was doing it, but by breaking her heart. By using her.

In his head Ford tried to separate his behavior from Devin's and stumbled. As if he didn't get bombarded by guilt enough on a daily basis already.

Tasha stood up straight and motioned for Harlan to come over. "I can't believe I have to say this, but we don't use multi-billion-dollar surveillance equipment to track down ex-boyfriends of the woman you're currently dating. You can't aim a drone at him either."

"We're not—" Ford gave up when she raised an eyebrow at him. "Damn, fine."

"Exactly."

"I would point out you're invading my privacy." And he tried to do it fast because Harlan was making a beeline in their direction and Ford wanted the conversation over before he joined them.

"If you're using Alliance resources it's not private."

Her authoritative tone and Harlan's closing advance took the fight right out of Ford. He'd managed to stall enough to avoid answering her questions. That would have to be good enough for now. "Fine."

Harlan stopped next to Ford. "Yes?"

"Give us a status on Trent's boss," Tasha said.

"Despite some persuasive methods and his constant calls for his lawyer, Matt isn't saying anything we don't already know from what he gave up and what we see in the records." Harlan's voice rang out as he gave the verbal report.

Ford had to give Harlan credit. He could be arrogant and far too by-the-book for his taste but Harlan didn't flinch at having a woman give him orders. He fell into line like the good soldier he was.

While he respected the hell out of Tasha, Ford didn't possess the obedience gene. "Anyone have news on the missing guard?"

"Unfortunately." Harlan pulled a piece of paper out of his pants pocket and unfolded it. "I was just putting the report together but it looks like the DC police got a domestic call and found the guard this morning. Hanged in his girlfriend's bathroom. She was shot, bled out on the tile floor. They're saying it was a murder suicide."

Tasha swore under her breath. "Great."

"No surprise there." The loss didn't even measure as a hiccup for Ford. He saw this coming. The only true victim was the girlfriend, and at some point, when this all ended, he'd spare a thought for her.

The guard had played a role and it was over. Whoever

ranked above him couldn't afford to keep him alive.
It was the method Ford found interesting. It showed
thought and planning. Pulling off a fake scene that convinced law enforcement took skills. It suggested a level
of professionalism that passed Trent and pointed to the
bigger presence behind the plan.

"Here's the name and address information, along
with the detective in charge." Harlan handed over the
paper without looking at it.

The cycle would now start. Tasha would work her
magic and commandeer then steer the local investigation. Lines connecting that guy to Trent would be
erased and the public would never know the danger
that lurked while everyone slept.

The only good news out of all this was that they
could now chase other leads. "Any chance of a money
trail from Matt to Trent or anyone else?"

Harlan shook his head. "Ellery is searching but Matt
is so clean he squeaks."

Too perfect. Too convenient. Ford knew from experience that when things looked shiny and new they
were often dull underneath. This Matt guy seemed
pretty damn dull. "I don't like it."

"Me either," Harlan said.

The piece of paper disappeared in Tasha's hand then
into her black pants pocket. "Look at you two, agreeing
on something."

Harlan waved off her comment. "We both want
Trent stopped. Only our methods differ."

He sounded reasonable. If Ford was the type to care
about someone else taking the high road and making
him look bad, he might get ticked off, but no. "Except

that I think you screwed up Hampstead and almost turned me into the juicy center of a fireball."

"And that ends my attempt at team building." Tasha added an eye roll to her long-suffering sigh before turning to Harlan. "Keep looking. Our time is almost up. We have to stop this before it gets to Yemen. Once there our only chance is an all-out assault which will leave everyone dead, including most of Alliance."

Not all of them. "Bravo would be fine."

"Sometimes I honestly think you believe you and your team can outrun a bullet."

Ford would bet money they could. "Pretty much."

"Right." Harlan nodded and left without acknowledging Ford.

Not that Ford blamed him. "I do like the way he says 'right' and a few other words. His accent matches yours."

They both watched Harlan leave the floor and head in the direction of the interrogation room they'd been using for Matt. Tasha piped up. "You could be less of an ass where Harlan is concerned."

"Not really."

She moved to stand in front of him and block his view of the rest of the room. "He's right. You are on the same team."

"Something about him sets off my alarm bells. I don't know what it is yet." His lack of love for the guy wasn't exactly a secret. Ford had told Ward from the start something smelled wrong with the tall Brit.

They were all burnable assets. Expendable, if it came down to either of them versus the world. Ford accepted it. With Harlan's background, Ford guessed the other man did too. But none of that made the stink go away.

"Well, try not to piss him off in the meantime. Despite the refined accent, he's deadly," she said. "He also ranks above you."

"Technically."

"No, in fact."

Ford conceded this round to her. "Understood."

"You need to know I think Ward is taking a risk by keeping you on this assignment."

"No, he's not." The denial shot out of Ford while a sudden flash of anger burned in his gut. "And if you're so worried, why haven't you tried to kick me off?"

" 'Tried'?"

It was never a good idea to challenge her authority. He didn't intend to do that anyway. "That was the wrong word."

"Because I think you being invested in something other than your wallowing is a good thing."

Yeah, the cryptic side of Tasha he didn't like so much. "Meaning?"

"Between the odd T-shirts"—she pulled at his sleeve—"and bitching at Harlan, your sole focus for the last few months seemed to be on causing trouble."

"That's not true." Damn, he hoped that wasn't true. No question, regret ate at him, stealing his sleep and ruining his focus, but he hid it. He showed up and got the job done, even with bad intel.

She broke eye contact for a blip then returned again. "I worried your last CIA assignment made you—"

"Wary."

"Self-destructive."

Ford preferred his word. "I'm fine."

Images flashed on the biggest screen as Ward stood at the end of the conference room table with a file. The guard's face and the crime scene photos appeared. Now Ford knew what Ward had been doing for the last half hour—preparing the briefing on the guard and his suspicious death.

Tasha ping-ponged between watching Ward and watching the photos on the screen. "Hmmm."

"What is that sound about?"

"I'll remind you of this moment and how *fine* you were when we have Trent in custody or on a slab and the assignment is over."

"You mean after I catch the bad guy and separate him from his deadly toxin." Because that was the only answer here. Trent had to be stopped and the toxin collected. No matter what. And he and Bravo team would be the ones to do it.

"I mean after Shay knows you played a part in bringing her cousin down."

The words cut through Ford, pinpointing his weakness and drilling in there. "He's a terrorist."

"Possibly."

Ford didn't see any other scenario that made sense. "If he is, I don't have a choice."

"I wonder if Shay will see it that way."

So did he.

18

Shay thought about calculating how much time she set aside each day to handle plumbing problems. She didn't even want to know what the building's residents kept shoving in the toilet. Whatever it was required her to make weekly visits to one unit or another. She now dreaded any sentence with the word "toilet" in it.

With plunger in hand, she unlocked unit ten and stepped inside. Ron was at his job on Capitol Hill, but an assistant or secretary or someone with a female voice had called and asked that the toilet be in working order by six. The job fell to her unless she found that it blew past her regular, limited expertise.

Lucky her.

Floorboards creaked under her feet. Since she wore light sneakers, the unexpected sound made her stop. No way would Ron's downstairs neighbor tolerate that for very long. She made a mental note to figure out what kind of handyman she should call to correct this newest issue.

But one disaster at a time. This afternoon's focus should be on water. Still, the squeaking grabbed her attention. She crouched down and tapped on the wood. A hollow thud greeted her.

Another knock and a creaking sound echoed back at her. Not from where she stood. From the short hall leading to the bathroom and bedroom.

"Ron, are you here?"

She strained, trying to peek past the corner of the wall. The lack of lighting cast the part of the hallway she could see in shadows. "Hello?"

If he were there, he'd speak up. Ron was the chat-by-the-mailboxes type. When you asked him how he was, he actually took ten minutes to tell you. He loved to hear himself talk. No way would he not walk out and say hello on his way to complaining about the toilet issue.

That meant something else was at play. Unease zipped through her. She tried to calm the acrobatics in her belly, but sitting back on her heels, vulnerable and waiting, sent her into a full body shake.

With her palm on the floor, she scooted her body closer to the front door. A quick glance back and she measured a rough eight feet to hit the doorway and get out of there. Her brain clicked into action as she tried to mentally explain away the noises and focus on the fact the door had been locked when she arrived. Thanks to her uncle's insistence and a good portion of his wallet, this was not an easy building to break into.

Something thumped and the tip of a shoe appeared. She didn't wait to reason that out. She jumped to her feet at a dead run. Footsteps hammered behind her but she didn't waste time looking back. Every self-defense class she'd ever attended talked about getting in front of people and screaming her head off. She planned to do both things.

Sweaty and shaking, her hand slipped on the knob. She fumbled, finally getting it open when a solid weight crashed into her back. She kicked out and yelled. Banged on the door. Anything to get someone's attention even if it was the middle of the workday.

Her body slammed into the door as a hand covered her mouth.

"Hey. Stop."

She heard the male whisper. Rage and terror whipped through her as she flailed and bucked. She tried to throw off the attacker's hand and shove her body back against him to throw him off balance.

"Shay, for God's sake. Stop."

The voice registered then and she fell limp against the door. "Trent?"

"What the hell is wrong with you?"

"How did you get in here? What were you . . ." She spun around, planning to shove her hands against his chest as she lectured him about scaring women. Then she saw his face, drawn with an unkempt and scraggly beard. Gone was the smooth skin and glint that trumped the geeky side of him and attracted young women everywhere he went. A mousy brown had replaced his previously blond hair.

She put her hands on his shoulders as she looked him up and down. "Oh, my God. What happened?"

This had to be about more than a girl. She couldn't believe this was a case of lovesickness gone ballistic. He wore a heavy jacket she'd never seen and looked like he hadn't had a meal in weeks.

"I'm in trouble."

She didn't need his brains or advanced degrees to ferret that part out. Her mind went to drugs. To a lot of bad choices and wrong roads she could see him taking. "What kind?"

"At work."

The place where he practically lived. She couldn't believe performance was the issue. He gave every task his all. "I thought you took a few days off."

His hands were still on her forearms, and he tightened his hold. "Days? I haven't been there in weeks."

Wrapping her fingers around his, she tried to loosen his stranglehold before he bruised her skin. To peel his fingers away one by one because much more of this pressure and her wrist would go numb. "How is that possible? Your boss said—"

"I had to get out of there." Trent dropped his hands and started pacing. He somehow missed the boards that made the noise earlier.

For a second her mind zoomed to how she'd ended up in this unit. "Did you set this up?"

"A woman in the diner made the call for me." Trent glanced around as if he thought someone was about to attack from behind. "I needed to talk with you."

He'd lured her. He somehow broke in. It wasn't a stretch to think he set up the floorboards as some sort of early warning system. Sure, the idea had a Hollywood bent to it, but it fit with the secrets and multiple stories in this circumstance.

But none of it fit with the story Anthony told her. "This is all because you fell for a woman in your lab? I'm sorry, I don't know her name."

Trent stopped and threw her an open-mouthed stare. "What are you talking about?"

"Your dad said you were in Charlottesville nursing a broken heart." The explanation sounded as dumb now as when she'd heard it the first time.

"That's . . ." Trent shook his head. Looked confused as hell, too. "That never happened."

If that story was a lie, then she had to wonder what else Anthony had said to appease her. He'd sold the infatuation-gone-wrong story. She'd never quite bought it, which turned out to be a good thing. "You haven't talked with your dad?"

"Shay, listen to me." Trent's hands went to her biceps. This time he shoved her hard enough for her back to hit wood and her head to bounce against the door. "I'm being set up."

She fought off a wave of dizziness. She didn't have room in her head for anything but confusion. Keeping up the divergent stories proved hard enough. "For what?"

"There's some missing stuff at work and everyone thinks I took it. Serious, really bad stuff."

The comment was such a convoluted mess, too vague and almost meaningless. But the way his voice bobbled and he glanced around the room every two seconds suggested he believed something had gone very wrong.

She tried to get him to calm down and focus. "I don't—"

"I need you to help me throw people off my scent." He shook her, then let go again. When he took off pacing a second time, his moves were jerky. He rubbed his hands together and stared at the floor.

"This isn't . . ." She stepped in front of him and forced him to look at her. "Trent, I don't even know what we're talking about."

"*Money* and an *alibi*." He punctuated the first and last words.

Two words she heard on television cop shows but never in real life. They spelled trouble, and Trent appeared to be in a load of it.

She ran through the possibilities in her mind. If not an imploded romance, then maybe drugs were the answer or he'd messed up a project at work. Being so smart, people sometimes forgot his age and clamped down hard when he made mistakes. No matter what it was, she was sure they could work it out . . . if he would just settle down and tell her the issue step by step.

But she couldn't wade through this alone. "We should talk to Uncle Anthony."

"No." The word came out as a slap. That old anger clicked back into place, and for a second his scared facade fell.

Whatever ate at Trent had him spinning and snapping. Her mind zipped back to the possibility of a drug issue one more time, and the life drained out of her. The family had been lucky on that score. Not on any other, but addiction hadn't hit their radar. If that was the issue, she'd read up on it, talk to experts, do whatever Trent needed to help him get clean and well.

She had to get him to a place to accept help first. "Trent, I can't—"

"I'll figure out a way to contact you in the next few days. You need to go to different banks, cover your tracks. You can take money off credit cards."

The comments sounded crazy. She turned them over in her head and couldn't make sense out of the rampant paranoia. He hadn't been right for months but now she feared he'd unraveled and she'd missed it.

When he grabbed for the knob, she put a hand against the door to keep it shut and him trapped inside with her. "Trent, listen to me—"

"Do not tell anyone you saw me."

"This is—"

He yanked on the door and managed to move her body a few feet out of the way. "And don't let me down."

Then he disappeared down the hall at a run and was gone.

19

Ford put the last of the dinner plates into the dishwasher and threw the towel on the counter. Night had fallen. Except for the streetlight outside the window over Shay's sink, darkness blanketed the side yard.

They'd eaten in near silence, which only added to his unease. The surveillance video from yesterday showed her roaming all over his apartment. Hell, she'd even dug around in his coat pockets. Good thing he'd stuck with protocol and didn't keep anything other than items relating to his cover in the condo.

There'd purposely been nothing for her to find, but that wasn't the point. She went looking for something and that spelled trouble. Ward sure thought so. Ford still wasn't sure how the response to his request for a video review ended up on Ward's desk first.

Ford tried to sell a story about Shay checking to see if he was cheating. The frown on Ward's face had suggested he didn't buy the ploy at all. Reviewing the tape meant telling the team. They took it well, except for Reid, who announced he could have held cover and kept Shay satisfied without causing a problem. Ford landed one hard shove before West stepped in and broke up the potential testosterone battle. It was a shame since Ford welcomed the energy release.

The back and forth with Reid had been a way to burn off tension and nothing more, but the problem remained. Shay had doubts. Ford knew his cover could blow the op, which should have been the most important issue. For some reason, all Ford could think about was the shitty possibility of having to break it off with her before it was too late.

He leaned against the counter and eyed her. She bit her lip and stared into space. Gone was the rapport from their restaurant date. Her mind wasn't there, in the room with them.

Reading women was not his strength so he didn't even try. "You okay? You seem distracted."

She lifted her arms and flipped her hair around into a ponytail, then she was on the move again. "Long day."

Not the most helpful answer. "Were you able to fix the plumbing problem?"

"What?" She stopped staring at her hands and shifting around inside the U-shaped area of counters.

"You texted that you had another leaky pipe issue." Not something he would normally have to remind her about. She tended to chatter about her day the minute he walked in. He found it endearing even though it sometimes took him a few minutes to catch up. "I'm thinking your uncle needs to spend some money to upgrade some of the basics around here."

"He doesn't really open his wallet all that willingly." She reached over and picked up the towel Ford had dropped. She matched up the ends and folded, then undid it and tried again.

He took the material out of her hand and hung it over the bar to the oven door before she accidentally strangled herself with it. "Would he rather the building fall down around you?"

"Good question."

Ford wasn't even clear on what they were talking about anymore. Pipes and towels and nothing that got to the heart of her being here in body only. "You sure you're okay?"

She looked at him and some of the haze cleared from her eyes. It was as if she'd forced her mind to snap out of whatever world it had landed in and come back to him.

"I'm thinking we should go to bed early," she said.

That sounded good, but the usual heat that flushed her skin was missing tonight. "And bed means . . ."

She smiled. "Bed."

Well, damn. "Ah, okay."

"Sorry." She gnawed on her lips again. "I understand if you want to go back to your place."

"I'm not an animal, Shay. I can go without sex for one night." He took a step and brought her into his arms and against his body. His hands linked at the base of her back. The tension finally left his muscles when she relaxed against him.

"That hasn't been my experience with you so far. Not that I'm complaining. I was a very active participant in those nights."

"I'll be happy just to hold you." Strange thing was, the holding worked fine for him. Sure, he wanted more from her, but he liked the quiet moments, too.

She snuggled into the space under his chin and

rested the side of her face on his chest. "That sounds good tonight."

He liked the position more than he wanted to admit. Naked and screaming his name still ranked as one of his favorites, but it felt right just to hold her. To give her comfort because tonight she seemed to need it.

He rubbed a hand up and down her back. "Maybe by morning you'll tell me what's really wrong."

"With a good night's sleep it will all be fine."

Ford rarely found that to be the case, but he let the comment drop. She'd find out soon enough. Then they'd both pay for his job choices.

Ward sat on the bench in front of Ford's locker outside the Warehouse gym. He'd seen Ford working out and knew he was nearing the end of his hour-long routine of punishing weight-lifting and modified push-ups that would have made a Marine proud.

Ford turned the corner, spied him and stopped. "Ah, damn." He slammed an open hand against the metal lockers, making them rattle. Not the most subtle of reactions, but exactly what he expected.

"Good to see you, too," Ward said.

Pushing past Ward in the small space, Ford reached for his lock and spun the dial to enter his combination. "Is this lecture time about the video? Because I'm not really in the mood."

Not willing to back down or buy into that grumpy-as-shit attitude, Ward just sat there, totally in the way. "Poor baby."

"Okay, then. I see this is going to happen no matter what I say." With a scrape and a clunk, Ford opened the locker and threw a pair of jeans and a tee on the bench next to Ward. "Let me shower first."

Nice try at avoidance, but he had known Ford too long to let it fly. "Hold off."

"Why?"

"If it helps, I'm skipping the 'I told you so' part on Shay and jumping over the million questions about whether your cover is blown."

Ford straddled the locker room bench and sat down a few feet away from Ward. "For some reason that makes me more nervous than your yelling."

"Proves you're smarter than everyone thinks."

"Insults. That's great."

Now that he had Ford's attention, he planned to use it. "I want to talk about the other issue we keep circling and ignoring."

"Another one? Shit, how many issues do we have right now?"

Ward got up and walked toward the showers. He turned a faucet and the water came on. The steady fall against the tiles functioned as white noise as it sent steam billowing in the shower area. He gestured for Ford to join him in front of the pounding water.

Ford hung up a towel on the hook just outside the open stall. "I don't usually shower with a guy on the first date, but if Tasha's okay with it—"

"A mole."

The amusement left Ford's face as his mouth flattened into a straight line. "What?"

"You and I both know someone leaked intel about our operation in Hampstead. There's no other explanation for the armed guard and the timed explosion."

"And the DC warehouse shootout had all the earmarks of a setup."

Ward didn't need to say more. He knew from the comment and how out of sorts Ford had been on this job that they were on the same page. The idea might also have been in the back of some team members' minds. For Ward, it stayed at the front, drilled into his brain. "The bad guys seem to know when we're coming."

Ford nodded. "That's what I've been saying."

Taking the final step, Ward put his latest concern on the table. "I'm thinking Matt's records might have been cleaned up before we got to him."

Droplets of water splashed against Ward's arm, and the humidity made his shirt stick to his back. His office might have been a better place for this conversation, but when you didn't trust your coworkers to keep quiet, you couldn't trust them not to plant listening devices either.

They had sensors to pick up and block those sorts of things and Security conducted an office sweep every morning. But they all knew the schedule. Someone who really wanted information could handpick a way to listen in and move devices around in time.

Ward hated the paranoia and how it infected everything.

"You know I agree with all of this, right?" Ford asked. "I'm the one who's been shouting about a double cross from the beginning."

"I know." While they were laying out the factors, they might as well hit the one where his view differed from Ford's. "I also think you like Harlan for this."

"Could be he's working both sides. Not sure why—money, boredom, whatever."

All possible in the abstract but not in fact. Ward had decided that much. "No."

"Because he's one of us? I know you think that matters, but agents turn. The pathetic pieces of crap."

"Because I've been watching and planting pieces of intel and he's not biting." This was the part that had ticked Tasha off this morning. She'd stormed out of the kitchen and hadn't said a word on the ride into work. Ward guessed she was storing it up and he'd have a yelling match on his hands when they got home.

Ford whistled. "Damn, Ward. That's cold."

"I know."

"Sounds like something I would do." Ford shrugged. "I'm kind of pissed you did it first but I like knowing you can still go there despite being in management."

That didn't make Ward feel better about his actions. "You're not the only one who thinks something is wrong there."

"Does Tasha know your theory and about your Harlan surveillance?"

Ward was trying to block her reaction from his head so he could get through the day. "Let's just say we don't agree on all office procedures."

Ford made a face that suggested he got how much trouble Ward had created on the home front. "So, what do we do now?"

"You get ready to move Bravo on Anthony's house." When the water puddled around Ward's feet, he shifted to the side but still within noise-covering territory. "He won't keep anything damning at his office, so it has to be the house."

"Ellery says the place is locked up with a military grade security system."

They'd had briefings and gone through blueprints. Taking a closer look at Anthony had been a priority for days. Problem was, Ellery kept finding intel that suggested getting close to Anthony would not be easy.

Which is why he had her handling work-arounds. The sooner Bravo got in there, the better. "I'll figure out a way. You just need to break in according to plan but be quiet about the tactics."

"Meaning?" Ford asked.

"Only Ellery, Tasha, and the two of us know the real date and time you're going in." Ward's paranoia spiked and adrenaline surged through him as he talked. The temptation to close that circle even tighter hit him and he fought it off. Ellery had to be included because if the tech experts were working against them, all of Alliance was doomed. "That means no backup and limited tech support. Your guys would be out there on their own."

Ford shrugged. "We can handle it."

"It's dangerous shit."

"For you maybe. My guys are professionals."

The ego and self-assurance—Ward counted on Ford for both. "You keep your team on alert, and ready them at the last minute with an order to go radio silent about it."

It was the best imperfect plan he could come up with out of all the imperfect plans. They were hunting a toxin and a known arms-dealer-turned-potential-terrorist, waiting for an auction that could change the geopolitical dynamics for years to come and now trying to flush out a traitor in the Warehouse. The UK and U.S. created Alliance to handle just this sort of catastrophic perfect storm, but damn, that was a lot to take on, even for these guys.

Ford stepped back and shook his head as he stared at the floor. "I fucking hate going after our own, but this person, whoever it is, needs to go down hard. You should know my inclination is to kill not capture."

"You can use my gun." And that was no joke. Ward viewed Alliance as his baby, and having someone fuck with it made him itch to attack.

Ford didn't stick around for the details. He grabbed the towel and shut off the water. Steps took him toward the lockers again.

"What are you doing?" Ward asked.

"I need to go shoot things."

Times like these, Ward wished he didn't have the damn injury and still could grip his gun.

20

THE MINUTE Ford walked up to the Warehouse's underground, inside gun range, all conversation among his team members stopped. He really wasn't looking for quality time with the men. Certainly didn't need conversation. After talking with Ward he wanted to burn shit down.

They definitely had a mole. The last time he'd dealt with someone out for his own interests and switching sides for cash or cover, a good operative had died. An inside guy snitched then, too. The weasel, worried his boss had traced the missing weapons to an inside job, had sold out Tom to buy time and save his own ass. The gunrunner sent mercenaries to cut up the most important person to Tom, Kelly, while he watched and begged for her life. Ford had arrived in time to hear the pleading, then see the knife slice across Tom's throat.

With the fury running wild inside him, he hadn't left a single mercenary standing.

Now he faced a repeat. Another weasel, this time selling out Alliance. Death would be too easy for whoever the person was. Ford wanted torture. Lasting pain and a moment where the guy knew his life meant nothing. That's what a guy who helped a lethal toxin see daylight deserved. Agony.

Reid unloaded his gun, checked and rechecked it before setting it down and shifting to the side to make room for Ford at the bay. "Surprised to see you here."

"I practice now and then just so I don't accidentally shoot one of you. Ward thinks that sort of thing would break morale." Before Shay, he'd come down to the gun range and fire round after round. The bangs couldn't silence the restless anger in his brain, but he'd tried. Now he lost himself in her instead.

Yeah, forget falling. Between the face and the hot mouth, the way she made him want to walk into the light and stand with her, he'd fallen. Past tense. It was too late. He'd blown it and turned the corner from truly liking her—something that was already foreign to him—to loving her.

For the hundredth time since he met her he thought the same thing: he was fucked.

"Do you ever shower?" Lucas asked. "Dude, you stink."

Ford didn't try to hide his sarcasm. "With your mom, but she asked me to wait and come by later tonight. We like to wash off after."

West lifted the portable gun vault onto the counter. Opening it showed off a line of shiny weapons. "Those jokes never get old."

Lucas laughed. "Are you sure? They seem stale to me."

"I meant I thought you'd be sleeping in. What with all the late night activity you're having. You look tired, by the way." Reid leaned against the cement block wall as he toyed with his karambit.

He handled the curved knife with a precision and expertise people trained years to accomplish and never got close. Reid flipped the karambit around, swiped it through the air, and slipped it back in its sheath on his belt. The man and the knife had proven equally lethal. Together, no one within cutting range stood a chance.

"Something you're trying to say about what I do in my off time?" Not that Reid hid his idiocy on that topic all that well. Ford knew he meant Shay and that the team was more than a little interested in how much time he spent at her place. As far as he was concerned, they could watch porn if they needed to get off because his private life was going to stay just that for now.

"She is pretty," West pointed out as he shuffled through the guns in the case.

Ford was not in the mood for a pile on by his men. "Shay?"

"No, Harlan," Reid scoffed, and threw in a few profane words as well. "Of course we're talking about Shay."

West dropped boxes of ammo on the counter. "He doesn't want to talk about her."

"Yet you guys keep trying." Ford reached for his gun but got cock-blocked by West standing in the way. Ford settled for exhaling as he waited for the next round of annoying questions he had no intention of answering.

"When did you break cover?" Reid asked.

"I didn't." And he wouldn't. Still, he had no idea where that shot came from. Could be rumors about the video had started making the rounds in the Warehouse. Lucky him.

"You didn't leave out something and she found it?" Reid asked.

What the fuck is this about? "Like what?"

West shrugged as he stacked the ammo boxes in a line. "Your gun, maybe."

Reid smiled. "Or your employment agreement with Alliance."

Now Ford knew they were just busting his balls. They'd probably seen his separate meetings with Tasha and Ward and figured something was up. He wasn't ready to set the record straight just yet. "Shut the fuck up."

West looked around the room. "Who are you talking to?"

That was the easiest question Ford had gotten since he started with Alliance. "All of you."

Reid came away from the wall to stand next to Lucas. "Ellery almost has the security system at Anthony's place cracked."

"We're changing the topic?" Lucas asked.

Reid threw out a hand in Ford's direction. "Poor bastard looked ready to bolt, what with all that romance talk. I took pity on him."

"You can transfer to Delta." Not that Ford wasn't grateful for the diversion. For any diversion away from his love life.

Lucas whistled. "Harsh."

"That sounds ridiculous with the British accent." And with that, the power shifted again. Ford had regained the upper hand and moved back into the leadership chair. He much preferred being in charge and holding the floor to getting question whiplash from the team.

"I don't think so."

They all turned at the sound of the female voice. Ellery stood in the doorway wearing her usual short plaid skirt and sweater. She had barely reached her mid-twenties but the big eyes and relaxed wardrobe made her look even younger.

Ford didn't notice much about her except that she was pretty in a friend's baby sister kind of way. Cute and off limits. At least he thought so. But from the way Lucas shot glances in her direction about a hundred times a day, he doubted that Lucas thought of her in a sisterly way.

"Ellery." Reid smiled and waved her inside. "Give us some good news."

"Not today. Sorry." She walked in with a folder in her hand and stopped next to Lucas.

He shifted until their shoulders almost touched. Dumb bastard. Ford bit back a warning on what happened when you dated someone on the job. He knew all too well how it had the potential to backfire.

West groaned. "Now what's wrong?"

"Anthony is officially investigating Ford." She handed a folder to Ford. "The alarms went off about an hour ago."

Lucas glanced down at her. "Alarms?"

Her gaze went to his then skipped away. "I set up a system where I get notified if anyone tries to check any of your aliases or covers."

Reid frowned. "Sounds like standard operating procedure."

"Not quite." Ellery talked with her hands. They waved through the air as she explained. "Most systems notify when people try to go behind firewalls and get into places they shouldn't be. Mine goes off if anyone checks your names anywhere."

West winked at her. "I feel safer."

"Well, I can't stop the searches. I just redirect them if they get close to information they shouldn't have."

That brought up a topic Ford didn't want to consider but needed to, especially if he was going to take Bravo into Anthony's house on a secret mission. "How often does that happen? That someone gets that close to us."

"Never."

Lucas lifted a hand but stopped just short of touching Ellery's hair. "Spooky computer genius."

She sighed and directed it toward Ford. "We have another problem."

He knew that expression couldn't be good. "I'm no longer enjoying your visit."

"Shay ditched the car that was following her." Ellery made the comment and then winced as if waiting for the fallout.

Ford guessed he should blow up but he'd clearly missed a step. He had no idea anyone but him was watching over Shay. "What?"

"Ward's orders."

There came the anger. It rumbled in Ford's gut and built to a crescendo. "Who and when?"

And then there was the problem about being out of the loop. He'd just stood almost in a shower with Ward and the guy never mentioned the Shay recon. Interesting what facts Ward shared and which ones he didn't. Ford trusted the man with his life, but this sucked.

"Someone not in Alliance," Ellery said. "I'd give

the name but you'd probably try to drown him in the
shower."

"Damn straight."

Lucas held up a hand. "Take it up with Ward."

Ford ignored the way Lucas acted as if he had to protect Ellery from him. As if he'd go after her. She was
the linchpin of Alliance. They all knew it but rarely
admitted it. She could shoot, but her real strength lay
in being able to use her computer to get them out of
most jams.

"This tail lost her?" he asked.

"He said she was stopping at a series of ATMs."
Ellery motioned to the folder in Ford's hand. "It looks
like she went into one bank, and after he waited for a
long time for her to come out, he went in and she was
gone. He didn't expect the subterfuge and is stomping
around swearing about it."

West made a tsk-tsking sound "Her behavior sounds
bad, man."

"Does she have money issues?" Lucas asked.

Ellery answered before Ford could. "Not according
to my file on her."

Standing there, Ford tried to block all of the questions. He needed to concentrate and think, to work
through the possibilities of what Shay could be doing
and why she felt the need to hide it.

"Thanks, Ellery." He somehow got the words out
even though thoughts and excuses for Shay flooded his
brain.

Ellery headed for the door then stopped and turned
around again to face them all. "We're tracking her
movements out of the bank using security and govern-

ment cameras. We should be able to piece together the trail soon."

West looked at Ellery then back to Ford. "Then what?"

"I don't know." That's all Ford could get out right now.

As if taking pity on him, Reid stepped in. "We have to see, but your cover could be blown."

"No." That answer floated through Ford's head and refused to leave. "Not that."

"How do you know?" Lucas asked.

"She's had plenty of chances to kill me in my sleep and didn't." If she were engaging in subterfuge and really part of Trent's plot, then getting rid of him would be no issue for her. Ford understood that much.

"Maybe she's not the type." West shrugged. "I've heard not everyone kills when they're angry."

Right, because anger was that rational. When he had seen Tom drop, dying and bleeding, he'd lost it. Broke into an animalistic rage he couldn't control. Ford had no trouble seeing any human who was pushed too far going off. "You know any woman who could be betrayed and not think about doing the deed?"

Ellery took that question. "Nope."

21

Shay was two seconds away from a full-on brain explosion. No, not really. She wasn't that lucky. No matter how hard she tried, she couldn't get away from her uncle. He stood on the other side of the breakfast bar asking all sorts of questions but refusing to answer hers.

"Is it really that weird I want to know exactly what Trent does for a living?" After getting pinned down in the upstairs unit and listening to Trent's ramblings, she was more confused than ever and looking for clarity.

"He works in a lab."

She knew she should just tell Anthony about Trent's visit, but something kept stopping her. She'd get close to saying the words then call them back. Whatever fear moved through Trent—and that's definitely what she'd witnessed—it attached in some way to his father. She'd bet what little money she'd scraped together for Trent on that.

Trent specifically mentioned his dad but didn't go to him for help. Anthony had the resources and the cash. Hell, he kept a safe in his office closet no one was allowed to go near. That housed something impressive. Something Trent could likely use right now.

She found some money and maxed out her Visa with a cash advance to get more, but Anthony possessed piles and owned enough properties to keep Trent hidden for a long time. The fact that Trent didn't seek out the obvious solution to his problem, whatever his problem was, shook her. He ran and lied and talked like his thoughts had been scrambled, and had her waffling on whether to even hand over the cash.

Her uncle smiled as he came around the bar and put his hands on her upper arms. "He works at a government lab dealing with top secret programs. That's all we get to know."

Anthony explained it to her as if she were a child. He talked slow and shot her a look that suggested he pitied her for being unable to understand his point. Other people, his staff and Trent, grumbled about Anthony's tendency to talk down to everyone.

For years she'd overlooked it because of all he did for her when he rescued her. She saw him one way and blocked the rest. Then she got older and struggled to ignore the negative and demanding pieces of his personality.

Tonight she found the whole "lying for her protection" thing too much. She was a grown-up, and being pulled apart by Trent and Anthony no longer worked for the stable life she craved.

This would teach her to accept the job running Anthony's properties over taking the office manager job at the small law firm in the Maryland suburbs. To be beholden to him for a paycheck gave him power over her. Now she got why Ford left home and never looked back. Sometimes you had to forge a path and realize that accepting help meant getting wrapped up in strings.

"You never wanted Trent to work there," she said. Anthony held up the job as being so important now that she wondered if he'd forgotten all the insults he'd lobbed when Trent took the position.

"The more lucrative careers are outside of government and academic work. My son has the brains, there's no reason for him to settle for a lower paying job." Anthony held up both hands and stepped back from Shay. "Seems like an obvious position to me, but he didn't listen to me and now we're here."

"Where?"

"Dealing with his broken heart."

Her uncle kept doing a verbal dance. Saying one thing one minute and the opposite a few minutes later. She was just about to call him on the Trent-girlfriend story when the front door alarm to her condo beeped.

"Hello." Ford came in and closed the door behind him. He didn't stop walking until he halted at the threshold to the kitchen with his gaze traveling back and forth between her and her uncle. "Sorry, did I interrupt?"

Anthony shook his head. "No."

"Family stuff," she said at the same time, going for purposely vague over dragging Ford into their mess.

He looked adorable in his pink I LIKE HOT DOGS tee and jeans that rode low on his hips. The damp hair and extra scruff around his chin gave him that scoundrel look she loved so much.

Ford moved around as he stood, shifting his weight and clinging to his gym bag and a white plastic bag filled with Chinese food containers. No question the tension in the room had hit maximum force because he didn't do much more than stand there until he looked over his shoulder and pointed toward the door. "I can come back."

"Stay." She'd tackle him if she had to. She wanted him here, on the couch, with her. Not across the hall waiting for the familial smoke to clear.

Another minute alone with Anthony and she might say something she'd regret. After a lifetime of thanking him and praising him, some of the shine had worn off. She no longer blindly accepted everything he said as gospel. He'd ruined that with the overprotection and careful parsing of what he told her and what he held back. She'd always love him and respect him, but some days she wanted to scream at him.

"Things seem a bit tense in here." Ford dropped the gym bag on the floor and came in closer to put the food on the counter.

"It's been a long day." She knew that was the lamest excuse on the planet, but saying it let her skip over the frustrating parts.

He reached into the bag and took out a fortune cookie. The paper crinkled as he ripped it and cracked the shell open.

Much more of that and she'd dive into the bag in search of the cashew chicken container. "Maybe we should—"

"You sure it doesn't have anything to do with what your investigator found on me?" Ford popped a piece of the cookie into his mouth and eyed Anthony.

Shay stopped in the middle of reaching for the closest food container. "What are you talking about?"

"Your uncle has someone digging into my back-ground and finances." Ford smiled as he said it. Actu-ally smiled.

Her uncle couldn't. Wouldn't. Not after she'd been adamant about not wanting Ford investigated, and An-thony promised not to . . . Or did he? She'd been firm, but now that she thought about it, she wavered. "An-thony!"

"Stop shouting." Her uncle snorted and held up both hands, as if that would hold back her anger. "It's normal in these situations."

Normal? She didn't even know what that meant any-more. "What situation would that be?"

Anthony turned away from her then. He faced Ford as if they could work this out with some sort of man-to-man chat. "Shay stands to inherit some money. You can't blame me for wanting to protect that."

Heat warmed her cheeks as she stepped between them and forced Anthony to look at her again. "Yes, I can."

"It's fine." With his hands on her shoulders, Ford moved her to stand beside him.

"It's offensive." And he was superhuman or wore emotional Teflon or something. She had no idea how his voice stayed even and he held onto his usual blank expression.

Part of her wanted him to explode, to start arguing and yelling. Any reaction so she would know he could be as human as her and lose his temper like any normal person. She loved how even he was, but, man, some be-haviors called for frustration, and she wanted it to seep out of him and go wild.

"Honey, I get it." Ford's hand landed on her lower back and he snuggled her closer to his side. "He's trying to protect you."

"See, your man understands." Anthony peeked into the bag and frowned.

Recovery took Shay another second. Ford rarely used endearments and never in front of anyone else. The gesture threw her, which was the only reason her uncle's hand got near the cashew chicken.

"Good news is the investigator didn't find anything." Anthony opened one of the boxes to reveal white rice then closed it again. "This isn't another case of being manipulated like with Devin."

The wind rushed right out of her, leaving her gasping and sputtering. "I don't believe this."

Shock gave way to a white hot rage. She broke away from Ford's hold because she couldn't stand to be touched right then. An investigation into Ford, lying about Trent, mentioning Devin. The trifecta of things guaranteed to tick her off.

"If it's easier for you, Anthony, tell me what you want and I'll gather it for you," Ford said. "There's no need for you to waste money on this."

They talked over her. She hated that even more than the overprotective thing.

"Ford, my God. What's wrong with you?" When he frowned at her, she started to wonder if she really was the one who was losing it. "Don't volunteer information for him."

"I don't know what the problem is here." Anthony threw up his hands as his voice grew louder. "I told you he's clean. Ford has earned my seal of approval."

She pressed her fingertips against her chest. "Well, thank goodness."

"I don't appreciate the sarcasm."

"And I don't appreciate your constant interference."

"Wait a second. This is not worth family disharmony." Ford put a hand on her arm. "Shay, really. It's okay."

"No, it's not." The soft touch knocked the bubbling fury inside her down to a simmer. Something about his continued calm started to rub off on her, even though she tried to grab onto her frustration and keep it running.

Anthony wagged a finger at her. "One day you'll be grateful for my protection."

It was her least favorite gesture, and one step too far. "Like Trent is?"

The tension ratcheted right back up and buzzed with the force of an electrified fence. "Excuse me?"

"Do you have his number in Charlottesville?" Once she started pushing she couldn't stop. If she could get Anthony to fess up with Ford there, all the better.

Instead, Anthony's features were drawn and the life seemed to drain out of him. "Trent has his cell."

"He's not answering it."

One of Anthony's eyebrows lifted. "Maybe he isn't ready to hear from his meddling cousin."

Ford took a step forward and angled his body in front of hers. "Okay, that's probably not necessary."

She gripped the back of his shirt and held on with all her strength. Right now he served as her lifeline in an argument she hadn't even planned on having tonight. Anthony had come over and sent the stress whirling.

Exhaustion smacked into her and she fought it off. "Ford and I are going to head down there to check on Trent."

Anthony swore under his breath. "Leave the boy alone."

"Or?"

"Don't test me on this, Shay."

Ford clapped and got them all focusing on him instead of the rising battle. "Maybe we should all head back to our respective corners and calm down."

Silence buzzed through the room. No one moved. After a few seconds, Anthony's shoulders fell and he moved out of the kitchen.

"No need. I have a late meeting." He pushed past Ford and headed for the door. He stopped and shot her one last look. "But leave Trent alone."

She couldn't have obeyed even if she wanted to, and she didn't. Trent had come to her, and now she had to figure out how to help him, even if she picked a way that contrasted with his pleading for money. "Okay."

"I'm serious, Shay." Anthony turned and put his back to the door. "Tell me you understand."

"I do."

He left then, slamming the door behind him without saying another word. It still rattled on its hinges when she looked at Ford again.

"I feel like that whole conversation was code for something else." He grabbed two plates off the open shelves. They landed on the counter with a soft thud.

Now that the tornado of stress had subsided, she slipped her thigh onto the bar stool as she watched him move around the kitchen. "He really checked into you?"

"Yeah." Ford opened the drawer and took out forks and spoons. Cool and collected, he acted like nothing had happened. Just went about setting up dinner and getting them both fed.

"How do you know he was digging?" she asked.

"My boss gave me the heads-up that a guy was asking questions." Ford unloaded the bag and lined the cartons up in front of her. "I assumed the rest about the financials and criminal record check and all that, and used some computer skills of my own to double check."

The idea intrigued her, but now wasn't the time to ask for details about his work.

"I'm sorry." The words weren't enough to undo the damage, but they came from her heart. The part of her that ached right now.

He winked. "It's fine."

It wasn't. Her entire family seemed hell-bent on invading his privacy. "First I looked through your place and now Anthony is paging through your life."

"Your family does have some trust issues."

"With Anthony at the head you can see why."

"Enough about him." Ford came around the end of the counter and took her hand. With one pull, he had her on her feet and in his arms. "What did you do today?"

"Errands."

"Sounds boring." He acted as if he actually cared. Even if he forced it out, she appreciated the change in topic. The only problem was, the switch led her straight into her bigger nightmare—Trent and his unexpected visit.

Determined to drag her mind to a happier topic, she brushed her hands up and down Ford's arms, loving the bulges and firm muscles. He was so solid and strong. Being with him helped ease the stress out of her.

"I had to go to the bank." Banks, as in multiple, but she wasn't ready to launch into that explanation either.

After wrestling and debating, she'd decided to tell Ford about Trent once she worked through what was happening. The last thing he needed was to be saddled with her family problems. Any sane man would run, and she couldn't stand the thought of that.

"Can I help with the banking?" he asked.

She pulled back and stared up at him, not sure whether to be offended or go all gooey soft at his charm. "Are you really offering me money?"

He hissed as he winced. "Clearly that came out wrong."

"Sort of, yeah."

"I was trying to say if you're short, I can help." When she lifted her eyebrows, he tried again. "Still not good, huh?"

She looked deep into those eyes and felt the intensity radiating off him. She focused on the pressure of his hands on her and his warm breath brushing over her cheek. The closeness, the caring . . . yeah, she'd fallen for him. Like, stupid and silly and out of control in love with him.

Nowhere near enough time had passed, and there was so much she still didn't know about him, but in that moment the pieces she hadn't filled in didn't matter. What she did know attracted her, sent a surge of feminine power through her.

She touched her hand to his cheek and took a sharp intake of breath when he turned his head to place a kiss in the middle of her palm. His tongue licked out and his hand held hers. As far as sexy come-ons went, this one deserved a medal.

"You're being sweet." And growing hotter by the second.

He gave her one of those so-cute-he-could-melt-butter smiles. "So, no?"

"No. I'm not taking money from you." She kissed him then. Long and lingering, falling against to him as her hands slipped up to his shoulders. "I know I'm being sensitive. It's just that . . ."

He kissed her forehead. "Yes?"

The support helped her get it all out. "Sometimes I feel like the men in my life think I'm an appendage, like some sort of extension of them."

His face fell. "Okay."

"Not you." She traced a finger over his bottom lip. He didn't pout and whine like Devin had, and she gave him a quick kiss to silently thank him for that. "I'm talking about Anthony, who thinks he runs my life, and Trent."

"What does this have to do with your cousin?"

"He acts like I'm his assistant." She hadn't thought about it that way before but now it hit her. There was a lot of Anthony in Trent. He acted entitled and as if he were smarter than everyone else, which he basically was.

"Did you talk with him today?"

Answering that would take them into a new round of conversation. She could unburden and Ford would listen. He'd probably stroke her back and tell her everything would be okay. That's what he did. It was the kind of support she'd come to depend on from him.

All good but not what she really needed right now.

"I don't want to think about him." She slipped a hand down Ford's body, hesitating over the broad expanse of his chest and smiling at the dip of his stomach.

"You'll probably feel better if . . ." When she got to the top of his jeans and started unbuttoning them, his body froze and he glanced down. "What are you doing?"

So much for thinking she was being obvious. She pushed his tee up and kissed his bare chest. Kept nibbling a line until her tongue flicked over his belly button.

Slipping down, she ended up on her knees and stared up at him. "You have to ask?"

His hand went to her hair and his fingers slipped through the strands. "You were upset a second ago."

"And now I want you in my mouth."

She lowered the zipper one tick at a time and rubbed her cheek over his erection. When he moaned, she did it again. Those fingers flexed against her skull as she peeled his briefs down and caught him in her hand.

She could smell him. Feel him. When she licked her tongue over his tip, she tasted him.

His scent wound its way into her head as his strong hands caressed her face. She was on her knees but felt powerful, cared for. Maybe even a little bit loved.

Taking him deeper, she sucked and held him. Her hand moved up and down and her mouth followed. The grumbling at the back of his throat spurred her on. Need built inside her until all she wanted was to pleasure him.

"Shay, I don't think—" But his hips shifted as if to help her take him deeper.

"Yeah, don't." She slid her hand down to his base then up again.

And when she swallowed him, he stopped protesting and started chanting her name.

Harlan paced back and forth across Ward's office. The space barely allowed for a desk and chair. Having Tasha and Harlan both in there made Ward downright claustrophobic.

But it was either handle the difficult situation now or have Harlan out on the floor yelling. Ward couldn't risk that. He had no idea how Harlan found out that the stated timetable for the run on Anthony's house wasn't accurate, but he knew and was pissed off. Forget the fancy education and proper accent. Harlan had been in there, swearing and fuming for ten minutes.

Showing no signs of winding down, he stopped in the middle of the floor and scowled at Ward. "Why wasn't I informed?"

Ward looked to Tasha for guidance, but her face remained blank. She stood in her favorite uniform of olive cargo pants and a slim black long-sleeve tee. She skipped the suit whenever she could get away with it, and tonight was one of those times. Looked good to Ward, since this situation seemed to call for combat gear.

"There's nothing to know yet." That wasn't exactly a lie. Ward hadn't finalized the go ahead.

Harlan went to the glass window and jammed his finger against it. The knocking sound had more than one person on the floor looking in their direction. "You think I can't see Ellery working round the clock on something?"

"Trent is in the wind. She's been working nonstop since we figured that out."

"Bravo is revving up to go out." Harlan tuned back, the fury evident in his eyes. "I want to know where and why."

"The timing is Ford's decision." Tasha's cool voice broke through the male madness. She dropped the line and stopped talking, as if her word should end the discussion.

Harlan clearly thought otherwise because he turned his wrath on her. "Since when do we let the team leaders decide operation protocol? They are in charge of on the ground tactics. That's it."

"Not this time." She maintained the monotone voice.

"And I'll ask again, why?"

Ward knew Tasha didn't need rescuing, but he'd created the situation and felt obligated to step in now. "Ford is in deep with this family. He knows their schedules and can call it without warning."

Harlan shook his head. "I don't buy it."

When he started to say more, Tasha held up a hand to stop him. "That's how it's going down, Harlan. My word is final."

"Fine." He broke their staring contest and threw open the door. A second later he disappeared like the ghost operator he'd once been.

Ward watched his MI6 counterpart leave the Warehouse floor and wondered if he was off to complain to the people above Tasha. "That went well."

She exhaled and frowned and engaged in most of her I'm-pissed-off gestures. "If you think I like lying to him, you're wrong."

"I don't think it's Harlan either. I will fill him in the second after Bravo moves in." Maybe a few seconds, but Ward wanted to make the point the subterfuge would only last as long as it needed to.

"You're on a short leash."

"Right." Ward nodded as his gaze scanned the documents on his desk. Floor plans and security system information. Anthony lived in a minifortress in an area frequently patrolled by private security and guards watching over ambassadorial residences. This job bordered on impossible.

He finally noticed the room had gone still. He glanced up to find Tasha staring at him. The small shake of her head telegraphed her displeasure.

If possible, the line of her mouth flattened even more. "I'm serious."

"We all are, Tasha."

22

HE WAS a piece of shit. Ford had decided that last night as he watched Shay drop to her knees in front of him in the kitchen. He didn't stop her when she stripped his briefs down his thighs. Or when she took him in her mouth. Or when he came on a crashing wave and wanted nothing more than to carry her to bed and start all over again.

He didn't feel any better about himself tonight. She was part of an assignment and he shouldn't care about her feelings, but that was no longer possible. Every hour wrapped their lives tighter together and magnified his deceit. She depended on him and shared with him . . . and he'd lied to her every fucking minute he'd known her.

Standing at the tree line on the side of her Uncle Anthony's impressive house, with the team spread out and crowded into the branches of the tall trees, Ford fought to bring his focus back to the operation. They had Ellery and Ward on the com and Tasha listening in somewhere. But this was all up to Bravo. Lucas and Reid at one end. He with West at the other.

Before they started tonight Ford had given the "prepare for a fuck-up" speech. They had limited eyes on this op but that didn't guarantee success, and there were a lot of variables out of their control, the biggest being Anthony.

They'd picked now as the go time based on Ford's personal intel. He'd called Uncle Anthony then gone to his office to talk early that afternoon. Anthony gave a speech about Shay that set women's rights back by at least three decades. He saw her as an extension of him and would someday be an extension of her husband. He didn't say it in a nasty way. More like in a protective-to-the-point-of-stifling way.

Ford had nodded and played along with the male bonding game because he had a role and information to collect, but inside he wanted to punch a wall. The idea Anthony saw Shay as almost fragile, as someone to be coddled, made Ford crazed. He defended her until he realized, in Anthony's mind he wasn't doing anything other than loving her.

But the thought that this bright, energetic amazing woman needed a keeper made no sense to Ford. He didn't see Shay that way. The vibrancy, how she was so even and sure and didn't pretend to be anything other than who she was, attracted him the most.

He tried to rationalize and remember that Anthony moved in a world where a woman was only as impressive as who she married. But damn, the walk through the 1950s' mind-set had Ford biting back bile. He also made a mental note to call his mom and apologize for men everywhere and their stupid ideas when the assignment ended.

But the visit did give Ford a chance to plant the

device on Anthony's computer. One that let Ellery into
his closed system. Even now Anthony sat in a restaurant at a late business dinner meeting with a man he
thought wanted to talk about bringing a major hotel
chain to town. Since Ellery faked the meeting on Anthony's agenda and the businessman in question was
really Pearce, that deal wouldn't likely go through.

Ford tapped his ear to open communication on his
end. "Ellery?"

"I need one more second to trick the alarm into
thinking it's set." The typing almost drowned out her
voice but she kept going.

"Copy that." They'd held tight for five minutes already. They could hang in for a few more.

Ford delved deeper into the trees and listened to the
sounds of the night. Cars passed by, down the small hill
and through the break line in the stone fence guarding
the front of the house from the street. The sound of
crickets played around them, and the lights from the
upstairs windows reflected onto the thick green lawn.

When Ellery took out the alarm, she'd take out the
sensor lights set up in a grid across the property. That
still left the neighbors' systems and roaming guards,
not to mention the stray walker who might pick up
movement if he were looking in the right place at the
right time.

"Any change in our time inside?" West asked the
question from right over Ford's shoulder.

"No, we need to get in and out in ten." Hardly
enough time to accomplish anything, but then this job
wasn't exactly what it seemed.

He'd briefed Bravo yesterday and they all agreed to

use this assignment as a mole test. They didn't share information. They'd been trained to act on command, and that's what they did when he'd sent out the call signal an hour ago. No one complained and no one balked. Ford loved that about his team. Also loved that they'd fire if they had to.

"That's a big house to search in ten minutes," Reid said.

They'd seen photos, but Ford agreed it towered over them in person. He had no idea why one man needed all that space. Then again, he'd seen no evidence this guy needed the extra cash selling a toxin might bring.

West whistled. "Three floors of expensive shit."

They didn't have to recon all of it. This was about getting inside and beating the security. They could look around, but the idea was to plant devices and see if the mole made a play. "We put ears in the most reliable places and photograph anything we question."

Reid's low chuckle rumbled on the line. "And if we happen to see a few vials of toxin laying around, grab them."

"Right. Simple." Ford liked to say shit like that even though he knew it was pure shit.

"Let's hope," Ward said. He'd stayed silent until then, but the sound of his voice reminded them all that someone was home at the Warehouse and watching over everything.

Ellery's soft voice broke in across the line. "One minute."

Time to go. In a second they'd know that either Ellery's computer magic worked or the motion sensors and video surveillance would light up. If that happened,

Ford wouldn't need to worry about Shay because she'd figure out the IT story was a ruse pretty fast. He could also end up in jail or a shootout before Ward and Tasha could smooth it all over with the local police.

Nature of the business, but what a damn stupid business it was. Protect and defend he got. Run around and almost get blown up needed a bit more explanation.

Ford glanced at his watch and hit the button that would synchronize the timepieces they all wore and buzz them at the same time when they had only seconds to get out of Dodge. "Start countdown."

Ellery kept up a steady countdown, raising the volume when she got to the round numbers. "Forty . . ."

"No casualties," Ward said.

The Warehouse crew liked to say that. Ford always ignored it. "Tell that to the other guys."

"No authority to neutralize targets." Nothing unclear about Ward's directive there.

Of course, it was easy for the guy in the office to throw out no-kill orders like that. Ford believed in survival. That meant he could shoot anytime someone leveled a gun at him. He passed that edict onto his team and he knew they would all follow it.

Not that he wanted bloodshed or trouble if they could avoid it. Some field operatives grew to love the power that came with killing. Ford wasn't one of them. Every death plagued him and stole a bit of his soul.

"Thirty . . ."

When Ellery hit the main mark, Ford nodded to West. "Going dark on this end."

The team went silent. Not even heavy breathing filled the line. From here they'd only talk in the event of emergencies, depending on the preplanned protocol, memories, and their watch timers to get them in and out without injury. The spare team listening in back at the Warehouse had the ability to break in and talk, but Ward ran these ops clean, like he'd want them to go if he were still in the field. That meant minimal distracting chatter on the line.

"Ten . . ."

Ford and West broke through the tree line to the edge of the property. They knew exactly how far they could go before bells started dinging. About fifty feet away and deeper into the yard Lucas and Reid appeared through the brush.

"We're a go." Ward almost whispered the command.

Bravo team didn't wait. Wearing all black and loaded down with weapons they hoped they wouldn't need, they headed for the gate that led around the side of the house to the back. They hit their beats, and as they arrived at the gate, a green light clicked on and the latch opened.

Score one for Ellery.

Footsteps thudded in the grass and the cool night highlighted the steam from their breathing. Still they ran. Crouched down and blending in, they snaked their way around the frames of outside furniture, missing the padding, and headed around the edge of the kidney-shaped pool and fire pit.

A smoky scent slapped Ford in the face. He couldn't exactly see Anthony out here making s'mores but he could see him hosting a party for fellow bigwigs as they complained about paying taxes or whatever rich people did.

Taking up positions on either side of the double French doors at the back of the scaling wall, they could see into the family room with its massive stone fireplace and overstuffed furniture. Everything looked expensive and oversized and nearly untouched, as if real people rarely hung out in there.

With most of the back wall of the house glass, hanging around on display was probably not a great idea. The whole setup made Ford feel exposed and twitchy. It also meant they had to stay low once they were inside, which was not an easy task in the limited time they had to get this done.

Lucas slipped a card through the back alarm pad and numbers flashed on the small screen. Ford didn't want to know what Ellery did to hack into the alarm company and steal the code. Normal people would never sleep soundly at night again if they knew how easy cracking their systems could be.

With a simple credit card he could take out a bolt. A well-placed kick against the doorknob would shatter a door. Yeah, safety was an illusory thing, and little did the fancy neighbors know a toxin might be sitting right on their street. The mad rush to safety if that got out could almost be as bad as the toxin seeing daylight.

West reached over and lowered the handle. The door pushed in without an alarm screeching through the night. That meant they'd gotten through the second hurdle. Both had been the usual for this neighborhood—alarm codes on the door and motion sensors on the lawn. Now to confirm that Ellery had disabled the inside motion sensors.

Lucas got down on his stomach and slipped a small pair of glasses out of his pocket. They looked thicker than most with black frames but otherwise ordinary. They were anything but. He'd see the infrared beams with them, and when he gave the thumbs-up, Ford knew they were in the clear here, too.

Round two also went to Ellery. The woman deserved a raise.

They filed in, one after the other, and took off in different directions once they crossed the threshold to the inside of the house. Ford headed for the home office. It might seem obvious to hide something there rather than in one of the eight spare bedrooms or seven bathrooms, but Ford viewed Anthony as old-school, and old-school types thought of their offices as sacred.

With his gloves on and his weapons at his sides, Ford slipped into the room. A quick scan of the obvious hiding places uncovered a small camera in the corner directly opposite the door. Out of experience, he knew Ellery had cut this feed, replacing the real-time footage with a loop that would show the status quo.

Ford headed for the desk, searched through the stacks and opened drawers. No locks and nothing out of the ordinary here. He moved on to the bookshelves and stuck a small black dot to the bottom of one of the shelves. The device would pick up all conversations in the room. The small square he put on the back of the computer monitor would give Ellery a look at whatever Anthony had hidden in there.

A tiny camera tucked into the corner of the framed print across from Anthony's desk came next, and then one near the top of the curtains. The devices looked innocent. For anyone but an expert, they'd be thrown away as lint or broken pieces of something.

Whether Anthony qualified as an expert or an innocent wasn't clear yet. If he found the devices, he'd know someone was on to him, so whatever intel they collected they needed to turn around and use fast.

Ford opened the closet and rummaged through the hanging clothes and the boxes on the floor. He tried to move one of them and it didn't budge. He knocked and heard the distinctive hollow thud of metal.

He recognized the sound as a safe. "Damn it."

Not a surprise, but the guy had two safety deposit boxes and a safe at the office. How many things could one man have to hide and protect?

"Incoming."

Ellery's voice was so low Ford nearly missed it. He almost shoved his earpiece into his head to get a better sound. "Repeat?"

"You have company in the driveway."

"Anthony?" That didn't make sense. Pearce had him targeted. They were in a restaurant close by, with plenty of time for Pearce to provide a heads-up if Anthony started moving.

"Yes." Ellery's voice stayed small.

Ford wanted to yell. He fought to keep the calm in his voice. "Calling time."

Giving the modified abort signal grated against his nerves, but he had men all over the house. Any one of them could run right into Anthony of they weren't prepared. They would have heard the warning call, but he knew they wouldn't scatter unless he gave them the okay, so he did.

Looking around, Ford checked for signs anyone had been in the room. No leave-behinds and nothing out of place. He shifted around the door frame and mentally called up the blueprint of the house for the nearest quick exit. They had minutes to go on the alarm hack but that didn't mean he could find a door without Anthony standing in front of it.

Ford listened for the sound of the front door closing. For footsteps. He heard nothing.

In the hall, he moved fast enough to cover ground but not make noise. Keeping his back against the wall, he skipped the kitchen and any of the back exits and opted for the side exit next to the downstairs laundry room. Not to be confused with the upstairs laundry.

With one last glance down the long hallway behind him and the doorway to the office, he slipped around the corner and headed for the mudroom. Right as he reached the doorway a light flicked on, which meant Anthony was inside.

Motherfuucker.

Ford slid back into the dark hallway before Anthony spied him, but the guy was on the move. Any direction he headed out of the mudroom would put him face-to-face with Ford. No way could he allow that to happen.

Time for an alternate plan. The one where Anthony got hurt.

Ford pulled his cap low and listened to the click of Anthony's shoes against the tile. Closing in meant Ford had limited time to act. His fingers hit the edge of his karambit, and all of Reid's training on how to best use the blade came rushing back. Ford's breathing slowed as he prepared to fight.

This could be a bloody end. He would not hesitate.

Anthony rounded the corner with his attention focused on a piece of paper in his hand. Looked like the mail. Ford knew because he was close enough to reach out and grab it. He went for Anthony instead. He hit him, slamming him into the wall with his face smashed against it.

Pitching his voice low and gravely to hide his identity, Ford issued his first threat. One he'd carry through with if he had to. "One wrong move and you'll wish you hadn't."

The older man struggled. Even with fifty pounds on Ford, Ford won. He had the strength and age advantages. All those hours in the gym blessed him with more muscles than fat, unlike the man trapped between his chest and the wall.

Anthony threw his shoulders and tried to launch back and get in a head butt. "Who the hell are you?"

Ford decided right then if the guy gave him the "Do you know who I am?" speech, he might put a bullet in him just on principle.

"Don't move." Ford flashed his blade to highlight his point. He didn't have any intention of cutting the man. Just wanted to scare him. Ford knew from experience the sight of a knife often paralyzed people, even for the briefest of seconds. That was all the time he needed.

West liked to show off his sleeper hold, but Ford had a few moves of his own. He wrapped his left arm around Anthony's throat with the crook of his elbow right on his windpipe as he ignored the flailing and ducked out of striking range of Anthony's slapping hand. Ford's fingers touched the inside of his right arm and he pushed Anthony's head forward.

In five seconds the blood flow cut off and Anthony's body went limp. Ford guided the unmoving body to the floor and stood over him.

West walked up beside him and joined in the staring. "You used the Marine stranglehold on him. That's cool as shit."

"You Marines take credit for everything." He clapped West's shoulder then spoke over the open com. "Let's get out of here."

Ford waited until they got to the van parked two blocks away at the end of a cul-de-sac, and hidden amidst the construction equipment for a house teardown and rebuild, to let the fever in his head work its way into his brain. He stripped off the combat gear in case someone decided to look outside and get antsy. The rest of his team stood nearby, grumbling and restless. But at least they all got out.

No thanks to Alliance's famed consultant. "Where's Pearce?"

"Here with us," Ellery said.

"Someone explain," Ford said, the Bravo team listening in.

"Seems Anthony went to the bathroom and didn't come back to the table." A mass of voices sounded behind Ward, and he talked over them. "Ellery has pinpointed a call to Anthony's cell just before he got up and left."

The mole. Jesus, Ford hated this assignment.

"Why didn't Pearce warn us?" Ford asked. That was the million-dollar question and the one that required an immediate answer or West might just greet Pearce with a bullet the next time they saw each other.

There was a brief hesitation on the line that had the Bravo members staring at each other. Then Ward came on again. "He was too busy watching Harlan."

Heat burned through Ford. "What?"

And by that he really meant Harlan needed to be held down while they all took turns beating the shit out of him as they worked him over for answers. Ford didn't believe torture resulted in reliable intel, and he held loyalty among the team members as one of the highest required characteristics. When those two belief systems battled each other, loyalty always won, and it was beginning to sound as if Harlan had none.

"He walked into the restaurant while Pearce and Anthony were there, and Pearce admits it threw him off." Ward cleared his throat. "We'll talk it through when you guys get back. Rendezvous tomorrow morning."

No way was Ford letting this lie for twelve more hours. Harlan could make up all sorts of shit and cover his tracks by then. "No waiting. We do this tonight."

"Damn right," West mumbled.

"You heard Ward," Tasha said, breaking into the conversation. "Everyone stand down."

Fucking Brits.

23

SHAY GRABBED the underside of the headboard and threw her head back into the pillow. Ford had been home for a half hour and already stripped her naked and crawled between her thighs. Energy pulsed off him, as if he were wired with a shot of adrenaline.

He spread her legs wider and kissed his way over her soft skin to the very heat of her. He licked, and a finger pressed deep inside her and her body grew wet with each touch. Her nerve endings already sensitive from the loving attention seemed to fire and spark.

Ignoring the way her hips arched off the bed and her thighs clamped against the sides of his head, she fought for control. Tried to hold off the orgasm and concentrate on the heady sensations battering her. But her internal muscles kept clenching and the pleading hovered right there on her tongue.

"Ford, do it now." She moved her leg.

He used his palm to pin it to the bed. "Almost."

But he kept up his sensual torture. His tongue. His fingers. He stretched her and prepped her until sweat formed between her breasts and her head lolled from side to side.

To get him to listen, she slipped her fingers into his hair and lifted his head. Looking down her body, seeing her softness and his dark hair right there, started a whirring deep within her. "I want you inside me."

Wetness covered his lips and his fingers kept drawing tiny circles over her clit. "Soon."

Much more and she'd lose it. She was two minutes away from passing out from pleasure. She hadn't known that was even possible until the first orgasm ripped through her. She headed straight for the second one right now at maximum speed.

Needing to move, to ease the tightening inside her, she drew her knees toward her chest. The shift opened her even wider and he added a second finger inside her.

"You are right on the edge." His voice was filled with awe and his focus never wavered from her body. He kept up a constant stream of touching and kissing.

But if he kissed there one more time her insides would flip and land outside. "Payback is hell, Ford."

She managed to pant out the sentence. Just when she decided he planned to ignore her and drive her insane forever, he moved. On his elbows, he crawled up her body, stopping every few inches to land a kiss or brush a finger over her. By the time he took her nipple in his mouth, she couldn't hold still. She shifted her hips and clenched, trying to throw her body over the edge.

"Nu-uh." He lifted higher and stared down at her.

They were locked in a staring contest, with her unable to move, when she heard the telltale rip of paper. His hand slipped down his body and she knew he'd finally found the condom lying next to her shoulder.

It wouldn't take much to push her over, and when he

pushed inside her, slow and steady, her breath hissed out of her lungs. Her body went limp as he moved, pressing in and out, changing up the rhythm and shifting his hips from side to side until it felt like every muscle and every cell inside her would break apart.

Her hunger for him raged like an angry beast. She grabbed for him, trailed her hands over him. Her legs held him tight inside her even as her heels dug into the back of his thighs. The lovemaking was sweaty and wild. They rolled over the sheets and knocked the pillows to the floor.

When she finally wrapped her arms around him and forced his body to plunge one last time into hers, everything inside her let go. She lifted her head to scream but the sound came out as a gasp. The orgasm raced through her and rattled her bones, bringing a wave of exhaustion right behind.

She stayed in a sprawl across the mattress. Her breathing, her heart, if anything still worked she didn't know.

As the strength of the pulses died down to tiny blissful aftershocks, his shifting inside of her sped up. The thrusting moved the bed and the final push smacked the headboard against the wall. He moaned and whispered her name through it all and then collapsed on top of her.

With all movement stopped, quiet washed over them. She closed her eyes as she ran her fingertips across his shoulders. His weight on her felt good. Anchored her. She could sleep this way all night, and resigned to do just that.

She'd almost drifted off when he finally lifted his

head and brushed her hair off her face. His sexy grin said he'd brought her to the edge just like he wanted.

He kissed her nose. "Hi."

"Welcome home."

More than an hour later Shay lay on her side and watched the minutes tick by on her alarm clock. The lovemaking had exhausted her, and Ford's warm body pressed against her back lulled her into a state of relaxation, but her eyes refused to close. Every time she drifted off, the memory of her cousin and his disheveled appearance flickered through her brain.

Trent said he'd get back in touch with her. Two days had passed and she'd collected as much cash as she could and still be able to pay her bills . . . still, nothing. No word or check-in. She started to worry he was as unstable as she feared, and it bothered her that she'd failed to hold him there and get him help. He could be anywhere, doing anything, as the paranoia took hold.

Ford's arms tightened around her waist. "Why aren't you sleeping?"

The words rumbled against the back of her head as he nuzzled her hair with his nose. Surrounded by him, she slid her legs, tucking them, and warmed her feet on his calves.

He brought her back tighter against his chest. "I'm serious, what's up?"

Maybe it was the concern in his voice or the way his hand spanned her stomach, making her feel protected. Whatever the combination, the soft caresses and low voice, she didn't pretend to be asleep. But she did try to ease his concern. "You expect me to doze off after that lovemaking session?"

"I can barely keep my eyes open. You wrung me out, woman." He exhaled, blowing a breath into her hair.

"Blame yourself." The one thing sure to block out her desperate memories of Trent was the memory of Ford's touch. The way he ran his tongue over her and plunged into her. For a blissful hour he could make all the bad parts burn away.

He kissed her cheek. "You're thinking instead of relaxing."

"How can you tell?" She turned over because she wanted to see his face and run a finger over the sexy stubble on his cheek.

"Energy thrums through you. It's weird but I can feel it." His hand traveled over her bare stomach and stopped just under her breast. "This isn't still about your uncle and his poking around, is it?"

The reminder shut down her brain. "I don't want to talk about him."

"Okay."

The words hung there. Ford didn't push or demand. He leaned up on an elbow and watched her. His hand rubbed circles on her skin. She welcomed the lack of pressure and let it lure her in.

"Something happened." She dragged the back of her fingers over his collarbone, loving his hard body and every dip and muscle. In their rush to get into bed they had failed to turn on the light, but the sconce from the hallway made his skin glow and provided enough for her to make out his expressions.

"What?"

"Trent came to see me."

"When?" Ford's hand stopped moving and he pulled back. "Wait, he's back in town?"

"I don't think he ever left." Letting her arm drop back on the bed next to her head, she looked at the ceiling, concentrating on the seams where the crown molding met in each corner. "He was crazed, Ford. Talking about people being after him and needing money."

"He doesn't have money?"

She looked at Ford again. Took in the furrowed brow and obvious concern. Sharing the news and her fears lifted a weight off her, but she knew she'd shifted some of it to him. "I don't think Trent wants to touch his accounts. It was all so paranoid. Like, if he accessed his money he'd be tracked down."

"This doesn't sound like a love life problem."

That part didn't make any sense to her either. She needed to confront her uncle but she couldn't do that until she understood what was happening with Trent and tried to help him. She got that he might not want to go to his dad and hear Anthony spout off about what a failure he was, but the dynamic between father and son only added confusion to an already complex situation.

Maybe Ford could help her make sense of it. "Trent had no idea what I was talking about when I told him about the love life thing. My uncle clearly lied to me about Charlottesville and the young woman."

"Why?"

"Protecting Trent. Trying to keep me from worrying. Who knows." She thought back to what Anthony's assistant said and the concerns they'd shared. "My uncle seems to be running wild, like he's desperate and losing control. I think the lies were part of that."

"That's nuts."

One of the many crazy aspects of what seemed to be unraveling her usually somewhat stable family. "Something happened at work and he's running."

"Okay." Ford rubbed a hand over his forehead. "Where is Trent now?"

"I don't know. He said he'd contact me but he didn't." Just talked about it started that ball of anxiety in her stomach spinning again. "I collected as much cash as I could but—"

"Go back for a second." Ford leaned across her, brushing his body against hers, and clicked on the light on the bedside table. "Why are you collecting money?"

"He needs it."

Ford started shaking his head before she finished the sentence. "No. We need to get him help. It sounds like he's had some sort of mental break. Giving him money so he can race around is not the answer."

"I go back and forth. I thought if I could get him the money, then meet him and talk, this time without him attacking me—"

Ford sat up, taking the sheet with him. "What?"

"It was fine." She made a grab for the edge of the covers, but he'd shoved them aside and now they were draped low on his hips and over hers. Being naked in front of him didn't shake her. He'd seen her and she didn't shy away from sharing her body with him. But she already felt exposed and vulnerable. The sheet gave her some shield, even if it was an illusion. His eyes burned with intensity. "What did he do to you?"

All of his anger centered on Trent. She got that, but seeing the burning fury, hearing Ford's voice vibrate with anger, shocked her. Strangely, it also comforted her, because all that protectiveness was meant for her. Not in a suffocating way like her uncle. In a way that told her Ford would keep her safe no matter what.

That comfort allowed her to spill the rest. "Trent lured me into one of the units and scared the crap out of me, but that's just because I wasn't expecting to see him."

"The plumbing problem the other day. That was him?"

"Yes."

Ford swore under his breath. "Why didn't you tell me then?"

She shimmied until she sat up with her back resting against the pillows. His palm rested on her thigh and his shoulder touched hers. For all the crazy family stuff, Ford wasn't running. That meant something.

"He was lost and scared, Ford. I'd never seen him that way and didn't know what to do."

"We'll meet him. Together."

Temptation pulled at her to accept the offer but she instinctively knew it wouldn't work. "No, he'll bolt."

Ford's expression tightened. "Shay . . ."

He was worried about her. It was sweet and caring, but misplaced. Trent had lost his way and some demon hounded him, but he would not hurt her. She had to believe that.

They were practically raised as siblings. She'd put her body in front of his when Anthony's demands got to be too much. They had a bond. It strained as they got older, but she trusted it still existed. He wouldn't have come to her otherwise.

She took Ford's hand in hers. "You have to let me do this my way."

His gaze traveled over her face. Whatever he saw must have changed his mind because the tension eased out of his shoulders and he exhaled in a way that said *I'm going to regret this.*

"Fine." That's all he said. One word.

She didn't debate but she did reach over to kiss him. And ended up hugging air. He got up and slipped on his jeans, not bothering with underwear or the zipper.

Seeing him walk toward the door sent her heart on a hammering rampage in her chest. "Where are you going?"

Without turning around he held up a finger and kept moving. "I'll be right back."

His shadowed figure disappeared down the hallway. Minutes ticked by and she scooted to the edge of the bed with the abandoned sheet wrapped around her. She was just about to get up when the alarm chirped and footsteps echoed in the hall.

He walked right over to her and handed her a brown envelope. "Here."

Afraid to touch it, she stared at it instead. "What's this?"

"Cash."

She held up both hands, not wanting to touch it or entertain the offer, whatever it was. "I can't—"

He sat down next to her and wrapped her fingers around the envelope. "I'm not asking what you had to do to gather the cash or why Trent came to you instead of his rich father. I'm not even insisting you stay away from him or bring me along, which I really want to do because I need to know you're safe—"

"He'd never hurt me."

"—but if you're not going to let me help any other way, you are going to let me do this." Ford nodded at the thick package in her hands. "It's about a thousand dollars, and maybe if he sees you have it, he'll trust you enough to come back here with you."

"I can't take your money." She tried to push it over to him but Ford held her hands still.

"I'm not giving you a choice."

She looked at his face, then down to the brown package on her lap. The gesture didn't solve everything but it relieved some of her anxiety.

Made her love him even more.

She nodded. "Thank you."

His hand went to the back of her neck and treated her to a gentle massage. "I'm pissed off about this, Shay. About him and about you being dragged into the middle of it all."

Tears pushed against the back of her eyes. She wasn't a crier but the lump in her throat got stuck there and she teetered on the verge of losing it. "He's family."

"You keep saying that, but do you notice how much life your family is sucking out of you right now?"

She couldn't deny it. For years they had the usual family squabbles. She wrestled with the best way to deal with Anthony, on how to love him and not want to strangle him. But a shift started when Trent took the government job, and the last few months something changed and Trent's personality changed along with it. They'd been off-kilter ever since.

Right now Ford provided the solid ground. She put the envelope to the side on the bed and leaned into him. "Then it's good I have you."

He dropped a quick kiss on her mouth as his arm wrapped around her. "I'm still pissed."

She pushed him down on the mattress and hovered over him. "Then let's redirect some of that energy into something fun."

He flipped her over. "I like the way you think."

24

Ward hated this part of the job. Turning on one of his own. He still didn't believe Harlan could sell them all out, but there he stood, indignant and nonresponsive in the small conference room they used for the rare interrogation that took place at the Warehouse.

This was the second time they'd put the space into action. First with Matt and now Harlan. Both instances left Ward feeling hollow and disappointed. When the people tasked with serving and protecting turned, no one was safe.

Tasha sat at the desk with one leg crossed over the other, looking every bit the in-charge professional she was. Ward tried to block her and his knowledge that Josiah and Ford waited just outside, watching.

Refusing to sit down and concede the upper hand in any way, Ward stood across from Harlan. "This isn't adding up."

"You were keeping me in the dark. I didn't have a choice." With his hands linked behind him, almost as if standing at attention, Harlan didn't move.

Not a surprise since the man dedicated his life to the clandestine service. He knew how to hold his body and not give anything away. He didn't fidget or stammer. He spoke in his usual clear, calm voice with his accent highlighting his upper crust upbringing and his disdain obvious in his expression.

They'd gotten along fine from the beginning. Ward knew Harlan's exacting style worked on the nerves of some of the more wild among the Alliance bunch, but Ward got it. Harlan had been trained a particular way and led a very successful career. Seeing strange T-shirts and hearing takedowns joked about in the Warehouse turned Harlan off.

Not Ward. He knew the guys liked to blow off steam. Problem was, Harlan never did. Never wavered in who he was, which made the idea of him being a traitor of some sort all the more ridiculous.

"You could have come to me," Tasha said.

Harlan's eyes narrowed a fraction. "Would it have done any good? After all, you're sleeping with him."

Something screeched in Ward's brain. "Be fucking careful there, Harlan."

Ward had a high tolerance for nonsense and joking around. He had zero tolerance for anyone taking a shot at Tasha. Neither did she, which made him wonder how many seconds would tick by before she flew out of that chair and knocked Harlan into the wall. If he didn't change topics fast, that attack would come. No question.

"Ford and I don't agree on much but we both know there's an internal problem at work here," Harlan said as he verbally pivoted. "Someone is leaking intel on our operations. We are getting beaten at every turn."

Tasha drummed her fingernails on the top of the

oversized desk in front of her. "You understand that by showing up in the restaurant that spotlight shines on you, right?"

"You can't believe that."

Ward expected some reaction but Harlan just stood there. He didn't even blink.

The need to push, to knock some of the practiced cool out of his contemporary, battered Ward. "Why did you go?"

"Anthony is under suspicion and his travels are being traced. I saw him with Pearce and investigated. I didn't see a reason to call in the team just yet, which brings me back to my point about had I known there was an operation under way, I would have backed off." Harlan tipped his head to the side. "I'm actually surprised Pearce saw me."

Cryptic. Ward knew the pieces Harland left out were the ones that mattered. Now he needed to fill in those blanks. "That's the part I don't get. You just happened to see them at dinner?"

Tasha stopped tapping and rested her palm against the table. "He's been following Pearce."

It took a second for the words to register in Ward's brain. When they did, a well of rage burned through him. "Are you kidding?"

"No joke. I am," Harlan said.

A new sensation settled in Ward's chest. He glanced at Tasha. "Is that part of an op *I* don't know about?"

"No, but it fits. Harlan having a hunch and checking it out on his own." Tasha's eyebrow lifted. "Like as payback for us keeping him in the dark. Am I right?"

"Search anything, I don't care. This is about the team

and the job. My private life is open." Harlan looked
from Tasha to Ward. "I'm not sure everyone who works
here can say that."

Ward ignored the shot. "There's nothing in Pearce's
background that points to a problem."

"Is there anything in mine?"

Ward couldn't argue with that logic. Which pissed
him off. "What would he gain?"

"What would I gain?" When Ward started to reply,
Harlan held up a hand and shook his head. "Look, we
can do this all day, but the fact is we're not one step
closer to locking this down and ferreting out the traitor."

Tasha seemed to size Harlan up as her gaze wandered over him. "That's a big word."

"What would you call someone who almost got Ford
and West blown up?"

With a nod to Tasha, Ward left the room. He got two
steps into the hallway before Josiah and Ford closed in.

Knowing the answer and wanting it on the unofficial
record between them, Ward turned to Ford. "What do
you think?"

He shrugged. "It could be anyone who works here.
A random person in Liberty Crossing or anywhere in
the intelligence community."

"That's not the response I expected from you." Not
even close. Ford had been banging on the Harlan-is-
the-problem drum almost from the beginning of Alliance's existence.

"Where's Pearce?" Josiah asked.

"We're about to question him." The Warehouse had
turned into a damn hotel for suspected moles these
days. The idea and the safety issues involved with

keeping cleared operatives penned in had Ward sleeping in his office even as he preferred to walk out and not come back.

Josiah didn't let it drop. "So, you do or don't think it's Harlan?"

"I'm not sure yet."

Josiah hummed. "His actions are suspicious."

"We might be able to get a handle on this in a few hours." Ford slipped a small handheld out of his back pocket. It looked like a small cell phone but was really a GPS unit.

"How?"

"The tracker I put in the envelope for Shay is moving." Ford flipped the screen around for Josiah and Ward to see. "She wouldn't need to carry it around unless she got the message to meet Trent."

That explained the stark look in Ford's eyes and the way his skin pulled taut over his cheekbones. He'd tagged her. Her and the money. It was the right call and something Harlan pushed to happen sooner, but now that they knew Trent lurked around town and wanted his cousin's attention, Ford had no choice. She might not be in on it but she was a pawn and everyone was using her, which mean Ford had to as well.

"I don't like this," Josiah said. "Why would a guy holding a billion dollars worth of deadly toxin, someone holding an auction, be scrounging around for cash?"

"Good question." One that Ward couldn't answer no matter how he tried.

"Maybe this is all a ploy." Josiah shot a quick side glance in Ford's direction. "I'm not pointing the finger at Shay, but something doesn't smell right here."

Ford didn't react. He acted as if he were locked in stone. Not even the thought of going after Harlan cheered him up.

No doubt about it. The guy had it bad for Shay. Ward knew how it felt to fall that hard, and didn't envy his friend the days ahead at all. "Be careful, and we'll hold these two here. No communication with the outside world until you track Trent down."

"Done." Not waiting for more, Ford nodded and left as if he wanted to get the whole assignment over as quickly as possible.

Ward didn't blame him one bit.

Trent's note said to meet him at the place where he got lost as a kid. That meant the National Air and Space Museum on the Mall downtown. She'd been babysitting him after school that afternoon all those years ago. He'd insisted on going to see the space shuttle. Pitched a fit like the type only a kid could do.

She'd wanted to stay home on the phone with her friends. She settled for the cell and the museum at the same time. One second of not paying attention and he'd disappeared. She could still hear him begging the security guard not to call his dad when they finally did find him in a back hall that was restricted to anyone but employees.

Today Shay sat in the reclining planetarium seat and stared up and at the scene above her. Open space and a smattering of stars. The narrator talked about the attempts we'd made to figure out if we were alone in the universe. She'd seen the presentation probably twenty times but the words hit home in a new way today.

She touched the envelope in her cardigan pocket. She'd been moving it around for the last hour. From her purse to the pocket to holding it in a death grip. At every sound, she jumped. Whenever a man approached her, she tensed.

Yeah, this had to end. She had to convince Trent to come home with her. She'd call Ford for help and she knew he'd step in.

"Shay." Trent said her name as a whisper as he slid onto the seat beside her.

The touch of his hand against her arm had her jumping. She bit back a scream just in time. Getting her heart to slow down to non-heart-attack levels took a little longer and a few deep breaths.

"Are you okay?" She tried to assess his expression but the room was dark. She saw a shadow and his blue shirt.

"Do you have the money?" The jitteriness came back in the way he shifted in his chair and kept looking around as if expecting to be attacked from behind.

"Trent, please. We need to talk." She put a hand on his knee.

He knocked it away. "Give it to me."

"No, I—"

"Fuck." He got up and stormed off.

Panic surged through Shay as she rushed after him. She heard angry mumbling in the dark planetarium when she hit the bar across the door and light poured in as she opened it. Unable to stop her momentum, she ran and hit the landing of the second floor before skidding to a halt.

Looking around, she went to the ledge and scanned

the main exhibit area below. A mass of people moved around her. Schoolkids and tourists dragging coats, people winding their way around rockets and planes. She targeted that blue shirt and the familiar profile, spying him as he jumped off the bottom step and pushed his way to the opposite side of the floor.

She ran down after him, taking two steps at a time and grabbing onto the banister for balance when her ankle overturned. Her hands held the envelope in her pocket so it didn't bounce out and her purse bobbed against her shoulder. It was an awkward sprint made worse when she called out his name and people turned to stare.

By the time she got down the steps the sea of people had closed in around her as they shifted in unison to the far sides of the room. Everyone pushed and tried to get by. She stood there, spinning in a circle while she looked for any sign of Trent.

She'd been in the position before, desperate to find him and convinced he was in danger. It was no less intense with Trent being a grown-up. His decisions had bigger consequences now. And his panicked escape from the planetarium only confirmed her worst fear that he'd gone over the edge.

She felt a tug, her cardigan yanked, and she grabbed for the envelope, sure in the chaos someone would take the money. While she looked down, the crowd seemed to part. She thought to shift out of the way when a rough hand slammed around her neck. The envelope slipped out of her hands and she slapped and tried to lunge and steal it back when the grip tightened.

"Stay calm." Locked in a vicelike hold, Trent's voice

filled her head. Gone was the nervous edge to his tone.
He sounded in control and dangerous.

A woman looked over then grabbed her young son
back. People nearby shifted away as well. Shay could
see confusion and then terror in the faces as they
watched her get manhandled and didn't know what was
happening. Hell, she didn't understand it either.

She grabbed at Trent's arm and tried to turn around
to look at him but his hold locked her in position.
"What are you doing?"

"That's enough, Shay."

"Trent, please." None of it made sense. This was
about giving him money but now he held her so tight
she had to scratch onto his forearm to keep him from
crushing her windpipe.

She moved her head to the side, trying to catch some
air, but her lungs refused to fill. "You're hurting me."

"You're my insurance."

The comment could have been in another language.
Her brain rushed to keep up but nothing unfolding now
fit with how she thought this meeting would go or who
her cousin was. His actions revved up the panic in the
crowd as more and more people saw her being held to
match the mass swirling inside of her.

She tried to focus and struggled to find the right
words. She thought she could reason Trent out of this
until she saw the man in a plaid shirt coming toward
them with a gun in his hand. No badge or uniform.
He looked like the average museum visitor only bigger,
with shoulders broad enough to knock against a door
frame and an expression that said he would unload that
weapon and not lose a minute of sleep.

Terror ripped through her as an alarm wailed and security filed into the building. Museum patrons were running now and many screamed. Noises clashed, and she tried to separate them out and analyze them over the sound of Trent's heavy breathing in her ear.

When she opened her mouth to try to calm him down, he dragged her backward. A squeak left her throat. Her sneakers scraped against the floor as she tried to stay on her feet. She stumbled but the headlock kept her upright as she coughed and wheezed.

When a second gunman appeared, her vision blurred. Fear knocked the breath out of her and her stomach rolled. All that nonsense about being hunted . . . Trent was right. These men with intensity bouncing off them wanted him and would go through her to get him.

Her head spun and the room began to tilt. "Who are they?"

"They want me dead," Trent said in a harsh whisper loud enough for the two gunmen and the few security guards scattered around to hear.

The uniformed guards weren't taking down the gunmen dressed in casual clothes. They acted as if the men in street clothes ran the show. When that registered, her mind began spinning again.

Flashing lights from police cars parked outside reflected through the museum windows. A crowd had gathered outside and she could see a helicopter flying low and close to the building. Everyone watching and covering Trent, clearly fingering him as the attacker in this scenario.

The pieces didn't fit. She mentally put it all together but no answer made sense. "These men—"

"The people setting me up," Trent said. "The ones saying I stole the toxin."

He'd asked her for money. Now there was talk of a toxin. Terror was too passive. A word didn't exist to describe her alternating waves of bone-shaking fear and rabid nausea.

She forced a few more words out as the blood drained from her head. "I don't know what you're talking about or what's happening."

"There's no way out, Trent." One of the casually dressed gunmen stepped forward. The slimmer one who looked no less lethal than the bigger one. "Let the woman go."

"No way!" Trent screamed.

Her ears rang and she tried to make eye contact with the gunman, get some clue what was going on. They both stayed focused on her cousin. "Trent, I—".

He shook her. "Stop talking."

"You don't want to hurt her," the bigger gunman said.

She saw something out of the corner of her eye. A gun. Trent held a weapon and was aiming it at her. No sooner did she realize it than the barrel pressed against her skull. "No, please."

"Let me get out of here," Trent shouted.

The big one shook his head. "Not going to happen."

People talked about what moved through their heads in the final moments. Flashes. Memories. She saw darkness and felt a paralyzing sadness at never seeing Ford again. Every thought went to him and what could have been.

Trent shifted behind her. His hold loosened and

she thought he was going to turn himself in. Then the bigger gunmen's eyes went wide and one held up a hand. "Trent, don't do it."

She tried to turn around to see what was happening behind her. One move and her brain exploded. A shock of pain vibrated through her and her knees buckled. She tried to draw in a deep breath as the world went black.

25

Ford ached to put the kid down. One bullet to the forehead. Trent would drop and Alliance could rush in and grab Shay. Get her out of there and to safety.

Seeing panic race across her face almost did Ford in. Even with an obstructed view, it heightened his rage. Sent it spiking.

They'd entered the museum dressed as tourists, with weapons hidden and the guards on alert. While Shay and then Trent went into the planetarium, Bravo assisted the guards in quietly moving people out of the way.

Evacuating without an announcement proved tough, and some people refused to leave their spots in line for exhibits. It was a frustrating exercise that fell apart when Trent bolted from the upstairs room and ran down the steps. Ford ordered West to "Take the shot" and repeated the mantra until the older couple standing next to him rushed out of the museum. West couldn't get a clear look, not with all the people shuffling around.

After that Ford had made the call to execute the takedown, weapons up and a kill order approved. One sight of Shay at the top of the stairs sent him racing around the side and giving West the go ahead to move in. Reid and West approached while Lucas blocked the exit Trent had been headed for.

It all worked, tense and a bit off script, but they headed for a quick end until Trent spotted the weapons and grabbed Shay. The public scene turned into pandemonium. Maybe that was Trent's goal from the start. Meet in a place where collaterals literally lined the wall.

People yelled and ran in every direction. The guards had their hands full with crowd control. That worked for Ford. It meant no one would try to be a hero and end up getting them all killed.

"Take the shot?" West asked over the internal com, his voice steady in the middle of the chaos.

Ford saw Trent's gun pointed at the back of Shay's head and calculated the chance of Trent getting a shot off before West could take him down. The chances of her getting caught in the cross fire were remote, but Ford couldn't tolerate even a possibility.

"Negative."

Reid's gaze shot to Ford and he backed up the order with a shake of his head. Being trained, they didn't question or balk. Ford issued a command and trusted them to follow. They didn't let him down.

As Ford watched, West moved in with Reid by his side. They exchanged words with Trent and it looked as if he might surrender. His grip around Shay's neck eased. Ford could tell by the way her body relaxed.

Shay hadn't seen him yet because he stood off to the side. All of her attention seemed focused on not being choked to death and on West coming toward her.

"Careful," Ford whispered as he approached Trent

from behind, twenty feet away. If Shay saw him now, he would have to deal with it. Cover or not, he needed to be in there. From this vantage point he had a shot, but keeping her alive was his priority.

Her anger he could handle. Her death he couldn't.

West acknowledged Ford's series of hold orders with a slight movement of his head. To anyone else, the gesture would have passed unnoticed. Ford knew it meant that West had heard him.

In the middle of all the gestures and sharp phrases, Trent's attention shifted to West's feet, as if assessing the distance between them and his chances of survival. Whatever he saw had him moving. With a quick smack, and before they could rush him, Trent hit Shay with the gun he held and dragged her falling body tight against him.

Ford's breath pounded in his chest and his knees went weak. He hadn't been prepared for Trent to sacrifice Shay—he hadn't telegraphed the attack. But there was no play for Trent here, nowhere for him to run, and he'd just added dead weight.

Bad decision or not, a killing rage moved through Ford. Seeing her body turn boneless hit him in the gut and he almost doubled over.

This little shit was going to die today.

With Shay out cold and a dribble of blood dripping from her hairline, Ford stepped into Trent's line of sight. He raised his gun and kept his finger on the trigger as he fought back the need to open fire. "Time for this to end, Trent. There is nowhere for you to go."

Trent's gaze stopped darting as he tightened his grip around on Shay's chest now. "The boyfriend."

Well, wasn't that just fucking great? The kid knew the players in the game.

Mole's existence confirmed.

Trent held Shay with one arm while reaching into his pocket with the other hand. "Nobody do anything stupid for a second because you will regret it."

Without taking his eyes off Trent, Ford nodded, knowing West would see the signal and fire as soon as Trent's hand cleared the pocket.

"You're in charge, right?" Trent lost some of his swagger as he looked to Ford, his words tumbling over each other. "Well, don't you forget I have this."

That fast Ford raised his fist and silently called a halt to the order to neutralize. They had a new problem. One deadlier than a bullet.

Even from a distance Ford could make out the object in Trent's hand. The vial was small. It could have held anything, but Ford wasn't taking a chance. Six vials of the deadly toxin were missing. It had taken Matt Claymore days to cough up that information and until that morning to admit he'd helped Trent walk out of the lab that day.

Ford had been right. All it took was fifteen minutes of West hovering over Matt, making threats and landing a few punches, to get him to open up. At heart Matt was a desk junkie and no match for West's fists or Ford's calls to keep hitting.

If this was one of the toxin vials and the kid used it, everyone in the building and outside—even those walking by and possibly those passing in cars—would die an agonizing and inevitable death before one minute passed to the next. That was the line on this supertoxin. It made sarin look like soy milk.

"What's your plan, Trent?" Ford walked around until he faced the kid head on, with Reid and West off to each side and slightly behind.

A couple more feet and Ford could reach out and snag Shay out of Trent's arms. Then it was open season on Trent. Bullets would fly and Ford would dive for the vial. They'd practiced so many scenarios, and while that wasn't one, his boys could improvise.

The arm wrapped around Shay held the gun. The vial sat in his other palm. Trent juggled it all. A lot of scary shit depended on him not falling or getting stupid or deciding the only way out was in a giant fireball of pain.

Trent shook his head. "One more step and I'll shoot her."

Even hearing the words ripped Ford wide open. He expected to see blood pour out of him. "She's your cousin."

"She's expendable." Monotone and cold. If there was anything human happening inside this kid, he hid it well.

In the background, the loudspeaker played an emergency message on an endless loop and the alarm continued to whine. Ford talked over the noise. "You want to die today, Trent?"

Because he would oblige. West and Reid looked ready to step in and assist. None of them relished killing but it was inevitable in their job. And right now, judging from the palpable fury aimed in Trent's direction, they all hated him more than the burden they'd carry for putting him in the ground.

"I'm not going in or being questioned or whatever you have in mind." Trent put his cheek next to Shay's.

"And I'm betting her life and yours that you're going to let me walk out of here."

"Wrong."

Trent smiled. "Not even for her? I hear you like her. More than you should."

A red-hot flush of anger crept over Ford. The mole had spilled it all. Trent knew about the cover and Shay's role, yet he'd dragged her deeper into his mess.

Fucking bastard.

"Last time. Put the woman down." West issued the order as he drew up even with Ford. His tone suggested he'd take them both out if that's what had to happen to end this sick game.

"I said no." Shay's head bobbed and fell forward as Trent pulled her back and used her limp form like a shield. "Tell your guy behind me to come around where I can see him, and clear this room."

For a second no one moved. If it weren't for the vial, Ford would have given the signal for a shot to the back of Trent's head. Lucas was in position and had Trent in his sights. Even now Ford watched him aim.

Trent shook the vial. "You should know, this isn't the only one I have. It's the one you can see, but anyone touches me and the others get released."

Ford knew Trent meant to scare him. The threat did the opposite. The more Trent talked, the more crucial information he gave away. Ford's mind clicked as he changed strategies. If he played this right, he'd pick up all the pieces because Trent, with his ego and obvious strain of narcissism, would show off and eventually give away just the right detail. Then he and Bravo could rush in and bring the whole network behind the auction down.

"Stand down." Ford barely made a sound as he spoke, and almost wanted to call it back when he saw the look of satisfaction cross Trent's face. But he gave the call for the guards to file out, and cleared the large open room of anyone except Alliance members.

The police argued back. Voices debated jurisdiction. It all whirled around him until he dropped Tasha's name.

"No one takes any action without my okay." He cut off the com before anyone could talk back, and stared Trent down. "Done."

There, let the weasel think he'd won.

"Call your other guy out here," Trent said, giving orders as if he were still in charge.

Ford nodded but didn't say a word. The gesture was enough to bring Lucas skimming along the side of the group.

Trent spared him a quick glance. "There you are." His focus switched back to Ford. "Now, unless you want all these people to die, I'd move your men back."

"No go." Ford's response was as much an answer to Trent as a command for his team.

Trent stared at the vial, pretending to study it. "All I have to do is crush it in my hand and we're all done. And that's only the beginning of what will happen to this town. To the East Coast."

Looked like they had moved into the uncontrollable ego portion of the program. Ford doubted reason would work with Trent's type, but maybe appealing to his mercurial side would have an impact. "You do this, then you don't get to collect all that money you want."

"Maybe this isn't for money."

Ford followed the comment through to its end. If Trent wasn't looking for a fast payday, that left only devastating options. That made him either a true believer or a nutcase. Ford knew you couldn't effectively negotiate with either.

"What do you want?"

"I'm going to leave here and you get to keep Shay." Trent glanced down at her. "Though I doubt she'll keep sleeping with you once she knows you've been using her."

Ford blocked the words. Stayed on task. "Like you."

"I asked her to bring money and she did." Trent tapped the top of the envelope sticking out of his pocket. "We're family."

That would be too easy. Ford almost smiled. He loved when a spur of the moment plan came together. And he made a mental note to remind his team of the benefits of using a simple tracker.

"You're a sick fuck." West's comment started with a growl and turned into a low, cool grumble.

"I'm going to walk right out that door." Trent nodded behind him, toward the main exit.

The dumb shit only had to turn his head and look out the window to see the people crowded around out there and the yellow police tape holding more back. Ford had to fight off the urge to shoot him as a public service. "There are cops everywhere."

"And they are going to part and let me pass."

Ford wondered if Trent battled delusions as well as his massive ego. "No way."

"You get to keep the vial I have on me, but know if I don't walk out of here in the next two minutes, my partner will release another one and keep doing it until I'm free."

Now all Ford had to do was flush out that partner. More than likely that would answer the mole question as well. "You're going to run out of toxin eventually."

"Is that what Matt Claymore told you? That I had a finite amount?" Trent held the vial with two fingers now. "I created this and I have access to all I want."

Looked to Ford like he hadn't let West hit Matt nearly hard enough. The guy held back intel? Ford vowed to fix that as soon as he had Shay.

"Let me shoot him," West said.

Trent's attention shot to the men next to Ford. "You do and the first ten thousand deaths—including yours and your friends here—will be on your head."

Ford had reached the end of his patience on hearing Trent ramble. "Let her go."

"Not until I'm out the door."

With the tracker. "Fine."

Reid eased his aim and broke attention. "Ford?"

Ford had one card and it looked like he'd need to play it and fill in his team afterward. Maybe give Trent enough space to trip him up. Ford could handle that so long as Shay was all right. "Our choices are limited."

"It's nice to see Shay is dating a smart guy," Trent said. "A shame it's not real."

West snorted. "You sure do like to talk."

"I'll take you two as bodyguards." Trent gestured toward Lucas and West.

Forcing his hand to move, Ford opened the com. "He's coming out. Let him go."

"I have a ride."

Even better. Once away, Trent would celebrate his "win" and not be prepared when the attack came.

Reid shook his head. "Of course you do."

Ford barely heard the back and forth over the yelling in his ear over the com. Everyone had an opinion, and all of them seemed to think he was an idiot. He could live with that because he had a plan. One that maximized their chances of ending all of this—mole, auction, and toxin—in one jump.

He focused on Ward's voice. "Trust me."

"Any move and we're all dead." Trent nodded at Lucas to take the lead. Never turning his back on West, Trent shot Ford a quick look. "Nice meeting you."

Plan or not, bile churned in Ford's stomach as he watched Trent drag Shay out. She had protection in the form of two of Bravo's best men, but seeing anyone but him touch her was starting to piss Ford off.

Surrounded by Lucas and West, Trent hit the open air. Ford wanted to rush in and grab her. They disappeared down the sidewalk to a waiting cab.

Reid grabbed Ford's arm. "What the fuck was that?"

"Necessary."

This time Reid stepped in front of Ford, breaking his view of the action on the sidewalk. "I know you care about her, but—"

"The tracker is still in the envelope, right on one of the bills." It was the final play. He could lead them right to his partner. To someone other than Matt. They had minutes only, but they needed all of the vials and whatever else Trent had in storage. One vial didn't get the job done.

"So?"

Ford looked at Reid. "The envelope is on Trent."

"I'll be damned. You baited him."

Ford tapped his watch and the small screen with the green dot. The dot that followed Trent's every move. "We all need to be ready. When he stops, we grab him."

Reid smiled then. "I guess that's why you're in charge."

26

THE SIDE of Shay's head ached. She reached back and touched a hand to the spot where the pain radiated. Her fingertips skimmed over the cotton bandage and she winced. The shot fired next to her ear had rattled her teeth and shook her brain.

When she woke up in the ambulance, medics asked her questions and Ford appeared out of nowhere, his face drawn and pain in his eyes. She remembered grabbing his hand and answering. Everything else was a blur.

Not everything. She remembered Trent. He ran, he grabbed her. Gunmen closed in. She rubbed her forehead and tried to clear out the last of the cobwebs.

The gunmen. Every time she closed her eyes she saw them. She'd repeated the story about how they walked right up to Trent. She stopped every law enforcement person but no one appeared concerned that there might be trained killers on the loose.

The pain in her head had kept her from jumping around and demanding attention. She'd said Trent's name over and over and was assured "it would be handled" . . . whatever that meant.

Even now, she sat on the edge of her couch and

tried to rally enough energy to get up and turn on the news. Some lifeline to what happened after she passed out. The pieces she did have didn't make sense. Trent seemed to be making the story up as he went, and when he hit her . . . she couldn't make that work in her mind.

She should also call Anthony but her cell had gone missing and Ford said something about her uncle being questioned. It all ran together until she wondered what was real. If it hadn't been for the blood on her shirt, she would have chalked the whole afternoon up to a terrible dream and crawled back into bed.

"Here's your tea." Ford appeared in front of her with a steaming mug.

Rock solid. That's how she would describe him. He'd worn a permanent frown since pulling her out of the ambulance. Even now he sat on the edge of the coffee table in front of her and watched her as if she might disappear if he blinked.

She had so many questions and knew he had to have even more inside him fighting to get out. Instead of interrogating, he just sat. He rubbed a hand over her knee as she gripped the mug with both hands, letting the warmth seep into her chilled bones.

He gave her thigh a squeeze and let his hand drop. "You should crawl into bed."

That meant giving in and not seeking answers. Even though her eyelids drooped and she'd bet she could curl up on the table and fall dead asleep, there were still too many unanswered questions.

And her family was scattered and in trouble. "Trent—"

"Not tonight, Shay."

It was the right answer. Her thoughts were too

scrambled to make sense. Even the police gave her a pass and told her to come in tomorrow. She didn't know if she should be afraid of Trent or the gunmen. Tears welled in her eyes and she fought to hold them in.

"Hey." Ford switched to the couch beside her and lifted the mug out of her hands. With his arms wrapped around her, he dragged her back against the couch cushions with a gentle rocking motion. "Your uncle will come over tomorrow. He's trying to help locate Trent right now."

A memory rushed through her brain and she grabbed a fistful of Ford's T-shirt in her hands. If she held onto him, he couldn't disappear like everyone else in her life. "The money."

"I don't care about the money." He kissed her cheek and lowered her head to his shoulder. "I care about you."

Snuggling into his arms and letting him chase the demons away felt right. She wanted to burrow deeper into his shirt and close her eyes. Not let the real world close in, even though she knew it knocked and scratched to get to her.

"He insisted the gunmen set him up." For some reason that excuse popped into her brain. Turned it around in her head and realized it didn't quite make sense.

"You said he mentioned a toxin."

And that was the bigger shock. For days she'd heard about a love affair gone wrong. Then she thought about how hard he worked and how much pressure he put on himself. She figured he was strung out and needed a break. That maybe his mind cracked and time away would help him heal. None of that centered on a toxin.

The need to know more kept stirring. "Is it all over the news?"

Ford ran a hand over her hair and pressed soft kisses around the edge of her bandage. "We're not going to find out."

She debated arguing until exhaustion pushed through her in a final wave that made it hard for her to even hold up her head. She decided to fight that battle tomorrow and aim for a much smaller victory. "Did you find my phone?"

"It's over at my place." He threw her a wince. "I admit I took it because I didn't want you reading the headlines."

"Trent could get in touch with me."

Ford's face fell again. "I don't think he's that dumb."

Trent was anything but, and Ford knew that because she'd told him. Once again her mind went blank when she needed it to reboot. "What does that mean?"

Ford stood up and held out a hand to her. "You need a shower and bed."

"What will you be doing?" So tempting to make a suggestion. He stood there in his usual jeans and black long-sleeve shirt. Attraction sparked then fizzled again. She wasn't sure she had the strength to even engage in a long kiss.

He smiled as if he'd read her thoughts and realized he had to be the grown-up tonight. "Checking you for a concussion."

"Romantic."

He extended his hand. "Isn't it?"

This time she slipped her hand into his and let him pull her to her feet. Her hands landed on his chest as she wobbled. "Please get my phone."

His frown could cut glass. "Shay—"

"You can hold it. I just want it in here in case." She practically slept with the thing. Some might call it an addiction but it made her antsy not to have it nearby.

Ford glanced at his watch before looking at her again. "Only if you get in the shower."

Working up some energy, she leaned in and kissed him. Soft and sweet without much pressure, but she tried.

She pulled back and shot him a smile. "Deal."

He walked out, all his focus on that watch. For some reason that struck her as strange. She didn't remember him having it on earlier but she guessed he did. But really, she didn't have the energy to do much but watch him walk. Even in her haze she loved seeing him move.

Now that she was up, she did some walking of her own. The kitchen was right there. There was no reason she couldn't pop in, maybe find the chips. Eating junk food might refuel her. Had she thought about it, she would have had Ford stop on the way home, but—

"You have no idea who he is, do you?"

She spun around at the sound of the familiar male voice. "Trent?"

He stood in her doorway with his hands in the pockets of his jacket. "Where's your sweater?"

The words barely registered. "What?"

Seeing him in her house so soon after everything, knowing Ford was right next door and people were looking for him—it constituted an emotional pile-up. The kind that made a person want to curl into her pillow and never go outside again.

"The one you had on today. Come on, I don't have

much time." He stepped inside and shut the door behind him. The bolt came next.

"I don't . . ." She watched him pick up and throw down Ford's jacket and sweater. "Maybe the police have it."

Trent flipped her purse to the side. He was on the hunt for something and she had no idea what, but the drug theory came around for a second time.

He scanned the room, then his eyes widened. "There it is."

Pushing past her, he went to the bar stool and grabbed her cardigan off the seat. She didn't even remember how it got there. She had no idea how he knew she wore it today. He'd never been a big women's fashion person.

He ran his hand over the material, clamping his hand on it as if searching for something. Turning the one pocket inside out, he dumped out a plastic container with vials of liquid resting in individual slots. The whole case was half the size of a cell phone.

She took a step toward him, trying to figure out what she was looking at and how it got in her pocket. "What is that?"

He held it up and sort of waved it at her. "My insurance."

That had to fit in somehow. Money. He'd needed cash. Her mind skipped to that topic and she glanced at the sweater looking for signs of the envelope weighing down one pocket. Did he take . . . did she give it to him? She didn't remember.

But she remembered the headache. "You're not making any sense You hit me and—"

"I created the toxin. My boss wanted to take credit, but it was me. He made all these plans for it and I played along. But as soon as I stopped, armed men came after me to get it back."

None of that made sense. Not to her. Not with what she knew. "You said you were set up."

"Yes."

They weren't saying the same thing. His own version put the guilt, at least part of it, squarely on him. She couldn't believe he didn't hear that. But that was only one of many inconsistencies. Despite her injury and the exhaustion, she'd heard the whispers. The policemen at the scene outside the ambulance had talked, and all the blame seemed to land on Trent.

"How did you get away from the museum?" That part wasn't just fizzy, it was gone. "They're saying you threatened people."

"Is the 'they' your new boyfriend?" Trent shook his head. "Damn it, Shay. He's dangerous. Tell me despite the state college degree you're smart enough to see that."

The odd shot pummeled her. He'd never talked about her school before. Never suggested she was dumb or beneath him. She'd heard him put on the entitled act with others but she'd been spared. Until now.

But his comment raised a bigger question. Ford was right next door and would be back any minute, but Trent had never met him. She didn't know how he even knew she was dating someone. "How do you know I'm dating?"

"He's been stalking you to get close to me."

Each accusation sounded crazier than the last. "He works in computers."

"Get away from her, Trent."

Shay glanced over and felt the blood drain from her head. Her previous case of dizziness morphed. Her head actually moved in circles now. Her computer hottie stood there with a gun and looking far too comfortable aiming it at Trent's head.

Her world collided and the questions piled up. "Ford?"

"How did you get by the bolt?" Trent asked, sounding more intrigued than angry.

"Had a feeling you'd stop by, so I disabled it. Removed the internal mechanism so you'd think you locked it."

"Do you hear that, Shay? See the weapon?" Trent leaned in close to her and pointed at Ford. "That's what I'm talking about. He's an assassin or a mercenary."

Ford's expression never changed. He wore the same unreadable look that made her twitchy even on a normal day, and this was not one of those. "You can stop being dramatic now."

"He's not who he says he is," Trent said. "He hunts people, kills people, and now he's come for me."

It sounded ridiculous, but Ford wasn't laughing. She wanted him to break out with a comment about how this was nonsense.

First, he needed to explain the gun.

Desperation clawed at her insides. She'd gone from sleepy to wide-awake and walking in a nightmare. "Ford, tell him what you do for a living."

"I doubt his name is even Ford." Trent's eyes narrowed. "Who are you working for?"

"Who are *you* working with, Trent? There's no way you did all of this by yourself."

Did what? They kept talking and Ford wouldn't answer her or look at her. He'd gone from the World's Greatest Boyfriend to a stranger in the last minute. "I don't get this. The toxin, the museum. You know about all of it?"

Ford's gaze bounced to her for a second then back to Trent. "Step away from him, Shay."

She needed answers. She wanted to understand. This was the man she'd been weaving a future around. He played in every vision she had.

"I don't—"

"Damn it, Shay, right now. Step back." Ford reached out and snagged her arm, pulling her closer to his side. "He attacked you once today already."

Trent dropped the container into his pocket. She thought he might have edged closer to the door. He no longer stood near the kitchen. Now he was within bolting range of the exit.

"Your boyfriend was there. He showed up after you passed out."

"After you hit her," Ford shot back.

She scoured her memory about the museum. The gunmen and the tourists played in her head. If Ford had been there she would have seen him . . . right?

"This doesn't make any sense." Her life was unraveling in front of her. Every aspect of what she thought she knew turned out to be wrong.

She tried to grab the pieces and hold them together. She loved this man and it was all disintegrating around her.

"You're going in this time, Trent," Ford said. "I don't know why you were dumb enough to come back here, but this is over."

Trent's smile could only be described as feral. "No."

"Looks like you need to learn the hard way."

A loud boom echoed through her condo. She heard the noise, and then the room flipped into slow motion. Her gaze switched from Ford's outstretched arm and the gun in his hand to Trent. As she watched, his mouth dropped open and he screamed with rage as he dropped to the floor.

She couldn't speak. Her body stood frozen as red stained Trent's upper thigh and spilled through the fingers he pressed there.

"Maybe now you'll listen."

Before she could scream—and one was trapped in her throat—a figure appeared in the doorway. Loomed was a better word. With massive shoulders and a gun of his own.

"Looks like your plan worked." The man towered over Trent where he rocked back and forth on the floor.

She recognized the man from the museum. "Get away from him."

Ford caught her in mid-protective lunge. "Shay—"

She squirmed out of his grasp and stepped away from him, moving back as he shifted forward. Her hands went up to ward him off. "Don't touch me."

"I need you to—"

She shook her head and immediately regretted the sudden movement. "Who are you?" She wanted to ask both of them, but only Ford mattered.

"I am the same man you've known for weeks."

In her mind she'd already tied her life to his. She'd spun sexy thoughts about them being together and growing closer. She'd actually believed he might tell her he loved her one day soon.

She's been a stupid idiot. She could see it now. The lack of anything personal in his house. The rooms that looked more spare and clean than most hotels. All the travel and how he moved.

He oozed confidence. Probably because he knew he could kill anyone who got in his way. He hadn't even hesitated to threaten Trent. Her gaze went to Trent and she started to drop to her knees to check on him.

"Shay, listen to me." Ford, or whatever his name was, stepped forward and reached for her again.

She dodged this advance just like the other. "No."

She meant to help Trent. His wailing cry finally wound down as his head fell back. She didn't know if he'd passed out or if something else had happened.

Ford pulled her attention back to him. "You have to—"

"No." Her mind screamed with the need to run. Her insides turned icy and she wrapped her arms around her body and rocked. "No, no, no."

The other guy dropped to the floor and wrapped something around Trent's bleeding leg. "Ford," he said, "maybe ease up for now."

Her attention zipped back to the guy from the museum. "You're one of the gunmen. A killer."

Ford stepped in front of her and blocked her view. "He's with me."

As with everything else today, that didn't explain anything. She turned on the newcomer because concentrating on trying to get the full story kept her mind off the shredding in her chest. "How did you know to get here so fast?"

"The tracker."

"What is that?" She waved a hand in the air and wished it had the power to sweep every awful thought away. "Forget it. I'm calling the police."

She reached for her land line but Ford got there first. "No."

"You don't get to tell me what to do. Not anymore." Not since she fell in love with him and he kicked it back at her.

Love. Despair washed through her, pushing out all the good thoughts and happy memories. Every muscle ached. Her body felt limp, as if flu symptoms beset it and her strength drained from inside her.

Ford clenched his jaw as if fighting back a rough case of fury. "You might be pissed off, but you are coming with us. You and Trent."

Why would she ever go near him again? And trust . . . that was gone. He stomped it out, erased all the good, in just a few minutes.

Before she could say anything, Ford tapped his ear and started talking. "We need medical transport and a clean-up crew. I have the vials and Trent."

The words tumbled over her and the reality smacked her square in the gut. She had no idea who Ford really was. She finally found the words to go with the question bouncing around in her head. "Why would I go anywhere with you?"

He finally lowered his weapon. "So I can prove we're the good guys."

She shook her head. "Too late."

A half hour later Ford stood in one of the Warehouse's back rooms, watching Shay. Sitting at a conference table, she looked small and vulnerable. The bandage didn't help.

He wanted to storm in there or balance his head against the screen—anything to be closer to her. After the quiet car ride over he was desperate for any reaction. Hell, he'd be fine with angry. He'd welcome it. It was as if she'd emotionally rammed into a wall and had nothing left but pieces. The indifference, treating him like a stranger, chipped away at his control.

Of course, that's what he was to her right now. A stranger. He'd set that up and didn't tell her fast enough. Trent always seemed to zig when he expected him to zag.

Ward came in and stood beside Ford. They both watched her. "She just sits and stares at the wall."

"Do you blame her?" Ford silently begged her to at least blink.

He rubbed that area of his chest that ached. The dead center where he felt as if he'd been kicked with a near-killing blow.

"Why did Trent go back to her condo?" Ward asked. "It was pretty risky."

"He needed the vials. Where are they, by the way?"

"Locked up."

Of course they were. Ward would have them in the deep freeze or destroyed in no time. "Something Trent said to Shay made it sound like he planned to double-cross Matt and whoever else is in on this." In the end the kid's ego and disregard for other people's greed, tripped him up. "But he needed the vials to do that."

Ward shook his head. "Idiot."

In the chaos at the condo this good part almost got

lost. This was good news. Not the best news, but a major step forward. "There was one vial on him and we recovered three more. If Matt is right, that leaves two out in the open."

"Let's hope we're only chasing two."

Nothing else had gone right on this op so Ford doubted this would. "Trent claims to have more."

"He's a lying sack of shit."

A terrorist, a liar, and possibly a deranged psychopath. That pretty much covered it. Ford would see him strangling Shay every day for the rest of his life. He'd felt so useless that he couldn't get to her and ease the pain.

And now he'd caused more. Him, not Trent.

Ward kept talking shop. "You took a big risk with the tracker."

"Not really." Trent might know science, but Ford knew human nature and his job, and the plan had been calculated. It also worked, though looking at Shay sitting there, he had to wonder at what cost.

"It could have gone sideways on you."

"No, I would have killed him before I let that happen. I had eyes on him the whole time, so did Ellery and West . . . and you." That part was true. Shay or not, Ford would not have let Trent get away free. West tailed him the entire time and Ellery watched, however it was Ellery watched over these things.

"Thanks to you we've shut part of the danger down."

Part but Ford wanted it all. If he was going to lose Shay, he sure as hell better get everyone involved, including the elusive, faceless Benton. "It's the job."

"Still, West said he was about to move in when

Trent made a move toward Shay's place." Ward made a clicking sound with his tongue. "I have to wonder, why come out and cause a scene?"

"Maybe Matt can help with that question," Ford said as he barely concentrated on the conversation.

Shay still didn't move. Not a shift or a head nod. Seeing her lifeless ate at him until his insides hollowed out.

Ward shrugged. "I'll try."

Ford snapped out of his stupor. It took another few seconds to tear his gaze away from the woman who had come to mean everything.

"Let me have a shot." He needed to hit something. He'd keep his hands off Matt but scaring the hell out of him was fair game. "If you fail, I get ten minutes with the guy."

After a brief hesitation, Ward nodded. "Fine."

"And I want West in the room with me again. That produced some results last time." Because that guy could terrorize just by standing in a corner.

Ward closed his eyes and exhaled. "Keep the blood-bath to a minimum."

"I can't promise that."

27

S HAY'S INSIDES shook so hard she could barely sit still in the chair. The cold room and metal chair didn't help, but this wasn't about temperature. The need to throw up hit her in waves. Her throat felt thick and if she shifted even a little the room blurred.

Reaction, misery . . . she wasn't sure what had her body falling but she knew who. The combination of Trent, the betrayal by Ford. It was too much.

Taking a deep breath, she started a mental count-down. When she reached zero she went back to the be-ginning and tried again. One the third time she finally stood up. Wobbly but on her feet.

A few steps and she'd be at the door. She'd bang the walls down if that's what it took to get someone in this place to let her out. She turned, closing her eyes to ease the vertigo. When she opened them again, Ford stood in front of her.

She had no idea how long he'd been watching her. Chalk the moment up to one more example of her not knowing what was going on in his head.

Still wearing the black pants and dark shirt she'd thought was some sort of dress outfit but now guessed was what he wore when he whipped out his gun, he stood frozen. She'd seen him in action twice now. He wore a weapon at his side even now. Amazing how something she hadn't known about even a day before now seemed like a natural part of him.

She wanted to shove him aside and go into the hallway. To scream until someone came running. From there, who knows where she'd end up. No one had explained anything to her. Oh, people flashed badges and she noticed all the security. A government agency of some sort, she guessed, but who knew.

He nodded toward the chair she just abandoned. "Sit down."

"Go away," she shot back.

He shut the door and slipped around her to stand in the space across the desk and in front of the open chair. "We have Trent in custody. His leg is fine though he likely will have a limp."

The comment sounded like the beginning of a lecture, or a bad movie. Ford's posture was perfect and he kept his hands folded in front of him. She caught glimpses of the man she thought she knew, but the steel veneer, the serious affect, didn't match with the guy who'd worn a T-shirt with possums running a car wash the other day.

No, this guy was someone else. Something else. Before she left this building and walked away from him forever, she wanted to know who had ripped her life and heart apart. "Who is 'we'?"

"My team."

She hadn't expected a real answer. She doubted anything he'd ever said to her was real. "Your hit squad."

"You've got this wrong." He tightened the grip of his hands on the chair back, his knuckles turning white.

"Oh, really?"

"We're the good guys in this scenario."

"Screwing women who never did anything to you and shooting up a museum?" The first one made her stomach heave and the second sent an unwanted series of memories running through her head. "Do you really believe that you're on the side of right here?"

"We're a black ops task force, pulled together from British intelligence and the CIA." Never one to show a lot of what he was feeling, he gave away nothing now. His flat mouth matched the flatness in his eyes.

And now he was going to try to sell her some sort of James Bond garbage. She reached for the knob and found a round disk. She pushed and tried to turn it. When that failed she slapped the door with her hands.

"You need the security access card."

Whatever that meant. "Open the door."

"Trent is accused of stealing a weapons grade toxin from his workplace. It's believed he intended to sell it on the open market. The only purpose would be for terrorist activities."

She looked at the black square next to the door, then at him. His words rumbled inside her, and her mind spun back through every bad spy novel she'd ever read. About the boy Trent had been and the angry and distant man he'd become.

Every minute of the last few months played in her head. Trent had become more self-focused and withdrawn. His ego raged and his behavior changed. She'd chalked it up to a range of possibilities. Becoming a

terrorist or a madman with the power over a toxin was
never on her list. What he'd said to her in the condo
made it sound like this was about having his work
taken and losing control, but she had no idea.

It all raced around in her mind until it was too much.
Too cloak-and-dagger. "This is crazy. Everyone I know
is suddenly crazy."

Trent talked about people chasing him, men aimed
guns at her. Now Ford thought he was some superagent.
Hell, maybe he was. Everything he'd ever said was a
lie, maybe he finally stumbled into telling the truth.

He came around the desk and reached out for her.
"Listen to me—"

"No." The second his fingers touched her arm she
shrugged away. Her back hit the door as she tried to put
as much space between them as possible. "Don't touch
me. Don't ever touch me."

Waves of nausea hit her then. She'd actually been
dumb enough to fall for this man. She'd accepted the
frustrating parts and welcomed all of him into her life.
For the first in a long time she hadn't held back. She'd
ignored the little voice in her head that told her to wait.

She'd even yelled at her uncle for investigating Ford.
Not that it did any good because none of this—the
gun-toting guy with the line about being a good guy—
came up.

All of the thoughts and shocks piled up until she
couldn't take on more. Breathing in deeply, she tried
to choke back the lump of whatever was lodged in her
throat and get her body under control. She would not
lose it in front of this guy . . . whoever he really was.

"Let me out of here."

Most of the color had drained from his face. He reached for her, then stopped as his hands dropped to his sides. "I had a job to do. I need you to understand that and listen to me."

Slowly her insides thawed out and twisted. The shattered feeling gave way to something raw and sharp. "Me, I was the job. That's what you mean, right? You used me."

"No, baby."

Now he used endearments. Now when they truly meant nothing. "Don't do that. Don't call me that."

His eyes closed, and when he opened them again there was a stark darkness there. "This toxin has the power to kill a lot of people, Shay. In the wrong hands innocent lives will be lost. Your cousin created it and stole it from his lab."

He didn't deny her claims. Didn't even let her keep the fantasy that she'd come to mean something to him. Just bounced to a new topic about this toxin. This was about getting control of some stupid vials, and she wasn't even sure she understood what that meant.

"Then why not question me? Just bring me in here, wherever this is, or to a police station or some office you superspies use to get information out of people." He didn't say anything. Suddenly he didn't have to. "Oh, because you thought I was in on it."

He winced but quickly covered it. "It was a possibility."

With both hands up, her palms hit his chest and she shoved as hard as she could. "Go to hell."

He barely moved, so she did. She slipped past him and walked to the other side of the small space, as far as she could before she hit another wall. The room could be a metaphor for her life lately, bouncing from roadblock to roadblock and not even knowing it.

"It wasn't all a job, Shay."

His words sat there, in the air, in her head. This was it, the big play where he tried to salvage something of his humanity while shredding hers.

No, he couldn't have this.

With her back to the wall she lifted her head and faced him down. "Shut up."

"Shay—"

She waved her hand in the air as if it could bat back the words and knock away the pained look in his eyes. "Don't you say anything. You don't get to act like it's no big deal that you slept with me and held me and then let me think I mattered."

"You do." He took a step forward.

She slammed her body tighter against the wall. "I hate you."

He swallowed. She could see his Adam's apple move.

After a shuddering breath he started talking again. "I know. You should."

This was a new game. A fresh way to torture her. As if luring her in and letting her fall in love with him wasn't enough of a joke on her.

"Everything you say makes me . . ." She lost the words. Lost everything.

This man had come to mean so much, and now he stood there, just a few feet away, not apologizing or saying this was all some huge misunderstanding. He wasn't. He'd reduced her to a puddle and had her on the verge of screaming and pummeling him and he acted like they were still friends.

"What do you feel?" he asked.

No, she would not give him that, too. She wouldn't beg or tell him what was going on inside her head. He probably didn't want to know. Hell, she could barely handle it. "You had a choice, Ford . . . is that even your name?"

"Honey, I had to get close enough to figure out where Trent was and see if your uncle knew anything."

She could hear the pleading in his voice and blocked it. "You think Anthony is in on it?"

"That doesn't matter right now."

For a second the haze cleared and she saw the truth. Ford was trying to ruin her family, had succeeded in crushing her, and he brushed it all aside. She had to move again. No matter how fast her head spun or how her feet stumbled, she couldn't just stand there.

She circled around until she got to the chair and rested her hands on the back. Leaning brought some relief. So did grabbing the frame with all her might.

"There were points, so many points, where you could have filled me in. Or you could have watched from a distance and not slept in my damn bed every night." There it was, the part that kept jamming in her throat and making her gag.

"I would give anything to go back. To not hurt you."

Rage swept over her, burning out the chill. "Get Out."

"I was doing my job. Trying to keep people safe."

But not her. He said all the right words but acted as if she didn't matter at all. "Shut up."

"It's dangerous and shitty and sometimes people get trapped in the middle and hurt." He shook his head. "Decisions, hard decisions, have to be made. The choices suck. Do you honestly think I want to make them?"

"I don't care." But part of her did and she hated that.

"Please listen to me." His hand came out again, as if he planned to touch her. Like so many times in the past where he grabbed her and hugged her close. Where he gave her comfort instead of inflicting pain.

She gave in and hit him. Rammed a fist into his chest then did it again. She hit, the sides of her fists thudding against him. Punched as she thought about all she'd lost and the pile of lies he'd told. She closed her eyes and let the anger wash over her. She hit until her arms ached and her chest heaved.

She could have gone on for hours or just a few seconds. Time blurred and the thoughts running through her brain, the replay of their time together, jumbled. He didn't touch her or stop her. He shifted his head out of the way but that was all.

God, even as a woman fell apart in front of him he stayed stoic and distant.

With heavy breaths hammering her chest and adrenaline still fueling her muscles, she tore herself away and stepped back. "Leave me alone."

This time he touched her. His hands wrapped around her biceps as he leaned in, almost willing her to believe. "I need you to believe me. To give me another chance. Hell, I just need you."

She'd longed to hear the words, and now he'd said them, buried them, in all the confusion of the day. "No."

His hands shook where they held her. "Don't you understand that this started as a job but became something else? What we have is real."

So many lies. That's what they'd had. And he kept stacking one on top of the other.

She shook her head. "I can't listen to this."

"I need you." He repeated the words. So harsh and pained, it sounded as if they were ripped out of him.

His rough voice cut through the haze winding its way around her. It gave her the strength she needed for one last shot. She slammed her hands into his chest and shoved. This time he moved. Stumbled back as his mouth dropped open.

"You need time." His voice sounded hollow.

"You could give me a lifetime and put an entire country between us and it won't help you." The ache inside her spread to every cell.

"Don't say that." His voice came out as a harsh whisper.

But that's not what killed her. The words. She'd never heard him beg for anything. Figured he'd waited until now, when she didn't believe a single word, to act like he gave a damn about her. "Go to hell."

He reached around her and touched the keypad. The door opened with a click. "Already there."

He slipped out before she could find the energy to try to follow.

Anthony's gaze flipped from Tasha to Ward. "I want to see my niece and my son."

Seeing the strong man now, pale and drawn, shifting in his chair as he rubbed his hands together, almost

made Ward feel bad for him. Then he remembered that
this man created Trent. He played some role, if not in
the stealing of the toxin, in forming the psyche of the
guy who did the deed.

"Trent is being questioned. Shay is fine," Tasha said
from her seat directly across from Anthony.

"I'm supposed to believe you?"

Ward balanced his hands on the back of the chair
next to Tasha. "You should be more worried about
yourself."

"I am going to bring in my lawyer and shut this
fucking place down."

That would be interesting. Not that Ward hadn't
heard threats like that before. People always launched
into bullshit when cornered. The inevitable squealing
about tough attorneys and lawsuits was part of the right
guy's handbook.

Of course, none of that mattered here. This building,
the Warehouse, the work of Alliance, operated just outside of the law of two countries. It was a dirty business
upholding the Constitution by shredding it, but sometimes that was the only way to keep people safe.

Not that they could print a handbook or put the
slogan on a T-shirt. No, they quietly worked, and in
moments like these, when Ford was being emotionally
ripped apart and Shay wore her defeat like a blanket
so heavy Ward had to look away, you had to believe in
something bigger. Somehow Ward still did.

Anthony had issued his threat, now Ward gave one
of his own. "If I want to ship you away and put you
in a hole so deep you won't see sunshine ever again,
I can."

"That's—"

"I can make you disappear. Let the people who know you think you're dead. Watch your business and your properties fall apart." Sad thing was, he didn't exaggerate. He had the power, and the woman next to him would sign off on all of it. She had no compassion for people who ruined the lives of others. "And, Anthony, I can do all of that without leaving this room."

His face went from pale to ghostly white. "Who's in charge? I want your boss's name."

Tasha raised her hand. "That's me."

Ward enjoyed the drop. For one second in a shitty couple of weeks, he wanted to laugh. The look of shock on the other man's face was priceless. "Yeah, she's the boss."

The older man gasped as he tried to gulp in air. "What the hell is this place?"

"You don't need to worry about who we were. Be more concerned about what we can do to you. What we do to terrorists." The practiced way Tasha said it sounded as if she were reading from a manual. Precise and clear.

"For the record, that's how we refer to your son." Ward nodded. "As a terrorist."

Anthony's body slumped. It looked as if all the fight seeped out of him and took a good deal of what was left of his life with it. "No, he wouldn't—"

"Yes, he clearly did."

Anthony's mouth dropped open as his eyes glazed over. "He's a scientist."

He repeated the phrase several times, more to himself than the room. He'd clearly suspected something had been going on and made up excuses and lies to cover for Trent. Now he knew the kid had blown well past a simple screw-up that daddy could smooth over.

"You knew something wasn't right," Tasha said.

"Trent's always been . . . different. He was working long hours and his boss said he was on this special project." Anthony shook his head. "I tried to find out more, used all my contacts. Went to his lab and got turned away before getting through the gates."

The man was lost in his thoughts but his words kept flowing. Ward wanted to encourage that. "And?"

"I needed Shay not to worry while I figured it all out, so I lied to her." Anthony's head shot up and his face pulled taut. "He's just a kid."

Ward could tell by the reaction that reality had begun to sink in and make sense in the man's mind. Anthony didn't get indignant. Didn't throw around his status or talk about his money and power. He took the news like a body blow. Looked only a few short steps before catatonic.

In that minute, Ward knew in his gut that Anthony wasn't involved. He might be crappy father and an all-around dick, but not a traitor to his country. This guy cared about public perception. He was demanding, and according to his file could be ruthless in business. He walked the line on appropriate behavior in some of his contracts and might have crossed it once or twice, but he wouldn't take this last step.

"Trent stole a lethal toxin from his workplace and threatened to wipe out half of DC yesterday, all while holding your niece and others hostage at the museum. That story on the news was absolutely real. You probably saw some of the footage," Tasha explained, dropping the pretense and using her British accent.

"You did a great job with him, by the way." The rub was unnecessary and Tasha scowled at Ward to let him know it.

Not that Anthony even acknowledged it. He shook his head and stared at Ward, then Tasha. "I want to see Trent."

"No one is going to see Trent for a while."

Anthony shoved back his chair and started to get up. "You can't—"

"Sit down." Ward waited until the other man obeyed. "The only good news for you is that the more time passes, the less likely it is I think you're involved in all of this."

"Me?"

"Your son has a partner."

Anthony dropped his head in his hands. "This can't be happening."

"Maybe this will convince you." Tasha unfolded her arms and showed off the small remote in her hand. A few clicks and a screen lowered on the wall to reveal the scene from the museum already playing.

Seeing the footage again rocked Ward. They'd dodged a catastrophe. He could have been looking at the cleanup of a lot of dead bodies and mourning the loss of his men. Ford and his team had prevented a disaster, but the danger was far from over.

Ward pointed to the image of Trent putting Shay in a stranglehold. "I especially like the part where he talks about the first ten thousand deaths he'll cause. That's coming up."

Anthony squinted and leaned in. "Is that Ford Decker?"

"He works for me."

Anthony started to say something but he ended up mumbling, and Ward couldn't catch it.

"I can tell from your expression you're starting to see how big this situation is."

"Is Shay okay?" Anthony actually sounded concerned.

"Your entire family is in a load of shit." Really only one of them, but if it worked to let Anthony think the whole clan was going down, Ward was fine with that.

"I didn't do anything. I would never . . ." Anthony closed his eyes. "I don't know anything about a toxin."

Tasha glanced up at Ward before responding. "Then help us figure out who does."

28

FORD FOLLOWED West into the main briefing room. Putting one foot in front of the other took all his concentration. Every time he let his mind wander or closed his eyes, he saw Shay's pale face.

He could pinpoint the exact moment when she went from trying not to believe to realizing he'd used her all along. He would see her shredded expression for the rest of his life. His chest still ached, and not from the pounding she gave him. He would let her hit him all day, hell, give her his gun, if it helped wash away some of her anguish at being betrayed.

That made him one more man in her life who'd betrayed her. She'd said Devin had treated her better, and Ford wondered if she was right. They both used her. The difference was, he actually loved her, but that wouldn't matter now that he'd crushed her.

His sins wouldn't wash away that easily. The wounds he inflicted festered like open sores. He'd seen anger and confusion and blinding pain in her eyes.

He almost envied her, because he couldn't feel anything. He loved her but that was buried deep under a pile of guilt. He planned to wrap all of it up and use those emotions right now to tear Matt apart.

West moved in front of their guest turned prisoner. "Matt, you are about to have a very bad day."

"No." He shook his head as his gaze bounced from West to Ford. "I've told you everything."

Ford hated this guy. Hated everyone involved in this case. Wanted to rip them all to shreds and burn the ground behind them. "Just like you told us everything but then later remembered about all the vials Trent stole, and how you basically escorted him to the parking lot? Try again."

Grabbing the yellow legal pad in front of him, Matt tapped the lines of writing. "I'm cooperating."

Ford had no idea what the guy had written and didn't care. He wanted to hear Matt say the words. Look his accusers in the eye as he admitted all he'd done. "You're going to be dead in two minutes unless you tell the rest of the story."

"There is no rest." Gone was the pontificating preener who clearly thought he was smarter than everyone else. Matt hung on the verge of tears as he dropped the pretense.

It was a shame Ford still knew he was lying.

"Benton." Ford dropped the name and waited.

Matt frowned. Almost looked genuine. "Who?"

"Nice try." Just went to show, book smarts didn't have anything to do with street smarts. "I didn't say Benton was a who."

"Dumbass." West mumbled it under his breath.

"See, Matt, I just watched some stupid prick hit my girlfriend and threaten to kill thousands of people." Ford stumbled over "girlfriend" but kept going. "She's angry, which makes me angry. My patience is gone."

West took out one of his weapons, a Glock, and ran a finger along the side. "And I like to shoot things."

"What?"

"By things I mean people."

Matt tried to push back but was handcuffed to the table, and the chain didn't let him get far. "You can't do this."

West nodded. "We are."

Looked like it was time for a walk down memory lane. They'd held back before. Not this time. Ford made a promise that this was the last time he'd walk into this room to get information from Matt. Bureaucrat or not, he either spilled now or left the building in a body bag. "Remember what happened when West hit you? I think you might have cried."

West scoffed. "That was a damn embarrassment."

Ford shook his head. "Imagine what he'll do when I let him go and don't try to restrain him."

"I need a lawyer."

Matt asked for the wrong professional, as far as Ford was concerned. "A mortician might be the better choice."

"I'm going to start shooting in one minute." West checked his watch then aimed the gun at Matt's head.

He was squirming now. Shifting and ducking as he pulled on the bonds confining him. "No, you can't—"

"I'll start with your foot then maybe go to your knee." West moved the barrel of the gun through the air as he talked. "It's kind of my specialty area. Knowing where to hit to inflict the most pain."

Matt looked to Ford, pleading with his eyes and then his words. "For God's sake, stop him."

Funny how people brought up God at a time like this. It never failed. Lawyers and God, the two staples of the guilty. "No, see, I asked him to come in here and do this favor for me."

"The gut shot will be the rough one." West made a tsk-tsking sound. "You won't die immediately but you'll want to."

"Let me out of here." Matt started screaming. He yelled about his title and who he worked for. Said something about the people he knew and how they'd all be sued.

Ford waited until Matt exhausted himself and wound down again. "In case you're unclear, that's not going to help. This is a sealed room. You're in one and Trent is in the other."

West slid a thigh on the edge of the desk and leaned in as if talking to Matt man-to-man, just shooting the shit. "How long do you think pretty boy will withstand the torture? Trent is in there nursing a bullet wound. He'll crack fast."

"First one to break wins." Actually, no one won. That's how this worked. Everyone was going down for this mess. Ford vowed that would be the case, and Ward and Tasha had promised to back him up. "You tell us what we need to know and we put in a good word for you with the prosecutor. Hell, we'll let you have a trial instead of deciding your fate and locking you up somewhere nasty without anyone knowing."

"I want immunity." Matt nodded, looking more secure in his position. Like he'd hit upon the right solution.

West snorted. "Now you're just wasting our time."

He got up and came around to the same side of the

table as Matt. Pulling the chair out as far as the chain would allow, West kicked out Matt's leg and aimed at his foot.

The guy begged and tried to push West's massive frame away. Finally he threw his head back and looked at them through his panicked panting. It took all of five minutes to bring the egomaniac to his knees. "Stop!"

Ford beat back the satisfaction soaring through him because this was far from over. "Say something worthwhile."

"Trent needed money because I was in here and couldn't get him what I promised to help him wait this out. He'd moved forward with the plan on his timetable and taken the toxin before I could get all of the funding and resources in place at the beginning."

That explained the part that never made sense to Ford, but he did wonder if the game went deeper than Matt knew. "He probably also thought about taking the cash and leaving town with the vials and cutting you out completely, but go on."

"There's a sale coming up."

"The auction." Ford balled his hands into fists to keep from launching at Matt. The guy acted like it was no big deal he conspired to open the floodgates to a new form of chemical warfare.

"Yes, exactly." Talking now, Matt didn't stop. "A man approached me about making some money. I knew Trent believed the government was stealing his ideas by taking control of the toxin and not giving him enough credit. He'd complained during his review and tried to take the issue over my head. The kid didn't understand how this works."

Ford had heard enough about Trent. Now he needed

to know about this other man. "You put the two of them together, the man and Trent."

"And collected a check," West said.

"Bad investments and a divorce that—"

"Spare us." Jesus, if Matt went down the road seeking pity, Ford might just take out his gun and shoot him right now. "Where does Benton fit in?"

"I have no idea who that is."

Ford found that believable. Matt was too low on the power chart to deal directly with Benton. The guy hadn't been seen in years. No way would he pop out to negotiate with a scientist.

That made it more likely Matt's contact was the mole, someone with access and resources who might know how to contact Benton. Who might work right in this building. "Who was the guy you talked with?"

"I never got a last name. He refused to give it." Matt sped up when West shifted positions. "He's British with dark hair. He claimed to have a black ops background and a way in. His documents and leads checked out. He said he could find a buyer for the toxin, and I left that part to him."

Ford turned the description over in his head. It all fit. He could see how this played out. Matt, however, seemed clueless about the extent of his fuck-up. "You know what that makes you, right?"

West exhaled. "A terrorist."

"It wasn't like that." Matt kept shifting around in his seat. He twisted and turned as he looked from Ford to West and back again. "The plan was to make some money and have Trent work on a way to counteract it so we could make even more money. Everyone won."

No, that last part was never part of the plan. Not for anyone but Matt.

West delivered the news. "For a smart guy, you're pretty fucking stupid."

Ford had reached his maximum tolerance point. He knew what the answer would be but asked anyway. "What's the Brit's first name?"

Matt swallowed and his gaze went to West's gun. "Harlan."

Ward watched it all. Stood there and waited for West and Ford to come out so they could walk through the new information. So he could test his theory and see if they all agreed.

He looked at West first. "Well?"

Ford answered. "Too easy."

"You think Matt is lying?" Not exactly where Ward was going but he'd listen. Even lost in a funk over Shay, Ford's instincts were good. Probably the best Ward had ever worked with.

"I think he's spitting back what he's been programmed to say." Ford put it out there and West nodded in agreement. "No way would Harlan give his real name and use his accent."

Ward had come to the same conclusion. "Agreed."

"The guy has been undercover all over the world and speaks how many languages? Yet we're supposed to believe he walked into this situation and didn't try to hide his identity." Ford stared at the floor as he shook his head. "No fucking way."

"He's being set up." Those were the first words West said since leaving the room.

Ward knew the threats took something out of the guy. He pretended it was part of the job, and they called on him to be the muscle so often he no longer blinked, but that didn't mean he enjoyed bloodshed.

"There is only one answer here. Harlan is being railroaded by the person who gave us bad intel on the Hampstead job and who had dinner with Anthony and didn't do anything to stop him from coming home early and finding us." Ford's voice dropped lower and grew rougher with each sentence. "It's been right in front of us all along. He came out of retirement to help and all he's done is screw us over."

"Pearce." Ward said the name on all of their minds.

This was a fucking nightmare. Pearce knew everything. He'd helped put the security protocols for the team and building in place. He knew the security codes. People in the building trusted him and wouldn't think to stop him, especially since they'd kept his lockup quiet to everyone but the two guards watching over him. Even they believed the security measures were somehow for Pearce's protection.

"But why do it after all these years?" West asked.

"Doesn't matter," Ford said almost at the same time.

Ward wanted to be the one who put a bullet in Pearce. Then he would stand over him and ask why, after all those years of service, he changed sides. Money couldn't be the only answer. Ward hated that fucking answer. "He's in the building."

Ford's hand went to the gun at his side. "Locked down?"

Ward's gut tensed. "He has a guard in with him and one at the door."

West already had his weapon out and started moving. "Only two?"

Before they could get very far, Ford stepped in front of them and held up a hand. "Wait, we can use this."

"How?" Ward was willing to try anything, and Ford rarely made a misstep. Despite the background and deaths on his last CIA operation, there was a reason Ford led Bravo team. A reason the team was so damn lethal.

"Maybe it's time for us to set a trap." Ford lowered his voice. "Pearce is making some sort of move. Let's give him a chance to do it. We have everyone in the holding cells in the main building. It's only a matter of time before Pearce feels the walls closing in and makes his big play."

West smiled. "Then we bury the fucker."

"I'd like to gut him, but no. We need Benson and Pearce's connection to him and this auction." Ford looked like he was mentally thinking out that scenario in his head.

"You two are scary together." And Ward slept better knowing that.

Ford nodded. "Let's hope Pearce hasn't figured that out yet."

Ward doubted Pearce would miscalculate that badly, but he did seem to think he was in control. They could use that to their advantage. "We need some luck."

West waved that off. "Nah, we've got skills."

For the first time since he walked out of the museum Ford smiled. "Oorah."

29

THE DOOR opened and Shay turned, half expecting to go another round with Ford. This time she was ready. She'd spent the minutes, or hours since he'd left—who knew in this place—replaying every minute of their time together. Every supposed work call he left her to go on. Every time he slipped into her bed at two in the morning and stripped off her underwear. All the conversations and the times he screwed her, literally and figuratively.

It all built up until she thought she might be able to kill him with her bare hands.

Thinking to do just that, she looked up ready to do battle. Instead, Trent stood there with another man. Someone she'd never seen.

Trent motioned for her to walk into the hallway. "Shay, come on."

"How did you get out?" Last she knew, he was in some sort of holding cell or sealed room being questioned.

"It's time for us to get out of here."

The spark of relief she felt hearing those words died almost immediately after she heard them. This was

wrong. Trent being out didn't make sense. The quiet
didn't make sense. As usual, nothing made sense.

Something bad had happened. He whispered her
name again, and the rough sound cut through her. Her
instincts flared and her priorities shifted. Forget killing Ford, she wanted him with her. Now. He carried
a gun, and she assumed he knew how to use it. That
would come in handy while she asked Trent the questions swirling in her brain.

She backed up farther into the small room. A second
ago she would have bolted from the building—from
the entire metro area if she had the chance—only now
the room felt like the only safe space to be. "I don't
think so."

"We only have seconds before Ford figures out he's
been played," the other man said as he glanced behind
him down the hall.

She detected a British accent and thought back to
Ford's comment about a joint group . . . or something.
Before she could take it all in, the man reached for her.

She pulled back, but too late. His hand landed on her
wrist and his fist tightened around it. She could almost
see the bruises from under his fingers.

"Get away from me." He wrapped a hand around
her arm like a vice and tugged. She flailed and kicked
but couldn't break the punishing hold. "What are you
doing?"

The man dragged her into the hallway and shoved
her against the wall. His hand went to her throat.
"That's enough."

"Who are you?" After days of little making sense,
she'd found something new to be confused about. An-

other player, another angle. Men kept jumping out with guns and she'd reached the end.

"One more word and I leave you here." The man's smile was almost feral as he shoved his elbow into her throat. "And trust me when I say you won't want to be in this building in a few minutes."

A now familiar panic shook her. She couldn't breathe. No matter how hard she tried, she couldn't draw in enough breath, and she began choking. Guttural and hacking, she made enough noise to bring the entire Army running.

Frantically looking around, she prayed for help to arrive. When it didn't, she slapped her hand against the wall and felt around, hoping to hit on something that would help. Maybe a light switch or an alarm. Anything that would buy her a few seconds but only smooth cool concrete greeted her.

Trent grabbed the other man's arm and pulled. "Pearce, what are—"

As the men struggled, the hold on Shay disappeared. She doubled over, as coughs wracked her body, and she gulped in air. Her legs had turned to jelly or she would have run. All she could do now was clear her throat enough to scream. That was the plan, until she looked up again.

The man who'd had his elbow on her neck was now pinning Trent against the wall and held a knife to his throat. "Don't use my name," he said, and pricked Trent's skin with the edge of the wicked-looking curved blade. "Ever."

Her mind raced as the fear pumping through her threatened to drop her to her knees. "Trent, what's happening?"

"I think in his own messed up way, he was trying to save you. Chalk it up to guilt."

The voice came from behind her. She looked over her shoulder and saw Ford and two other men coming down the hall, guns drawn. A similar sight had terrified her at the museum. For some reason it sent relief pouring through her now.

"Who are you?" She asked the man who had just spoken, but would settle for anyone supplying an answer.

"The man next to you is Trent's partner, or one of them, Jake Pearce," Ford answered. "Isn't that right, Pearce? You're in with this stupid kid in the hope of making quick money selling a lethal toxin and getting into bed with a known arms dealer like Benton. Good for you."

"Who the hell is Benton?" Trent asked.

"Son, you're a step behind," Ford said, but never broke eye contact with Pearce. "Benton? What the fuck is that about?"

Pearce loosened his grip. "He has a vision."

"Yeah," Ford said. "Death by toxin."

This time Pearce laughed. "Not a huge loss. Have you taken a look at humanity lately?"

More on the toxin and another crime to lay at Trent's feet. She'd refused to believe it before, but something in Ford's tone convinced her now.

She focused on him, the one man she knew. "You know Pearce?"

"He works for me," said the guy in the middle with the gun.

"Disappointing, isn't it?" The bigger one from the museum added the question.

She thought she remembered his name as West, but who knew at this point. With the nightmares running together, she didn't understand what was happening. But she got that Pearce had trouble picking sides. She also looked into Ford's eyes and knew he would cut the man down with a bullet if he had the chance. To help that happen, she shifted to the side.

"Trent?" Ford called out. "I'm guessing Pearce let you out."

"This can end easy. Just let us go." Trent sounded hopeful, like he actually believed it might happen.

Even she knew it wouldn't. Three men stood over Trent with guns now, and two more came up behind them at the other end of the hall. She doubted Trent even knew he was surrounded. Pearce did. He glanced at her and smiled, and dread filled her. He would push this to the end. Probably sacrifice them all.

"That worked at the museum, but not this time." Ford's gaze flicked to her then back to Pearce. "This time we predicted the run and everybody stays where they are."

Pearce shook his head. He stepped away from Trent and slipped his knife back into a slot on his belt, but he made no move to surrender. "I don't think so."

"You can't possibly think you'll get out of here," the one who seemed in charge said. "Even if you make it upstairs, this building is filled with black ops experts." His voice never wavered and he kept his body perfectly still.

Ford and the other men coming toward them were a matched set. The ones she now believed probably were the good guys, or whatever qualified as good in a situation like this. They held their bodies the same way. Shared the same intensity.

"I'm not even sure I know where we are." She hadn't meant to make the comment. It just slipped out.

"In the building that's hard to escape," the man in charge said.

She had no idea what that meant but got the basic idea: they were as lethal as the toxin they kept talking about. But seeing them all there eased the anxiety spilling through her stomach. She still had to lean on the wall to stay upright but felt as if they might have a chance. Slim, but possible.

Instead of looking worried, Pearce just stood there. "And that's exactly why I'm here."

The big one looked ready to shoot. She bit back a gasp and tried to slide tighter against the wall and out of the line of fire.

The leader swore and adjusted his shoulders. "Pearce, this is a losing game. Tell us where Benton is holed up and let's end this thing."

"It's worse than you think." Pearce opened his palm and a small vial rolled around in his palm. "It looks innocent, doesn't it?"

She didn't need an explanation for that. She'd seen the same thing in her cardigan pocket when Trent barged in, wild and demanding. The toxin. It was right there, with them, a few feet away from her.

She grabbed the wall, dug her fingers into the grout lines between the concrete blocks and tried to stay still. Ford's expression told her how bad this was. A nerve ticked in his cheek as his finger moved off the trigger.

Trent pushed his way around Pearce and stared down at the vial. "Why do you have that here?"

"That was always the plan, Trent. One toxin drop and they're all gone." Pearce made an exploding gesture with his other hand. "Poof."

Ford's frown grew even more severe. "That's your big fucking move? To kill everyone in the building?"

Pearce held the vial between his thumb and forefinger. "Well, to use one vial to wipe out the service and sell the rest. Unfortunately there were only two vials hidden in the apartment upstairs from you two. Trent should have hid it all there instead of taking some with him to the museum."

Trent clawed at Pearce's arm. "That wasn't the deal."

"Shut up." A backhand sent Trent flying across the hallway. He slammed into the concrete wall and stayed there. "You get to live for the sole purpose of making me more."

Silence rained down as a wave of tension swept through the corridor. Walls of anxiety pushed into her from every direction. She could almost feel Ford's pulse from where she stood. It raced like hers. Like all of them, except this Pearce, who seemed to have ice in his veins and death on his agenda.

"So, in the end, this is about money," the leader said in a flat tone.

Pearce scoffed. "Shit, no. It was never about the money."

"What then?" Ford lowered his gun. "You served in intelligence for years and now you want to destroy it?"

"You wait, Ford. You'll see." The amusement left Pearce's face. He was a giant ball of simmering rage

now. It radiated off of him and into those around him.
"They spin you up and send you out to kill. They give
you training and you sit through briefings. They convince you that you're one of the good guys and all the
bloodshed and stomping on rights is for the greater
good."

"Jesus, you've lost it."

Pearce's gaze shot to the big man in front of him
with the gun. "No, West, I finally found my common
sense again. You, of anyone here, should know what it
feels like to be used for your killing skills and not appreciated."

"That's what's happening here?" Ford's voice rose as
he talked. "You didn't get enough praise? You needed
another medal? You can be that pathetic?"

Pearce raised his gun. Aimed it right at Ford.

Despite everything, she wanted to race in front of
Ford. Guard him. Wipe the mixed look of pain and
hatred off his face and give him back his blank expression.

"I got a government pension and was shown the
door."

"Poor baby." Ford shook his head. "Trent, you picked
the wrong fucking partner. This one is a whiner."

"I'm the one with a vial." Pearce shook it, probably as a reminder that despite all the guns, he was in
charge.

Ford shrugged. "If you say so."

Pearce's gaze shot to her. "You've served your purpose. Now say goodbye to Ford. If it's any consolation,
I think he really did fall for you, the stupid bastard."

"Shay, move."

But it was too late. Pearce held her with one arm hooked around her throat.

Her eyes widened and a gasp escaped her lips. For a second time, Ford saw Shay clawing at a hand holding her while she couldn't break free. Even though this was all part of the plan, a strategy that put her in danger, he had to stand there and watch. It took every ounce of control for him not to lunge.

Fuck the toxin and Trent and Pearce. He wanted her out of there. "Let her go."

Pearce glanced around, even spared a look for Harlan and Josiah coming up behind him, Reid and Lucas behind them. "Everyone back away so I can finish my work."

"You think we're going to let you kill everyone in here?" Ward asked. "You can't be that stupid."

"It's too late to save them." Pearce held the vial. "One goes into the vents and everyone in here dies, but I'm giving Ford the chance to let her live. She can leave with me and the other vial."

Ford knew things Pearce didn't, but still his heart ripped open. He looked at Shay's scared face and thought about the time he'd been with her. This was not a choice he could make. Not that he could trust Pearce or could guarantee her safety, but he couldn't say the words Pearce wanted.

"I'm getting tired of seeing men touch her." She could hate him forever. He just wanted her to have a long healthy hate. Not to die today. Not here, not while she still believed he'd done this all for a job and that she didn't mean anything to him.

"Pearce, don't do this." Trent reached out.

Pearce shoved him away. "If you want to exit this building, you will shut up and stay out of my way," he said, then turned back to Ford. "You don't get that chance. Does she live or does she die first, when I slit her throat? It's up to you, Ford."

The memories of the last time Ford faced a knife on someone he cared about came rushing back. Pearce probably thought the comment would paralyze. The opposite happened. Fury like Ford had never known welled up inside him. Instead of tamping it down, he let it fill him. If there were a sacrifice to be made, it would be him. His body for Shay's life. He was fine with that.

This time he would not be too late.

But he had to move fast. He could see Harlan and Josiah ready to make a move. He had full control over his team but those two were wild cards. He glanced at Harlan and held eye contact a beat too long. The message was clear. Ford's job would be to grab the toxin while one of them put a bullet in the back of Pearce's head.

Any way you measured it, this was ending today. Right here. In this hallway, in the secure building in Virginia. Maybe with all of them dead, but definitely with Pearce in a pool of blood.

But Ford had one last vow to make. "I will fucking kill you."

Pearce laughed. "Is that what you thought while those killers carved up your old partner in front of you?"

There it was. The emotional attack. Ford pushed it all away.

The hubris would do Pearce in. He'd been told too many times that he was the best, and now he seemed to breathe it in and believe it above everything else. It's what allowed him to set up Harlan without any guilt, and what pushed him to throw in on this job. He'd grown to see himself as invincible.

He didn't know he'd been lured into this hallway. That the building had been evacuated and the ventilation system shut down. This was all about drawing him out, getting him to talk. The only potential issue was that one last vial.

Pearce missed another important fact. His skills were nothing compared to Ford's fear for Shay and his determination to keep her safe. "You might want to remember," Ford said, "I killed the men who killed my partner."

"You won't kill me." Pearce tightened his hold on Shay. "Not while I have her."

Ford was about to give the silent go ahead for Harlan to do just that when Shay cleared her throat.

"Ford?"

No, this couldn't happen. He needed her quiet. He couldn't look at her or hear her.

Ward must have known what the sound of her voice did to Ford because he spoke up. "Shay, just be still."

She ignored Ward. Ignored them all and focused on Ford. He felt the intensity burn through him.

"Do it." She tried to nod, but Pearce held her too tight.

She couldn't mean . . . "What?"

"Do whatever you have to do to stop him." A lone tear ran down her cheek.

He felt gutted. Knifed and ripped open. He almost dropped his gun as he forced himself to stare at her and take in what she'd said.

Pearce wasn't impressed. He shook her. "You're as big a pain in the ass as your cousin."

She struggled to push his arm down. Her voice came out raspy and her words tumbled into each other. "I love you. Do you hear me? I am furious and hurt, but I get it."

Jesus, she was begging him to do his job but she didn't understand his training or that he had a plan. She was willing to sacrifice herself for him. "Shay, no."

"I understand now why you did it . . . this guy and the toxin." She visibly swallowed. "I love you."

The words crashed into his skull and his vision blanked. Ward gave him the side eye, but it was the last thing Ford saw. The emotions he blocked on the job poured through.

Pearce's laughter brought him back. "Isn't that sweet? Ford, I think she means it, which is a fucking shame."

Her eyes grew even wider. "Do it."

Ford saw Ward nod and Josiah move. Everything spun in slow motion as men piled in the small space, following the instructions he'd given before they put their plan into action. Both Alliance teams appeared and the shouting started. Trent ducked down but Shay stood still. Ford had to get to her but Josiah moved faster.

"Josiah, no!"

Pearce spun around, easing his hold on Shay. Ford reached for her then and got enough of a hand on her arm to shove her out of the way. He couldn't be gentle because he needed her out of the line of direct attack. And he had to hope he succeeded because he couldn't stop to check.

The first shot nailed Pearce in the neck, just above his protective vest. Blood spurted as he let out a vicious yell. His hand went to the wound and he swore to take them all down.

Knowing he meant it, Ford lunged and tackled. Shots rang out as Pearce managed to grab for his gun and fire before his back slammed into the ground. Shots went wild and Trent yelled.

On cue, the building siren started wailing and the blue emergency lights clicked on. That was the all-clear signal. No one but them stood in the firing line, but the building was in lockdown so if that damn vial got broken, the damage would be minimized.

Not that Ford would let the worst case happen.

Josiah jumped over Trent's slumped body and slid on his knees beside Pearce's head. The move knocked the gun out of Pearce's hand.

But that wasn't the real problem. Ford's only thought was the vial. He saw Pearce's tightened fist. Saw his arm go into the air as if to slam the glass tube against the hard floor. Josiah and Ford both grabbed Pearce's arm.

Fury gave Pearce disproportionate strength. Blood poured down his throat and covered his hand, but he held on. Josiah held the arm still and Ward jumped in as Ford pried Pearce's fist open.

"Move!" Harlan, still on his feet, swung his gun through the air like a bat.

The bones in Pearce's hand crunched and he let out a scream of agony as Harlan made contact. The vial fell and Harlan knocked it over their heads and into the enclosed interrogation room where they'd held Shay. Ford watched the glass container fly through the air. His first reaction was to land on it.

His second thought made more sense.

Jumping to his knees, ignoring the pain that shot through him, he thrust his hand at the doorknob and dragged the door closed. If Ellery was right about the ventilation system and building design, the airtight room should contain the toxin. Ford didn't know, but they were all still breathing, so he that was a good sign that the toxin hadn't penetrated into the hallway.

His gaze went to Shay, who lay against the wall with West's body in front of her.

Leave it to West to protect as ordered no matter what spun around him. Ford could count on the guy for anything. "Thanks, man."

West nodded and lifted his body off her.

"We need a medic," Ward yelled into the com.

Panicked, Ford slid across the floor to Shay as Josiah and the others watched over Pearce. Above the yelling and crashing as more agents flooded the area, Ford ran a hand over her. "Are you hit?"

The dazed expression didn't clear from her eyes. "No."

Ford looked to Pearce and saw all the blood. Then he noticed the shift of people in and out across from Pearce and saw Trent. A bloodstain spread across his stomach as his breathing turned shallow.

But Shay was staring at Ford, her gaze searching his face. For what, he didn't know. He did the only thing he could think of. Wrap his arms around her and protect her from one last bit of pain.

30

"TRENT IS the hospital and your uncle is with him."
The woman Shay knew as Ford's sister but clearly
wasn't handed her a cup of coffee as she stepped
around her desk and sat down in the big black leather
chair. "Your uncle is yelling and demanding the guards
keep back, so that's a good sign."

"Okay." Shay didn't know what else to say, so she
went with that.

"He's always insisting we treat you right or he'll
have all our badges." The other woman smiled. "I
didn't have the heart to tell him we really didn't have
traditional badges."

Shay still couldn't process it all. The crimes Trent
committed and the way he'd dragged her into them.
The shooting, and seeing his still body on the floor as
the medics rushed in. She pushed it all out, that and
Ford. It was the only way she could keep functioning.
"You need to look up the definition of a good sign."

"True." The blonde laughed. Her nameplate said her
first name was Tasha, so at least that part wasn't a lie.
The space was as cool as the woman, with blue walls
and photographs of what looked like places in Europe.

Behind her there were bookcases filled with binders and a big safe with an even bigger lock.

Shay had no idea while she was still in the building. Something about needing to be debriefed. Since no fewer than five people—including Tasha and the man Shay now knew was Ward—had asked her a series of questions.

Now she had one of her own. "So, you're not Ford's sister."

This time the other woman smiled. "No."

"And you're British." Even in her emotional stupor, Shay had picked up the accent. It kind of went with the rest of the package. Tasha seemed confident and professional. Finding out she was the boss didn't hit Shay as a surprise. Thinking about her trying to rein in all the men under her did.

And there seemed to be a lot of them. She'd walked through a room of Fordlike guys wearing weapons. All were cordial. When she'd stopped to thank the big one she now knew as West, he shook her hand and winked.

That was a lot of testosterone to handle. Shay didn't envy Tasha that. She also didn't need to stick around for more.

She had wounds to lick and a heart to repair . . . eventually. "I want to go home."

"Soon."

"We're removing the last vial of toxin." Tasha said it as if she were talking about a guy being in the building to repair an air conditioner. No fear, no worries.

That made one of them. Shay heard the word toxin and was now trained to break into a cold sweat. "You found it?"

Tasha's calm slipped and a peek of anger slipped though. "Pearce had set it on a timer to leak through the ventilation system. We wrecked that plan. Our tech people are quite good."

Again with the casual comments. Shay sat in a building with more security than she'd ever seen, surrounded by people who whipped out weapons if they heard a noise. It all seemed normal to them. A few hours there and she needed to go home and rest. "This is what you do? What you all do?"

"I think you're really asking if this is what Ford does, and the answer is yes."

Her heart clenched. It felt like a giant fist reached in there and squeezed. Her breathing hitched as she thought back to what she'd said to him, in front of all of them.

In that moment, she'd wanted to give him permission, to make him understand. She didn't regret the admission. She just didn't know, in light of all that had happened, if the words mattered. "He also lies and sleeps with women while pretending to be someone he's not."

Tasha tapped her fingernails against the armrests. "You probably want me to apologize for sending him to you, but I won't."

"Thanks." Yeah, okay. It was time to go. Shay decided she'd had enough of the cool detachment routine. She could take a lesson but couldn't sit for one today, so she stood up.

"We were fighting having a catastrophic substance get into the wrong hands." Tasha sighed. "As it is, we still have an arms dealer hiding in Yemen and it's only a matter of time before he finds someone like Trent and makes another play."

Shay had no idea what that meant but it sounded pretty damn terrifying. Maybe there were some things the public didn't need to know. "I should leave so you can get back to that."

"You might want to see this before you go." Tasha picked up a remote and turned on the television.

The last thing Shay needed was a show. "What are you doing?"

"Letting you see top secret footage from the museum attack."

Shay's stomach rolled at the idea of reliving that. "I was there for the live version."

But she couldn't move. When the screen came to life and the video started rolling, she was rooted to the ground.

Tasha got up. "I know you're doubting us and thinking maybe all that screaming Trent did was true and maybe he is innocent. But we aren't wrong."

Shay didn't want to point out that they missed the truth about Pearce and he worked for them. She also couldn't admit yet that she believed it all. There was no doubt Trent had gotten mixed up in a terrible crime. He hadn't bothered to deny the charges as Pearce said them only a few hours ago. Part of her wondered if her misguided cousin took pride in the mess he'd created.

"Ask yourself how he had all those vials if someone was setting him up and he didn't really steal them." Tasha fast-forwarded then stopped the tape. "Then watch this part."

As far as Shay was concerned, she didn't need to.

She'd actually seen enough. But still, her curiosity was piqued. "Why?"

Tasha handed her the remote. "So you can see how many chances Ford and his team had to kill Trent at the museum but didn't because of you."

Everything inside Shay stilled. "What are you saying?"

"That when it came down to sacrificing you and his job, and the safety of who knows how many, Ford picked saving you." Tasha reached over and hit Play. "He's not an emotional guy. He'll never write you a poem, but he is worth the risk."

Shay's mind rebelled. All the denials rushed into her head. "How can you say that? He's done nothing but lie to me."

"He kept you alive. Seems to me that's more important." Tasha shrugged. "For Ford that's the very definition of love."

Two days after the building almost exploded in a chemical haze, Ford sat in a chair at ten at night. He occupied his usual seat at the conference table in the main building but would rather have been in the Warehouse. Be anywhere his mind might shut off. He spun it from side to side, clearing his head and refusing to think about her.

Ward and Harlan came into the empty room and stopped in front of him. Harlan was the first to speak. "Why are you here?"

There was a temptation to ignore both of them. To shrug them off. "Where should I be?"

"Ah, home?" Ward's eyebrow lifted as he asked the question.

"I don't have one of those." It wasn't a lie. The condo he lived in across from Shay was part of the cover, but he'd given up his real place when the op started. Figured the nicer condo would do him some good, be a step up. Not that he was in it all that much. He preferred staying with Shay.

That damn ache hit him in the chest again. Much more of this and he'd need a medical check-up.

Harlan frowned. "Now you're just sounding pathetic."

"Fuck you."

This time Harlan nodded. "And insubordinate."

He didn't sound angry, and Ford didn't suspect he was. They'd reached a silent truce since the Pearce disaster. Tasha and Ward told Harlan that Ford had stuck up for him. Likewise, Ford understood that Harlan's quick thinking and telegraphed directions likely saved them all from having to spike the toxin right next to Ford's face.

Speaking of which . . . "The conference room detoxed yet?"

"Give it forty years or so." Ward pulled out a chair and sat down.

"Benton's still on the loose." Ford would give anything to blow up whatever cave or house or car that guy lived in. He'd make it his life mission to identify him and hunt him down.

Ward swore under his breath. "We didn't even get close to him and Pearce isn't talking. Unfortunately, we trained him in how to survive interrogation, so this might take some time."

They could bury him in a deep hole for all Ford cared. "The fucker."

"We have him," Harlan said. "Benton will come later. Alliance is exactly the right group to find him."

"I will. Bravo will take him out."

Ward glanced at Harlan before facing Ford again. "I believe you, but stop trying to change the subject."

Ford did not want company. He didn't want conversation. He wanted the one thing he could not have. "I'm not talking about her."

"You should be talking *to* her," Ward said.

Harlan had the nerve to smile. "Seems obvious."

For some reason Ford found Harlan's accent even more annoying when he was talking about Shay. "Did you miss the part where she told me to go to hell a hundred times?"

Not really, but close. She said she hated him. Really, he could recite every word. At the end when she scrambled to help her cousin, she pushed him away one last time. He'd gone to touch her and she shrank from him.

Lesson learned.

"Since when do you get sidetracked so easily?"

Ford tried to block out Harlan's presence and concentrate on Ward's question. The answer was far too easy to call up. "I lied to her and put her in danger."

"Ahh, now I see. That's really the problem," Harlan said. "The danger."

Ford hated this conversation. "Shut up."

"Harlan is right."

"Shouldn't you be home with Tasha?" Ford thought about adding a smart remark, something inappropriate, but he admired Tasha too much for that.

"She told me to straighten your sorry ass out first."

"I liked you better when you weren't getting sex on

a regular basis." Sex, love . . . Shay. Ford groaned as he buried his face in his hands.

"We all did," Harlan said under his breath.

Ford lifted his head. He felt the speech coming and walked right into it, hoping to end the torture faster. "Just say it, Ward. Whatever you came to say, spill it."

Ward held up his hands. "You fell for her."

Every muscle ached and his raging headache came back with a vengeance. Ford said the word anyway. "Yes."

"Huh." Harlan looked at Ward. "Didn't think he'd admit it that fast. I owe you twenty."

They skipped over one important fact that Ford couldn't forget. "It's over."

"Nah, it's in a holding pattern until you get over there and beg." Ward stood up again.

"Excuse me?"

"You fought me to keep your cover. You refused to put a tracker on her until it was almost too late. You wouldn't let West shoot when he should have at the museum, and when Pearce unleashed the toxin your sole concern was to rush her to safety." Ward nodded. "That's love, my friend. Stupid, crazy, and complicated, but love."

"You keep missing the part where she hates me."

"And you keep missing that you were willing to fight with all of us to keep Shay close to you. How about you go fight with her to win her back?" Harlan asked.

The support from that quarter threw Ford off. For a second he sat there and stared. "The danger—"

Ward waved the comment off and started talking before Ford could make his point. "Will always be there. No one gets that more than me, but you've got to decide."

"What?"

Harlan smiled again. "If you can stand being alone while she marries someone else."

31

Eɪɢʜᴛ ᴅᴀʏs. It had been eight days since she'd heard from Ford. Tasha had come over and brought Ward with her. They told office stories, mostly administrative stuff, and about how they met in Fiji with Ford tagging along. They talked about Ford, slipping his name into every story, until Shay thought her head would explode.

Then West showed up the next night to give her the status on Trent, that he was okay and in custody along with his old boss. West hung around, looking uncomfortable. Right before he left, he told her how miserable Ford was without her.

Her uncle even called, strangely sheepish, and asked if they could have dinner next weekend. He said to bring Ford along.

It was a conspiracy to keep throwing the man in her face.

To block it out, she watched the news every day, looking for a story about Trent and the toxin, but it never came. Tasha said it never would, but she was still surprised. The excuse was that there were some things the public didn't need to know. In the past Shay had heard that excuse and rolled her eyes. Now she believed. There were certainly things she'd rather not know. Things she'd pay to forget.

Her doorbell rang. Not the outer door buzzer. Her personal doorbell.

A rush of anxiety filled her belly and she fought the urge to run and hide in the closet. She wasn't one to live in fear, but having experienced so many shocks in such a short time, she still hadn't adjusted to normal again. If she even knew what that was anymore.

One day the hurt and sense of loss and vulnerability would fade away. One day she'd go to the door and not expect to see Ford on the other side.

Going up on tiptoes, she looked through the peephole. Her feet fell flat again.

Ford.

She leaned her forehead against the door as conflicting emotions bombarded her. Love and anger. Frustration and a tiny flicker of hope. She tried to crush it all down and act like nothing mattered. That she was over him and them and everything that happened.

But, man, no one was that good an actress. She opened the door anyway.

He stood there with a hand balanced on the door frame and a bag of take-out Chinese in his other hand. His beard looked a bit scraggly and his frame suggested he'd lost weight, though she didn't know how that would be possible in just a little over a week.

Basically, he looked as crappy as she felt. All dried up and hollowed out. But that didn't mean they were sharing dinner.

"What are you doing here?" She was impressed at how strong her voice sounded. How she didn't pass out.

"What I should have done from the beginning." He pushed past her, leaving her holding the door behind him.

"Not come in at all?"

He stopped in the center of the room and turned around, still holding onto the bag like it was a shield or something. "Adam."

The name came out of nowhere. Another agent, or whatever he called them. She didn't know. "What?"

"My real name is Adam Ford." He put the bag down on the stack of magazines on her coffee table. "Other than my parents, of course, and a few people at the office and a few more at the CIA, you're the only one who knows."

She turned the name over in her mind and decided it fit. But a rush of confusion came right behind. "Should you be telling me this?"

"No, but I trust you."

Her body clenched and her heartbeat sped up. It was as if her mind and her heart engaged in an epic battle and just seeing him tipped the scales.

She had to shut it down. She was too raw and too exposed. "Don't do this. Not now."

"Missouri." He slipped his hands into his back pockets.

"What?"

"I'm from Missouri, not Montana."

"I don't care." But she did. Every morsel went to that part of her brain that was desperate to know more about him. To hold onto him even though he'd bruised and battered her beyond recognition.

"My parents are married, have been forever. That

was all true." He shot her a crooked smile. "They're going to love you."

Oh, no, no, no. "How dare you tell me this now?"

He shrugged. "I want you to know."

He stood there saying all the things she wanted to hear, but it was tainted by his deception. "They are never going to meet me."

"University of Virginia."

He just kept spitting out facts as if he'd stored them up to use them now. "Your school?"

"I went into the CIA right after. Have been all over the world and seen some fucking awful things."

"Like the toxin."

"Much worse."

"How is that possible?" More information she shouldn't know. More things that shouldn't matter, but the more he said, the more her heart opened back up to him again.

She leaned the front of her thighs against the back of the couch because she needed something to hold her up. Maybe it would work as a barrier between them and help to hold onto her anger.

But that got harder each day. Seeing the tape Tasha showed her started that healing. Clearing her mind and remembering his face when he saw Trent grab her, and then Pearce grab her. There was no way Ford could fake that concern.

"I do what I do because I believe I can make a difference. That there are shitty people out there and they have to be stopped using whatever means are necessary. That stuff Pearce said? All garbage." Ford's eyes darkened and anger showed on his face but he quickly pushed it out again. "It's not a perfect job by any means, and I've wanted to walk away more than once, but I do believe in what I do, especially in the group I'm with now."

"Even if it means setting up a line of innocent women and pretending you like them." She said it, but there was no heat behind the words.

When she'd told him she got it, she wasn't lying. Seeing the team in action and knowing what could have happened, she could only respect the danger they threw themselves into. But that didn't mean she understood his willingness to hurt her.

They stood there, staring at each other in some weird standoff. She was about to hand him the bag of food and show him he door.

"Love."

He didn't say anything else and she refused to hope. She would not get sucked back down a second time.

She held up a hand and shook her head. "Stop."

"With you it wasn't pretend. From the beginning I knew I was in trouble." He moved then, walking until he could turn her and stand directly in front of her. Leaning in until his nose touched her hair.

"I said stop." But she didn't push him away or kick him out. She was stuck there, reeled in and pathetically hopeful.

His hands brushed up and down her arms. "I ignored the rules and my training."

She should pull back. Walk away. Stop and eat the Chinese food—something. Instead she dove in. "Tasha says you kept West from killing Trent at the museum out of respect for me."

Ford kissed the tip of her nose. "Love, but yes."

A shiver raced through Shay's body. Actually shook her then shook her again. "West says you've been a mess."

"That's nicer than how he says it to me, but yes to that as well." Ford kissed the area where her bandage had been. "Did you mean it?"

The closeness, the warmth of his body, that soothing voice . . . it all lured her in. She loved this man. Right or wrong, stupid or not, she loved him. "What?"

"When you said you loved me?"

She shook her head, refusing to give him the final bit of satisfaction. "Please don't—"

His hands rested under her elbows and brought her closer. "I screwed up. I should have come clean and gotten off the assignment. Hell, I probably should have left you alone, but I couldn't."

"How many times have you given this speech at the end of a job?" She would say anything to put the brakes on. This was headed for heartache for her, and she didn't know what to do to make it stop.

"Never."

Oh, God. "Ford . . . Adam . . ."

His hand went to her hair and he brushed his fingers through it. "Call me Ford."

"My life is pretty simple, or I thought it was." Hard to keep up that illusion what with the dangerous toxins and armed gunmen roaming around.

He stepped back, not breaking contact but far enough that she didn't have to look up to see him. "I'll leave Alliance for you. That's the group I work with."

Her brain shut down. Every argument against trusting him screeched to a halt inside her. "You just said—"

"You want me to be a handyman or learn a skill, I

will. I don't know shit about computers, but I'll take courses." There was nothing blank about his expression this time. Worry played in his eyes and on the lines on his face. "I will be whatever you need me to be, just give me another chance."

This could be another ruse. A way to win her over . . . but he didn't have to anymore. That thought hit her and she couldn't let it go. He could walk away now and go to another job. But he was there, in her house, begging.

"Ford."

"I love you. All of you, exactly how you are and for who you are." He gave her arm a gentle squeeze. "I love how you make me feel and who I am when I'm with you."

The last of her resistance broke. The wall she'd tried to erect against him shattered and crashed. "You're killing me."

"Mostly, I love you more than anything else in my life or anyone I've ever known, so I will walk away from my job and never regret it. If that's what you need, I'll give it to you."

She had to swallow back the lump in her throat. This time, a good one, one filled with hope and love and possibility. "And for all those people who won't get help because you've left the field?"

"There are other operatives." He pulled her in close again and his palm cupped her cheek. "I have spent my life rescuing. You don't need that from me. You're strong enough to stand in a room and accept death if that means saving everyone else. Damn bravest thing I've ever seen."

"I thought I was going to throw up." He should know that because it was true.

"See, Shay, the reality is I'm the one who needs you."

That hope flamed to full life. She wanted to hold back but the words spilled out. "I love you."

He closed his eyes, and when he reopened them some of the darkness had cleared. "Say it again."

"I am angry and want to punch you and know we'll have to replay every conversation so you can tell me the truth this time around." She wrapped her arms around his neck. "But I do love you."

He rested his forehead against hers. "Thank God."

"And no."

His head shot back. "What?"

"You don't have to leave Alliance."

"I will."

She knew he meant it and that was enough. "I've seen you in action. It's where you belong."

"I won't lie to you again, but there will be things I can't say."

"I get that."

He winced. "Danger."

"Apparently, being the manager of this complex is pretty dangerous."

He finally smiled. A real smile, big and wide and sexy as hell. "So are museums."

She felt his erection press against her and saw the way his expression went from happy to something heated and wanting. She put a hand on his chest to let him know it would not all be easy. "We have a lot of work to do."

"Is it too much to hope you're talking about the building's plumbing?"

Nice try. "Yes."

He winked at her. "It doesn't matter. I'm in. No matter how long it takes to rebuild the trust. I'll be here."

With just a few words he'd said exactly what she needed to hear. Somehow it would be okay. They would rebuild and put the trust back together. She'd keep on loving him and he'd keep being the guy he was. "I want you here, with me."

"And I hope you mean *here,* since I don't have a place to live."

It was too much, too fast, but still she wanted it. "You're in luck. I know about this building."

He kissed her then. It was a kiss filled with promise and a touch of regret that deepened the longer it went on. Nothing tame or modest. His mouth covered her's and his hands toured her back until heat flushed through her.

When he lifted his head, all that intensity she loved was back in full force. He nibbled on her bottom lip. "Start by showing me the bedroom."

"That's playing dirty." But she loved it.

He dropped another kiss on her mouth, this one short but no less loving. "I will play however you want."

And she believed he would keep that promise. "Show me."

ACKNOWLEDGMENTS

A QUICK BUT heartfelt thank you to Jill Shalvis and Allison Kent for reading an early draft of this one and letting me know I was on the right track.

My deepest gratitude goes to May Chen for being the amazing, enthusiastic, and thoughtful editor she is (and everyone told me she would be). Your guidance on this book was invaluable. And to everyone on Team Avon and at HarperCollins for making me feel appreciated and welcome—thank you!

This may be an odd thank-you but . . . thanks to the television show *Strike Back,* which indirectly inspired my series by making me say, "I want to write something a little like that but with real romance and bigger heroes!"

As always, much love to my husband and thanks to my fantastic readers who make it possible for me to do what I love for a living. I appreciate you all.

At Avon Books, we know your passion for romance—once you finish one of our novels, you find yourself wanting more.

May we tempt you with . . .

- **Excerpts** from our upcoming releases.
- Entertaining **extras**, including authors' personal photo albums and book lists.
- Behind-the-scenes **scoop** on your favorite characters and series.
- **Sweepstakes** for the chance to win free books, romantic getaways, and other fun prizes.
- Writing **tips** from our authors and editors.
- **Blog** with our authors and find out why they love to write romance.
- **Exclusive content** that's not contained within the pages of our novels.

Join us at
www.avonbooks.com

AVON

An Imprint of HarperCollins*Publishers*
www.avonromance.com

*G*ive in to your Impulses!

These unforgettable stories only take a second to buy and give you hours of reading pleasure!

Go to *www.AvonImpulse.com* and see what we have to offer.

Available wherever e-books are sold.

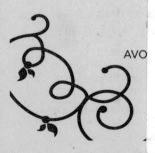

AVO